THE WIDOW'S BOYFRIEND

An unputdownable psychological thriller with
a breathtaking twist

E.V. SEYMOUR

JOFFE
BOOKS

Joffe Books, London
www.joffebooks.com

First published in Great Britain in 2023

© E.V. Seymour

Cover art by Nick Castle

ISBN: 978-1-83526-004-3

For Carrye and Richard

PART ONE

CHAPTER ONE

There were all sorts of horrors in this world, but the arrival of your sister-in-law at seven forty-five in the morning on the first day of the school summer holidays was right up there with them. I stumbled out of bed to see what all the fuss was about. Before you wonder how I knew it was my brother's wife, Dido took the same extreme approach to inanimate objects as she did to people. Before she could give the brass knocker another hefty clout with her manicured hand, I opened the front door.

'I was having a lie-in,' I protested, which was pretty obvious. My cropped blonde hair stuck up at angles. Last night's mascara — shame on me — decorated my cheeks and I was wearing my favourite *Sleep Tight* top over rumpled striped black-and-white shorts. The paint on my toenails was chipped and my legs needed a shave important personal-care issues designated to receive my full attention that very morning. Fortunately, Dido — no slouch when it came to appearances — was too exercised to notice. In full-on work mode — in charge of marketing for a "recud" label — all five feet ten of her swept in like an iceberg in the middle of the Sahara. A lock of recently styled hair, the colour of fresh ash and up-to-the-second cool, swished past and almost caught me in the eye.

I trailed her through my open-plan sitting room, study and kitchen.

'Well,' she said, twirling around, one hand on her designer-clad hip. I wasn't sure whether this was the prelude to drama or a negative observation of my living quarters.

Hastily, I picked up a half-eaten packet of ginger biscuits and a selection of end-of-year thank-you cards from the kids — *Best Teacher Ever. We Love You, Miss Finch.* My laptop had mysteriously found its way onto the polished wooden floor — this, too, I collected. Organised in my work life — I taught at a local primary school — I verged on haphazard when it came to my tiny, "bijou", as Dido once described it, garden flat in a quiet back street of Cheltenham.

'Do you know about your mother's boyfriend, Verity?' The tone was accusatory.

I wondered if last night's drinks with colleagues — shots at the Urban Fox — had messed with my brain. A single glance at Dido's predatory expression told me there was nothing wrong with my cognitive functions.

'What boyfriend?'

'His name's Roger.'

I knew it was childish but I couldn't help but grin. Dido's thin top lip curled. It reminded me of a dog before it took a bite out of you.

Mum had been a widow for the past five years, after my lovely dad collapsed in the family bathroom from a stroke and died. She'd never expressed any interest in seeing another man and had carved out a fulfilling life for herself without one.

'If Mum has found happiness at her time of life, good for her.' To be honest, although I agreed with this in principle, I wasn't entirely sold on the idea of someone taking Dad's place. 'After all, she's still young and beautiful.' I wasn't kidding, or blinded by prejudice. At sixty-two years of age, my mother was attractive enough to model for *Saga* magazine, or an online fashion site for oldies. She'd look knockout in one of those posh cruiseline TV adverts.

'*I have youth and a little beauty*,' Dido said loftily.

'The Duchess of Malfi,' I retorted. 'Bit early for literary references, isn't it?'

Dido fixed me with an ominous expression. 'Maybe so, but we all know what happened to *her*.'

Yeah, she died young, but I wasn't going to get into a debate about John Webster's dark little play in a game of "Who's The Cleverest" with Dido. She'd win hands down.

I chewed my lip. Nice people would say that my sister-in-law was caring, protective of her mother-in-law's best financial interests. I knew better than that. Dido always had an agenda. To put it bluntly, my mother represented a family-sized meal ticket. While I loved my brother, who, on the cusp of middle-age (forty, if you're interested), was almost ten years older than me, Alex had been a drain on my dad's resources from the moment he was on solids. Nothing had changed since our father's death. An expert in hare-brained ventures destined to fail, he simply went to *Mummy* now instead of *Daddy*. The thought of my mother's resources being possibly channelled in other directions would not play well with "after the main chance" Dido.

Humour her, I thought, plastering on a smile. 'How do you know about Mum's new man?'

Now that I appeared to be taking an interest, Dido softened. She swept a ton of magazines off the nearest chair and gracefully arranged herself in a way guaranteed to display her perfect size-ten figure and lean, toned legs. I reckoned the dress she was wearing was more than I paid for my mortgage each month.

I curled up on the sofa, hid my bare feet with their shoddy nails beneath me. *All girls together and isn't this lovely?*

Dropping her voice by several decibels, Dido began, 'I spotted them having dinner at Henry's.'

A chic seafood restaurant in Cirencester, I had it down on my culinary bucket list.

'When?'

'Last night.'

5

Didn't waste much time in reporting it, I thought.

'They were *intimate*.' She said it like it was a dirty word. Mistaking my numb expression for stupidity, she explained breathily, 'They were all over each other. In fact, at one point, I thought they should get a room.'

Uncomfortable at the deeply unpleasant picture attempting to take shape in my head, I said, 'Where was Alex?'

'Alexander was at home looking after Kitty and Fred.' My sister-in-law was the only person on the planet who called my brother by his full name. 'It was Dana Hervey's hen night,' she explained.

'If Mum and this Roger seemed close,' I said, clearing my throat, 'perhaps they've been seeing each other for some time.'

'Who knows?'

Well, I certainly didn't. 'So what's Roger like?'

'I have absolutely no idea.'

'You didn't introduce yourself?'

'That would have been rude.'

I blinked. Dragging me out of bed to complain about my mother's personal life was rude. 'How do you know his name, then?'

'I overheard your mother speaking.' This was accompanied by a tetchy sigh and big eye-roll.

'Then you must have had a good look at him. Is he fat, thin, bald, tall, short, has chest hair, nose hair, or what?'

Dido inhaled sharply and flicked back a pale grey lock. Her large, solid-gold hoop earrings jangled. 'If you're not going to take this seriously.'

'I am — honest.' It was possible that Dido just wasn't very good at describing people so I tried a different approach. I had to do this all the time with little kids when they couldn't grasp what I was on about. 'Did you get a sense of his personality?'

'Louche,' she said. 'Sleazy,' she added. 'His hair was stupidly long for a man of his age.'

I gave a start. 'Ponytail?'

'Christ, no. He had two buttons of his shirt undone.'

'Is that a thing?' I asked, mystified.

'Should only ever be one.'

'Even when it's thirty degrees?' Which was what the temperature had soared to lately. For the past week we'd been more concerned with keeping the children cool and plastered in sun block than teaching them anything of note.

'*Even.* He's the type of man who leaves the lavatory seat up,' she said, in evident disgust.

My brother had many failings, but he deserved a bloody medal for putting up with Dido. I waited a respectable beat, creating the impression that Dido's observations were worth consideration.

'How did my mother *seem*?'

Dido arched an eyebrow. A versatile facial gesture and one I aspired to, it can convey *you look cute/you must be joking/are you serious?* Dido's didn't fit into any of those categories.

'Did she look happy?' I pressed.

'That's not the point.'

'Of course it's the point.'

'That man could be manipulating her. He might be after her money, for God's sake.'

And there we had it. 'He could be lighting up her life,' I countered.

Dido was one of those women who could express without expression, yet still pin you to the wall. 'Honestly, Verity, I thought you of all people would be concerned.'

'Not sure what you mean.' I did, but wanted Dido to say it out loud.

'We all know you're Eleanor's favourite. How come she didn't mention *the new man in her life*?' Dido made speech marks with her index fingers to emphasise the point. 'She tells you *everything*.'

'Apparently not,' I said with a cutting smile.

CHAPTER TWO

Was I narked by Mum's omission? No, although I admit I was a tad shocked.

We've always been close. I once overheard her say that she loved the fact that she could talk to me about the things that mattered. Not quite sure what she meant exactly because, quite often, I did all the talking and she listened. There was a kind of understanding between us, I guessed, that we were on the same page about most things, although I confessed that I was never absolutely certain what was going on behind my mother's eyes. A quiet and reserved woman, self-contained, she exuded calm and patience. Every crisis, big or small, was dealt with in the same composed manner: the time Alexander got expelled (again) and Dad went ballistic; the time Grandma had a fall that finished her off and my father cried. He'd definitely felt things more deeply. As quick as he'd lose his rag one moment, he'd be hugging the life out of you the next. Plain-speaking and dependable, there remained a Dad-sized hole in my life. I missed him. I always would.

And why the thought of Mum with some random man hurt more than expected. Not that I'd ever let on to Dido. The second she huffed her way out, I removed the offending nail varnish from my toenails, shaved my legs to baby-smooth, showered, dressed, drank a glass of orange juice, cleaned my teeth and, picking up my car from my rare-as-rocking-horse-poo allocated parking slot, drove the twenty-five-minute journey from Cheltenham to Cirencester. I generally headed out of town on the London Road, through Charlton Kings, because it was prettier and I was moderately less likely to get snarled up in traffic.

I'll be honest. I'm a nervous driver. I passed my test first time and had an accident three months later when taking a bend too quickly, no other car involved, writing off my Corsa, although — thankfully — not me. I now drove a Suzuki Swift, which was a misnomer because I barely got beyond fifty miles an hour on a good stretch. Fortunately, living in town, the opportunity to piss off other motorists was limited. If a journey could be walked, I walked it.

Milk-white skies and hazy with heat, it was already murderously hot outside. Due to the great holiday exodus, traffic was lighter than usual, although still demonic in nature. Cheltenham was a place of fast and large cars, the animal equivalent of bison crossed with antelope. Tootling along, once I was clear of town, I tried not to overthink things. Dido was a drama queen. To see my mother with anyone was bound to seem a little odd, nothing to get worked up about. I simply needed to deal with it.

* * *

Mum lived in one of the narrowest streets in Cirencester, maybe even the country (an exaggeration). It looked as if the buildings on either side were leaning towards each other, about to shake hands. It was in a maze of roads off prestigious Dollar Street and packed with Cotswold stone houses, mostly Grade II. Dad had been an architect so I appreciated these things. He'd also instilled in me the need to get my foot on the property ladder, which I'd done with the money he'd left me. Frankly, I'd rather have had my dad. For many years the family home was a grand Regency semi in Pittville,

Wellington Square. After me and my brother moved out, Mum and Dad decided to hotfoot it to Cirencester. I got it. The pace of life was quieter, less cut and thrust. Vets, dog groomers and hairdressers covered more square miles than seemed feasible. Recently, it had blossomed with lots of little independent shops and become quite boho. It was not unusual to see incredibly well-dressed elderly folk, women in their seventies gorgeously made up, strolling alongside a fair collection of 'yummy mummies'. Sadly, my dad had only been retired a few years when he passed away so he didn't really get to enjoy their little coach house. Gated, with more than enough room for my car, in theory I could drive straight in. I preferred the Pay and Display in the grounds of the old Abbey. There was bags more space and less chance of me having a prang.

Mum did a Pilates class on Monday mornings, which rather suited my purposes. The coach house was still my home and I had a key.

After a short and sweaty walk, I let myself in through the bright yellow front door, which I believe Farrow and Ball call 'Babouche' and I call 'English mustard,' and briefly basked in the cloistered shade of the interior. The hall was wide and cool. A keen collector of art, Mum used it to display some of her eclectic pieces, works by Nic Joly, and wooden and bronze sculptures by Ed Elliott, plus the odd piece of contemporary African pottery.

Slipping off my sandals, the porcelain tiles cool beneath my feet, I sauntered into the kitchen with its central island and overhead pendant lights, top-of-the-range Italian gadgetry and fittings. As usual, everywhere was uber clean and tidy. For years, my father had nagged my mum to have help in the house. She never did and didn't now. She'd never liked the idea of someone else in her home. Privacy was important to her and I felt more than a twinge of guilt entering the utility room to check out the calendar that hung off the back of the door. I wasn't interested in dental appointments or doctor's check-ups. I couldn't give a toss about lunches or cinema nights with Hazel Tranter, my mother's closest friend — as much as she was close to anyone, that is. I was hunting for dates with Roger. There appeared to be quite a few and, to my astonishment, extended as far back as March 15.

Coo, I thought, *over four months*. Had she seemed different? Did she look more radiant? Were there signs all along and yet I'd been too wrapped up in my own stuff and failed to notice?

At the sound of a key in the door, I flicked the pages back to July and hung the calendar hastily in the right place. Stepping back into the kitchen, I swooped up the kettle purposefully, perfectly timed to my mother breezing in. A morning of surprises and there was another: she was singing. Her rich contralto voice tripped with happiness and pleasure. Don't get me wrong, she isn't a sad person, but this was incredibly out of character. Mum didn't do light and carefree. She's a serious woman who let you believe that the rooms in her mind were quiet and peaceful. What if they were really ripping with parties and raves?

'Hello, darling. How lovely to see you.'

And there she was, with that same slightly enigmatic smile, not a hair out of place, no sheen of perspiration on her brow. She had the deepest brown eyes, like dark pools of espresso. The lines just above the corners of her high cheekbones served to make her look interesting, rather than haggard or gaunt like they did with some older women. Looking at her, I suddenly wondered if Dido's choice of hair colour was modelled on my mum's.

I gave her a hug, felt the slight resistance as usual because my mother could never be described as tactile. Some things had not changed, I realised, despite Dido's verbal hand grenade about my mother's alleged behaviour with Roger.

'Coffee?' she said brightly.

'Please.'

I hopped up onto a breakfast stool and watched as she glided about, bare-footed, spooning this, shaking that, wondering how I could roll the conversation around to "the new man". I needn't have worried.

'Have you spoken to Dido?' She gave me a slow, amused sideways glance.

'Do you mean has Dido spoken to me?'

'About last night?'

'Yes.'

Two cups of coffee were placed on the island, together with a plate of Digestives. Mum sat down beside me.

'Verity,' she said, lightly touching my hand with her slim fingers. 'I'm truly mortified you had to find out like that.'

'Find out what exactly?' Did that sound a bit silly? Probably.

'That I'm dating a man.'

Dating? Whoa — sounds serious.

'It's very important for you to know that nobody will ever take your father's place in my heart.'

There was a *but* coming, I knew it.

'But I've been quite lonely these past few years and thought it was time to spread my wings a little. Do you understand?'

She looked at me a little forlornly, willing me not to criticise, judge or condemn her. How could I? 'Of course, Mum. How did you meet him?'

'Through the Internet on a dating website for seniors.'

I was speechless. Mum has a laptop but I'm not sure she's ever switched it on. The biggest technophobe on the planet, she literally has no digital footprint. The best she can manage is WhatsApp and her half-arsed messages are usually fraught due to her failure to understand the significance and meaning of emojis. I could no more imagine my mother swiping left than me being invited to take part in *Love Island.*

Spotting my confusion, she explained, 'It was Hazel's idea. We had a few drinks one evening. I was saying how much I missed Artem and Galyna.' The refugees, to whom she had given a home, had briefly channelled my mother's naturally caring nature. I remembered she'd felt quite bereft when they left. 'Before I knew it,' she continued, worryingly dreamy-eyed, 'Roger stepped into my life.'

God, was she going all Mills and Boon on me? 'When was this?' A trick question, I was ashamed to admit.

'We had our first meeting here in Cirencester, at the Fleece, in March.'

Matching the date on the calendar. 'So what's he like?'

'Very nice,' she said, which, in my book is the kiss of death. Nice is for cakes and functional sex. "Nice" people are bland. From what Dido described, Roger was anything but. Picking up on my less than knocked-out response, Mum qualified her answer. 'He's younger than me.'

Dad was considerably older than Mum. I swallowed at the prospect of a toy-boy. Bloody hell, I hoped he was nowhere near Alex's age, or God forbid, mine. 'How much?' It came out a bit squeaky.

'Fifty-three.'

Thank fuck. 'Divorced?'

'Never married. Want a biscuit?' She reached for the plate.

I shook my head. 'Long-term relationships?'

'Not that he mentioned.'

Black mark. Had to be something wrong with him. How do you get to that age and not have had a significant other?

'Don't look like that, Verity.' Her tone was only half-reproving.

'Like what?'

'Like Roger's odd, which I can assure you, he is not.'

'I'm sure he isn't,' I said with a warm smile. 'What's his surname?'

'Scott-Jefferies.'

Double-barrelled surnames are legion in the Cotswolds, to the point of being common.

'Does he live here?'

'Cheltenham.'

Good, I could suss him out on home territory. 'Does he work?'

At this my mother looked slightly vague. 'Something in finance.'

Hmm, no wonder Dido was getting palpitations.

'Look, if you want to know more about him, how about coming for supper tonight?'

'Great,' I said. *Shit*, I thought.

Mum rested her hand on my thigh. 'Good, that's settled.'

'Want me to bring anything?'

'Only your good self. Roger normally sorts out the wine.' I nodded blindly. Dad had always "sorted out" the wine. Before I got sentimental, the postman arrived and dropped what sounded like a brick through the letterbox. Glad of an escape route, I jumped up. 'I'll get it.'

The brick was, in fact, my mother's latest prescription for contact lenses. In amongst a couple of flyers advertising new ventures locally, a postcard arrived with a picture of Hereford cathedral on one side. Naturally curious, I turned it over. It was addressed to Eleonora Kaminska. The script was in capital letters and looked as if it had been written by one of my six-year-old schoolchildren. It read: *BLISS HERE.*

'What's that?' Mum asked, taking the postcard from my hand.

'Obviously been delivered to the wrong address.' Except it was the right address. 'Who lived here before you and Dad?'

Mum didn't answer. Her lips were silently moving, yet no words came out.

'You okay?' I asked. She hadn't gone pale, or anything like that. She just seemed, I don't know, peculiarly focused. 'Odd it's addressed to an Eleonora,' I murmured. 'With you being an Eleanor.'

'Total coincidence.' She snatched a smile. 'And explains the confusion. I'll have a word with the postie.'

She slipped it underneath the plate of biscuits. 'Right,' she said with a meaningful look. 'I need a shower and then I must pick up a few things for tonight.'

'Oh, okay.' Conscious that I was expected to leave her to it, I slid off the stool.

'About seven, is that all right?'

14

'Fine, two nights with Roger on the trot,' I said with a cheeky smile.

'Yes.' She beamed. 'I suppose it is.'

Walking back to the car, irritation coursed through me. What had possessed Mum to have dinner so publicly, the night before, on the anniversary of my dad's death?

CHAPTER THREE

I'd arranged to meet Nicola and Rinelle at Clementine's, an artisan café that used to be a butcher's shop. We'd been to school together and counted ourselves as close friends. Handily, the café, in Queen's Circus, was not far from my flat.

As usual, Nicola was already there and had commandeered a table at the back, with a view of the entrance. Her capable-sounding name, which, according to Greek sources, means "victory", defined her. She was not a Nic and definitely not a Nicky. A Nicola through and through. She glanced up at my approach.

'Rinelle's running late.'

This came as no surprise. Rinelle couldn't be anywhere on time if her life depended on it.

I slung down my bag and ordered a Pepsi. 'How's things?'

I never ask Nicola directly about work because she's based at the "doughnut", which is how people refer to the third arm of the intelligence services, GCHQ. To be honest, I had no idea what she did. I thought she might be an analyst. I didn't believe she skulked around meeting shady characters on trains, or catching terrorists. Having said that, she'd be ideal because she looks so ordinary. I didn't mean this unkindly. She had dark brown hair, held in place with slides, and wore massively big spectacles. Her only concession to make-up was a certain shade of brick-red lipstick. *Floral* best described her dress sense — the bigger the pattern, the better.

'Busy. You?'

'Doing my best not to be.'

'I envy you having six weeks' holiday.'

'It's not all rock and roll.' It came out unintentionally snippy. It was true I did slouch around in the first few weeks. It's called "decompression". After that, there was always a fair amount of preparation for the start of the school year. There's basic admin to do, and a lot of printing and laminating. I made a point of learning the names of the new intake from Year 2, paying attention to those who needed additional support. In my primary there were a number of kids who came from difficult backgrounds. Nurturing them, as best I could, presented certain challenges. The results of seeing them shine bright and fly high were worth more than increased status and extra money in a pay packet.

Nicola flicked me an appraising smile. 'Is this burnout talking, or is something bothering you?'

I grinned. 'Typical spook.'

'I simply know you too well.'

So I told her all about my mother and Roger. 'I feel rubbish about it and rubbish for feeling rubbish,' I finished awkwardly.

Before Nicola could offer me her wisdom, my mobile phone rang. I let out a groan. It was my brother. He rarely called unless it was to spout about a new business venture. This time, I suspected Dido's interference.

'Hey,' he said.

'Hello, Alex, how you doing?'

'Fine, fine,' he said 'Lots on, as usual. Got an idea to run a venture, involving buskers and street musicians.'

Good luck with that, I thought. There were loads of buskers in Cheltenham. They ventured from sublime (I could think of one) to, frankly, abysmal.

'I want to sort of manage them.'

"Sort of" summed Alex up. 'Aren't they all one-man bands?'

'Oh, very good.' Alex snickered. 'High end, of course.'

'Right.'

'Wondered if you'd seen Ma lately.'

So not subtle. I glanced across at Nicola, whose smile was as wide as the table. 'This morning, actually.'

'How is she?'

'Great.'

'Good, that's good.'

'Kids okay?'

'Yes, all fine. Potty-training Fred. Bit of a nightmare. Kitty is driving our nanny crazy.'

'Get a new one. Nanny, that is, not child.'

Alex gave a guffaw of laughter.

I could almost hear his brain clicking at the other end and I wondered if Dido was standing next to him, breathing ice and fire down his neck.

'Thing is . . .'

'Yeah?'

'Her boyfriend.'

I pulled a face. It sounded a weird description for a man who was almost elderly. Not that I was ageist, and my mother was spectacularly fit — in the old-fashioned sense of the word, that was.

'What about him?'

'Aren't you bothered?'

'Bothered?' No, I wasn't going to make this easy.

'That it may not be a good idea.'

'*It?*'

'Roger.'

'How so? Mum is having fun. Isn't she entitled?'

'Yes, but—'

'Alex, who are you, or I, to make that kind of judgement?'

'Well, I see where you're coming from . . .'

That, I very much doubted. 'Look, I'm meeting him tonight.'

'Are you?'

If I'd told him I was upping sticks to go backpacking in China, he could not have sounded more astonished. I silently cursed for being too open and honest. I wasn't trying to upstage or hurt Alex, but he really was driving me nuts. 'If I get the creeps about him, I'll be sure to let you know.'

'Deal.' He spoke with such relief that I definitely got the impression that he was as uncomfortable asking questions as I was giving answers. 'Until then, relax and let things be. Oh, and good luck with the new venture.'

I ended the call.

'You sounded upbeat,' Nicola said.

'That's because it's Alex.'

Rinelle arrived. She looked fantastic in a loose-fitting pale blue linen shirt over tan-coloured shorts, white pumps on her slim feet, her hair tamed by a wide orange silk scarf. I was more of a sundress, denim jacket and Doc Martens type of girl. No disrespect to Nicola, but Rinelle was the prettiest woman in the café, if not the whole of Cheltenham. She had small, delicate features and incredibly long painted nails. It was a marvel to watch her pick things up without snapping one of them. They could hardly be called functional but, crikey, she had style.

Rinelle pulled up a chair. 'So what's the latest?'

'I'm going to the loo,' I announced. 'Nicola can fill you in.' I gave her a meaningful look.

I did what I had to do and took my time about it.

'I ordered our usual,' Rinelle said, as I sat back down.

Orange juice and smashed avocado on toast with a couple of poached eggs plopped on the top. 'Great.'

Rinelle looked at Nicola who looked at me.

'What?' I said. 'Oh, I get it, you think I'm being super-sensitive.'

Rinelle flashed a big smile. 'Just a teensy bit.'

'We get it,' Nicola said. 'After all this time it must seem weird.'

'You could say.'

'But your mum is so grounded,' Rinelle said, doing her best to reassure me. 'Some people get intolerant as they grow older. That's not your mum. She wouldn't choose someone who wasn't special. My mum always says that your mother is as beautiful on the inside as on the outside.'

'That's lovely.' Out of anyone else's lips it could have sounded cheesy. Rinelle's sincerity shone through and I felt a vicarious thrill. It's nice when your friends' parents like your parents, or in this case, *parent*.

'Have you met Roger? Rinelle asked gingerly.

'I'm meeting him tonight.'

'You might really like him,' Nicola said.

'Unlike you to be optimistic.'

She grinned. 'I save my pessimism for the workplace. Do you know anything about him?'

I gave the broad brushstrokes, which, I realised, amounted to very little.

'Where does he live in town?' Rinelle asked.

'What are you suggesting, I stalk him or something?' I couldn't deny the thought had crossed my mind.

She hitched a shoulder. 'Might be fun.'

'No way.' The sturdy note in Nicola's voice was unmistakable. Out of the three of us, she was the sensible one. I suppose I should be grateful that one of the guardians of the realm had her head screwed on.

'Mum had dinner with him on the anniversary of my dad's death,' I blurted out. *How's that for pessimism?*

Rinelle pulled a face. Nicola was totally unfazed. 'You could argue it's a healthy sign she's moved on. It doesn't mean that she's forgotten your father.'

I pressed a hand to my mouth. My eyes prickled with tears. The weird thing about people you love dying is that grief can sneak up on you and catch you unawares. The passage of time never seems to make that much difference. Emotions are not so raw, but they're still there.

Rinelle rested a warm hand on my back.

'Sorry.' I sniffled into a tissue.

'Don't be daft,' she said. 'It's deep, I know, but whatever happens tonight, whatever you think of the situation, we've got your back.'

And I knew they had. They'd been with me every step of the way, including when Dad died. 'Thanks,' I burbled.

'Drinks at mine tomorrow night,' Nicola announced. 'I want a full debrief.'

'You're on.' Cheered up, I clean forgot about the weird postcard.

CHAPTER FOUR

What could I say? Roger was *hot*.

The guy before me in his crisp white shirt, two buttons undone, had no hint of a gut. His stone-coloured chinos were not disastrously tight. He didn't wear flip-flops or loafers without socks. His were dressed-to-impress Versace trainers. His hair was not dull grey, like Dido had described. It was silver with flashes of wet slate. His hair was not too long, and he hadn't dyed his moustache and beard in a lame attempt to appear young like some older men desperate to "get down with the kids". His eyes, the colour of one of my favourite cocktails (vodka, blue curaçao and prosecco) were kind, slightly downturned at the edges, and he had a tan that made him look as if he'd been dipped in honey, with a golden smile to match. I'm a sucker for men with deep voices and he spoke in a rich baritone. He laughed a lot, and it wasn't down to nerves. Instantly, I could see my mum's attraction to him. He was easy-going and laid-back. I'm not being horrible about my dad, but he was more your strong and stable type. God help me, but I was actually rather impressed that my mother had been able to snare Roger Scott-Jefferies.

Then an unsavoury thought crossed my mind: *was he a player?*

'So, Verity, Eleanor tells me you're a school teacher.'

'That's right.'

We were sitting outside under a big shady umbrella that failed to protect from the suffocating heat. It felt as if every atom of oxygen had been sucked out of the atmosphere.

We drank Pimm's, which Roger had concocted: strong, sweet and with the right amount of mint and cucumber, no strawberries. I was looking for an alcohol hit, not the regulatory daily intake of five fruits. Or was it supposed to be ten now?

'You enjoy teaching?'

'Yeah, I do. Mostly.' I didn't enjoy the moments when some little kid threatened to get their "dad on me" for ticking her off.

'You're obviously a patient young woman. Must get that from your mother.' He stretched over and casually took her hand, like they'd done it all their lives. I clocked her dreamy-eyed expression again and wondered if I'd ever seen her this way with my father. Maybe when she was young and in the first flush of lust and before my brother and me arrived. At the back of my brain I heard Nicola whisper: *Stop it.*

'Mum says you live in Cheltenham,' I said brightly.

'Got a place in the Park.'

'Nice — been there long?'

'A few years.'

'But you're not from here originally?' I thought I'd detected a slight rural accent.

'Devon,' he said.

'Like Mum.' Only my mother's accent was not in the least bit discernible. Proper Received Pronunciation, it had rubbed off on me.

'Whereabouts?'

'South Hams.'

'That *is* a coincidence.' The second today, I registered, darting an enquiring look at my mother, who smiled.

'Yes, I was born in Kingsbridge and moved to Totnes,' she said.

Roger gave her hand a squeeze. 'We share so much in common.'

I wondered if he too was a late, if joyous, surprise to relatively elderly parents, like my mother.

'We're going to eat soon,' she said briskly. 'Top up, or shall we move on to wine?'

'I've bought a couple of lovely bottles from my cellar,' Roger said with a wink.

'You have a cellar?' Blimey, which mansion in the Park did he inhabit?

'Only kidding. It's a cupboard under the stairs.'

'Oh, right,' I said, feeling daft and gullible. 'Wine for me, if it's white. Only a glass as I'm driving.'

'You're very welcome to stay,' Mum said.

'Well, I . . .' Christ, I didn't fancy staying if Mum and Roger were shacking up for the night. He appeared to read my hesitation with a hint of amusement.

'I mustn't be late either, got an early start in the morning. Important business meeting,' he added.

'Right,' I said. 'Thanks, Mum. I'll stay.'

After that Roger switched to low-alcohol lager and I rather went for it. Booze made me bold. I might as well have asked what his intentions were towards my mother.

'Mum said you work in finance.' I forked in a mouthful of spicy chicken with harissa, lemon and olives, one of my mum's specialities.

'Wealth management.'

'Sounds lucrative.' Dido would be appreciative.

'It's interesting and gives me a good living.'

'You have an office in town?'

'Rodney Road.'

'Tooth Row,' I said with a laugh. 'Full of dentists and dental technicians.'

'Ah, yes, you're right.' Roger topped up my glass.

'You never married?'

'For goodness' sake, Verity, leave the poor man alone.' Mum spoke in a jolly tone. Underneath, there was a definite level of frustration and annoyance.

Roger flicked up both palms. 'It's fine, honestly, Eleanor. Verity has every right to quiz me.'

'Sorry,' I said. 'I don't wish to be rude.'

'I should think not.' Mum's smile had an edge so subtle most would miss it. Not me.

'To answer your question, I almost got hitched a couple of times.'

'Really?' Mum said, wide-eyed.

Reaching for my glass, I could tell this was news to her.

'So glad I didn't.' Roger gave my mother another smooth look.

Steady, I thought. 'You never wanted children?' I persisted.

'Not sure I'd be a great influence. I'm naturally subversive.' His laughing eyes met mine. He ate lustily, not messily, thank God, although I noticed he put salt on his food as though he were crop-spraying.

'Nothing wrong with a little subversion. Kids love a maverick.' I turned to Mum. 'We're always thinking of ways to shake things up with my nephew and niece, aren't we?'

'I wouldn't put it quite like that.' Mum seemed strangely put out by the suggestion. I guess she wanted to create a good impression of her maternal skills.

'I'm looking forward to meeting them — and your brother, of course.' Roger stood up, withdrew a packet of cigarettes from his pocket. 'Just popping outside for a smoke. Filthy habit, but can't quite kick it.'

'You don't have to go into the street,' Mum protested.

Yes, he bloody does, I thought, taken aback. My mother had only ever gone ape-shit with me once in my life, and that was when she discovered a pack of B&H in my handbag. Condoms were fine, ciggies definitely not.

'Wouldn't dream of it,' he said. 'Gives you girls a chance to catch up.'

I watched him crunch across the gravelled path, listened as the wooden gates swung open and closed.

'You hate people who smoke,' I hissed.

'I don't hate anyone, Verity. I *dislike* the habit. Roger's a grown-up and makes his own choices.' She broke into a smile. 'Apart from his most obvious vice, what do you think?'

I picked up my glass, took a swig of wine, put on a serious expression. 'Actually . . .' I began.

'Yes?' She looked painfully anxious, trusting even.

I burst out laughing. 'I think he's lovely.'

She let out a long breath that I hadn't realised she'd been holding. 'I'm so pleased. I couldn't bear it if you hadn't liked him.'

'Dido might be another story,' I said.

'Dido will have to lump it.' She raised her glass and chinked it with mine.

Roger returned. Feeling stupidly happy, I topped up my glass; some wine sploshed over my hand. I wasn't thinking of anything to say in particular; more a case of the first thing that popped into my mind.

'Did you solve the mystery of the postcard, Mum?'

'What postcard?' Roger said.

'It's nothing,' Mum said with a dry laugh.

'A mystery isn't nothing.' Roger leant forward. I caught the briefest whiff of nicotine.

'Someone mistakenly sent a postcard to this address,' I said. 'The woman's name happened to be Eleonora.'

Roger's expression was vacant, possibly because I was slurring my words. I gave it another shot, this time articulating them more slowly.

'Oh, I see.' His eyes lit with recognition. 'How weird is that. You never mentioned it, darling.'

Mum quietly sipped her wine. 'What's there to say?'

'The surname looked Polish,' I said.

'Verity, you're making something of nothing.'

Roger nudged my arm. 'You obviously have a taste for the dramatic, young lady.'

In my addled state, I let it go. Too familiar, for my liking, this could possibly be Roger's first bum move.

'You should meet my sister-in-law, Dido. People generally tell me I'm stubborn.' As if to prove a point, I added, 'Do you have it, Mum?'

Her face tightened. 'Of course I don't. It went straight in the bin.'

CHAPTER FIVE

I woke up disorientated and with a monster hangover. My head felt like it had been pumped with concrete and I had an acute form of gut-rot, like I'd swallowed the stuff they used to clean out blocked drains. Already hot from an indoor temperature of twenty-seven degrees centigrade, I leaked boozy perspiration. If someone lit a match near my face the fumes from my rancid breath would ignite and singe my eyebrows.

Barely able to focus, and with the walls still drifting and shifting, I snatched up my phone and saw, firstly, that it was past noon and, secondly, I'd received a host of messages from Dido.

So, what's he like? Can you speak? Is he solvent? MESSAGE ME.

Ashamed to say, the thought of Dido's frustration elicited a warm thrum of pleasure. It didn't last. To my dismay, I *had* sent messages to Nicola and Rinelle.

He's great. Mum is weird. Had a shitload to drink. Mum doesn't like me. Roger is hot.

This elicited an *'Awesome xx'* from Rinelle and *'Haha, amazing,'* from Nicola.

Jesus, in the cold light of day, I'd definitely overhyped him.

With a groan and a hand pressed to my temple, I tottered out of bed and stood underneath a cool shower for a long time and felt sorry for myself. Nothing like a heavy night to plunge your self-esteem to the level of the gutter. Snippets of conversation drifted back from the night before. Had I made an arse of myself? Short answer: yes.

Towelling myself dry, I smoothed on White Company body lotion that Mum had left in the guest bathroom, ignored my knackered reflection in the mirror and slipped on a pale green sundress that matched my eyes. This morning, I was making allowances.

Slowly and softly, I inched my way downstairs. A huge bouquet of flowers, awaiting my mother's attention, sat in a sink filled with water. The card next to it said: *Thank you for a marvellous evening, love R xx*

Smooth operator. Roger must have organised delivery before he discovered how marvellous the night would be.

Helping myself to a glass of sparkling water from the fridge, I ambled outside to where my mother was deadheading roses. She looked up at my approach. Her calm expression was reproving, or was I scratchy because I'd had more alcohol than was good for me? An overload always put me in a bad mood.

'I saw your lovely bouquet,' I said.

'He's very thoughtful. Did you sleep well?'

'Fine.' As much as you ever sleep when you're wasted. The thought of drinks tonight with the girls, usually a rowdy affair, lacked appeal. 'About last night, Mum—'

'Oh, don't be silly,' she said with a big smile. 'I was stupidly brittle. I'm not good in the heat, to be honest. Honestly, you said nothing wrong.'

There was nothing like receiving absolution from the person you love most in the world, but did I believe her?

That she might not be telling the truth would be a novelty. Honesty ran through my mother like the interior of a stick of rock. You could say it was her watchword. I wanted to delicately pursue the postcard connection, but Roger arrived and the dynamic instantly changed. The glow from my mum could light up the darkest night.

She handed her secateurs to me and slipped her arm through his. 'Hello, stranger.' She tipped up on her toes and kissed him softly on the cheek.

'Morning, Verity.' He flashed a smile. Plain black T-shirt over jeans, he looked as crisp and fresh as he had the night before. I suddenly remembered that he'd said he had work that day. Wasn't that the excuse he'd given to head off early? He was very casually dressed for an important business meeting.

'Don't ask her how she is.' Mum laughed, cutting into my thoughts.

'Yeah, feeling a bit rough,' I admitted.

Mum offered to make me a bacon sarnie, which I declined. I didn't think my stomach could cope. Roger also passed on food, but accepted a cup of tea.

'I'll have some tea, too,' I said.

She beetled off, leaving the two of us together. I really wanted to go inside and escape the heat. Roger had other ideas. He sat down and patted the seat next to him. Dutifully, I sat.

'Is your mum okay?'

'She's fine.'

'Only, last night, she seemed, a little . . . I don't know, off.'

'Off?' I suddenly felt protective of my mother and I really wasn't too happy discussing her feelings with a man I'd only met twenty-four hours earlier, however pleasant he seemed.

'Out of sorts.'

'Not at all.'

'That postcard business.'

'A misunderstanding.'

'It seemed to upset her.'

'The heat was too much. That was all.' I was comfortable with thieving my mother's excuse because now I was more certain than ever that something was up. I didn't yet know what it was.

'If you say so.'

The mood changed. There was a nasty undertone. I looked him sharply in the eye. He was in grave danger of moving from hero to zero. He flicked both palms up. 'Sorry, that came out wrong. I care about her, that's all.'

'And so do I,' I said stonily.

'Here we are.' Mum bowled out with a tray of food and drinks. 'I made a pot,' she said, setting it down.

Roger sat while my mother poured out three cups, adding sugar and milk.

'Have you wound it up?' he asked, playfully.

Bloody hell, I thought. *Can't you stir your own tea?* Mum caught my vibe and flashed a *behave* expression, as she dutifully obeyed. I silently sipped while they prattled on about going for a walk through the Bathurst estate. Eventually, I stood up and announced I was heading out.

Roger stood up and rested both hands on my shoulders. 'It's been quite lovely to meet you, Verity. All the good things your mother said were true.' The intensity of his expression could have cut through tungsten, the strongest metal in the world. *Charmer*, I thought, pulling away before he could kiss my cheeks.

'Bye, Mum,' I said, giving her a hug.

Darting back inside, I collected my overnight bag, deciding to leave through the front door so I wouldn't need to cross the courtyard.

Opening it, I gave a start and let out a yell. A large dead bird of prey, a buzzard, perhaps, lay on the doorstep. Wings splayed, blood congealed where its head should have been. What really turned my tummy was the glut of maggots crawling in and out of its flesh. I wanted to run away screaming.

Next, I heard thundering footsteps and my mum's concerned cries followed by Roger's baritone voice. I shuffled aside and her eyes shot wide.

'Get rid of it.' White-faced and tight-lipped, she was a picture of distress.

'Must have been accidentally hit by a car,' Roger said. 'Got any bin bags, Eleanor?'

'Somewhere.' She put a weary hand to her head. 'In the utility.'

'Go and sit down, Mum. I'll get them.'

She turned on her heel and I unearthed some bags and handed them to Roger. It had to be said he was a star. He disposed of the bird with his bare hands and disinfected the entire area afterwards. I sat with my mother who stared into the distance and didn't say a word.

'All done,' Roger said. 'You girls are safe with me around.'

He sounded hearty, as if getting rid of a dead creature was no big deal. Maybe his Devon country-boy roots had kicked in. Whatever, it pleased Mum no end. She came back to normal, composure thrown around her shoulders like a cloak.

'Rightio,' I said with affected brightness. 'I'll be pushing off — again.'

'Text when you get home, Verity.'

I assured Mum I would.

'Drive safe,' Roger called after me.

Outside, the heat boomeranged off streets and buildings and smacked me in the face. I could barely breathe and felt a sudden bubble of panic.

It was odd for the bird to be so far outside its natural habitat. An accident was simple and straightforward, I told myself on the walk back to my car.

What if it wasn't?

CHAPTER SIX

On the inevitably slow journey home, I tried out various scenarios. Cars hit birds all the time, usually when the vehicle was moving at speed. It was impossible to drive fast through the narrow streets of Cirencester so the buzzard, a big bird and normally savvy, would either have been unlucky or slow. Perhaps it had been ill, which would explain why it was so far outside its comfort zone. Another scenario: someone had left it there deliberately, which, I told myself, wasn't as chilling as it sounded.

I'd once stayed at a friend's in the Cotswolds. Her parents had a lovely new home on a small, exclusive development. Some random woman drove a banged-up Fiesta onto their drive, stopped, dragged out a large branch of a tree that had got stuck underneath the chassis and dumped it in their front garden, said, 'See you later,' and drove off. Annoying and anti-social, it wasn't an act of malign intent.

I frowned.

Would someone run over a bird somewhere else, pick it up off the hot tarmac, keep it a few days to rot and then, after decapitating it dump it randomly on a stranger's doorstep?

Despite the strangling humidity, I felt a sudden chill.

If it were deliberate, I thought, *why*? Was it a targeted action? Mum posed absolutely no threat to anyone. She had good neighbours. She had friends. She didn't get into rows because she was entirely risk-averse. Could it be a case of mistaken identity and, again, if so, was it intended as a threat, warning, "we've marked your card", or what?

Don't be so ridiculous.

Despite giving myself a mental talking-to, I crunched gears and automatically ducked as a guy in a souped-up Ford Sierra shot past and showed me his middle finger. *Well, fuck you, too.*

Speeding up a little, I told myself I was looking for answers when there were none to be had. Inexplicable events coupled with excessive alcohol consumption contributed to paranoia and, consequently, I made a promise to stay sober that night. Might even pick up some low-alcohol lager on my way to Nicola's later.

I'd barely got one foot over the threshold when Dido phoned. Not a woman to fob off, I answered straightaway.

'So?' she said, the tiny word punching above its weight and conveying *dish the dirt, spill the beans* and *make it worth my while.*

'Morning,' I said.

'It's afternoon. How did it go last night?'

'We had a very nice evening. Mum cooked her signature dish and we sat outside in the courtyard.'

Dido clicked her tongue. Obviously she wasn't interested in the menu.

'Oh, *that*,' I said, as if it had just dawned on me. 'Happy to report Roger seemed like a regular guy.'

If silences could be stippled with expletives, this was one such example. I almost felt sorry for her. 'Although, to be fair—'

'Yes?'

'It's impossible to sum up a person after a single meeting.'

'Exactly,' Dido said. 'That's how people get taken in by serial killers. The worst are the most charming.'

Could you have a "worst" serial killer? Weren't they all evil as fuck? Not knowing what to say, I decided not to mention the corpse on the doorstep.

'I think discreet enquiries should be made about him,' Dido continued.

Dido was as discreet as a nuclear explosion.

'I hope you're not expecting me to snoop on your behalf.'

'God, no. I was thinking of your friend. The girl who works at GCHQ.'

How did you tell someone to take a hike, without being very rude? 'The *girl* is too busy looking after national interests,' I said, a touch haughtily. Muttering about having things to do and places to be, I ended the call.

Rattled by the Dido effect, I banished her from my brain by pottering around the flat, tidying up, cleaning the loo, picking the clothes up off the bedroom floor, shaking out the creases, and hanging them back in the wardrobe. I picked up a novel and, armed with an energy drink, sat outside, reading among the plants that had managed not to keel over and die in the heat.

As brilliant as the story was, Dido had inserted a worm of suspicion in my mind. When I wound up reading the same paragraph three times, without taking in a word, I put the book down, stretched my arms up and over my head and yawned.

Not for one second did I think Roger was a serial killer, a philanderer maybe. If this were the case, my mother stood to have her heart broken. Pressure expanded in my chest at the thought.

A bit emotionally untethered and with time to kill, I grabbed a wide-brimmed sunhat and headed out towards town. Shade was hard to come by and I was forced to negotiate my way from one tree-lined side of the road to the other.

Cheltenham was one of those lovely places where you see humanity in all its variation and colour. Kids on skateboards skedaddling down pavements at breakneck speed (I know they shouldn't), forty-year-olds on E-scooters (similar criticism), corporate types attached to their mobile phones, arty folk (or at least giving the impression of being so), the inebriated, the stoned, the glossy and the glamorous, mum and dads, and everything and everyone in between.

Soon I was passing Montpellier Gardens and Imperial Square, where I turned right and veered left into Rodney Road. The sun blazed down, threatening to incinerate me.

Apart from the aforementioned dental establishments, there was a language school at the far end of the street and, roughly opposite it, a fabulous "high days and holidays" restaurant I'd been to once. The offices of an "ethical wealth-management consultancy" appeared about halfway along, the nameplate failing to reveal whether Roger worked there or not. I wasn't really certain if he was a one-man band, or operated as part of a team.

Tapping the name of the company into my phone to view the website, I discovered there wasn't one. A number of other financial services companies popped up in neighbouring streets, with proper contact details and information. *Didn't mean a thing,* I told myself, trudging back home.

* * *

Nicola's apartment — too posh to call it a flat — was in what was euphemistically known as Spook Row because of the number of GCHQ personnel who lived there. There were no gardens. Who cared when there was air-conditioning? Currently, the temperature was set to a deliciously cool sixteen degrees. I felt better already.

Nicola had gone to town on tapas, which I tucked into about as much as my abused tummy could stand. I insisted on drinking my own supply of 0.05 % hooch while Nicola and Rinelle got stuck into a bottle of Pinot Grigio. George Ezra was singing in the background while I lounged, feet up, on Nicola's expensive sofa.

Nobody asked me about the night before until we were all settled. There was a degree of theatricality about it. Nicola liked to control things, and Rinelle was happy to fall in until we were all good and ready and the stage was set. Predictably, Rinelle was first to enter from the wings.

'How was it?'

Good in parts, odd and freaked out in others. 'Okay.'

'Is that it? You said he was *hot* in your drunken messages, you hussy.'

'That was several pints of Pimm's and Pays d'Oc talking.'

Deflated after the hype, neither of them bought my bland response, a point Rinelle made with the tip of her dagger-like fingernail in the sole of my foot. I let out a yelp and then a sigh and gave them the lowdown.

I'd expected interruptions and interjections, at least from Rinelle, although there was plenty of eye movement. Nicola maintained a poker face, because that's Nicola for you. I stuttered to a halt after relating the birdie balls-up.

'Gross,' Rinelle said, pulling a face.

Nicola asked how my mum reacted.

'Upset and rather shaken.'

'Who wouldn't be?' Rinelle interjected.

'The evening before,' Nicola continued. 'How did she seem?'

I took my time answering. 'Loved-up.' Infatuated, more like.

'That's so sweet.' Rinelle swooped on a cocktail stick and speared a double anchovy stuffed olive.

'And you've no idea how the headless bird got there?' Nicola took a slow steady sip of wine.

I shook my head.

'Can't we change the subject?' Rinelle said, mouth full. 'I'm trying to eat here.'

I did as asked, although not in the way expected. I told them about the strange postcard.

'Maybe your mum has a connection to Hereford,' Rinelle said, chewing vigorously.

'She's never mentioned the place to me.' I reminded the girls that she'd been brought up in Devon, same as Roger. She was a late arrival to her parents who were well into their forties when she was born. Unfortunately, they hadn't survived long enough to meet my father.

Nicola's gaze intensified. 'The message, what was it again?'

'"BLISS HERE". Uncontroversial and almost friendly,' I commented.

'When was it sent?'

'Yesterday morning.'

'Did you notice the postmark?'

It hadn't occurred to me to look. 'I assumed it was sent from Herefordshire.'

Rinelle grabbed a handful of crisps. 'Two slightly peculiar events, so what?'

Nicola didn't seem convinced. She doesn't do short term. She only does big picture. Her entire education was devoted to wanting to get into intelligence. Not content to simply walk down a road, she had to peer around the corner and spy on what's at the end of it too.

'What was your mum's reaction?' she enquired.

'Dismissive, initially. Although there was no mistaking the address, she reckoned the confusion emanated from the similarity in her Christian name.'

'Eleonora Kaminska sounds Polish,' Nicola said. 'What's your mum's maiden name?'

'Hannaford.' I took a gulp of wine. 'Anyway, I mentioned the whole episode again in front of Roger, last night, and she was plain spooky. I mean she tried to laugh it off, but I know when she's concealing her feelings.'

'Hiding from him, or from you?' Nicola said.

'Good question.'

'And she got rid of the card, you say?'

I nodded.

'Any way you can find out if that's true?'

'Fuck's sake, Nicola, you're making out Verity's mum to be a liar.' Rinelle's voice lifted a few notches. Two sharp lines appeared between her eyebrows.

'I'm saying she might be being economical with the truth. There's a difference.'

Rinelle spread her hands. 'What would be the point of that?'

'To protect Verity.'

I was sure that if Nicola had the dubious honour of telling us that the world was going to be blown up tomorrow and there was nowhere to hide, she would speak in the same slow and calculated manner. She reminded me of Mum, in that way, and it's equally annoying. Rinelle and I spoke in unison. 'From *what?*'

'I have no idea. Safe to say, if your mum kept the postcard, it has meaning for her. Might be worth checking.'

I rubbed my chin. I didn't like the idea of snooping on Roger (and was too embarrassed to admit I'd tried to check out his office in town) but I positively hated the idea of sticky-beaking through my mum's belongings.

'Is anyone going to eat anything?' Rinelle's hungry gaze fell upon the salami with marinated peppers and aubergines.

My appetite had gone walkabout. The intense expression on Nicola's face didn't help.

'Do you think the two events are connected?' I asked tentatively.

'Probably not.'

Thank goodness for that. I picked at crisps and prawns and smoked trout and was persuaded to have a small glass of wine that made me feel instantly better. Rinelle dived in to the food like a prisoner recently released from a lengthy jail term. Conversation turned to Rinelle's work. She was in marketing for a company specialising in energy-efficient products for the manufacturing industry. We discussed their expansion plans and her potential for promotion.

'When I worked in Croydon,' she said, 'it was really tricky to recruit cool applicants for the marketing team — absolutely no takers. Different story in Cheltenham — we practically had a stampede. My crew are full of bright ideas. They're never off Insta and we've just launched a series of podcasts.'

I started to relax. Nicola had other ideas. All the time we'd been eating and talking, she'd been ruminating.

'You said Roger arrived while you were outside.'

Rinelle let out a groan and theatrically pressed a hand to her forehead. 'Can't we leave the poor bastard alone?'

Ignoring Rinelle, I replied, 'We were in the courtyard, yes.'

'And he entered through where?'

I could see where Nicola was going with it. 'The wooden gates into the garden, not through the front door.'

'But, theoretically, he could have deposited the bird beforehand.'

'I guess,' I said unhappily.

Rinelle was incredulous. 'Fuck's sake, why would he do that?'

Nicola looked to me for an answer that slapped me smartly across my face.

'To make my mother emotionally dependent upon him.'

'What's wrong with you two?' Rinelle burst out. 'You're reading too much into a common situation: man meets woman.'

'Calm down, it's only a theory,' Nicola said.

'And a dangerous one. Verity, you have a good relationship with your mother. Don't screw it up. If you're really bothered, talk to her about your concerns.'

This time, *I* looked at Nicola.

She gave an enigmatic shrug. 'It's not a bad idea.'

'*Thank you,*' Rinelle said, taking a bite out of a crusty piece of bread.

'Not being funny,' I said, the most insincere phrase in the English language, 'but one more thing to throw into the mix: Roger works in wealth management.'

Rinelle stopped eating.

'Pour me more wine,' Nicola said.

I grinned and topped up our glasses. Good intentions and all that.

'Why didn't you say before?' Rinelle asked.

'You didn't ask before.'

'Coo — do you reckon he's after her loot?'

'Now who's reading too much into it?' Couldn't help myself. Rinelle ignored the implied criticism. 'I have to admit Dodgy Roger has a certain ring about it.'

'You sound like Dido.'

'I bloody hope not,' Rinelle said, spluttering. 'No offence, but your sister-in-law is one prize heifer.'

Harsh, but fair. I'd once witnessed Dido roasting my mum for forgetting that Freddie was lactose-intolerant. It wasn't pretty.

Nicola was on silent mode, sipping her wine with deadly intent. I couldn't ask for her technical expertise directly. I needed to tap her knowledge in a more roundabout way.

'Hypothetically, if I wanted to profile Roger, you know, work out if he's on the level, or not, how would I go about it?'

Nicola flashed a smile. 'No way.'

Rinelle rolled her eyes. 'It's only *hypothetical*.'

There was a momentary pause when I wasn't sure how Nicola would respond. Those big spectacles she wore obscured any possibility of reading her properly.

'Generally speaking,' she was keen to emphasise, 'you need to look for the blanks in his past, the stuff that doesn't add up.'

'And how would one do that?' I was careful to keep my interest objective even though it was entirely subjective.

Nicola gave me another of her inscrutable looks. 'Finding out about someone is reliant on intelligence, checking out digital footprints, scouring social media, unearthing bank accounts, financial stuff, that kind of thing, and discovering if the target has a history of documented violence, spells in prison, or whatever. Combing through fine detail is ninety per cent of the work.'

I stood no chance. Nicola had access to information denied to the general public. My best shot was Google. I didn't hold out much hope.

'But human intelligence,' Nicola continued, 'is more a case of following, watching, checking routines, finding out who a target hangs out with, his associations.'

'Isn't that stalking and weren't you dead against it?' Rinelle said.

Nicola slow-blinked. 'I'm not endorsing it. I'm simply answering Verity's question.'

'What are the risks?' I asked.

'A professional would be what we call target-aware. He'll cover his tracks. He'll be security conscious. He might not use digital devices at all but prefer to pass on and receive information through word of mouth only. We're talking terrorists here,' Nicola said emphatically. 'Not flaky members of the public with questionable agendas.'

I'd known Nicola for almost twenty years. She came across as a closed book in all things: relationships, holiday destinations, hopes and dreams. Now I thought I knew why.

'With the big kids, your life is on the line,' Nicola said.

'This is just a random bloke who's taken up with my mother,' I said with an uneasy laugh.

'Then why are you making such a meal of it?' Nicola asked with a flat stare.

CHAPTER SEVEN

Because I had a hunch, because I didn't believe in coincidences, because some deep protective instinct kicked in, I Googled Roger first thing and got precisely nowhere. It's claimed that it's easy to find someone with a name on the Electoral Register. It wasn't. Undaunted, I set out for the Park after most people had hit the office with their first takeaway coffee of the day.

I strolled to Tivoli where there's a nice pub that served prosecco and nibbles as part of their Summer Nights Special. Victorian terraced houses were so tightly packed they looked as if they huddled together for warmth. From there, it's a stone's throw, via one of my very favourite roads, to the Park and the best that Cheltenham had to offer: a lavish loop of ferociously priced homes surrounding the University of Gloucestershire campus. The central conservation area was leafy, with wide pavements for runners and walkers, and, it had to be said, the odd cyclist. Looking for Roger was like hunting for Nemo. Paying attention to Nicola's advice offered my best opportunity to catch a break. I needed to study Roger *in situ*. Besides, what else was I going to do that Wednesday? The thought I might actually run into him was banished from my brain. That kind of stuff happened in novels. It didn't occur in real life.

I pottered along as the temperature continued to climb. Now that the students had departed for the summer, it was extraordinarily quiet, apart from the insistent drone of a lawnmower. Deciding to follow the noise, I fetched up outside a pretty Regency-style villa that, judging by the coded entry panel, had been compartmentalised into flats. A young guy, my age, was cutting the lawn of the communal grounds. A long shot was better than no shot so I applied my warmest smile and approached him. He had a proper hipster beard and dark eyes. A white T stretched over a firm torso that I'd bet was as tanned as the rest of him. He looked up and instantly killed the motor — an encouraging start.

'I'm looking for someone who lives around here,' I began boldly. 'The name's Roger Scott-Jefferies.'

I could tell from his blank expression it meant nothing.

'He's late fifties, about your height. Shock of silver hair, blue eyes.'

This was met with a slow shake of the head.

I tilted my chin towards the apartments. 'Think anyone inside might know?'

With another shake of the head, he started up the mower.

'Well, thanks for your time,' I yelled over the din. Not so much a man of few words, a man of none.

Chastened, I stopped a woman walking a Saluki — we ended up talking about the dog whose name was Shakira — and after that an elderly gent on a mobility scooter.

'No idea,' he said, gliding away.

I'd almost done a full circuit of the Park. The little toe on my right foot rubbed dispiritingly against my new pumps. Footsore, I dropped down onto a bench underneath a tree, let the peace steal over me, and watched the world go by.

My intelligence-gathering operation had stalled at the first. Despite all the excitement of the night before, Roger's occupation was no different to thousands of others involved in the financial-services industry.

Feeling bad and a little silly, I was forced to admit that Rinelle was right. I should cut Roger some slack. What harm had he done me, much less Mum? A chat with her would put my stupid suspicions to bed, once and for all.

Limping back home, I passed the entrance to Merestones Road and noticed an estate agent board with a "Let" sign outside a modern brick house with ugly grey cladding and a dustbin parked as if it were an ornamental feature. Estate agents countrywide had a habit of leaving signs up for ages — it's a cheap form of advertising. I hobbled past then hobbled back towards a stout woman in a kaftan loading a car with suitcases in the drive next-door. Call me contrary.

'Hi,' I said brightly.

Hot and bothered, she shut the boot with a dull clunk and turned her friendly face towards me.

I went through the usual routine.

She puffed out her cheeks and dabbed her brow with a tissue. 'I don't know his name but someone matching that description moved in about six months ago.' Her face fell. She placed a plump hand against her chest. I was worried she was about to have a heart attack. 'Is he in trouble?' Code for: *am I in the shit and do I have an axe murderer living next to me?*

I gave a giddy laugh and assured her that he was a fine upstanding citizen. Well, I thought he was.

'Only he comes and goes all times of the day and night,' she said. 'Not sure he lives at the property full time. Keeps himself to himself, if you know what I mean. Not that there's anything wrong in that. Town living for you, isn't it? Nobody has time to talk, or pass the time of day. I'm from Norfolk, see? Different there. Folk are friendly, not standoffish. Ah, well, best be getting on.' She walked towards the driver's door. 'Shall I mention you called, if I see him?'

'Nah, it's fine. I'm sure our paths will cross.'

I watched her drive away. Unease hooked a finger into my chest and gave my heart a yank. If this was Roger, and I was pretty sure it was, he'd arrived in town a month before meeting my mum. I'd assumed he owned a property when, according to the lady with the orange hair, he rented it. Lots of people did this. *I'd* done it. There was no call for alarm. He hadn't misled me when he said that he lived in the Park. It simply wasn't the kind of property I'd imagined. The coming and going at all hours meant he spent more time at Mum's than I knew. Again, nothing wrong with that, was there?

Determining to phone Mum later, my mobile rang.

'Great minds,' I said, glad that we weren't on a video call. Me skulking outside Roger's house would not look cool. 'I was about to call you.' Close-relation telepathy, we do this a lot.

After the usual social preliminaries, Mum said, 'I need a favour.'

'Ri-ight.'

'You're not busy, are you?'

I felt my cheeks turn pink. 'Not at all.'

'Roger is whisking me away for a few days.'

I curbed an *oh* and said, 'Anywhere special?'

'It's a surprise.'

'Does it require a passport?' Where the hell was he taking her?

She gave a girlie laugh. 'Not that exotic. I suspect we're heading for Cornwall.'

I should be pleased for her. How often had Mum been away in the last five years? Spending time with Hazel and Justin in their Spanish villa, like a third wheel, didn't count.

'Anyway, would you be a darling and housesit? The plants need constant watering and you know I hate leaving the place empty.'

'Fine. When?'

'Today.'

'That's sudden.'

'Oh dear, do you have plans?'

Most of my friends were either away, or gainfully employed. 'Nothing that can't wait.'

'You sound a little down, darling.'

'I was hoping for a chat, that's all. When are you leaving?'

'In the next half an hour, I'm afraid. There's nothing wrong, is there?'

'No, I'm good, fine, actually.' It came out a bit strangled.

'You're sure?'

'Yes, when will you be back?'

The line went briefly quiet and I heard a muffled exchange. Obviously consulting with Roger. 'Sunday. You don't need to stay for the full four days, if it isn't convenient.'

'It's not a problem,' I said. 'Have a lovely time.'

After she ended the call and before I lost my nerve, I headed for the dustbin outside Roger's let, flipped open the lid, swooped on the single rubbish bag and spirited it away.

CHAPTER EIGHT

There was nothing nice about trawling through other people's rubbish. It stank, made a mess and sapped the soul.

Armed with a strong pair of Marigolds, I'd unearthed empty juice cartons, eggshells, plastic wrappers and an eclectic number of takeaway containers that confirmed Roger's global tastes. General detritus, which should have been put in a designated food waste bin, was bad enough to make the climate-minded at the borough council antsy — a sin, maybe, but not a crime.

For a finance man, I thought it odd that Roger chucked away credit card receipts. I'm so scared of being scammed anything leaving a financial footprint gets put in my shredder. A bunch of restaurant and hotel bills told its own story. Roger was, indeed, generous with my mother. They'd recently dined at the Lion at Winchcombe and the Royal Oak at Gretton. A bill for a room at the Feathers, Ludlow, made for interesting, if not exactly illuminating, reading. Details were scant, due to the fact it had been torn up. No guest names, no date, just food and beverages itemised for a three day stay. Of possibly greater significance, an old luggage tag with a flight number, barcode and a destination for Malpensa airport, in Milan. I had an unpleasant time unsticking junk mail and flyers, leaflets for painting and decorating services, window-cleaning, cheap food deals and cheap broadband services. There was nothing incriminating or condemnatory, nothing to suggest that Roger was anything other than on the level and I felt foolish for doubting him and embarrassed that a tiny bit of me was jealous of his place in my mother's affections.

After I cleared away, I messaged Rinelle and Nicola and told them I'd be out of town, staying at my mum's. They didn't need to know that my mother was holidaying with Roger.

I ate a few dry crackers standing up because I thought I should eat something, threw some toiletries and clothes into a bag, packed my laptop, switched off appliances that didn't need to be on, and drove along the familiar road. I reached Cirencester around three o'clock in the afternoon.

Steeling myself, I drove down the street, thankfully, one-way, negotiated the gates without incident, and tucked the car in the courtyard, next to Mum's Evoque.

As soon as I was inside I went straight upstairs. The door to the family bathroom, or "death-trap", as I privately referred to it, was open. More people keel over, have horrible accidents, strokes and heart attacks in this one small room than in any other area of a home. It's connected to two things: the sanitary ware is bloody hard if you come crashing down; and the fact that people often stumble into it for a pee or glass of water, half-asleep, in the early hours. That's if they haven't tumbled down the stairs first. When I'm old I'm going to live in a single-storey dwelling to cut the risk by half. Not that this would have helped my dad. His stroke was a proper "lights out" job. It had nothing to do with unyielding surfaces or stairs.

Mum had refurbished the bathroom with new tiles and a softer paint colour. To my eyes, it made no difference at all. I could still see him lying there. What would Dad have made of Roger?

Fleeing to my room, I found Mum had left a sweet message on my pillow:

Thanks so much for this. Help yourself to anything. There's fish pie in the fridge. Roger's put in a bottle of wine to chill. See you very soon — love and hugs, Mum xx

Hugs? My heart swelled. Roger must be good for her, I told myself. As soon as she returned, I'd be open and honest and we'd talk properly and my silly fears would all disappear.

Feeling more sorted I treated myself to an early drink courtesy of Roger — a delicious unoaked Chardonnay, and sat outside under the umbrella with a collection of Mum's inspirational "homes" magazines, thick with design tips. She let me have the old copies for school projects. Good with my hands, the curtains and covers in my tiny place were all homemade, without looking naff. If pushed I'd say I was a better seamstress than my mum, and she's pretty special.

After I repainted my toenails dark blue and let them dry, I took out the fish pie, heated it up and ate it flopped in front of the TV in the living room. Home had a soothing effect and my eyes grew heavy with sleep. I must have dropped off because I woke with a start.

My mouth was dry and it took me a few seconds to realise I wasn't at mine. I stood up, switched off the TV and wandered into the kitchen for a glass of water. At 9.30 p.m., the light had dimmed, the air clammy and humid. I wasn't afraid. I didn't think that something, or someone, had woken me up, yet I felt stale. In a funny mood, all the good feelings I'd experienced earlier had vanished, sucked out into the night.

Thoughts scuttled through my mind: sudden trips away, a man who comes and goes, a dead bird and random piece of mail.

Safe to say, if your mum kept the postcard, it has meaning for her.

I started downstairs. I scoured the contents of the recycling bag. With repugnance, I went down the bin inside and bins outside. I opened cupboards, drawers, checked through shoe-cleaning boxes in the boot room, containers in the utility. I eased paintings from walls for anything that might drop out from behind the frames. After scouring the desk in the study, I lifted up the old-fashioned phone to see if the postcard lurked beneath. After ransacking the contents of the vanity unit in the downstairs cloakroom, I continued my search upstairs.

The medicine chest contained all the usual medications. The guest bedroom was clean, as was Alex's old room, which now contained children's beds for when Fred and Kitty stayed over. I left Mum's room until last because it was undoubtedly crossing a line and, if the postcard was anywhere, this was where it would be. The point was I didn't want to find it. If I did, its significance was unquestionable and then what would I do?

Bedroom side-tables yielded no surprises, other than the contents of the chest of drawers revealed that Mum had given her lingerie a serious upgrade. Feeling awkward, I turned my attention to her wardrobe, in which I found Dad's death certificate. Guilt stole over me. I shouldn't be here. This was wrong. I'd lost the plot.

Ashamed, I slumped down onto the carpet, my back against the wall, and covered my eyes with the heels of my hands. I stayed quite still, letting my breathing settle, and listened to the ticking silence. I'd been here before, I realised, remembering that same sense of things not being quite right, unable to identify it and then being powerless to stop it.

I let my hands drop and my vision return to normal. Opposite, under the window, there was an ancient and rather shabby chaise longue. Dad had proudly brought it home one day from an antiques fair at the Corn Hall. For sentimental reasons Mum couldn't bring herself to get rid of it, but she'd jazzed it up with a new cushion the colour of fresh corn and with a fleur-de-lys design. The stitching, I noticed, looked wonky to my critical eye. Scrabbling across the floor like a crab, I picked up the cushion and ran my fingers along the seam. Beneath the fabric, it felt stiff instead of soft.

Dread assailing me, I tugged at a loose stitch with my nails, then another and another. Already, I sensed with a kind of grim finality what it was. Tugging it free, the postcard stared back up at me, and then I knew.

CHAPTER NINE

Talk about shit and fan.

I went to bed confounded. Sleep was patchy. My emotions I felt hard to pin down, keen and raw. One question beset me when I woke bleary-eyed the next morning: why had Mum lied?

Throwing on a vest top in soft green over a pair of navy shorts, I padded downstairs. The postcard in my pocket chafed against my thigh. Still early, I went outside and dutifully watered the plants from the butt. The air felt cleaner, less heavy and I was grateful for the reprieve.

I made myself proper coffee and considered what to do. I began to message Nicola and, as quickly, scrapped it. She had weightier matters than . . . I didn't know what to call it: a family issue, a personal problem? If I confronted Mum, which was bound to be awful, I could hardly take the moral high ground after snooping in her bedroom.

Mulling it over, mug in hand, I did a couple of turns of the garden, watched butterflies flirt among the buddleia and several swifts fly in and out of a nest in the eaves until, fortified with purpose, I returned to the house. Slipping out my phone, I photographed the postcard on both sides and tucked it back where I'd found it. Taking the cushion back downstairs I found the cotton Mum had used to stitch it from her sewing-box in the study. It took me no time at all to repair the seam. The only giveaway, the needlework looked better than hers. Hopefully, she wouldn't notice. I put the cushion back in place, plumped it up and walked away. But I wasn't finished.

My mother's laptop was next on my list. If Mum had lied so easily to my face, what other lies had she told?

The password was a doddle to break. First, I put in her birthday — access denied (and thank goodness for that). Then I put in several amalgamations of "Verity and Alex" — access denied — until I hit on "Fred&Kitty1234" — bingo! There were no files, no folders and no record of messages going out or incoming. *She'd been careful*, I thought, *but had she wiped her search history*? A quick click told me she had not. And then I wished she had.

Mum had been viewing a sizeable property for sale in Shropshire. Called unimaginatively "The Stone House", there were loads of pictures of the grounds, which looked as extensive as they were neglected: apple orchards overgrown with long grass, weeds and brambles; mangled rusting iron-work propped against outbuildings with rotting roofs and missing slates. Estate agent photographs are supposed to tell porkies. These didn't because they couldn't. With a price tag of £850k, a belfry and clock tower, the main building looked like a gingerbread house inhabited by a coven of witches. Of stone construction (quelle surprise) and with "elaborate", according to the blurb, mullioned windows, it was quite obvious that it had seen better days. An inscription over a pointy porch announced that it had been built in 1890. Details of the interior were scant and I didn't think it was a deliberate attempt to intrigue a potential buyer. Powered by oil, with private water and a septic tank, "in need of some refurbishment" and estate agent-speak for "total renovation", it would be a monster to bring up to contemporary stand-ards. No mention of council tax band, that thing that affects our bank balances annually, and appears under "Go Figure" in the average estate agent's details. I'd been a property virgin when buying my home. Boy, had I wised up during the whole, horrible process. With this baby, I had images of lead plumbing and dodgy wiring. It probably had damp, wet rot and beetle, too. The energy rating told its own story; it was predictably pants. But my mother had viewed it over a dozen times in a recent forty-eight-hour period. And then I recalled the hotel bill during my ramble through Roger's rubbish, in which the Feathers, Ludlow, featured. Had they viewed the house together? The thought that she might be planning an impulsive move with Roger to "do it up", left me reeling. There was only one person who might be able to enlighten me: my mum's best friend, Hazel Tranter.

It's an extremely short walk from Mum's home to the Mead. A skip and a jump across Thomas Street and you were there. Big family houses, solid and thirties in style, you'd need a sizeable bank balance to enjoy the Mead lifestyle. Not a problem for Justin Tranter, a head honcho at one of the top five largest banks in the country. An old friend of my dad's, Justin had been best man at my parents' wedding. I wasn't sure of the chronology of Hazel's arrival on the scene, though she had been a part of it for the past thirty years. Most of the week Justin was up in London, leaving Hazel to her own devices. A social dynamo, she ran lunch clubs, cinema evenings, played golf, was an enthusiastic member of the Women's Institute and vocal on any topic you cared to mention. A less likely friend to my mother you could not find.

I rang her bell and set off the dogs. After a lot of barking and yowling, the pooches were contained and Hazel flung open the door, invited me in and asked if I'd had difficulty locating cucumbers recently.

'You'd never believe the problems I've had trying to get hold of the damn things. I mean, is there a shortage, or something? I know times are tough but really . . .'

Not exactly my field of expertise, I made some stupid remark about being sorry for her loss and followed her sturdy back into a garden room. She wasn't a ship in full sail, more an oil tanker blundering through the ocean waves. Of generous proportions, she was also generous in nature. I'd always rather liked her, even if she was dotty.

'Take a seat,' she said. 'As ever, lovely to see you, Verity. G&T?'

'It's a bit early for me.'

'Nonsense. I was just about to pour myself a drink. You'll keep me company, won't you?'

With Hazel, it was never a question.

'Great,' I said. 'A small one would be lovely.'

I watched her measure out a large one. Topping it up with one of those posh and expensive tonics I can't afford, she handed me a glass and we chinked *Cheers*.

'So do tell — what's new, darling?'

A great deal, I thought grimly. 'With the summer holidays, not a lot.'

'What bliss.'

I squashed a reaction, purposefully dismissing the turn of phrase and reminder of the message in the postcard from my mind. Hazel looked at me appraisingly and took a large swallow of gin.

'How's your mother?'

I explained that she was away with Roger.

'So you've met her new beau?'

'I wasn't aware she had an old one.'

Hazel snorted with laughter and waggled a thick finger at me. 'Oh, you're a naughty girl.'

I pretended to join in, not faking it well enough judging by Hazel's next remark.

'Am I to deduce you're not keen?'

'I've not known him long enough to decide.'

'You have to admit he's dishy.'

'He seems very nice.' That bloody word again. *And he's a dab hand at clearing up bird crap and feathers*, I should have added.

Hazel's big wide features softened. 'She's entitled to some fun in her twilight years, don't you think?'

I nodded and gave a glassy smile. The gin tasted lovely and astringent.

'It's lovely to see her more settled,' Hazel said.

I wasn't aware she was *un*settled. 'Is something troubling her?'

'Troubling? Goodness, no.'

'She's happy here, isn't she, I mean, in Cirencester? She wouldn't move away, out of Gloucestershire?'

Hazel seemed genuinely taken aback. 'Whatever gave you that idea?'

'New man, new life?'

'You're jumping the old gun, my dear. Anyway, it's not as if Roger lives in Australia. *Then* we might all be worried.'

'Has Justin met him?'

'He has. We had supper together only last week.'

Sounded like a regular event. My heart swelled with jealousy. I stifled a distinctly unkind remark.

'And Justin likes him?' I tried to make it sound as if this was no big deal, either way.

'Roger is a man's man,' Hazel declared.

'They get on well then?'

'You know Justin; he gets on with everyone, just like your father in that regard.' She placed a pudgy hand over mine. It felt soft and very hot.

What Hazel was trying to say was that Roger was not my dad and nobody could replace him. My mother had said the same, yet it sounded more sincere coming from her closest friend.

'Justin must miss him.'

'Oh, he does,' Hazel said solemnly. 'We all do, Verity.'

I nodded, choked back a threat of unexpected tears, and forced a smile.

'You really think Roger makes her happy?'

She gave my hand a little pat. 'Indubitably, darling.'

I knocked back the rest of my drink, resisted the invitation for another and said that I had to go.

'Oh, to be young again,' Hazel said, enveloping me in a hug. 'Come again, soon, Verity. My door is always open.'

None the wiser, I wished Hazel goodbye and cut through Park Street to Black Jack Street and ambled along the eclectic range of independents, that included a picture framers, butchers and bookshop. After a wander, I ordered lunch from a café with a courtyard and outdoor seating area.

Waiting for my sandwich to arrive, I took out my phone and clicked on to the Stone House. It had been on the market for several months with the same estate agent, which I phoned. The second I mentioned the property I was treated to a charm offensive.

'It's a fabulous buy — bags of potential. Scope to do something really special.'

Like knock it down, I thought.

'There's been substantial interest but, as yet, no takers.' This roughly translated to *viewings are slow and the vendor is threatening to dump and appoint a new agent.*

'What's your position?' I was asked tentatively.

'I have nothing to sell.' Which was the gospel truth. The agent would be mistakenly salivating over what he thought was a *cash buyer.*

'Fantastic. I could arrange a viewing this afternoon.'

'That won't work for me. I live in Cheltenham.'

'I *see.*'

It's genuinely assumed that if you're from Cheltenham, you're loaded. Actually, lot of kids at my school were on free school meals. I knew parents who struggled to pay the rent.

'But I could view tomorrow,' which came as much as a surprise to me as it did to the estate agent. What the hell was I thinking? I loathe driving. I especially hate driving long distances to places I've never set foot in. Normally, I'd take a train but the location was so far out in the sticks it would take me weeks. 'Could we make it around noon?'

'Wonderful, if I could take some details?'

I thought there'd be some recognition when I supplied my name. Its absence told me that, as much as my mother was interested, she had not arranged a visit, unless, for unfathomable reasons, she'd used another. Maybe she'd given Roger's. Christ, maybe that's where they'd disappeared to for a few days.

'Mr Croucher will be escorting you around the property,' I was told.

Flying blind on gin and curiosity, I gushed about how much I was looking forward to it.

CHAPTER TEN

Stuck behind tractors, caravans heading for Wales, motorists who actually drove slower than me, it took over three nerve-jangling hours to reach the Stone House.

Terrified of motorways, I'd admittedly taken the "scenic" route, skirting the riverside town of Ross-on-Wye, then Hereford — cathedral town and seat of mystery — passed through Leominster and then, sliding over the border to Shropshire into Ludlow, on to Craven Arms and then . . . well, it was hard to tell. I genuinely thought the sat nav had gone on strike. I was in among "them there" hills and a landscape that was as alien to me as Mars. Despite a South of France sky, with definitely a touch of the Côte d'Azur about it, the countryside smouldered with heat and menace. A single match thrown and the tinder-dry woodland would spark into an inferno, with me caught in the middle of a wildfire.

With every mile away from familiar surroundings, I felt more disjointed. I mean the countryside was nice, if you liked that sort of thing, and I recognised that farming was essential to the economy and for the table. As a committed urbanite, however, I couldn't get my head around what people did for fun out here. The winter months must be hell. When I finally clocked the For Sale sign at the top of a drive that appeared more pothole than road, I'd almost lost the will to keep breathing. Nevertheless, the sat nav nagged me to follow so, braced, I cut a zigzag route, and prayed a tractor would not be trundling along from the opposite direction. Reversing was not my strong suit.

Fields and fields of sheep could be glimpsed through high straggly hedges that threatened to scratch the paint off my car. It went on for what felt like miles. At one point I seriously considered calling the whole thing off and would have done if there had been a place to turn around.

The drive eventually opened out a little and I spotted a tree line of poplars in the distance. Two hundred yards ahead: the unmistakable Gothic proportions of the Stone House. Despite the fine day, the property and everything surrounding it felt darkly intimidating.

A stonking big Land Rover parked next to the porch indicated that the estate agent had already arrived. I drew up alongside as a hefty man, with a face the colour of rare sirloin, climbed out to greet me, brandishing a clipboard. Surprise briefly tweaked his features. He'd obviously expected someone older.

'James Croucher,' he announced, sticking out his hand, which I shook. 'Good drive?'

'Perfect,' I lied.

'Shall we? It will be cooler inside.'

He wasn't kidding. Supermarkets in summer could be nippy. The Arctic Circle was bloody freezing. This was next level. It was the kind of cold that seeped quickly into your bones, and stayed there.

We stood in a massive hall in front of a long-defunct fireplace. Shutters at the windows had been opened, yet the light failed to penetrate the gloom.

Getting straight to business, Mr Croucher said, 'A quick recap of the history of the property. It used to be a school managed by the local authority.'

I tried not to react. Being in the school business, I couldn't imagine working at such a place.

'How long ago was this?' I asked.

'It closed down in 1984. As you can see, it's empty.'

'What happened to the previous owner?'

'He passed away last year.'

In which case the price tag seemed unusually low. Yes, it was a forbidding pile, but the land alone made it a cheap deal and that didn't make sense. Talking Dido's language, beneficiaries, usually children, want as much as they can from the sale of a loved one's home. I questioned Mr Croucher on the subject.

'Mr Jones had no heirs or dependents,' he explained smoothly. 'The proceeds from his estate are going to charity.'

From the hall we entered a panelled drawing room that was as dingy as the hall and smelt noticeably of damp. An inglenook fireplace that hadn't been used in a very long time dominated the space. It was hard to picture it emitting warmth. Conversely, it was easy to imagine small boys being shoved up its chimney to clean it in decades gone by.

Croucher went into full-on estate agent mode. 'As you can see, it's generously proportioned and would make a wonderfully elegant entertaining space.'

'What's beneath?'

'The cellar.'

Our next port of call, it ran the length of the building. The joists looked as if they were doing a heroic job of propping up the house in a losing battle. I reckoned the whole structure would require underpinning. 'A straightforward piece of construction,' according to Croucher. Not sure Dad would have agreed.

Mr C kept up the patter and we returned to the first floor and a snug that in no way came close to the description.

'Where does that go?' I asked, pointing to a door.

'Ah, that's the entrance to a secret passageway. An interesting feature, isn't it?'

Not how I'd describe it. I found it positively disconcerting. 'Where does it lead?'

'Into the grounds. I have a key, I think.' He fumbled through a large assortment. Selecting and pushing one into the lock, it didn't budge.

'A bit more elbow grease,' he said with a laugh, putting his full weight behind it.

With a loud crack and bang, the heavy door flew open. A wave of musty, damp air greeted us. I peered inside into a dark tunnel, the length of which was difficult to deduce. From where I stood there was no light at the end.

'You can go inside, if you like.' Croucher flashed a mischievous grin. 'Don't worry, I won't shut you in.'

'No, I've seen enough.' A million quid wouldn't induce me to step inside.

Croucher shut the door and went to lock it. 'Damn,' he said. 'The mechanism's seized up. I'll have to get our maintenance team in.'

'Unlikely someone would come this way to break in.'

'You're right there,' Croucher said, reassured and completely missing my point. 'Its existence is hardly common knowledge.'

We strolled along corridors with walls that contained "moisture" and floors covered in linoleum. Into a vast kitchen with hideous strip lighting, where an Aga, for which people normally paid fortunes, squatted, like a relic in a village museum.

Up a wide staircase that creaked and complained with each step, we travelled through a maze of rooms which dripped silence, forbidden to speak, as if they'd been forced to sign a non-disclosure agreement.

Curiously, a connecting corridor between the west and east wings were lined with ten small chipped sinks. Puzzled, I asked Mr Croucher what they were doing there.

'For the girls,' he said, obliquely, 'although I'm not sure why old Mr Jones kept them all these years. It would have been simple enough to take them out. Same with the loos.'

I scratched my head. 'Was this a boarding school?' If so, it was hardly Hogwarts.

'A children's home and at some stage in its life an approved school.'

'God, how awful.' Injustice burned inside me. I couldn't help it. I could never imagine a time in the history of the house when it was anything other than a dump in the middle of nowhere. It might as well have been Alcatraz to my mind. The cruelty of grown-ups never ceased to amaze me. Who, in their right mind, would shove a child in a place like this? I said as much.

Croucher's smile was thin. 'Times were different then.'

Oh, that old maxim, I thought, following him along a landing to a small door that I would definitely have missed had I not been alerted to its existence. Opening it with a flourish, Croucher flicked on a light to reveal a steep stone staircase.

'This was used by servants in the nineteenth century. We think it led to their quarters.'

I sneaked a look. The steps seemed steep and I didn't really fancy going down, but Croucher took the lead and, not wanting to appear a wuss, I felt duty-bound to follow. With stone walls and a single metal rail to cling to, the narrow treads were worn smooth in the middle, no doubt from hundreds of pairs of shoes. Fortunately, I don't have big feet. The air was foetid, as though nobody had breathed it in for decades. Trying not to hyperventilate, I listened to Croucher's incessant commentary, thinking only of getting the hell out and hoofing it back to civilisation. Towards the bottom I noticed letters scratched into the walls and called to Croucher for an explanation. Already well ahead and probably as eager to get back to his office, as I was to go home, he was droning on about walking the grounds. Running my fingers over SUSAN MILLER, J.D., MORWENNA T, SARAH S and SARAH W, CHERYL CASTREY, I half-expected to stumble across Eleonora Kaminska. Relief that I didn't quickly calcified when I read a name that was confusing and unexpected: BLISS HANNAFORD.

Rooted, open-mouthed, wondering and thinking, I ran my fingers over the carving. Unequivocally, my mother's name had been Eleanor Hannaford before she married my father. As far as I knew, she had no relations called Bliss. Was it another one of those weird coincidences? For the life of me I had no idea what was going on and why Mum was viewing the property, unless . . . I fumbled my phone, took a lousy picture then, mentally spun out, chased after Mr Croucher who was waiting outside.

'All right?' he said.

'Fine,' I replied.

He strode through the grounds while I stumbled along behind. In spite of the sunshine, the landscape looked as grey as the building it surrounded; everything drained of colour and reduced to noir.

A number of outbuildings, in a hideous state of disrepair, clung miserably together. Flashing ripped off, roof tiles missing. Entrances boarded up to prevent vandals, which was a joke, their handiwork already plain to see.

'Some fruit trees in the orchard are quite ancient, with some rare varieties,' Croucher said to my deaf ears. 'The rest of the grounds are a mixture of woodland and clearings and the whole plot runs to around seven acres.'

'There's a lot to take in,' I said, without a word of a lie. The toe of my shoe blundered painfully against a stone sticking up out of the earth. I glanced down and noticed there were several in a line, like marker stones in cemeteries.

'Pets' graves, I shouldn't wonder,' Croucher said, catching my eye. 'Perhaps if you'd like a second viewing . . .'

The question hung in the air in suspended animation.

I said I'd get back to him once I'd had time to consider, thanked him for his time and we wandered back to the cars. 'I was wondering about the previous occupants, the girls. I'm a schoolteacher,' I said, as if this explained my interest.

'I see,' he said, in a way that suggested he didn't.

'Is there any way I could find out who they were?' I asked.

His large forehead creased in surprise. 'As far as I know, few paper records of staff and children remain. Everything's digitised these days. Local authority archives might be your best bet.'

Unlikely they'd reveal the kind of specific information I was looking for, I thought ruefully.

CHAPTER ELEVEN

I'd forgotten how hellish Friday afternoon traffic is. I was hot. My mind was travelling to places more awful than the place I'd visited that afternoon. I had random pieces of information that appeared to connect and then didn't connect at all. They only made sort of sense if my mother knew Bliss Hannaford. In the middle of the mess was Roger Scott-Jefferies. Everything had been fine until he appeared on the scene.

I had a banging headache by the time I arrived at my mum's. Pouring myself a chilled glass of lemonade, I downed it with two painkillers and flopped on the sofa. Little by little, I cooled down and calmed down. A rummage through the fridge revealed cold meats, salad and a nice piece of Gouda. I took the lot out, made up an eclectic plate of food, resisted a tempting glass of wine, and ate slowly. After I cleared away, I took out my laptop and investigated the origins of the Stone House, an institution that I fast discovered had a diabolical reputation.

Girls were sent there for minor infringements: theft, "being difficult to handle" i.e. with anger management issues, and, worst of all, for falling pregnant. The irony was that those banged up for promiscuity fell into the hands of sexually predatory staff. Physical abuse was rife, punching, kicking and slapping an everyday occurrence. Despite the clamour from whistleblowers and a full-scale investigation by the authorities in the 1960s, the place was not closed down for good until almost two decades later. Who knew how many young girls' lives had been ruined in the interim?

I'm not naïve. I know bad things happen to good people. I recognise that I'm super-privileged, that my protected upbringing has shielded me from casual cruelty and neglect. It doesn't mean I'm impervious to the suffering of the most vulnerable. Hot tears coursed down my cheeks and I cried for what I read and more for what I imagined.

Strung out and exhausted, I went to bed early and fell asleep quickly. I rarely dream and, if I do, never remember. I wasn't sure what time it was when I woke up, sheened with perspiration. Intensely humid, still dark, the only illumination from a hunchback moon, I reckoned it was around two or three in the morning. Checking the time would be like kissing insomnia full on the lips and inviting him to bunk up next to me. I resisted the urge and lay very still, willing myself to breathe deeply, relax each muscle and banish the more troubling aspects of the day. Slip-sliding between consciousness and oblivion, a shuffling noise wrested me from sleep. Eyes open, I listened hard. There it was again. I sat up in bed. The shuffling had given way to footsteps. It sounded as if someone was creeping around below and trying very hard not to be heard.

I'd often thought what I would do if faced with a burglar in my home. Hiding would be a first option. Second: screaming the place down. I did neither. Grabbing a robe, I picked up my phone; my finger poised over the Emergency number. Creeping out onto the landing, I expected to see torchlight. Instead, I was greeted with full illumination. Perhaps, Mum and Roger had returned early, although there was no sound of hushed conversation. Perhaps, Mum had come back solo. Maybe the trip hadn't been a success and they'd rowed, or something.

Peering over the banister, a figure crossed the hall and looked up, startled.

'Jesus fucking Christ. What are you doing here?'

'Thought that was my line,' I said drily. 'You scared the crap out of me, Alex, *and* you woke me up.'

'Sorry, I knew Mum was away. I didn't realise you were house-sitting.'

I stomped downstairs, gave my brother a clumsy hug. Mum's "darling boy", was a better-looking version of our father. He had Dad's brown eyes and olive colouring. His hair was a rich raven colour, as Dad's had been before he'd gone grey. Square-jawed with a big captivating smile, Alex looked dependable, which was a laugh. Unlike our father, Alex had vulnerabilities. Easily distracted and easily led, he couldn't stick at anything for more than five minutes and was hopeless with money. I loved him fiercely despite his failings. He was a great father and put up with a tricky wife with a stoicism only found in saints. 'So what *are* you doing here?'

'Dido and I had words.'

This was not an uncommon occurrence. Alex had occasionally slept on my sofa.

'Thought I'd give her some space,' he said, with a loose grin.

She's thrown you out. 'What time is it?' I yawned.

He looked at his watch. '3.40 a.m.'

'The birds will be up in twenty minutes. Tea?' I asked wearily. No way was I getting any sleep now.

'I'll make it,' Alex said. 'You look bushed.'

I followed him into the kitchen, slumped on the sofa under the window and watched as Alex assembled two mugs of Assam. He handed one to me.

'Budge up,' he said.

I shuffled along. 'What was the row about, or shouldn't I ask?'

'You shouldn't ask.'

'That bad?'

He let out a big sigh. 'Mad cow thinks I'm having an affair.'

'And are you?' I, for one, wouldn't blame him.

The rim of his mug clashed against his teeth. 'Christ, Verity, of course I'm not.'

He probably wouldn't dare.

'Thing is, she's paranoid,' Alex said in a rare moment of disloyalty. 'I wouldn't be at all surprised if she's having me watched.'

'Now who's being paranoid?'

He shrugged a shoulder, glowered into his mug.

'Kids all right?'

'Golden.'

I sipped my tea. He sipped his. I knew he wanted to talk about Mum, as did I, only he didn't know how to broach the subject and I didn't know how much to tell him. What did I actually know? Well, I had suspicions. I had suppositions. Without hard facts, there was no evidence.

'About Mum,' Alex began, rather woodenly, I thought.

'What about her?'

'This thing with Roger.'

'Yep.'

'Dido said you met him.'

'I have.'

'And?'

'Jury's out.'

Alex turned his gaze towards me. 'That's not very reassuring.'

'Neither is it cause for alarm.'

His face spread into a grin. 'You're such a liar.'

No, that's not me, I thought grimly. 'Keeping my options open, that's all. Cautiously optimistic,' I added.

'So where's the catch?'

'I guess it's all a bit sudden.'

'I asked about *him*, not the situation.'

I playfully punched his arm. 'You're not as dumb as you look. I don't know,' I said more seriously. 'Roger seems okay. He obviously cares for Mum. He appears genuine.'

'*Seems* and *appears*,' Alex murmured.

'Exactly. And there have been one or two odd events lately.' Alex's eyes darkened with suspicion. 'Circumstantial evidence, if you're a copper,' I said.

'Always knew your love of detective stories would come in handy for something.'

'Don't knock them. You can learn from the best writers.'

Unconvinced, Alex took a swig of tea. 'Go on then, what sort of events? I'm all ears.'

First, I told him about the postcard. Alex was so obviously dim I had to explain about the similarity of our mother's name and the one in the message. The dead bird met with an equally empty response. I didn't tell him I'd snooped through the family home, or on Mum's laptop. I didn't mention the Stone House, desperate young girls and tales of physical and sexual abuse. Perhaps, if I had, I'd have received a stronger reaction. *How* I wanted to offload, but Alex cannot keep his mouth shut. He'd tell Dido and then carnage would ensue. This was a situation *I* needed to control and I couldn't do that with a sister-in-law with her own agenda derailing me.

'Is that all you've got?' Alex said, unimpressed.

'I said it was circumstantial.'

'It's random and unconnected.'

What would Alex say if he knew the whole story? *No*, I thought, *can't risk it. Not yet.*

'Take Roger for a beer,' I said brightly. 'He's a man's man and will respond better to you.' Than to me, was the inference. 'Find out for yourself what he's like.'

'He'll think I'm vetting him.'

'What's wrong with that?'

Alex ran a hand underneath his stubbly jaw. 'When are they back?'

'Sunday.'

'Okay, I'll talk to him. You talk to Mum.'

'I've already talked to her.'

Conscience salved, I finished my tea, stretched my hands above my head and said I was off to bed.

CHAPTER TWELVE

I woke late. Alex had already left, no doubt to make peace with Dido. *Good luck with that*, I thought, and flipped open my laptop.

I Googled Bliss Hannaford and got nowhere, then Eleanor Hannaford. There was one born in 1749, another born in 1851 and who died the same year. A forty-three-year-old Eleanor Hannaford, from Nuneaton, could be found on Facebook. I tried both names again and inserted "Devon". A rundown and disused butcher's shop, bearing the name, Hannaford, popped up in Torcross. Studying the lineage of various brothers gave away no clues.

I turned my attention to court records. Was there some way I could search them to find out what had led Bliss Hannaford to the dreadful Stone House? Nicola would know how to access that type of information, I was sure. Then again, supposing I found out, it didn't explain my mother's secretive interest in a random relative. I thought again about the cryptic message. It could be interpreted as some woman, named Bliss, now living in or visiting Hereford on holiday. Except if she was reaching out to my mother, why had she addressed it to a Polish woman?

My brain fried and needing to clear it, I set off for the market held on the square in front of St John Baptist church. The produce was as eclectic as the shoppers keen to bag a bargain. There were stalls of cheeses, sweets, cakes, fish, meats and street food, as well as hats, cushions, rugs, scarves, hand-turned wooden bowls, jewellery and plants. I fell for a jaunty straw hat with a blue band and a long silk scarf in a vibrant shade of pink. Suddenly starving, I snaffled a chicken and bean burrito from a street stand and took it to a bench close to a statue of two boxing Cotswold Hares. Munching contentedly, my thoughts returned to the conversation I'd had with my brother. Alex was right. I did need to talk to Mum; otherwise I was going to drive myself potty. Approach was everything. I needed to be sensitive. It was critical I didn't blunder in. As if by telepathy, my phone pinged. Mum had sent me a picture of Moreton-in-Marsh.

We've had a lovely few days here. Hope all is well and you haven't killed my plants!! No need to hang around tomorrow if you have things to do xx

I smiled. She sounded happy and on hearing from her, everything felt suddenly okay and normal. All the other things that had driven me crazy were simply stuff. *Not everything in life can be explained*, I told myself sternly. I'd go back to her place, pick up my things and then call her later in the week for a chat. Nothing heavy.

Settled, I popped to Tidings to buy a birthday card for Rinelle, lusted over a pair of ritzy Wellingtons in LLB, Laurence Llewellyn-Bowen's interior design shop on the corner of Castle Street, before deciding that sixty quid was more than my bank balance could stand and returned to the house.

The postman had been and I crouched down to scoop up an appeal from a dog charity, two flyers from estate agents keen to give no-obligation valuations and another from a pizza restaurant. Among the mail: a plain brown A5 envelope with no name, no address. My previously happy mood vamoosed. The inside of my chest felt dry and tight, as if heralding an attack of bronchitis.

Setting the rest of the mail down on the console table, I stood and opened the anonymous and oh-so-innocent-looking package. My fingers slipped inside and curled around several shiny photographs. I pulled them out with a trembling hand. Photographs are such rare creatures in a digital age. These were not dodgy replicas taken from a mobile phone. These were classy, high-spec records of a life: my mother shopping in Cheltenham, another as she ventured into Morans on the Bath Road, another of her sitting outside Blancs with Hazel, sipping a glass of wine. Nothing threatening about them apart from the fact that someone was, in effect, stalking Mum. But when I saw pictures of me, Mum, Alex and my young niece and nephew together, I felt chills. It had been a fun day out at an adventure park, during half-term week in February. They were mundane, trivial, you might say, and yet their existence contained so much threat.

I put a hand to my temple, trying to still my racing mind. Was Roger on the scene then? I didn't think so but, wait, his neighbour said he'd moved in six months ago so it was possible, although he couldn't have delivered the photographs because he was with my mother. The inescapable truth: someone wasn't only watching Mum; they were watching her family. Cold fury streaked through my veins at the thought of someone deliberately waiting for me to go out so that they could deliver their nasty little message. Only Mum knew the reason why.

The thought of staying in the house another second was appalling. What if someone was watching now? I stupidly glanced over my shoulder as if someone would suddenly jump out from behind the curtains. What if the threat turned into something concrete and dangerous?

I quickly gathered up my belongings, shoved the photographs into my bag, and drove back to the sanctuary of my own place. On information overload, random thoughts flitted in and out of my mind, like marauding Red Admiral butterflies. Mum's father had been a carpenter, her mother a medical receptionist, though she'd given up work when she'd had her only child. They weren't poor, but Mum had not been brought up in a lavish environment, unlike my dad. They'd met when she'd sought the bright lights of the capital. By all accounts (and this was a problem, because I only had my mother's word for it) she'd been a bright child, but not one who'd sought further education. She'd trained as a secretary, which was how her path had crossed with my dad's. To my knowledge, my father had never met Mum's parents. She rarely talked about her past and I never thought to question it until now. My interest had always been in the present, my concerns focused on my own life. The past had nothing to do with me and I wasn't curious enough to find out. Except now I needed to know the details of my mother's life, because her safety might depend on it.

The short journey back seemed longer than usual. Thankfully, home felt safe and knowable and solid. No shifting walls here, nothing tenuous or dodgy about its foundations.

I set my bag down, slipped out the photographs and took them to my desk, a beautiful piece of furniture that had sat in my father's study until bequeathed to me. I laid them out like a croupier in a casino, photographed them on my phone. Next, I took out a writing pad and wrote a series of bullet points, detailing what had happened in the past few days. It was pretty cryptic: *postcard, dead bird, Stone House, photographs.* Under each, I made notes longhand. I thought better this way than banging things down digitally. On another page, titled *Roger*, I made more notes and I was fair: *nice to Mum, generous to me, witty and friendly.* Did asking my mother to stir his tea really count as controlling behaviour? *Simply me being pissy,* I told myself sternly, so I left it out.

I stood up, rolled my shoulders, clicked my neck from side to side to loosen the tendons, glad that by writing things down in a logical sequence, I'd regained an element of control. Tomorrow, I'd visit Mum. Tomorrow, I'd put everything on the line. Tomorrow, I'd get answers.

CHAPTER THIRTEEN

'You're back earlier than expected.' Not my greatest opening line, but it was the best I could find. I'd already phoned ahead to see if Mum was available for "a little chat". Made me sound like a gangster putting the squeeze on an informer.

'Yes, Roger had a few things to do at home,' Mum said. Meanly, I wondered what that meant: washing clothes, tidying up, making preparations for a client? It occurred to me that, so far, I'd seen very little evidence of him actually working. 'Besides,' Mum said airily, 'we don't live in each other's pockets.'

'But you had a *nice* time.' God, that word again.

'Idyllic.' She seemed to drift off to some faraway place. I hated to be the one to drag her back.

'Mum,' I began tentatively.

'Yes?' Her gaze was clear and true.

'Something happened while you were away.'

Her dark eyes shone. It meant I had her attention.

'Anonymous photographs were pushed through the letterbox.' I handed her the envelope. She slipped out the pictures, one by one, her lips thinning when she saw the shot of me and Alex and her grandchildren.

She glanced up. 'Was there a note?'

I shook my head.

'When was this?'

I explained it had happened between me leaving the coach house to go into town and returning a couple of hours later.

'Do you think you should go to the police?'

She gave a start. 'Whatever for?'

'Because it's obvious someone is stalking you.'

She slid the photographs back into the envelope. 'That's a little dramatic.'

'You think?'

She gave me a kindly smile. 'Police would need rather more than that to run an investigation.'

'They *do* have more than that: the postcard, the dead—'

'For goodness' sake, Verity, you're making something of nothing. Why are you so obsessed?'

It came out sharply and felt like a slap across my face. I took a breath. 'You don't think there's anything odd about it?' I let my eyes travel to the package.

'Odd, yes. Dangerous, no.'

Sometimes I think I'd have to slam my mother over the head with an anvil to get a reaction.

'Okay,' I said slowly, locking onto her gaze. 'Who's Bliss Hannaford?'

She blinked hard twice. Something flashed behind her eyes before a smile danced across her lips. 'Goodness me, however did you find out?'

'Find out?' I repeated dully. Two little words and they felt like chunks of ice in my mouth.

'My nickname as a child.'

Needing to hang on to something, anything, I gripped the strap of my shoulder bag. Bliss Hannaford was no relation. This was my mother. And the message in the postcard was no coincidence. But how could a girl from Devon, who'd been brought up by loving older parents in Totnes, wind up in Shropshire, in care? It would mean that her whole early life was a lie and one she'd sold to my father too — unless, for obscure reasons, he was in on it, and that was ludicrous. It had to be another Bliss Hannaford — had to be.

'Are you all right?' she said solicitously.

'It's hot in here,' I said lamely.

'Go out into the garden and I'll bring you a glass of water.'

I nodded and did as I was told. The air throbbed. The colours of the leaves in the trees seemed brighter, fused with energy. I'd once dropped acid. This was what it had felt like. I didn't like it then and I didn't like the emotions tumbling and spinning out of control in my mind now. Mum fussed around me, made sure I was quite comfortable and sat down next to me. In less strange times, this would feel companionable.

'Better?' she said.

I nodded dumbly and took a slug of water. Help me, I thought. Help me to understand.

'Years ago, when I was a child,' Mum began, 'I had a friend, who, for the life of me I cannot remember why, called me Bliss. She was the same age as me. We went to school together and played together.'

'What was her name?'

'Cherry.'

I flashed back to the carvings on the staircase at the Stone House. Was there a Cherry?

'Is that her real name, or nickname?'

Mum let out a laugh. 'Her real name. She lived in the street next to mine.'

'In Totnes?'

'Yes.'

'What happened to her?'

'Her father changed his job. She moved away, went to live in Shropshire. Sadly, we lost touch.'

'Is it possible that Cherry sent the postcard?'

'Why would she do that?'

I hiked a shoulder. 'To reach out to you?' I suggested.

'After all these years, I doubt it.'

'People do, especially as they get older.' I blushed. Mum didn't like me referring to her age.

'Then why not pick up a phone, or send a letter, like people of our generation still do?' Again, the enigmatic note in her voice, the tease in her smile.

I sipped my water slowly. Mum had not asked me how I'd unearthed the information. Furiously, attempting to think of a convincing cover story before she did, I asked what Cherry was like.

'A wild child.'

'A bad influence?'

'Cherry was prone to leading me astray.'

'I can't imagine that in a million years.'

'Oh, it wasn't so awful by today's standards. Nicking sweets and cigarettes.'

'Smokes? Really?'

'She introduced me to Dubonnet and Cherry B.'

'How apt,' I chipped in. 'Sounds disgusting.'

'It was.' She let out a laugh. 'Made me quite sick on one occasion.'

I'd never seen my mother even remotely drunk. It felt strange to picture it now.

'She was my best friend — my only friend,' Mum said with conviction. 'I'd have done anything for her.'

'You must have been sad when she left.'

'I was bereft, totally lost,' she admitted.

'How old were you?'

Her gaze slid away, lost in another lifetime.

'Fourteen, fifteen, something like that. I grew up,' she said more certainly. 'My parents never said, but I think they were glad she was gone. My father was strict and always said no good would come of her.'

He was right, I thought. Poor Cherry's wayward behaviour had finally caught up with her and I wondered what she'd done to wind up at the Stone House. Touching to think that she'd carved my mother's name into the walls after they'd lost contact. I wanted to find a way to tell Mum, but that would mean confessing to all sorts.

Mum lightly touched my cheek with her cool fingers. 'Your colour has improved.'

'I feel so much better,' I said, in more ways than one.

'There's something I want to talk to you about, actually.' Pale light shimmered behind her irises. It didn't bode well. I instantly braced. Was she ill? Was I in trouble? Fuck, was she about to announce she was getting married? 'Don't look so worried.' She laughed lightly. 'It's a small thing, really, but I wanted to be upfront so there are no secrets.'

My mouth dried and I was certain my eyes were wide with dread.

'I'm investing in a scheme recommended by Roger.'

I felt the air knock out of me. Why had I not seen this coming? It was so damned obvious. 'How much?'

'£300k.'

Triple fuck. Wondering what his commission amounted to, I dug my fingernails into my thighs. Keep it cool. Keep it calm. 'That's a lot of money.'

'Relatively speaking.'

'Can you afford to take a hit if it goes south?'

'It won't.'

'That's not what I asked.'

She didn't answer straightaway. 'It would prove a costly mistake, but I trust Roger.'

'You don't know him,' I burst out, unable to help myself.

The muscles in her jaw tightened.

'What about your own financial adviser, what does he say?'

My mother gave a shifty look.

'Don't tell me you've dispensed with his services.'

'Malcolm is not up to date with current trends.'

This did not sound like my mother talking. Roger had put the damn words into her mouth.

'Fuck, Mum, Malcolm has advised the family for years.' Never able to abide bad language, her expression sharpened. 'He got me my mortgage. He was Dad's financial man.' I was only aware I was shouting when I stopped.

'What you're really saying is that you don't like Roger and don't trust him.'

'This is not personal.'

She threw back her head and laughed without mirth. 'Of course it is.'

'I don't know Roger well enough to have an opinion on his character.'

'But, I do.'

'No, you don't,' I snapped. 'For all you know he could be a gold-digger.'

'How dare you and, for your information, what I do with my money is *my* business.'

'It's not about the money.' I wasn't bloody Dido, although right now, I thought she had a point. 'It's about a bloke who's just rocked up and is now controlling your finances.'

'He is not—'

'You were with Dad for thirty-five years. You've known Roger for less than six months. Have you run it past Justin?'

She bit her lip, stayed silent.

'Oh, great,' I said. 'So even your closest friends are frozen out when it comes to good old Roger.'

She stood up. Her honey-coloured cheeks flamed pink. She bunched her hands. In all my days I'd never seen my mother remotely lose it. She came as close to it as I'd ever seen. I hadn't hit a nerve. I'd whacked it with a sledgehammer.

'If you have nothing polite to say, I suggest you leave.'

I scraped back the chair, swept up my bag and stomped off across the gravel. Petty of me, but I left the gate to the courtyard wide open on my way out.

CHAPTER FOURTEEN

I sent SOSs to Rinelle and Nicola. A Sunday, both were eating lunch with their respective families and promised to pop around to mine afterwards. While waiting for them I alternately seethed and fretted while making up a witches' brew from leftover tequila, vodka and fresh orange juice. Already two down by the time they arrived, I felt stone-cold sober. As soon as we all had drinks, I brought them up to speed. I'd expected strong and expressive facial reactions from Rinelle, not so Nicola, who was less flummoxed by the eye-watering amount of money, than she was about the photographs. With Rinelle, it was the other way around.

'What are you going to do?' she asked.

'What *can* I do? Mum's right. It's her money. What she does with it is up to her. Roger has obviously made a strong impression and convinced her he's a safe pair of financial hands.'

Rinelle tapped the coffee table with a blood-red nail. 'You mean he's got his feet under the table PDQ.'

I felt the same way. 'I absolutely hate arguing with Mum. We never row about anything,' I said unhappily. 'You should have seen her. She was so full of anger.'

Rinelle slipped her arm around my shoulder and gave it a tight squeeze.

'Show me the photographs again,' Nicola said.

I handed her my phone. She studied the images. 'The ones of you with Alex and the kids were taken when?'

'February. Roger hadn't met my mother then, but he was renting his house a month before.'

'Doesn't mean he took the photographs,' Rinelle said.

'Inconclusive either way.' Nicola handed me back my phone. 'Your mum's right when she says she doesn't have enough to take to the police.

'You sound like her,' I said dryly.

Nicola hitched a shoulder. 'Look at the facts. You haven't found the evidence to suggest that Roger is after her money.'

'By the time I do he could have bankrupted her.' I took another grim swallow of alcohol.

'At least your mum had a logical answer for the inscription at the school,' Rinelle said.

Nicola let out a snort of laughter. 'I'm gobsmacked you drove all the way out there.'

Trawling through the gallery of images on my phone and finding the right one, I held it aloft. The girls leant forward.

'Hard to make out,' Rinelle said. 'It looks like you're in a dungeon.'

'It felt like it. You can just about make out the initials and names.'

Nicola took the phone, scrutinising the images closely, and read the names aloud.

'Do you think Cheryl Castrey is Cherry?' I asked.

'Could be.'

'God, you're turning into a proper detective,' Rinelle said.

'Relentless is my middle name.'

'Obvs not a familial trait,' Nicola said.

I didn't catch on.

'Alex,' she prompted.

'He is in his own way. Flipping unstoppable when it comes to chasing down the next duff deal.'

'Aw — poor Alex. I like your brother,' Rinelle said.

'Everyone likes Alex, but you have to admit he's not got a business brain.' I told them about his early hours visit.

'Bet that spooked the hell out of you,' Nicola said with a wry smile.

'I could have thumped him.'

'Does he know what's going on?'

'Edited highlights,' I replied. 'He said he'd take Roger out for a beer. This was before I knew about the money thing.'

'Be a good idea to fill him in before he does.'

So I did.

* * *

Alex and Dido live in Queen's Road. It's handy for the railway station and a convenient location for getting into town. A leafy street, with lots of the bigger buildings converted into flats, or, as Dido maintains, "apartments". Where basic homes fetch over £500k, they'd landed their attractive Edwardian semi with a little help from respective Banks of Mum and Dad. Dido has expensive tastes and she puts them on display at every opportunity: plantation shutters at the windows, enormous red Aga and top-of-the-range appliances in the kitchen. The contents of the children's playroom look as if they've been purchased solely from John Lewis.

A grudge merchant, she didn't look pleased to see me until she suspected I'd come over to her way of thinking. She didn't offer me gin, her normal poison, because she was on a health kick and, instead plied me with some green goo that I disliked intensely.

Alex sat opposite me. Dido perched on the edge of the window seat in front of the aforementioned plantation shutters and, without preamble, asked what had happened.

I filled them in on Mum's intended financial plans. 'This is on a strictly need to know basis so I'd appreciate it if you didn't go in like an armoured vehicle,' I finished.

Alex went quiet. Dido went ape-shit.

'This is preposterous. We can't let her do this. That odious, money-grabbing, grubby little man has to be stopped.'

I spread my hands. 'I'm not sure getting cross is going to help the situation.'

Dido fixed me first and then Alex with a look that could dissolve stone. Properly cross, her top lip practically disappeared it was so tightly drawn across her jaw.

'She's made up her mind, as far as I can tell,' I said softly.

'Alexander,' Dido's voice dropped to a low growl, 'you *must* talk your mother out of it.'

Alex scrubbed the back of his head with his hands. 'It might be too late.'

'Then talk to Roger straight and tell him to give it back.' Having dispatched her husband with a 'ha,' she turned her rabid gaze on me. 'I was right about that man all along, but you wouldn't have it.'

What could I say? Arguing was pointless. A glance at my poor brother told me he was blindsided. He didn't say it, but I suspected he was looking to Mum to finance his next crackpot idea. Perhaps, in the long run, if the money tree withered and died, it would do him good. He wasn't stupid and he'd be forced to find gainful employment. But this was a side issue right now.

I chewed my lip. 'I think it's important we don't lose sight of Mum in all of this.' Easier said than done. Before I left home, I'd dropped her a text to say that I was sorry we'd argued. I'd heard nothing back. This was unheard of. She was obviously really upset with me.

'I agree,' Alex said.

'But if this bastard is going to ruin her,' Dido protested.

'We don't know that.' Alex spoke sharply, an immensely brave move. Dido countered with an "I'll speak to you later" expression. I had visions of him on my sofa that very night. Uncomfortable with being caught in a marital spat and because I'm a coward, I stood up.

'I'll leave you to the rest of your evening. Sorry to be the bearer of bad tidings.'

I gave Alex a big hug and allowed myself to be stiffly air-kissed by my sister-in-law.

'We will fight this,' Dido said stoutly, showing me out.

Not a battle you can easily win, I thought.

CHAPTER FIFTEEN

On Monday morning I received a phone call from an unknown number. Disappointed that it wasn't from Mum, I ignored it. The text that swiftly followed upended any possibility of making plans for the day.

Roger wanted to "talk" over a drink. I didn't know whether this was his idea or Mum had put him up to it, although it wasn't her style. She never shrank from difficult situations and this was as tricky as it got. Roger, I reckoned, was a self-appointed mediator. I texted him back with a *when* and *where*. He came straight back with *noon* and *Brasserie Blancs*. He'd chosen well. It was nearby. I knew and liked the restaurant staff and, most importantly, the venue was too public for him to make a scene and get away with it. I didn't think he'd get violent or anything like that, but things could turn awkward. Once I started questioning what the hell he thought he was doing with my mum's money, it was possible he'd get snarky, not shouty: I'd intuited that much.

I dressed carefully in French-navy tailored linen trousers with a crisp blue-and-white-striped shirt and white pumps, the vibe grown-up, not primary school.

High noon, I thought grimly, pounding a pavement already sticky with latent heat.

As I pushed my way through the glass entrance, I saw Roger sharing a joke with a barman. Likeable, affable, approachable, all the "bulls", Roger had an easy manner, I had to give him that. Smartly dressed in a lightweight suit that matched his eyes, he turned towards me with a massive smile that lit up the grey furnishings. He strode towards me on "down with the kids" footwear, planted his hands on my shoulders and kissed both cheeks, as if we were old friends seeing each other after a long period apart. I stood straight and stiff and felt hopelessly out of my depth against the onslaught of such affection. Lunchtime trade was already brisk and it felt as if every eye was upon us, marvelling at the wonderful relationship on show. Shit, did people think he was my dad?

'Verity, what are you having to drink?'

'St. Clements,' I said with a tight smile.

'Nothing stronger?'

I caught the eye of the barman. 'No, I'm good, thanks.'

'Why don't you sit down?' Roger said. 'I'll sort these and bring them over.'

I set up camp in the corner, watched and waited. I'll be honest, nerves sent urgent little messages across my shoulders, pummelled the inside of my brain, darted in short painful bursts across my stomach. I should have felt more in command. I should have felt greater certainty of the ground on which I stood. In reality, I felt as if I were standing knee-deep in porridge.

Roger athletically hooked back a chair with his foot, set the drinks down. 'There you go.' He sat opposite, legs wide apart, at ease. He raised his pint of lager. 'Your very good health.'

I lifted my glass, chinked with his and took a sip. Lemon cut through orange like a sharpened blade.

'How's things?'

His watchful gaze upon me, I gave a bland reply. This was the warm-up before the full workout.

'Fine.'

He frowned, 'Not according to your mother.'

I felt a pinch of guilt.

'Was it her idea for you to come and talk to me?'

He puffed out his narrow cheeks. 'God, no, I thought it best to keep it between the two of us.'

I nodded agreement.

'Your mother's incredibly upset, Verity.'

'As am I.'

'I want to talk to you about that.'

About *that*, or about *me*? I swallowed some more drink and almost choked. *Get a grip*, I thought. *You've done nothing wrong.*

'If you don't mind me saying, you seem a little paranoid.'

I felt my eyes narrow to two slits. 'Did Mum say that?'

'Not in so many words.'

'Then I'd appreciate it if you kept your opinions to yourself, particularly as you weren't present at the time.'

'Point taken.' He calmly lifted the glass to his lips, took a long pull of his lager.

'You said you wanted to talk,' I reminded him. 'Or was that it?'

His smile spread far and wide. 'I like that about you. Straight and direct and down to business.'

This wasn't me at all.

'Okay,' he said, patting his thighs, belting out a drum roll. 'I think we need to clear the air. I can see exactly where you're coming from. New man in your mum's life, whisking her away, the whole money thing.'

The way he put it you'd think he was talking about a few quid. 'Tell me more about the investment,' I said, skewering him with a look. 'I'd be genuinely interested.'

'Yes, your mother said you might be. You bought your own house, didn't you? Not bad on a young school teacher's salary.'

I didn't rise to the bait. 'So what kind of scheme is it? What's the deal?'

'It's all rather irrelevant now.' His smile was warm, wide and smug.

88

At this, I snapped a look that could shatter the mirror behind his head.

'Don't look like that. I'm putting the money back into your mother's account today.'

I don't know what was most astounding: the fact that my mum had already handed over the dosh, or that Roger was giving it back.

'Ri-ight.' My red-hot hand of cards suddenly felt like shit.

'Not because I think it isn't a prudent investment — it could have turned a tidy profit for her long term, to be honest, but I can see how it might come across to you and Alexander.' His voice dropped to gravel tone and his eyes uncomfortably locked onto mine. 'Cutting to the chase: you think I'm after her money, don't you?'

Perhaps. Possibly. Not so sure. His revelation made me feel grubby for harbouring such suspicions. Maybe that was the idea, I thought, as I looked into his unsmiling eyes. I countered his question with one of my own. 'Have you spoken to Alex?'

Roger glanced at his watch. 'We're meeting for a late lunch. You're welcome to join us, if you fancy it.'

I didn't. I wondered whose idea that was. Seeing off the pair of us in a single sitting. *Stop it*, I thought, burbling an excuse that I was already committed.

'Another time then.'

His eyes were still on me. I squirmed under his gaze. This was so unpleasant. As charm offensives went, Roger seemed to have all the answers, all the bases covered. I feared he was about to step things up a gear, which he did by reaching across and placing his big hand over mine. It felt as heavy as a rock.

'Verity, I think it's really important you know how much I care for your mother.'

'I'm glad to hear it.'

'She's a magnificent woman.'

I nodded blindly. The pressure on my hand was enormous.

'She makes me very happy and I like to think I make her happy too.'

Still his hand remained.

'And, of course, I can see why you're so deeply emotion-ally attached to her.'

My fully functioning foe-detector switched on and flashed amber.

'A little incestuous from an outsider's point of view, admit-tedly, though entirely understandable in the circumstances.'

Flashing from amber to red. 'Circumstances?'

'She told me all about Colm.'

I yanked my hand away.

The greasy smile on his face matched the slippery look in his eyes. Homing in on my horror, he continued, 'It's okay. We've all been there. Rest assured your secret is safe with me.'

Stung into fury, I stood, picked up my drink and hurled it at his face. Sticky juice dripped from his hairline, down his not so self-satisfied cheeks, into the collar of his shirt, flecking his suit and corroding his smile. The glass smashed into a dozen pieces.

Throwing an apology in the direction of the bar staff, I staggered out and, on shaking legs, blindly headed out of the bar.

CHAPTER SIXTEEN

Bastard, bastard, prick, bastard.

Swept along in a blizzard of blind pain, I barely registered Dido coming out of the entrance to Montpellier Gardens until I heard Kitty excitedly calling my name.

I looked up as she broke loose from Dido and barrelled into my legs.

Her sweet face looked up into mine and then fell. 'Auntie V, what's the matter? You're crying.'

'I'm okay, Kitty. Honest.' I furiously swiped at my cheeks with the back of my hand.

And then I remembered the damn photographs, the way some horrible person had looked at my niece and nephew and thought they were fair game. Glancing anxiously around, the tears started rolling again.

Dido, who was pushing Fred in a buggy, charged towards me, grabbed Kitty's hand, and enveloped me in a hug.

'Goodness, Verity, sweetheart, whatever is the matter?'

'I . . . it's okay. I'll be okay. I'm okay.'

'You are so not.' She spoke briskly. 'Kitty, don't you ever run off like that again. Now take Auntie V's hand and don't run. You,' Dido said, addressing me, 'are coming with us, and I don't want any argument,' she added in response to my feeble protest.

With Dido leading the way, Kitty and I followed. Her warm little hand in mine, she chatted on about her swimming lesson that morning, her friend, Cosmo, who was coming for a playdate soon. Momentarily, I was grounded in the seemingly ordinary yet thrilling events in a young child's life. It's hard to be either angry or upset surrounded by innocence.

Cutting through by John Gordon's, we crossed into the courtyard to a child-friendly tearoom. Dido parked the buggy with Fred red-faced and sound asleep inside.

She followed my gaze. 'Why he can't do that at night is the great mystery of the universe,' she said with a wry smile.

'Can I have a strawberry milkshake, Mummy, and a brownie?' Kitty asked, wide-eyed.

Dido winked at me with a grin. 'She certainly knows how to exploit a situation and,' she said, more seriously, 'I take it we do have a situation.'

I fluttered my fingers. 'It's nothing.'

'It is *not* nothing.'

Dido ordered for Kitty and she and I settled on cappuccinos. After a rummage through nappies, wet wipes, small plastic containers of raisins and casting aside a squishy looking banana, Dido produced a colouring book with pens from a voluminous canvas bag. With Kitty settled, she turned her sympathetic gaze on me.

'Is it that beastly man? Alex is going to give him a damn good talking to.' She glanced at her watch. 'Around now.'

I deflected. 'No.'

'Well, whatever's wrong?'

I shook my head. 'I don't want to talk about it.'

'But you must, Verity. I've never seen you so upset.'

'Honestly, I'll be okay,' I repeated, with more conviction than I felt.

Charged with revelation, her eyes widened to the size of Frisbees. 'It's not me, is it?'

'You?'

'I haven't made life easy for you lately and I don't mean to dump this whole thing with Roger on you. Honestly, I don't.'

She looked so genuinely unhappy I made a muted 'there, there, it's okay' noise.

'But it's wrong for me to lay it on you,' she said, pressing a hand to her chest. 'I'm terribly sorry, Verity. Truly.' She touched my knee as if I had a venomous spider parked there, the gesture, I'm certain, kindly meant. At heart, Dido was like the rest of us: well-intentioned, vulnerable, a bit clumsy and didn't always know how to reach people.

She wasn't finished. 'I feel things deeply, Verity. I don't always come across very well. I can be a bit, oh, I don't know, pushy, a little sharp. I know that,' she said, looking up earnestly, 'And me and Alexander, well . . .' Her gleaming white teeth rested on her bottom lip.

I'd intuited from Alex that things were a bit iffy. This was such a normal state of their marital affairs that I'd paid it very little attention.

She twisted around, as if shielding Kitty from what she was about to say with her body.

'Things aren't so good at home.'

I trotted out the usual clichés about all marriages going through rough patches. How the hell should I know? 'It's particularly tricky, I imagine, when little people are involved.' I tilted my head towards sleeping Fred.

Dido smiled fondly and lowered her tone. 'I know this is a shocking thing to ask, but you don't think Alexander is—'

'Absolutely not. He adores you. End of.'

She let out a great sigh. Her eyes suddenly filled with tears of gratitude. I saw how strung-out she was.

'And he'd tell me if he was,' I assured her.

At least, I thought he would.

Dido tilted the rim of the cup to her lips. 'There's me going on about my problems. You still haven't told me why you're so upset. It's not a man, is it?'

Oh God, if Dido only knew.

I decided on a half-truth. 'It's this thing with Mum. I hate falling out with her and the whole situation clearly got to me.'

'Aw — poor you,' Dido said. 'She'll come to her senses soon. I guarantee it,' she said.

I so wished I had Dido's certainty.

* * *

Emotions are unpredictable creatures. I'd felt soothed by the children's presence. My sainthood was guaranteed by calming down my sister-in-law and giving her the reassurance she craved. Forced to park my own emotions, they ambushed me once I was over the threshold of my own home.

I seethed, wept and, swept along on a torrent of rage, despaired. Why had my mother exposed my most intimate pain to a man who would use it as a weapon against me? It felt like the ultimate betrayal.

Colm O'Connor was not "the one that got away", or any of those stupid and lame sayings that people trot out when they don't know what to say, let alone how to say it. He was the love of my life, the man with whom I'd wanted to spend the rest of my days. I loved all of him with every fibre of my being. After almost a decade, I still did. I'd never found anyone else. I doubted I ever would.

We'd met at uni. He was reading history for no other reason than he fancied it. Intelligent and naturally curious, he could have studied medicine, cosmology, modern languages or the classics. Dark-haired, with a pale complexion, he had slate-blue eyes that sparkled with wit. Tall, he was powerfully built, muscles toned not from hours in the gym, but from working for years on his father's farm. When his arms were around me I felt safe, like when my dad gave me a hug.

It wasn't so much his looks I fell for, but his patter, his ability to make me giggle until my sides ached. It's true what they say about a man's ability to laugh a woman into the sack. And I was willing. We laughed and loved deeply for almost three glorious years until the tragedy that befell him then felled me.

In our final year his older brother, Sean, was killed in a road accident after a truck driver took his eyes off the road to answer his mobile phone. Having taken over the running from his father, Sean was the mainstay of the family farm and, while Colm's younger brothers were happy to step in, the farm needed someone experienced at the helm in the wake of Sean's death. Colm was that man.

I thought I'd go with him. To uproot and move to Ireland, to a land and landscape with which I was unfamiliar, didn't scare me. I'd already struck up a relationship with Colm's sister, Róisín, a warm, capable and funny woman, who'd taken to me as I had taken to her. Their parents were good people. I liked them and they liked me. I was happy to give up every aspiration I'd ever had to be a farmer's wife.

Like I said, Colm was intelligent. He was also emotionally literate. Perhaps he knew that, despite all I claimed, it would be hard — too hard. Something deep inside, a sixth sense, told him it wouldn't work. I didn't know it then and, maybe I only believed it now because it made it easier to bear.

Fooling around one day, not long after we'd started sleeping together, he'd joked, 'What's a posh city girl like you going to do on a muddy farm in the middle of Cork.'

'I thought it's supposed to be the Emerald Isle.'

'That's because it rains and where there's rain, there's mud. No place for a girl with designer shoes.'

I never knew he meant what he said until later. At first, I was in denial. *He'd come around*, I thought. He was simply testing my resolve. Grief-stricken, he bore the weight of responsibility to his parents and his siblings. Colm's shock at Sean's death, leaving a wife and three small children, changed him from the laughing man I knew to a more serious individual, quick to shut down conversation, slow to smile. I tried to be patient, to be tender and coax him out of his misery. The greater my efforts, the more he slipped away from me. There was no sudden break-up; no dramatic "It's over". This was a slow, mouldering disintegration. Nothing felt right. The cold, twisted blade of rejection almost killed me. A broken heart, I quickly discovered, was not an imaginary idea. It existed. I literally felt as if the main muscle in my body, the organ that keeps everything pumping and working and living and breathing had let me down. I couldn't sleep. I barely ate. I had no desire, no purpose. Joy was for others. There was none for me. Grief is the price we pay for love, it has been said, and it doesn't only affect those whose loved ones have died. It affects the abandoned and lost and lonely. Had it not been for my mother, without a word of a lie, I would not be here.

She and my dad collected me from my room and took me home. Unanchored, my father kept out of the way, steeped himself in his latest project. It was my mother that nursed me back to physical and emotional health, my mother who knew when to sit with me in silence and when to talk, my mother who helped me see that I had a future, different to the one I'd envisaged for sure, but one that still had meaning and hope. So, yes, Roger was right when he'd observed my special emotional bond with my mother, which was why it hurt so much when she tore it apart for a man I now despised.

I splashed cold water over my swollen face, dried my eyes, changed out of my clothes and, bare-footed, slobbed about in shorts and T-shirt.

I made myself eat a sandwich I didn't want, checked my phone to see if Alex had been in touch. He hadn't. Childishly, I grinned at the memory of Roger's face drizzled with orange juice. Not so fucking smooth and charming now, you total shit.

Come early evening, I'd cleaned my flat and cooked chilli for dinner. Debating what to drink from my vast array of soft beverages (not), my mobile rang. It was Alex.

'Hey,' he said expansively.

The thing about being a sister is that you can spot within seconds whether your sibling is trolleyed. I could practically smell the booze travelling the airwaves.

'Good lunch?' Definitely long lunch.

'Smashed it,' he slurred, full *rah*. Alex might have been kicked out of two public schools, but he'd hung out with enough ex-pupils to talk the lingo. When he's with his mates, I sometimes think they've never progressed beyond fourteen years of age. An image of forty-year-old lawyers, dentists and corporates in short trousers flashed across my mind. 'You know he drives a top-of-the-range Lexus?'

What was it with men and motors? I did not know because Roger had always parked somewhere else when he visited my mother. Interesting, I thought, until I realised I did the same.

Alex was still blithering on. 'He's one hell of a guy and I mean he's sooo fucking hip and cool. He's like God, sister. He's the man.'

'I thought it was Mum who was going out with him.'

'Ha-fucking-ha! Seriously, he's smart and funny and—'

'Spare me the BS, Alex, what's he done?' As if I didn't know.

'What's got into you? He hasn't done anything.'

'How did he buy you off?' There was enough deadly intonation in my voice to deflect any more questions about me. Alex sobered up pretty damn quick.

'Verity, that's beneath you.'

'Well, did he?'

There was a long, offended pause. 'He's made me a very generous offer, if you must know.'

'How generous?'

'A hundred k.'

'For what?'

'You know, the busking thing.'

I closed my eyes and counted to ten. 'On what terms?'

'Terms?' he repeated, as if he didn't understand the basics of finance. Come to think of it, that was a distinct possibility.

'The Ts and Cs, Alex,' I said, exasperated. 'It's not an interest-free loan, is it? What percentage are you tied in for?'

A shifty squirming silence descended. I looked at my feet, at the wall, at the saucepan of food simmering and awaiting my attention.

'Haven't discussed the fine detail as yet,' Alex finally blustered.

I gave up and changed the subject. 'Did you talk about Mum?'

'We did.'

'And?'

'He makes her very happy *and*,' Alex said, appearing to briefly lose his thread, '*and* he's going to give the money back.'

Good — for a sickening moment I thought Roger was going to redistribute Mum's wealth to Alex. I still disliked the idea of "going to" and would have preferred "given".

'He's a top man. You really should give him the benefit of the doubt.'

On this we had to differ. Roger had upset my mother's life, and now he'd upset mine.

'Hell, that was risky.'

Nicola was not one to over dramatize. If she reckoned something was perilous, it's because she believed it was. Nonetheless, my response was pared down.

'I thought he was a philanderer, not a murderer.' I told her about the lovely Viola: she of the gold ankle bracelet and lithe figure.

'But Eleanor didn't believe you?'

'She says she met her.'

'You think Viola is an imposter?'

'Bit strong. She could be another financial victim.' Except why would she agree to meet my mother? It didn't make me feel any better at what was rapidly becoming an impossible situation.

'Either way, you don't believe she's Roger's sister?'

'She doesn't look like him and they didn't behave like siblings. Hell, what do I know?' I gave a weary shrug. 'After I told Mum my not-so-earth-shattering, game-changing news, we had another argument. My fault it was bloody.' I took a disconsolate sip of gin.

Nicola looked thoughtful.

'You said you were going off grid,' I said in a bid to change the subject.

'Yes.'

'Out of the country?'

'Yes.'

'That it?'

'Yes.'

'So why am I here?'

Nicola took a strong pull of her drink. She gave a little shiver. Dutch courage, or what?

'What I'm about to tell you is for your ears only. You cannot divulge or reveal it to anyone else, and that includes Rinelle. If you do, I will deny every single word and will never speak to you again.'

'Crikey,' I said.

'I mean it. I will block you from my existence.'

I swallowed and nodded numbly.

She snapped a look. 'Do you understand?'

Fingers of fear closed over my heart. 'Yes.'

'Good. You're right about Roger.'

'I knew it,' I burst out.

'For goodness' sake, keep your voice down.'

Chastened, I muttered a sorry. Nicola had a worried expression and Nicola isn't generally the worrying type. I indicated for her to continue.

Nicola lowered her voice. 'Roger's real name is Michael Yuill. He's a Canadian with British citizenship and has lived in the UK for the best part of thirty years. During this time he has adopted a number of aliases, which he uses here and abroad.'

I was too astounded to let the 'fuck' that was in my brain pass out through my mouth.

'His shtick,' Nicola continued, 'is conning rich men and women out of their fortunes.'

'Men?' I whispered, aghast. It had never occurred to me.

Nicola gave me a square look. 'He's a sexual chameleon and does what he needs to do to get what he wants.'

O.M.G. I'd thought things were off, but not *this* off. If he was stringing my mum along too, he was in a danger of giving her an STD.

'His last mark was an Italian count. That's when he was Gianni Romano.'

Suddenly, the luggage tag with the Italian destination made sense. I wished I'd keyed his car.

'He stays ahead of the game by moving around. He's rarely in one part of the globe for more than a couple of years.'

'But if you know this, why isn't he in prison?'

'You need charges to be brought and then they need to stick. Most victims willingly go along with the con until it's too late. They're so embarrassed by being duped they keep it quiet — even from their own families.'

'You said most. What happens if they don't?'

Nicola looked at me long and hard. In my head I was skittering for the exit.

'His first wife, Jane Mills, an American heiress to an international shipping firm, was found dead in her hotel room in Switzerland. She was twenty-nine, fit, with no previous medical conditions. Nothing was ever proven,' Nicola added, in answer to my horrified expression. 'Conclusions from the post-mortem were inconclusive. It looked as if she had simply died in her sleep. Interestingly, her family never bought their son-in-law's story of innocence and he never did get his hands on all the money.'

I reached for my drink, wishing it were a bottle.

'An undisclosed settlement was made for him to go away and never come back,' Nicola continued. 'After the heat died down, he used it to fund his next mark.'

I thought of all that had happened after Roger turned up on the scene and asked Nicola for her take on it.

'A guy like him is a professional. They research their victims in exactly the same way law enforcement and the intelligence services investigate suspects and criminals. In this regard they're not that different to the average hit man studying his target prior to a kill. They need to know their victims intimately. The big difference is that the con man is looking for vulnerabilities and weaknesses that he can exploit to ensure control.'

I recalled our last conversation with Rinelle. 'You think he was responsible for all those odd little incidents?'

'Classic moves designed to wrong-foot and make your mum emotionally dependent on him. Clever, really, if you think about it.'

I could barely speak because of the rage and fear punching the hell out of each other in my head.

'Do you think Mum is in danger?'

'Hard to say.'

I grabbed Nicola's arm. 'Are you serious?'

'If he's made to back off, he might go quietly.'

'Not very likely, is it?'

'Depends. The idea is to pull off the scam quickly, smoothly and with as little fuss as possible. Family members rarely spot what's going on until it's too late. In this case you might have rattled him enough for him to think it's not worth the trouble.'

'Is there any way of following his money trail and tapping his resources?'

'Above my pay grade,' Nicola muttered. 'People like him are adept at covering their financial footsteps. He's probably got an account in the Cayman Islands, or some place where it's hard to carry out a trace.'

'So what do *I* do?'

Nicola tapped the table with her finger. 'How did he react when you threw your drink over him?'

'I didn't stick around long enough to find out.' I told Nicola about Roger/Michael's lunch with Alex and the offer of financial help for Alex's crazy business enterprise.

'He won't deliver,' Nicola said, matter-of-fact. 'No more than that investment money will wind up safe and sound in your mother's account.'

'It's already in, although it hasn't cleared.'

'And it won't,' she said firmly. 'Making a promise he has no intention of keeping is another ruse to keep you all barking up the wrong piece of Scottish pine while he's planning his escape through the forest.'

'Think I should confront him?'

'Risky.'

'Surely, the greatest danger comes from doing nothing?'

Nicola sat back. 'Your decision, but if you do call him out, hit him with what you've discovered.'

'*Me?*' I said, catching the stern glint in her eye.

'Tell him that, should anything happen to you, or your mother, it will trigger the delivery of a confidential file simultaneously to the police and the press.'

I emitted a dry laugh. 'A guy like him won't fall for an old trick like that.'

Nicola's expression was sturdy and hard-edged. 'Tell him it includes new information, implicating him in the death of his wife.'

My eyes shot wide. I felt awfully sick.

'Should spoil his day, if nothing else,' she said with a grin.

CHAPTER TWENTY

A collective swell of hot emotions reared up and crashed down inside my mind. I found it impossible to sleep.

Scuppering his nasty little plan, and trashing six months of schmoozing and lying would seriously dent Michael Yuill's income stream. Turning over for the millionth time, I'd be surprised if he didn't cut up rough.

I rose early, dressed appropriately: vest top over cotton culottes and, very importantly, running shoes. As a precaution, I slipped a legal pepper spray bought off the Internet into my bag. I planned to corner him early before he had a chance to pretend to go to the office, visit Mum, or the woman I knew as Viola. I had to put a stop to him inflicting any more emotional damage on our family.

Alarmingly, he opened the door naked apart from a burgundy-coloured towelling robe, drawn so loosely across that I could see a profusion of dark chest hair, and a gold chain around his neck. The heady mix of testosterone and expensive shower gel almost floored me.

'I've been expecting you.' A wide smile, the size of a train tunnel, spread across his face. I'll be honest. I was conflicted. Should I stay, or should I leg it?

'You going to stand there all day?'

Beckoned into a narrow corridor, I hesitantly followed him into a kitchen that looked as if it had never been used. The view to the small garden revealed scrubland, empty pots and a dead tree. I wondered what was behind the closed doors in the rest of the house. I imagined empty or minimally furnished rooms, without personal touches and identifying features. The place had the feel of a motorway motel, somewhere to rest your head, a base. This was no home with books, and prints on the walls and fresh flowers in vases.

He didn't offer me tea or coffee and that was fine. All business, he leant the small of his back against the sink, folded his arms and viewed me with a crafty expression that robbed me of courage and certainty. Would he undo me with lies disguised as truths?

'I expect you've come to apologise for your behaviour at Blancs.'

'I haven't.'

'Or, perhaps, for spying on me with Viola.'

'I don't know who that woman is. She's not your sister. A co-partner in crime, maybe.'

He donned a wafer-thin, pitying smile. 'What a creative mind you have. See, that's the thing, Verity, you know nothing, and what you don't know you make up. Yours is a world of wild and sad accusations and delusions. I suppose it's understandable after dear old Colm dumped you. Not that I blame him. Nobody likes a neurotic bitch.'

Anger flashed through me like a blade in the night. *Hold it together*, I told myself. *Let him dribble on with his malice and deceit. He thinks I have a shit hand of cards. He doesn't know I have a Royal Flush.*

'Do you talk about my mother in that charming way?'

He barked a laugh. 'What do you take me for?'

'A conman.'

I'd like to say I wiped the self-satisfied expression from his face. Didn't make so much as a smudge.

'Wow! That's quite some allegation.'

'You deny it?'

'Jesus wept,' he burst out nastily. 'You silly little girl.'

It stung. Hadn't my mum used those same words?

'Spare me the insults and answer the question.'

Something shifty was going on behind his eyes, as if he was quickly reappraising the situation. I doubted he thought me worthy of respect. Reaching into my bag I wrapped my fingers around the pepper spray.

'I'm not here to play games,' I said, intent on slamming it to him. 'Why do you do it?'

'Do what?' His wide-eyed response did not align with the set of his jaw.

'Exploit the vulnerable and rip them off. Does it give you a kick? Does it make you feel the big man? Tell me how a sick bastard like you ticks. I'd be genuinely interested to know.'

'Pretty rich coming from a kid who's been given everything.' Again, that smug "take that" smile.

'Ah, so there we have it: envy and petty jealousy. I was hoping for something less banal.'

The smile vanished.

'I know what you did, the postcard trick, the dead bird, the photographs, *everything*.'

He rubbed his jaw and burst out laughing. It was rich and long — worryingly so. I stood mute, perplexed. Maybe this was where Viola came in. Maybe she'd been instructed to set it all up. It would explain how incidents occurred when he was nowhere to be seen. Except, the idea would still have been his so why did he find it funny?

'You're not on the wrong path,' he said, wiping his eyes with his sleeve. 'You're in the wrong county, sweetheart.'

Burning with anger, I hissed, 'I don't believe you, Michael.'

His top lip curled. His blue eyes faded to the colour of dead lavender. 'Believe this then,' he spat, merciless and predatory. 'Your darling mummy never set foot in Devon before she married your old man. She's Polish.'

Heat spread up from my neck to my hairline. I opened my mouth to protest. Too quick, he was on a snarling roll.

'Brought up by her grandparents in Ludlow, she got rebellious and difficult to control and they had to put the mad cow away.'

'Shut up,' I yelled.

'More than enough material for me to work on without fucking about with dead animals, pictures or whatever your sad little mind makes up.'

Shock grabbed my chest. I was breathing hard. Events were spinning out of control and there wasn't a damn thing I could do to contain them. 'You're lying.'

The card shark smile on his face revealed he was not.

'You stay away from her, you hear? You never set foot near our family again, or I swear . . .'

'Swear what?' He puffed out his full lips and, body coiled, took a terrifying step towards me. His hands flexed and balled into fists as he taunted me. 'I'm so scared. Are you?'

I was. My knees jackhammered. Beating hard and loud, I thought my heart would smash through my ribcage. I whipped the pepper spray out and waved it in front of his face. Did he jump back? Did he hell.

'If anything happens to her or me . . .'

'What will mad little Verity do next?'

'Send the police a file on who you are, what you've done and how you *think* you got away with murder. Fresh information should put you away for a very long time.'

And then I let him have a blast of mace and ran.

CHAPTER TWENTY-ONE

I recalled little of my flight home.

With the words "neurotic bitch" ringing in my ears, I barrelled out of the house, down the road and ran and ran. By the time I reached home, I was blowing like a steam train, my side pinched with stitch and my calves were burning.

He was a liar. Mum didn't grow up in Ludlow with grandparents. Hannaford was a Devon name. She must have confided in him about the postcard and that's how he'd stumbled across the Polish connection. Yes, that's what had happened.

What did he mean about putting her away?

An image of the Stone House loomed before my eyes. No, I told myself, stop speculating.

I threw my bag onto the table in the kitchen. It missed, and fell with a dull thump onto the tiled floor. I stooped down to pick it up, put my hand inside and pulled out my phone. The screen looked like a piece of crazy paving. God, could this day get any worse? At least I had that rare beast, a landline. All my friends had taken the piss when I'd let on. It was as if I'd announced I'd joined some weird sect. I only had it installed to appease Mum and shut Dido up.

'If you're buying a property, you need a reliable means of communication,' Dido had said.

'I have a reliable means. It's called a mobile.'

'Mobiles can be hacked and don't always deliver in an emergency.'

What sort of emergency? I'd wondered at the time. Shit, this was definitely one of them. Immediately, I went to the front door and dragged the security chain across. I checked the window locks in my bedroom and in the kitchen. If Yuill was capable of murder, it wasn't only my mum who was in danger. Shaken, I made myself a stiff cup of coffee and sipped it slowly, trying to gather my thoughts.

Then the landline rang.

Only certain people knew the number, family members principally, and I didn't want to speak to any of them.

On it went. Eventually, whoever rang off, rang again — maybe it was Yuill.

A weird pulse above my top lip ticked. I stared at the phone, willing the noise to stop.

I begged it.

I pleaded with it.

'Shut the fuck up,' I yelled.

And, to my surprise, it did. To make sure it didn't start again, I took the receiver off the hook, marched into my bedroom and shut the door behind me. Resting my back against the wall, I briefly closed my eyes.

Silence snaked around me. Exhausted, I recalled Nicola's words.

They research their victims in exactly the same way law enforcement and the intelligence services investigate suspects and criminals.

And then, like a sunrise on a summer morning, it dawned on me.

Yuill's unscrupulous snooping to research his "mark", as Nicola had put it, had unearthed something in Mum's past, putting in motion a chain of events that were as scary as they were unknowable. If Yuill's activities had dinged someone's alarm bell, those messages were not sent to wish her well after all those years. They were a warning.

The only way to test the theory was to challenge the veracity of Yuill's allegations. Opening my laptop, I started with Ludlow, a market town, with medieval streets that sloped down to the Rivers Teme and Corve. According to Wikipedia, it was a place that was significant in the history of the Welsh Marches.

My mother had always maintained she grew up in Totnes. Were the towns similar? I took a look. Totnes was also a market town, situated at the head of the River Dart, with a long recorded history, dating back to the tenth century. One discernible difference: Totnes was home to New Age travellers and those with an alternative way of living. In terms of size of population, they were not poles apart. Both had a similar creative vibe and, in Ludlow's case, a bit of a landed gentry twist. The best lies were the ones based on truth. In this context it wasn't a reassuring thought.

Next I typed Kaminska into obituaries and encountered the same level of obfuscation I'd encountered when trying to find Roger, which, as it now turned out, wasn't surprising given his weakness for pseudonyms and criminal tendencies.

Interestingly, a Polish artist had set up a gallery in Ludlow, but the name was Wozniak. I looked at landmarks, places of historic interest, of which there were plenty, including a castle, medieval walls and, bingo, the famous Feathers Hotel. Immediately, my mind flipped back to the hotel bill I'd found among Roger's rubbish. Had he stayed there for research purposes? Again, this was not reassuring. Hairs prickled on my bare arms, despite the heat. Then I stumbled across a news item regarding a much-loved character and former employee of the hotel.

His name: Eddy Kaminski.

I puzzled over that for all of thirty seconds. A quick Google told me that Kaminski referred to a male, while Kaminska referred to a female, as in wife and daughter.

The desire to find stuff out is not always matched by expectation. I'd wanted to disprove Yuill's allegations, unpick his lies, stake and pin them down, not corroborate them.

I got up, grabbed a glass, filled it with water and tossed it straight down. Why would Yuill come up with a story based on a real-life person in a real place? It couldn't be for the sheer hell of it. What would be the point? I'd heard that "Make My Day" bluster in his voice. I'd witnessed the bragging certainty in his eyes. He was telling the truth and if he was . . .

To squash the awful thought taking form and shape, I returned to the news item.

A former fighter pilot, Eddy Kaminski had settled in the UK after the Second World War, married an Englishwoman, Nina, and had spent his working life as a handyman and occasional hotel porter until his retirement. He had passed away in 1982, aged seventy-three.

I sat back. My mother was sixty-two. Her best friend's move was when she was fourteen or fifteen, around forty-seven, maybe forty-eight years ago, pinning the timeline between 1975 and 1976. Eddy would have been in his mid-sixties. *She was brought up by elderly parents*, Mum had said, *by her grandparents*, Yuill had said. If it were true, what had happened to her parents? And what must it have been like for her? My friends' grandparents were lively, fit and active. Sixty now equated to forty then. Knocking on in the 1970s was a completely different gig: old of body, old of mind. Was that why she'd admitted to being rebellious and difficult? I clasped my hands around the back of my head, annoyed for so readily buying into Yuill's lie. I mustn't. Not yet. Not until I'd established the facts.

I checked out the Feathers Hotel, an impressive Grade 1 half-timbered establishment, Jacobean in style with curved mullions and transoms. Dad would have adored it. The interior was distinctly quirky, with a mixture of petrol-blue furnishings; busy carpets in public areas and Prince of Wales feather motifs, from which the name originated. The food looked yummy — as did the cocktails, my personal weakness and totally superfluous because this was not about me enjoying myself. I chose the cheapest bedroom with an en-suite, without breakfast. Replacing the receiver, I picked it back up and booked direct. Car parking was an extra fiver as long as there was space. At this time of the year it was unlikely, I was told. Didn't bother me a bit. I came from a place where parking spaces were more valuable than gold bullion.

No sooner than I'd replaced the receiver, the phone started to complain again. This time, I snatched it up. Double trouble: Alex with Dido listening on speaker.

'I've been ringing and ringing,' Alex began.

Some people wrongly assume that you're deliberately avoiding them when in fact you might be out of the house or in an area where mobile signal is poor. In this instance, it was a fair cop.

'And you're not answering your mobile,' he added testily.

'It's bust. I dropped it on the floor this morning.'

'Was that before or after you upset Roger?'

'He's not called Roger.'

'What?'

How to condense everything I'd uncovered, convey them in logical order, explain coherently the implications, and inform my brother that his barking business venture was now officially tits-up? I fell quiet.

'Dido speaking.'

I gave a weary sigh. The beginnings of a headache threatened the area behind my eyes. 'Yes, Dido.'

'What do you mean he's not called Roger?'

'He's a conman.' I hoped Nicola didn't have my place bugged. Revealing to Dido and Alex Yuill's imposter status was literally the only way I could get them to see sense and take what I said seriously.

'Good God,' Dido burst out.

I gave edited highlights, not exactly chapter and verse, more headings. 'You were right all along,' I said to please her.

'So it means the funding is off?' Alex wailed.

Sometimes my brother is immensely thick.

'Of course it's off.' I heard Dido tut.

Before they got into a scrap, I said, 'What did Yuill say exactly?'

Alex answered glumly. 'That you'd been round making wild accusations.'

'You believed him?'

'I didn't want to,' Alex said defensively. 'Then he said that something had come up and he was going to be out of the country for the foreseeable future.'

Despite Mum's money being stolen, I let out a long sigh of relief. 'Until he's on that plane, get over to Mum's and keep an eye on her.'

'She'll be devastated,' Dido said with feeling. 'Wouldn't it be better coming from you, Verity?'

'Can't.'

'Why not?' Alex said.

'I'm going away for a few days.'

'But . . .'

'Sorry, Alex, but Mum needs a man around and that man is you.'

CHAPTER TWENTY-TWO

Welcome to Merrie Olde England.

After the motorway, the landscape changed. Travelling through Worcestershire, skirting Herefordshire, and into Shropshire, it seemed more spread out and under-populated. I drove for miles along pot-holed roads behind combine harvesters, tractors, vans towing trailers crammed with unfortunate-looking sheep and Land Rovers towing horseboxes. A lot of village shops and post offices were closed, some with tatty frontages as if on the verge of shutting for good. Sunlight streaked across fields dotted with sprawling farms and tiny cottages. Occasionally, a big manor house would rise up out of the trees, like a monument to the fallen.

I arrived in Ludlow at lunchtime and found a car park next to a tiny police station. I put three hours on the meter and walked uphill and into the belly of the town. Too early to book into the Feathers, I wandered down a narrow street, squeezed onto an even narrower pavement and was buffeted along by shoppers and people with dogs and pushchairs. Where it tapered to a buttercross, a man with a lined face and penny whistle played a plaintive song. I chucked a pound into his hat and stood back in the shade, observing a wider street beyond where 4x4s parked on either side of a road lined with more historic buildings than seemed possible for such a small place. At the bottom of the hill: the Broad Gate, a thirteenth-century medieval arch and, I guessed, former stronghold to the town.

Cutting through a short arcade of shops and pubs, I found myself in the middle of a market in full swing. Smaller than the ones to which I was accustomed in Cirencester and Cheltenham, the emphasis was on local food, booze and produce. Artisan doughnuts vied with artisan breads and cheeses. Veering left, I ventured into a tiny square of Grade II terraced houses in beautiful red brick, occasional shops and a restaurant at the rear. Back out into the market, my voyage of discovery continued and I passed a chocolatiers and wine merchant's. Opposite, a building called the Ludlow Assembly Rooms housed a cinema. Beyond, Ludlow Castle loomed, symbolic of power and reputation lost.

On the corner, near the castle, I bought a sandwich, a takeaway iced coffee and a bottle of water for later. I ate and drank sitting on a bench in front of the castle, a cannon in the foreground. As if I'd time travelled and stepped out from my Tardis, I watched a world go by I didn't recognise. I doubted things had changed very much since the War of the Roses. Everything, including people, moved at a slower pace. Dogs were not fashion accessories. They were beloved pets. Tattoos were flaunted. Designer clothes were not. Crusty-looking men with red faces and wine bellies sported checked shirts with frayed sleeves and collars, no doubt bought from a local outfitter. These were worn over mustard-coloured and pink trousers. This town and its inhabitants represented a huge contrast to the glitz and glamour, cut and thrust of Cheltenham, a "Lollyland" whose people sported for-eign-holiday faces. Out in the sticks, it felt less well heeled, but I could be wrong; less sophisticated, ditto; less chal-lenging, for certain. It had to be admitted, less unhappy. Whoever these people were they were welded to the fabric of the place. In Cheltenham, it was possible to be anonymous. Here, you'd find it hard to hide. Fundamentally, these were not my people, my tribe. What that made me, I wasn't sure. I remembered Yuill's stinging words: *Pretty rich coming from a kid who's had everything.*

And I had. I'd never lain awake at night worrying about my bank balance and my future. I'd always had a safety net in that I was loved and well provided for. I was never going to fall through the gaps and wind up on the slag heap of society. To my shame, I'd taken it for granted. A bit of do-gooding in my professional life — making sure that the poorest kids got fed and received the attention they deserved — was no different to big name celebrities banging on about saving the planet and paying indulgences to salve their consciences so that they could jet off on holidays to foreign climes.

Shame on me.

As I looked at all the faces, so very different to what I knew, I realised with a jolt, that these *could* be my mother's people; this *could* be her birthplace, where she'd spent her significant early years. If it were true, it confounded everything I thought I knew about her.

In reflective mood, I pushed the debris from my lunch into a bin and cut down a steep hill, past an emporium that sold woodburners, to where the river flowed.

At the bottom, a jolly café and paved area from which children could feed ducks and play on grass beneath the trees. Looking across to the other side, hearing the distant sound of farming at full throttle, I wondered if my mother had once stood here. Had she thrown pieces of bread into the water? Had she walked the same streets as me, visited the castle, bought cakes in the market, or played by the riverside?

And if she had, why lie? What secret life was she protecting? Committing an offence these days, whether online or for real, was almost a badge of honour. Celebrities wound up in prison all the time and came out and lived a life more exalted than the one they had before then went inside. Alex hadn't exactly covered himself in glory academically or professionally and yet he was stable, married and was the father of two adorable kids. That Mum was ashamed of her past enough to conceal it from those who loved her most was impossible to believe.

Or was I reading too much into this and letting my wild imagination run away from me?

I ambled back up the hill with a blazing sun punishing my back and thought, once more, about Eddy Kaminski.

Some years ago, there'd been a café in Cheltenham run by a Polish couple, who were devout Catholics. If Eddy were buried in the place he'd lived and worked, there was every chance he would be buried in the grounds of the local Catholic Church.

I returned to Castle Square and the tourist information centre. A quick enquiry pointed me in the direction of Henley Road.

'Is it far from here?' I asked a middle-aged woman.

'Take you twenty minutes.' She gave me precise directions, including landmarks, which were variously St Laurence's Church, the local hospital and a Chinese chippy, off a roundabout.

I dolloped a layer of suntan lotion on my arms and legs, took a slug of water, readjusted my sunglasses and set off.

The townscape quickly changed from historic and medieval to residential, functional and less attractive. This could not be said about St Peter's — a tall, imposing building with a round turret and curved form that was at odds with a roughly hewn exterior. It was as if an elegant piece of Italy, fashioned and built there, had been transported, in modular form, and crash-landed into the middle of a British housing estate.

I entered through sturdy, ornate gates and it quickly became evident that what set this church apart was the absence of graves.

At the main entrance, I spied a couple of cars parked outside. A man sped out towards a beaten-up Volvo, with an urgent expression on his face. Cutting in, I asked where I could find the nearest cemetery.

'Left out of here, down the road,' he called over his shoulder, driving away as if he had the devil on his back.

I turned on my heel, took another swig of water, and retraced my steps to the main road. The cemetery was further away on foot than I'd imagined, almost near a roundabout and main route to Shrewsbury.

I crossed over and trudged up a short hill to a wide car parking area, from which well-tended grounds rose gently up a slope to a small chapel.

Grave upon grave upon grave, the task ahead was daunting. I'd be here all day.

From a central path, lots of doglegs off, some marked with alphabetical letters, that bore no resemblance to those buried, but were simply handy markers for the bereaved. A tranquil spot it was occasionally interrupted by the noise of cars whooshing past on the road running parallel.

I followed the main route, past angels and recently laid flowers on meadow that looked as if it had been nibbled by sheep. At the top the path intersected, one way leading towards toilets and gates, the other to a bin and a bench placed against the walls of the chapel. I sat down for a few moments, drinking in the quiet, thinking about my mother and Eddy Kaminski. Mum had never displayed religious beliefs unless you counted being kind and respectful to others and observing the rules of the Ten Commandments. I knew little about the Catholic faith bar the basics, the cross of particular significance.

I stood back up and followed the path that ran around the chapel. Beyond, row after row of crosses, as if given a separate plot of land especially for them.

Treading carefully, hardly daring to breathe, I walked among those who slept peacefully, those who slept fitfully and wondered whether Eddy was here and, if he was, whether his rest was that of the honest man.

And then I stumbled across him in an untended patch, devoid of grass in a carpet of weeds, the grave marked out in a rectangle of plain stone, next to his beloved Nina in a similarly marked grave that was overgrown and unkempt. Despite the glowing description of Eddy Kaminski online, there was nothing to suggest he or his wife were mourned or missed. Nobody had visited for a very long time. It made me sad. I'd often find flowers left either by Mum or Alex, sometimes Dido, at Dad's grave. I guessed when we were no longer around to do it my father's last resting place would fade into obscurity too. It wasn't a pleasant thought.

I crouched down, picked up a handful of dry earth, letting it run through my fingers. *What was your story*, I wondered. *What tales could you tell? And would you have told me anyway?*

Check-in at 4.00 p.m., I trundled back down the path, pausing at the noticeboard to the entrance and did a mental 'Duh!' Had I not been so impatient, I could have saved myself a lot of trouble. A map of the cemetery clearly delineated the Catholic section of the church.

Under an immense weight of heat and anxiety, it took forever to get my bearings and collect the car. A town of hills, I drove away and back up the main High Street and through an archway and entrance to the Feathers car park. Luckily, someone was pulling out of a space as I pulled in.

Dating back to 1619, the hotel was even more impressive than the photographs. It was literally like stepping back into history but with all the benefits and functionality of modern living. There were quirky little style notes everywhere. Ornate ceilings and a magnificent staircase had been carefully restored and had stood the test of time.

I went through all the usual palaver associated with staying in a hotel for a couple of nights. I booked dinner, but didn't book breakfast and declined a newspaper. The receptionist was so young she was unlikely to have a clue about a previous employee from over forty years ago. I needed to find a historical bod, a keen amateur like one of those enthusiastic guides you find at National Trust properties, someone who knew the history of the area and its people.

Poking my head into the dining room, ladies (mostly), in floral prints and engaged in animated conversation, were taking afternoon tea. There was a lot of "haw, hawing" and I didn't think they'd welcome a random approach from a brash out-of-towner.

My room was very much what I expected. Cosy, with biscuits I liked, nice toiletries in the en-suite and a bed made with Egyptian cotton sheets and with a mustard-coloured throw that matched the curtains and toned with the tartan carpet. A feather motif was attached to the wall above the headboard.

Overheated and not a little tired, I stripped off, took a cool shower and tested the furniture. It was as comfortable as it appeared and, for a few minutes, I drifted off and came to when I heard someone closing a door from a neighbouring room and walking along the corridor.

Dressed again, I came downstairs and bowled straight into a youngish guy wearing a grey suit and open-neck white shirt. He was slim, had close-cropped hair, a straight nose on a clean-shaven face.

'I'm sorry,' he said, although it was my fault.

'I should have looked where I was going.'

A smile crinkled the edges of his pale grey eyes. I glanced at his lapel. What a happy accident. Stating the obvious, I said, 'You're the manager.'

'I am.'

'Then you're the very person I need to speak to.'

His smile faded marginally. He probably associated those words with guests getting uppity about lack of hot water or not enough biscuits in the room

'I'm trying to find out information about an employee who worked here.'

Immediately, the shutters went down. 'It's not a matter I can discuss. Are you a journalist?'

'Goodness, no.' I noted he hadn't asked me if I were a police officer. That obvious, huh?

'His name is Eddy Kaminski. He worked here as an odd-job man and porter in the 1970s.'

The shutters went back up and the smile returned. 'Well before my time. Was this in Peter Nash's day?'

Who was Peter Nash? A previous manager, I supposed. 'I don't know.'

'Irrelevant really,' he said, 'I believe Peter passed away some time ago. The hotel has been through many changes.'

'Right,' I said, not feeling very hopeful. 'Do you know anyone who could help?'

'Your best bet is to find one of the older locals.'

'Do you think they'd generally be happy to chat?' I flashed a brilliant smile.

'Hard to say. People are friendly enough. It's a very close-knit community.'

Wary of strangers was what he meant, but was too polite to say. So I said it for him.

'Especially those from the city,' he agreed with a grin.

That was me told, I thought, thanking him for his time.

CHAPTER TWENTY-THREE

I don't like eating alone in public places. It's sad and lame. Solo drinking in a bar is worse. I ordered a Grey Goose vodka and tonic in the dining room and went straight for the kill with a main course of wild mushroom and pea risotto. Come eight o-clock my tummy was pleasantly full, my mind edgy and feeling so far outside my normal surroundings, I could have been in a spaceship heading to another galaxy.

Older locals, the manager suggested. I had to locate them before I could persuade them. How to do that in a place I didn't know would push my boundaries.

I idled outside onto a stuffy street. Heat bounced off buildings, ramping up the humidity to suffocating and energy-sapping proportions. I quickly became drenched in perspiration. Not a great look.

Deciding to retrace my steps from the afternoon, I slowly walked back through town, travelled down Mill Street, past the Blue Boar and into Silk Mill Lane before doubling back to Broad Street, with its restaurants and the Angel Inn, a lively looking place that seemed a cut above.

A large number of people milled about, some off to pubs, or walks down by the river; all ages, few mixed-race faces. I glanced at some and shyly smiled, received the odd, occasionally puzzled, smile back. What the hell was I doing? What did I hope to achieve? Did I even want to uncover the secrets of my mother's past? Wasn't it enough that I knew what I knew?

No way.

Dejected and brittle, about to return to my room, I noticed the pub opposite my hotel. It was black and white and looked a bit rough. A number of men gathered near the car park entrance, puffing their lungs out. Wisps of cigarette smoke caught in shards of late summer sunshine. The irony was that the punters opposite could look directly at the customers in the Feathers. Yin and Yang, you might say.

With the bones of an idea in my mind, I headed down the hill — was there any other way — to the bright lights of Tesco. It was cooler inside and, after I got my bearings, bought a packet of B&H, that set me back over ten quid, and was a lot more than when I'd last bought smokes and matches. No matter. I had a plan. Might be a "wing it" plan, even a shit plan, but in unknown territory, without contacts, with no sense of the general etiquette regarding social interaction, an idiot plan is better than none. You can't smoke inside a pub and gossip. You can outside, or at least you could here.

I lit up, inhaled, coughed a bit, took another drag and realised that returning to a bad habit was like getting back onto a bike after you'd piled over the handlebars and hit the tarmac. It's painful but, somehow, you couldn't resist climbing back on board.

Ambling across the road, I made my way uphill and stopped outside a pub called the Compasses. Peering through the glass, one hand shielding my eyes, I felt like a child watching a party to which I wasn't invited. With a predominantly male customer base, the centre of attraction was a large TV playing sport. Lively laughter spilled out. Several faces turned towards me as if I were the focus of interest, instead of the other way around. Drawing abruptly away, I caught sight of my own distorted reflection. Dark shadows had crept underneath my eyes, unseen. Tight lines appeared at the corner of my mouth. I smiled, bared my teeth, determined to banish them.

Back up the hill and before the Bull, a National Westminster Bank with a hole in the wall, an image of modernity and entirely incongruous in "ye olde building".

Like a hot air balloon going up, a great guffaw of laughter erupted as I drew near to the car park entrance of the pub. One old boy who looked as if he'd been dipped in creosote wiped tears of mirth from his reddened cheeks. It was hard to tell the ages of the assembled. I had them pegged from anything between thirty and ninety.

Horribly aware of my posh accent, the way I looked, the vibe I gave off, I swallowed hard and put out my cigarette by dropping it to the pavement and grinding it with the heel of my bloody expensive gold sandal. Then I took out a fresh ciggie from the pack and made my approach.

Normally, I'd break in with 'I'm terribly sorry to interrupt, but do you possibly have . . .'

'Anyone got a light?' I muttered.

A burly man with tattoos on both arms patted down his shorts and pulled out a pack of matches. Selecting one, he lit it and beckoned me over.

'Here you are, darlin'.'

'Ta,' I said. Christ, I cringed.

'Hey blondie, what's a pretty girl like you doing out on your own?' The shouted question came from a tall, whip-thin man with cheekbones that stood out like rocks on a beach.

'Leave the lass alone, Spike,' one old man growled. With hair growing out of every orifice, he resembled a wild boar.

'S'okay,' I said, inhaling and trying to look cool, like I was one of them and, I suspected, failing miserably. 'Anyone want one?' I asked, brandishing the pack and cursing the desperate note in my voice.

'Well, if you're offering.' Spike's leer made me shiver.

All eyes on me, I pushed through, did the deed and stood awkwardly to the side. The smell of spilt beer was strong, as was the odour of laundry that hadn't dried properly. A couple of women, who appeared to be related and of indeterminate age, had slinked out to view the curiosity (me) and join the party. Fleshy arms matched fleshy eyebrows. When the more senior woman spoke in a rich Shropshire accent, her voice sounded as if it had been smoked and cured over a fire for a hundred years.

'You a reporter, or what?'

'No.' My laugh was dry, not in the least convincing.

'We had some bloke sniffing around a few months ago.'

Yuill, I thought. 'Really?' I hoped someone would explain to what degree *the sniffing* went. About to press, I was immediately cornered.

As information gathering went, I was the one under the spotlight. For the next five minutes the man with the reddened cheeks, who, I discovered, was called Riley, asked the questions, helped along by Enid, his cousin, and her daughter, Tammy. This lot could work for the security services. Within minutes they'd prised out of me where I was from, my name (thank fuck it wasn't too cultured, although it was a close run), what I did for a living and why I was pootling around a town I'd never visited before. With regard to the last, I lied.

'I'm researching for a school project.'

'Come to the right place, love,' Tammy said. 'You visited the castle?'

'I'm more interested in Second World War history.'

'Allied military occupied it during the war,' Riley informed me. 'Yanks used to play baseball in the castle gardens.' His tone lacked warmth. He obviously thought it a disgrace.

I inhaled a lungful, tipped my head to the sky, and blew out a perfect ring of smoke. 'A number of Polish fighter pilots settled in the UK after hostilities. That's really my area of interest.'

'Good luck with that,' Riley said. 'Men at the hard end never talked about their war experiences, didn't matter if they was from Poland or these parts.'

'Dead right,' the others muttered.

'Have you heard of a Polish guy who used to live here called Eddy Kaminski' I said casually.

'What about him?' Enid's eyes were hard.

'He fought in the war, didn't he?' Tammy said, looking pointedly at her mother.

'That's as maybe.' Enid's salty tone suggested she had no fondness for the man or his memory.

'Eddy was all right.' Riley spoke with quiet authority. 'Kind-hearted as they come.'

'He were that.' The man with the tattooed arms had been silent until now. He let out a chuckle. 'Showed me his service revolver once when I was a little kid.'

'He did what?' Enid burst out.

'Keep your wig on. It's not like now when kids can't play an innocent game of cops and robbers without being arrested. Back in the day I thought I was the bee's knees. Got to hold it too. It was that small. Fitted nicely into the palm of my hand. Mind, it was heavier than you'd think.'

''Cos you were a kid, dickhead,' Enid said.

'Weren't army personnel supposed to hand back their weapons?' I asked, thinking that handing a gun to a child threw an alarming light on Eddy.

The tattooed man exchanged looks with Riley and shrugged.

'Anyway, you can't talk to him,' Riley said. ''Cos Eddy's been dead these past forty years and his missus went before him.'

'Are there any relatives I could speak to?' I tried to banish the unease from my voice.

'None that live here,' Enid said with a "back off" glance.

'So no remaining family?' I persisted.

'Ay,' Riley said. Enid flashed a warning look, one that he ignored.

'He had a granddaughter. Nobody knew what happened to her.'

'Bad luck and trouble, that one.' Enid's mouth turned down. Tiny lines above her top lip deepened. 'Not surprised they sent her away.'

Sent her away? Chiming with Yuill's account, I prayed the tears welling in my eyes would be regarded as a physical response to the cloud of cigarette smoke enveloping me.

'Bloody hell, Mother.' Tammy cut in. 'Don't you listen to the fucking news? Stuff happened then that's still happening now.' She looked straight at me. 'The poor kid wound up in one of those fucking awful places where kids got sexually abused.'

Fear pressed its dirty hands around my throat. My tongue felt as if it had swelled to twice its normal size. 'And her name?' I asked. I had to be sure.

'Eleonora, though some folk called her Bliss.'

In a strangled voice I thanked them for their company, wished them goodnight and dashed back across the road to what passed for sanctuary.

CHAPTER TWENTY-FOUR

Life is like Russian roulette. You never know when it's your turn for a bullet. I slept the sleep of the damned.

Rising early, I made myself a mug of tea that never tastes quite right from a hotel tray, and sat listlessly by the window.

Everything had blown up in my face. My mother: the Devon girl whose childhood was a picture of innocence and joy. My mother: a woman of unblemished character to whom others aspired, *beautiful on the inside and on the outside*. In reality, she'd been a tearaway and troubled teenager and had endured an appalling childhood in a terrible institution.

On a late night when the wine had flowed and shots were downed, Nicola once randomly told me that to be an effective liar you need grains of truth to make any deceit stick. *Building a legend*, I think she called it. Mum had duped us all by borrowing pieces from someone else to create a life infinitely better than the one she'd experienced. It killed me to think she'd felt shame so deep she'd recreated her personality and lied for a lifetime.

Staring outside without seeing, I thought long and hard about whether I'd ever glimpsed her past. I'd never seen her lose her cool until lately and now it made sense. For clear reasons my mother found it difficult to trust. There was always that element in her that was unknowable and unreachable. Maybe we all have this armoured piece inside, as protection, yet in Mum it was stronger, like iron. You could maybe make a dent but you'd never break through. And yet she'd allowed a man like Michael Yuill to do so and cut up rough when I had challenged that decision. It begged questions. What did he have that others didn't? What made him special?

I had no more business in this place. With a strong urge to flee, I worried I'd be charged for checking out early. How I'd approach my mother when I returned, I'd no idea. She'd be angry and I'd be sorry, though not for the reasons she thought.

Reflecting my mood, the weather was on the change. The temperature had dropped a few degrees. Still hot, not insanely so, the sky no longer bright blue, more cobalt. Only the air remained dense and sullen and uncommitted.

I was about to slip down to reception when there was a tap at the door. Housekeeping, probably. Opening it, I found Tammy standing outside. I wondered if I'd broken some unspoken rule, caused offence, pried when I should have kept my beak out.

'Oh,' I said.

Looking at me kindly, she asked if she could come in "to have a word".

I stood aside and indicated the chair while I perched opposite, on the end of the bed.

She looked different in a lacy pink top over a long loose-fitting skirt and flip-flops. Unlike the night before, she was wearing make-up. Her badly dyed blonde hair was scrunched up into a ponytail so that her features were more strongly defined. Her lipstick had travelled outside her natural lip line and her short lashes were heavily coated in mascara. If she hadn't been smiling she'd have been scary. It was easier to tell her age in daylight. I reckoned she was late fifties, early sixties. That made Enid a lot older than I'd first imagined, unless Tammy had been born to her when she was very young.

Planting both feet firmly on the carpet, Tammy sat with a hand firmly resting on each thigh and surveyed the room with admiration.

'Nice here, isn't it?'

I agreed, wondering what she really wanted. I didn't have long to wait. Her eyes quickly found mine.

'Are you all right, lovey? Only you looked awful upset last night. Vanished as if someone had set light to you.'

Touched by her concern, guilty for making superficial judgements about strangers, I assured her I was fine.

'You didn't look fine.'

I forced a smile. 'It was the story about the girls, you know, at the school.'

'Ah,' she said shrewdly. 'Too tender-hearted for this old world. It was criminal what went on at that place.'

'What did go on?' I could hardly get the words out.

'I was only a little kid, but there were rumours.'

She reached out to the table and ran a thick finger across my rose-tinted laptop, as if it were a thing of wonder, then let her gaze fall upon the tea-making facilities. 'Is that a kettle I see? I'm that parched.'

I explained that I'd already used up my quota of teabags and coffee, but could perhaps order room service. I thought she'd decline.

'I'd love a latte,' she said.

A quick phone call to reception, during which I received the impression that this was not a routine service, I turned my attention back to Tammy.

'You were saying?'

She blinked, as if she'd forgotten her thread.

'Rumours,' I reminded her. 'About the school.'

'Oh, yeah, that. According to Mum, it was well known that men were regular visitors.'

I pressed my hands together in my lap in a blind attempt to control the shake in my knees. 'How could that be? What about the authorities?'

'Turned a blind eye, didn't they?'

'And people knew?'

'Common knowledge. That's what made me mad with my mum. She's a dear old thing, but she can be cruel. Those girls had a dog's life in there. No,' she raised a finger, 'worse than that. And it wasn't their fault.'

Satisfied she'd made her point, she asked me what it was like living in Cheltenham. 'Been there once,' she said. 'Good shops,' she added approvingly. 'Not that I'd ever want to leave here. I'm a small town girl, me. Born here, schooled here, worked here until my back got bad.' She winced, flexed her thick ankles. 'Got a water problem — fluid retention, they call it.'

Bewildered, I made a soothing apologetic noise. My mind could not be farther away from Tammy's medical issues, as sympathetic as I was.

'Fact of life.' She gave a shrug of her broad shoulders.

I needed to get her back on track. 'You must know a lot of people.'

'That I do, which is why I knew the man asking questions all them months ago was a wrong-un.'

'Did you get a name?'

She shook her head.

'Do you remember what he looked like?' It paid to corroborate.

'Tall, rangy, wore a Stetson and cowboy boots. Had one of them soft suede jackets, you know the ones with the fringes. Thought he was fucking Clint Eastwood.' She let out a snigger.

This didn't sound like Yuill at all. My responding smile was weak.

'How old was he?'

'Probably my son's age, around thirty-seven.'

A knock at the door announced the arrival of room service.

Watching in silence as drinks were dispensed, I rounded up my thoughts, waited until after the door closed and it was just she and I.

'This man,' I reminded her, 'was he local?'

Tamsin blew the surface of her drink with her overly made-up lips. 'No way.'

'Any idea where he came from?'

'Over the border.'

'Wales?'

'Herefordshire. Said he worked on a farm. Could just picture him on his horse.' She flashed a grin. 'Bunch of in-breds in those parts.'

The remark was so casually delivered, so matter of fact, it sounded as if it could be true. I had no idea where she meant and asked her.

She sipped her drink, placed the mug down carefully, leaning very slightly towards me, as if dispensing the security code to a vault filled with treasure. 'The Herefordshire Triangle.'

Familiar with the Bermuda Triangle, I was none the wiser about the geography nearby. My ignorance must have shown on my face because she continued, 'It's an area straddling the River Wye, made up of Staunton-on-Wye, Preston-on-Wye and Monnington-on-Wye.'

I made a mental note to check out the area as soon as Tammy left.

'This man asking questions, what about exactly?'

'Same as you, lovey. He wanted to know about Eddy Kaminski.' She scratched her chin. 'He especially wanted to find out if Eddy's granddaughter had visited.'

My mother, I realised, a breath hitching in my chest. 'When was this exactly?'

'Easter time.'

My life revolves around the school year. Half terms and holidays receive star billing on my calendar. I knew this to be the end of the first full week in April and after Roger had met Mum.

'Did he say why?'

Tammy shook her head, swallowed more coffee.

'You didn't think to ask?'

'None of my business.'

It felt like a rebuke. Heat rose up from my chin to my cheeks.

'So what did you tell him?'

'The truth.'

'Yes?'

'That she'd not set foot in the place she'd called home for decades.'

'You know that for a fact?'

'I do.' She inclined towards me again. The chair wheezed and groaned. 'People round here look out for each other. We see who comes and who goes.'

I let out a nervous laugh. 'Surely, you can't keep an eye on the entire population. What about visitors and tourists?'

'We'd spot one of our own from fifty paces.'

'And she was one of yours?'

Tammy slow-blinked. 'She was.'

'You knew her?'

'I was only a child.'

'But you *did* know her?'

Her eyes drilled into mine. 'Enough to spot the likeness in her daughter.'

Breath whooshed out of me. I tried to look away and, caught in Tammy's vice-like gaze, found I couldn't. I was like a fly about to be devoured by a very determined spider.

'Am I right, Verity?' Her small eyes glinted and there was an ugly twist to her lips.

'No,' I said. 'You're wrong.'

Tammy clicked her tongue, put her mug down, the contents half drunk, and, with effort, stood up. 'Must have a lookalike,' she said with a flat smile.

Eager for her to leave, I crossed the floor and got to the door before she did.

'Look after yourself,' she said as she left.

I was sure she didn't mean it.

CHAPTER TWENTY-FIVE

My knees trembling, I stumbled back to the chair and sat down with a thump. Was the man who thought himself a modern-day cowboy responsible for stalking my mother, for sending her things she didn't want, for taking pictures of me and my brother and his family? Was this man asking questions because Yuill, with his ulterior motive, had shone a spotlight on my mother and disturbed her past? What exactly had Yuill started when he'd done his homework? He hadn't kicked a wasp's nest. He'd kicked the lair of yellow jacket hornets.

I went into the bathroom, poured myself a glass of water from the tap and drank it straight down. My frightened reflection stared back at me from the mirror. It was as if a malign artist had grabbed hold of my chin in one hand and etched misery all over my face with the other. I wanted to check out, to lose a hundred quid I could ill afford. I wanted to go home and see my friends and drink wine in the sunshine and forget about Yuill and the school, with its predatory visitors, and the strange man asking questions, and run like hell from the fact that Mum had lived a double life and had lied to us all, even my darling dad.

I scooped up toiletries and packed the few things I'd brought into my bag. One last sneak at my laptop before I go, I thought, flipping open the lid, pressing my finger for identification, and Googling the area Tammy had called the Herefordshire Triangle.

The geography covered around twelve miles and could not be more than minutes apart by car. Monnington-on-Wye was a small settlement originally mentioned in the Domesday Book. Preston-on-Wye looked as though it had more going for it. Populated with homes and a village hall, it provided keen canoeists with a couple of campsites. Staunton-on-Wye, I discovered, was situated on the south bank of the river and had a church and a nature area known as "The Scar", a place dangerous to children due to its hundred-foot drop. One of the most under-populated parishes in the country, Tammy's allegation, according to historic information, contained a germ of truth. In the 1800s the wealth of the village was reliant on one man, G. Jarvis. On his death he bequeathed his estate to villagers on the strict condition his wealth must never leave or be given to outsiders. Families, consequently, married close members to carry out his wishes and prevent wealth from going outside the area, the result a shallow gene pool. After centuries had passed, I doubted it held true today, Tammy's warped opinion based on hearsay and folklore.

There were five working farms in the area. Studying the locations, I came across a little-known local mystery: the disappearance of blacksmith, Donald Birch, aged thirty-nine. He'd vanished during the long hot summer of 1976 and was never seen again.

A shiver travelled from the tips of my toes to the top of my head. The timeline bothered me. Mum would have been fifteen and, allegedly, an inmate of the Stone House.

He especially wanted to find out if Eddy's granddaughter had visited.

Why?

I closed my laptop and checked out of the hotel early.

'Was everything all right?' asked a concerned receptionist.

'Lovely. Family emergency,' I explained.

'I'm so sorry to hear. Perhaps you'll get the opportunity to come back and stay with us again another time.'

Not a chance. 'The woman you sent up to my room,' I began.

'What woman?'

I described Tammy. I mean, she wasn't exactly difficult to miss. The receptionist's face broke into a smile. 'Oh, her,' she said, pressing a hand to her chest. 'She told me about the charity event you're both working on.' Her face fell. 'I mean that's right, isn't it?'

I smiled in fake agreement and strode out to my car. Not averse to deception, what else had Tammy lied about?

I quickly stowed my luggage, climbed inside and drove out towards the Shropshire-Herefordshire border and Leominster.

After endless days of sunshine, the sky swelled up with grey cloud that pressed down upon the earth and robbed it of colour. I'd no reason to believe that anyone was following. Unsettled by Tammy's visit, alarmed by the stranger asking questions, I still checked the rear-view mirror to make sure.

Out of Leominster, I picked up the A44 and passed quaint sounding places like Dilwyn, which sounded more Welsh than English, and Weobley and a sign that announced a local art fair the following month. From there, it was a short drive to Letton and Staunton-on-Wye. I didn't pootle, tootle or dawdle. I was on a mission, with little hope of a glorious outcome or happy ending, truth and closure all I asked.

The sat nav took me past a pub and led me down nail-biting and bottom-clenching narrow roads with high hedges and estate fencing and "shut your eyes and pray" bends. I spied orchards and fruit farms and falling-down barns, but not the church I'd expected. A clutch of houses appeared as I drove downhill to a railway bridge. The road extended for two to three miles and at thirty mph the drive felt slower than the average snail. Warnings to KEEP OUT and PRIVATE and DOGS LOOSE did not lessen my anxiety. There appeared to be no epicentre, just a lot of nothing.

Coming to the end of the road, I turned around rather poorly in a gateway and headed back the way I'd come and turned left, back onto the main road.

Another left and past a war memorial, with an overhang of trees so dark it was as if the world had briefly eclipsed, I came across civilisation: a couple walking a lively black Labrador and homes that were either done up or in the process of being done up. Long drives flanked either side of the road and there were a couple of sweet thatched cottages. It bore no relationship to the blurb I'd read, or the slur Tammy had cast. This was a place where gentrification was in full swing. Even the sun broke through the grey to celebrate it.

Feeling more assured, I drove to Monnington, which was exactly as I'd imagined: orchards and the odd black-and-white dwelling, public footpaths and church.

Stomach rumbling, I headed back to the A438 and main route into Hereford, and stopped off at a fancy farm shop with the kind of prices I'd expect to pay in Cheltenham. Judging by the motors in the car park, there was nothing like it for miles and this was where the landed gentry hung out and did their food shopping. A bottle of Radnor Hills water, a sausage roll and a flapjack later and I was back in the car and driving across a wide bridge, underneath which the River Wye sparkled.

Glancing back in the mirror, I spotted two vehicles behind me, one a dirty old white van, effectively making me the lead car down more narrow lanes and bends. This always made me nervous. Hogging the road, a bloody great Land Rover appeared on the opposite side, except there was no side and it missed me by a squeak. Sweat beaded my forehead and the back of my neck as I, first, stalled and then crunched the gears on take-off. Cursing under my breath, I noticed the vehicles behind were having similar difficulty getting by. Relieving the pressure a bit, I had a head start.

More bends and then a jolly-looking pub painted retro-bathroom pink, with people drinking in the beer garden outside, and then past an abandoned-looking farm on a shit piece of road. Fields stretched out on either side, punctuated by the odd smallholding. Cold slithered up my spine. I felt as if I were being drawn closer to wilderness and No Man's Land: to somewhere I really shouldn't go. Glancing in my mirror again told me that I was alone. Me and my car and I didn't know what else. Just as the creeps were really starting to bite, the road widened out into a hamlet. It looked pretty safe and I decided to stop in front of a green, opposite a chapel that had been converted into a home.

With nobody else about, and certainly no Clint Eastwood lookalike, I climbed out and walked along a wide road with bungalows and views of a field of tan and dun coloured ponies.

Past a gateway, the road dropped down to tennis courts and a mighty oak tree. Bees buzzing. Birds singing, it was a picture of rural calm, fragmented only by the sound of dirt-track bikes in the distance. Still, I felt a tug of something not being quite right, like the memory of an old wound, the touch of an ancient scar. Did places absorb unhappy events? Was this why we tear down the dwellings of serial killers, as if obliterating the place removed the stench of death and the violence that had taken place within?

A crow cawed above my head. I glanced up, saw that the sun had beaten it and the sky had thickened. *Nobody about,* I told myself. Then why did I feel as if I were not alone?

Retracing my route, I stepped aside, flattening my back against hedgerow, as a battered van, more rust than red, driven by a pensioner, chugged past. Ahead, a triangular stretch of grass that stood quite oddly in front of a large executive-style home. I looked down a lane that bore left and downhill to a farmhouse with outbuildings.

Said he worked on a farm. Could just picture him on his horse.

The chance of it being this farm was slim, the idea that I would find the man with the hat remote, that he would answer my questions truthfully, should I discover him, non-existent.

But I had to try.

Half obscured by thick hedge, the road slithered round, briefly out of view. A red-brick barn with a corrugated roof could be glimpsed. Drawing near, I saw it formed part of a large courtyard of buildings, including a farmhouse, painted sky blue. Anyone inside would have a clear view of me. Feeling suddenly exposed and unsure, I ambled along and past a box of salt for gritting the roads, on which sat a welding mask, free to anyone who wanted it.

Further along, a scrap yard of old, rusting farming equipment, stacks of bricks and sheets of broken glass. I flashed with irritation. A child venturing inside could easily get hurt.

At the sound of footsteps, I narrowed my gaze and saw a thickset man, bull-necked, bare-chested, with thick eyelids and flat features, trudging towards me. He had one of those haircuts that was shorn to stubble at the sides, long and sticking up in gelled spikes on top. He didn't look threatening. With a sloppy smile, he looked benign, maybe a bit gormless, if I were unkind.

I made eye contact, acknowledged him with a nod, a sort of "Hiya". He slowed a bit and then I heard noise behind from an approaching vehicle with a sound system. I'm no country and western fan but I recognise Dolly Parton when she's warbling her heart out.

Time slowed. By contrast, my heart rate increased. A strange sensation, deep inside my lungs, put my body on high alert. I didn't sense danger. I smelt it and, in response, my mouth dried and my palms and underneath my arms broke out in a sweat.

A glance over my shoulder revealed that the vehicle was a clapped-out white van with rust on the wheel arches and blacked-out windows. Was this the same motor that had followed me into the village? Driving it, a man with impressive sideburns, long-jawed, wearing Aviator sunglasses, and a Stetson on his head. He rolled to a stop behind me, Dolly still blaring, and then he got out. Slowly. As if he had no place else to be other than here in this lane with me.

Panicked, I looked for help from the stray walker. His face a yellow sheen of sweat, he smiled and lumbered towards me. In an instant, I read his intentions to snatch, capture and take. Heart rate working at a dizzying speed, I swiped the pepper spray from my bag and, as his flabby arms shot out towards me, let him have it straight into his eyes.

Recoiling, his hands pressed to his face, and howling like a beaten dog, he thrashed, cursing and groaning. My fear was so great I heard nothing. It was as if someone had switched off the sound.

A rush of air and I twisted away as "Stetson" made a grab for me and clutched thin air. Another swipe and he knocked the pepper spray from my hands. Aghast, I ran.

CHAPTER TWENTY-SIX

The leaves on the trees turned grey, the road ahead a dark, unforgiving line. Red brick drained to white. It was as if I were in a black-and-white movie, a nightmare, and running for my life. Sound that had mysteriously disappeared returned with raw vengeance. I heard my shoes hitting the tarmac, my heart banging against my chest, Stetson man breathing close behind. I didn't shout or yell. I was too busy escaping. And I was not running well. My legs were like lead. My lungs were on fire. I wished I were fitter. I cursed that I'd always been happier going to a bar than going to a gym. Within metres, I stumbled, I felt blisters forming and I had a stitch. Still every piece of me focused on reaching my car, getting the hell out and never coming back.

Almost at the end of the lane, where it joined what passed for a main road, strong arms encircled my waist, pulling me back and down. I hit the road with tremendous force, chin, hands and knees taking the brunt. Stunned, I felt little pain though knew I was badly grazed and bleeding.

I wanted to check out, to curl into a ball, to press my bloodied stinging palms to my face to pretend that if I couldn't see my attacker, he couldn't see me, that none of this was really happening.

Resisting the urge to hide, I struggled to get up. A swinging kick made my hip howl. I let out a scream of pure anguish. Rough hands tore at my clothes. "Stetson" manhandled and dragged me to my knees. I squirmed and yelled as he scooped me up effortlessly with arms that were like rock and threw me over his bony shoulder as if I were a sack of swedes.

From upside down I saw my bag lying in the middle of the road with my wallet and credit cards inside. Stetson's accomplice stood next to the van, pouring water from a bottle into his ruined eyes, swearing his head off in a thick rural accent. Against two, I had no hope. Pushed into the back of the vehicle, there would be no way back.

A primal urge kicked in. I beat Stetson's back with my fists and wriggled and wriggled, feet kicking, arms flailing. His hat flew off, exposing a thinly covered scalp of lank hair, and he jerked to a stop.

'Fucking hell.' The first words he'd spoken.

Arching my back, I reared up, roared and dug my nails into his head. He dropped me as if I'd sprayed him with acid. Landing badly, I scuttled away and limped towards the open road where I heard the sweet sound of deliverance: a motorist was heading slowly along in a black Jaguar. Arms waving madly like windmills, putting myself in the path of the car, I flagged him down.

'Stop,' I screamed. 'Help!'

The driver must have pumped the brake because the saloon dramatically screeched to a halt. A man, late thirties, I reckoned, stuck his head out of the window.

'Bad men,' I gabbled, gesticulating wildly with my thumb pointing over my shoulder.

He scrambled out of the car and ran, long and lean, towards them. I heard him shout 'Oi' at my attackers.

Fast receding footsteps followed by the sound of two van doors slamming shut. An engine roared into life and then the sound of tyres spitting gravel as the vehicle moved off. One glance told me that the driver who'd saved me was walking back empty-handed. My bag had gone, with the important financial pieces of my life with it.

Letting out a groan, I pitched forward and gingerly rested my damaged hands on my knees. At least, thank God, I was safe and relatively unscathed. That it could have been so much worse I could barely admit. How stupid and reckless I'd been.

'You, all right, love?' I felt a warm hand upon my back.

I straightened up and looked into my rescuer's eyes. Downturned at the edges and of the deepest blue, they reminded me of Michael Yuill's. A scrub of black hair, with just a couple of strands of grey, revealed a high forehead. Faint lines on his brow and down the side of his nose suggested that he was possibly older than I'd first imagined. His lips were thin and his jaw set in a hard "Don't mess with me" expression, for which I was eternally grateful. He wore a white T over black chinos. It clung to his body, giving the appearance he worked out on a regular basis. The sleeve tattoo on his right arm was of a crown with crossed swords in red and canary yellow inks, the inscription "Lest We Forget" suggesting he was ex-army.

'Thank God, you happened to chance by,' I said, breathless.

'Looked nasty. Do you know those guys?'

I shook my head.

He viewed me with concern. 'Those cuts on your hands need dressing. Do you need a hospital?'

'I need the police,' I said, shakily. 'They've nicked my bag with my credit cards too.'

'I've got a phone in the Jag. Okay to walk?'

I mumbled that I was, which was a lie. Every step felt as if I'd wrenched muscles I didn't know I had.

'My car's up the road.' I indicated the green. 'Oh, bloody hell, my car keys are in my bag,' I wailed.

'Once we've called the cops, I'll give you a lift to the nearest police station.'

I couldn't quite place his accent. Underneath the northern intonation, there lurked a rural burr.

He walked slightly ahead and moved with purpose. I briefly wondered if he was in the SAS; Credenhill was stationed nearby.

'I can't thank you enough. I hope I'm not holding you up, or anything.'

'No problem.' He glanced at his watch. 'Nothing that can't keep, anyway.'

I noticed that when he smiled he did so more with his eyes than with his mouth.

We reached his car. I'm not a petrol head — as long as a motor gets me from A to B, I'm good with it. Despite my prejudice, I had to admit that the sight of the XF Saloon made me thrill, possibly because it represented safety and sanctuary and freedom.

'Hop in,' he said. 'I'll start her up and pull onto the verge before a tractor piles into us. Kids around here drive at warp speed.'

I climbed into the plush leather cream interior, glad to sit down. With the crisis over, the pain kicked in. My hands were a mess of raw flesh and gravel. Muscles in my calves and thighs felt as if they'd been stretched to breaking point. The soles of my feet felt chafed and blistered.

We moved off, the Jag gliding away then, to my disbelief, gathered speed.

'W-what are you doing? I need to call the police.'

I glanced across and noticed a pulse in the man's jaw ticking. Muscles in my stomach lurched and tightened.

'Please, stop,' I begged.

His response was to go faster. I twisted around and looked behind me at the disappearing village and civilisation.

I didn't care what speed we were doing. I wasn't staying with this Samaritan turned psycho, and reached for the door.

Before my hand connected to the handle, the locking mechanism kicked in. Chills swept through me. Either I'd blundered from one bad situation to another, or it was all part of a perfectly coordinated plan.

'Look, I want to get out. Drop me off, I don't care where and I promise not to tell.' How many women in this situation had uttered those same words and whose pleas had gone unheard?

He put his foot down and the motor, an automatic, clicked up a gear. Hedges and fields rushed by at an alarming pace.

Maybe I could attack him, claw at his face, but then crashing and getting killed or badly injured didn't seem a great option.

'Put your seat belt on,' he commanded.

If I did as he said, I'd be effectively shutting the only door marked "Way Out". On the other hand, it seemed that preserving my life was important. Reluctantly, I did as asked.

'Who the hell are you?'

'You'll find out soon enough.'

'Where are you taking me?'

'You don't get to ask the questions. There's a hood in the glove compartment. Put it on.'

'No.' I crossed my arms.

'Do it,' he barked.

I opened my mouth to refuse and then I noticed the blade. Terror swelled inside me.

His right hand on the steering wheel, the knife in his left, he jabbed it towards me, his thin lips drawing apart in a snarl. I'd no doubt he would think nothing of sticking it into flesh. *Mine*.

Tears streaming down my face, I did as I was told.

The hood was made of sack and had a drawstring around the neck. I put it on as loosely as I could. Rough against my skin, it smelt of earth and straw and despair.

'I can't breathe,' I said, my voice muffled.

'Then don't cry,' he said.

CHAPTER TWENTY-SEVEN

Terror was blinding white and razor-sharp.

Rough and scratchy, the sacking made it difficult to breathe. It was impossible to keep panic at bay. Sweat slicked my skin and plastered my short hair to my scalp. Surely, someone driving past would notice the person with the unusual head covering and call the police? Or would it be misconstrued as a joke? Would it be deemed safer to look the other way? Was this how men got away with the abduction of young women so often? Was there some unspoken code of *mustn't get involved*?

Silence crawled all over me. The smooth, fast ride induced waves of nausea and, terrified I'd throw up, I clenched my hands in my lap. I pictured my knuckles shining pale beneath the tightened skin like the new bones of the recently deceased.

Think! Where were we heading? Further west, I surmised, towards Wales, though I wouldn't have staked my life on it. A dry cynical laugh threatened to bubble up and erupt. *Keep it together.* I silently cursed. Knees jackhammering, I strained to understand the sequence of events of the last few hours.

Kind and considerate Tammy no longer existed. I saw how she had deliberately set me up. How else could those three men know I would be chancing this way?

Three men.

I tried not to think what they might have in mind. If I allowed my imagination to wander there, my spirit would break, untethered and be lost.

And yet . . . I hadn't been hurt, not really. Nobody had knocked me out with a blow to my head, or forced a roofie-laced bottle of water down my throat. They wanted me whole.

For what?

I shuddered inside.

At last, the engine note changed and the car slowed. The road beneath its wheels rutted, the Jaguar moved in a zigzag motion, bumping up and down. We drove like this for around a dizzying mile until the car rattled over what I presumed was a cattle grid, beyond which it travelled across a smoother surface until the engine dimmed and the Jag ground to a halt.

I heard dogs barking, men shouting. A fresh pulse of terror swept through my nervous system at the thought of people traffickers and stories of British girls sent abroad. Was I an intimate cog in the machinery of modern-day slavery? Would I be pitched into a dark cellar with a dozen other young and terrified women? *Stop*, I thought. This is about Mum. Did it make things better? *No.*

The driver's door opened and the shrill sound of a woman's voice cut through a gust of warm air. Orders were given to remove that 'bloody sack, Clay,' and let me out. *Schoolgirl error to mention a name*, the functioning part of my brain registered.

Someone opened the door on my side. I stayed rigid and compliant as the hood was whipped from my head. Blinking against the sudden flash of light, I looked up into the face of the man I'd christened Stetson. His hat was back in place and a blade of straw stuck out of the side of his mouth. Through clenched dirty yellow teeth and rancid breath that contained a sour note of cheap coffee, he told me to get out.

I moved slowly, partly because my body had seized up, mostly because I wanted to put off whatever lay in wait.

I looked about at a collection of shabby black-and-white cottages, paint peeling, guttering hanging, one incongruously decorated with a Sky dish, and a yard surrounded by barns with tin roofs and in a terrible state of disrepair. One had fallen victim to fire, judging by the blackened timbers and soot-covered bricks. Geese roamed freely among an assortment of old tyres, disembowelled cars, metalwork and planks of timbers that had seemingly been left out in the rain to rot. Piles of dung steamed in the afternoon sun. The van I'd seen earlier stood next to a mud-spattered pick-up truck, a couple of similarly filthy quad bikes, and an abandoned single-decker bus, the sleek-looking Jaguar very much the odd one out.

The larger of the two dwellings had a wooden stoop, on which there were three easy chairs. My "rescuer", the man I presumed was Clay, was in conversation with the bull-neck I'd first encountered on the road. Of the woman, who'd given the orders, there was no sign.

Stalling for time, I took deep breaths and let my gaze travel over a mixture of paddocks and pens housing goats, sheep and chickens and, more surprisingly, a pair of ostriches. Beyond, an orchard of fruit trees, a greenhouse with broken panes and vegetable patches. There were no other dwellings, only fields and an ugly pylon. With all its cables and wires and steel rods, it looked as if it powered the entire county. I doubted the nearest neighbour lived anywhere nearby.

From its elevated position, anyone approaching would be easily spotted. A glance back at the dusty and pot-holed drive revealed it disappeared around a number of bends and into the distance. If I took to my heels, I'd be easily caught before I ran out of steam.

'Move,' Stetson barked. Resistant, I jutted out my chin, stayed put. Clay and the other man stopped talking and moved silently off the stoop and fell in behind. To make the point, Stetson gave me a shove.

With three pairs of eyes boring into my back, I edged forward towards a broken-down cottage with logs piled outside. A stained mattress and a TV, with its screen smashed, lay propped against an open door and an entrance that was impossibly dark. Eyes darting right and left for some magical means of escape, I found none.

Hesitating, another thud in the middle of my back impressed upon me the need to cross the threshold. Although I'm five foot six, I had to duck a low beam, then squeeze past domestic junk, while my vision rapidly tried to adjust to the musty interior.

I was in a basic kitchen with range, sink and cupboards. A long refectory table, that had seen plenty of action, ran down the middle. Seated at the end, a woman with short, jet-black dyed hair and strong, almost Romany, features. A small window that looked out onto a tangle of garden bathed her in light. Lined and weathered she might be, yet her eyes shone tiger-bright and her generous mouth curled into a smile. No doubt, she'd been an attractive younger woman and, in her mid to late sixties remained so. A gold chain with a heart glinted around her neck. She sat, composed, her hands resting on the table in front of her as if about to play the piano. Her painted dark-blue nails were unspeakably long, reminding me of my friend Rinelle. No rings were on her fingers, the only other jewellery, apart from the chain, a pair of oversized gold hoop earrings. From another room, I heard a clock strike four.

'Sit down,' she said.

My feet wouldn't move. I glanced over my shoulder to where Stetson stood guard.

She inclined her head. 'Come near. I don't bite.' Her accent was strongly rural.

I went to pull out a chair.

'Not there, here.' She indicated a seat next to hers.

I walked on leaden legs and sat.

'That's better. You're very pale. Did the boys mistreat you? I told them not to be rough.'

Thinking it might be a cheap method to put me at my ease, I shook my head.

She dropped her gaze to my hands and frowned. Standing up, she reached for a tea towel, ran it under a tap and dabbed painfully at the wounds. A childhood memory of grazing my knee after I'd fallen off my bike and Mum picking out grit and dirt danced through my mind. 'There now,' the woman said, when she was done. 'You're young. You'll heal. Would you like some water?'

Again, I shook my head.

Suddenly she shot forward and clasped my chin in one hand. I tried to draw away. She hung on tight and studied my face like she was reading a map. I wondered if she could hear my heart bumping against my ribs.

'Gently,' she said, her voice almost a purr. 'I'm not going to hurt you.'

She *was* hurting me. I was too immobile to speak and say so.

'You're the spit of her, did you know? I always wondered what Bliss's daughter looked like.'

A pulse of realisation charged through me. I stared into her deep-set eyes. I knew this woman. She was the girl my mum had spoken about: Cherry B, Cheryl Castrey, the person I'd believed had carved my mother's initials on the walls of the Stone House. In the light of new information, I could no longer be sure. Perhaps Mum was responsible for leaving traces of her past behind. Strange, when she'd spent a lifetime trying to eradicate them.

When Cheryl let me go I felt indentations from her fingernails on my chin.

In a shaky voice I said, 'You can't do this. People know where I am. I'll be missed.' I imagined police running through my last movements, maybe they'd do one of those reconstructions and some bright-eyed viewer would notice my car and sound the alarm.

'True.'

It wasn't the answer I was expecting.

'I've got friends at GCHQ,' I said boldly.

'Yada yada.'

I stared at her venomously. 'Why the hell am I here?'

'All in good time. Brew first.'

'I don't want tea. I don't want anything from you.'

'Course you do. Why else would you be snooping?' She let that land before she gave a nod of approval and said, 'Fair play, you're quite the detective.'

I wasn't looking for accolades. 'I don't care anymore. I just want to go home.' I winced at the pathetic whine in my voice.

'And you will.' She patted my hand. 'Clint,' she bawled to the man I'd christened "Stetson", her voice carrying to the next county. 'Tell Chuck to make us a cuppa sharpish and tell Clay to let Yootha know we have a guest.'

I stood up. 'If I'm a guest, I can choose to leave.'

Cheryl's eyes drilled into mine. 'Sit down, or . . .' She gave Clint a meaningful glance. I didn't need for her to spell out what might happen if I didn't obey. I sat. Clint nodded, disappeared then returned. With a stony expression, Cheryl examined my face, her gaze snaking to my body, looking me up and down. The horrible thought that she was assessing how easy I'd be to get rid of sent a fresh shard of fear razoring up my spine.

'So how is Eleonora?' Cheryl asked the question conversationally, as if the last few menacing seconds had never taken place.

I spoke sullenly. 'She's good.'

'*Good?*' The smile on her lips did not match the cold in her eyes. 'Not how I'd describe your mother.'

'You were both at the Stone House, her crimes no worse than yours.'

'Is that so?'

I didn't answer.

'She still with her man?'

'My father died five years ago.'

'Not *that* man, the one nosey parkering.'

So I was right. Roger aka Michael's, enquiries had reignited old woes. I shook my head.

'Not surprised by his appeal, mind. Your mother likes a certain type.'

'You don't know my mother. You haven't seen her for forty-seven years.'

'Leopards and spots, my dear.'

She made my mother sound like some man-eater, which was utter crap. Sure, Michael Yuill had turned her head, but that was a one-off. For five long years Mum had mourned my dad. There had never been anyone else either during the marriage or after — until Yuill came along.

What about before? A voice in my head needled.

'Fortunately for us your mother's weakness worked in our favour. Men like him smell vulnerability in a woman.'

I scratched my head. 'You were working together?'

'No way, Mr Yuill was a crook and a thief. Anyone with half a brain could work that out.'

Even with half a brain I couldn't accept her version of events.

'Let me get this straight, Michael Yuill, a man you'd never met, rocks up right here, asks questions and magically provides you with a lead to your old childhood friend.'

'What of it?'

'It's too random and coincidental.'

'That's because you don't know how things work in these parts,' she countered with a smug smile. 'Folk know each other around here, not like where you come from. Someone takes ill in the next county, and we know. Our histories and friend-ships span the decades.'

'The rural grapevine must be an amazing thing,' I said dryly.

'You can scoff all you like, but I'm the one in the driving seat, missy.'

She had me cold.

'Yuill was quite the charmer when he came to snoop on your mother. Arrogant as hell, he thought himself better than the rest of us, according to my old friend, Enid. What?' she

162

said at my surprised expression. 'Enid and Tammy have been my eyes and ears for decades.'

I clenched my jaw at my utter stupidity. When Yuill had made my mother his research project, he'd obviously crossed paths with Enid. 'What else did Enid tell you about Yuill?'

'That he talked a good talk, perfect if you're wet behind the ears,' she said pointedly.

'My mother is not naive,' I countered.

'When it comes to men she is.'

Unhappy with the way the conversation was going, I shifted uncomfortably in my seat. I'd learn more if I kept my mouth shut and stopped trying to defend Mum.

'So then you talked to Yuill?'

She laughed. 'Did we hell? My boys followed him. *Put him under surveillance*, you might say. Silly sod led us straight to your dear old mum. I had to say, looking at the photographs they snapped I was surprised how well she'd worn. Must be all that luxury living: fine dinners, good booze, fancy holidays and private healthcare.'

So this was a straightforward case of jealousy and envy. 'Is that why you sent a cryptic postcard and left a dead bird on her doorstep?'

A cold smile lifted her lips in response.

I took this as confirmation. But why leave such a gap between taking the photographs in February and putting the plan into action in July? Did the month have particular significance for her? Or did she think I was less likely to be missed in the summer holidays? I'd no doubt that I was pivotal to her nasty little plan.

'Why did you do it?' I demanded to know.

'Why not?'

'You did it for kicks?'

Again the soulless smile.

'You did it because she had a nice life and you didn't?'

Her expression darkened. Her eyes held mine.

'I did it because she deserved to have her life ruined. It's why I've spent the last forty-seven years hunting her.'

Hunting? Who does that over some minor infraction and teenage squabble? Christ, a girl in primary school had once bullied me mercilessly. I heard she'd moved to London, to Balham, to be precise, in a road I knew well. I had absolutely no intention of tracking her down and telling her how much she'd made my life hell.

Chuck, with his pudding face, lumbered in. Tea arrived on a tray with a proper teapot, china cups and saucers, milk in a jug and sugar lumps in a bowl. It might have been misconstrued as a pleasant social occasion with an old friend of my mother's — if I wasn't being held against my will.

I watched him leave and waited as Cheryl poured and stirred and asked if I took sugar. As bad as my situation was, I thought it prudent to accept. This appeared to please her. *Keep it calm; keep it steady*, I thought, desperately needing to understand what was driving her, not that I believed she'd give it up easily. Cheryl was a drama queen, a diva, determined to stretch out and enjoy her moment of power and glory, maybe the only high point in an insignificant life. No way was she going to rush the grand finale.

She lifted the cup to her lips, drank, placed it back down so very carefully, and ran a fingernail over the grain of the table in a circular motion.

'How close are you to your mother, Verity?'

The tone was too familiar, a base method to exert power. Petulantly, I didn't answer and sipped the tea, which was strong.

'See, you only have bits of her story. You're missing all the big juicy headlines. Not your fault because your mother never told you. Am I right?'

Unfortunately, it was true. Whatever this woman was, whatever her real agenda, she was no bull-shitter. She displayed a rare animal cunning that stripped away lies, mine included. For a lifetime I realised I'd been deceiving myself about my mother. Any tricky questions, I saw now, were effortlessly deflected. She'd always been incredibly busy, which now I saw as distraction. I wasn't sure anymore that I actually had the first idea about her. The thought was devastating. I could feel the tip of my nose turning pink, a prelude to tears. If Cheryl noticed, she gave no quarter. She leant in so close I could smell tannin on her breath.

'Did she tell you, Verity, that she murdered a man?'

CHAPTER TWENTY-EIGHT

I cupped my hands over my nose in shock. Yes, Mum hadn't told the truth, but not *this*. She didn't have a violent streak in her. Rarely had I heard my mother raise her voice, let alone her hand. Only lately, after we'd argued, had I glimpsed anything remotely aggressive, and that description was pushing it.

'You're bloody lying.'

'Am I lying about your mother, the granddaughter of a Polish immigrant? Am I lying about her incarceration in the Stone House? Am I lying when I say you're no closer to your mother than my gormless sons, Chuck, or Clint, are to me?' She tilted her head in Stetson's direction. The hoops in her ears jangled.

'I don't believe you.'

'Then believe this.' She raised her hands behind her neck and unclasped the chain. With reverence, she opened the heart-shaped pendant and pushed it into my hands. It felt like a burning coal. I badly wanted to sling it back at her.

But I couldn't.

Inside: two tiny photographs. On the right, a teenage Cheryl, dark-eyed, dusky-skinned with the soft lusty bloom of youth in her expression. On the left, a man who wore a

Stetson and bootlace tie, just like Clint, who it seemed was channelling an ancestor, but it was the striking similarity to Clay, the man who'd driven the Jaguar, that was so astounding. They had the same shaped face, similar expression in their petrol-blue eyes. And then it hit me: Michael Yuill bore a similar countenance.

Your mother likes a certain type.

But why would she fall for someone who looked like the man she'd allegedly murdered?

I swallowed hard, pressed the necklace back into Cheryl's hands. 'Who is he?' I asked in alarm.

'The father of my daughter, he was my soul-mate, my everything.' She stared at me with cold certainty. 'His name was Don Birch.'

The name unfamiliar, I frowned. Then it hit me in sound bites: Donald Birch, blacksmith, vanished in 1976, never seen again.

'But his body was never found,' I protested.

Cheryl's nostrils flared in accusation. Her strong features tightened into a mass of angry lines. 'So you knew all along. That bitch told you.'

Every blood vessel in my body froze 'No, no. I read about it, okay?' I said, imploring her to believe me. 'I'm just stating you can't accuse someone of murder when there's no body.'

'Doesn't mean she didn't kill him,' a voice, as old as time, spoke behind me.

I twisted around and found myself caught in the sights of a grey-haired woman with long plaits that reached to her waist. She had small, alert eyes that looked as if they could see around corners. The skin beneath was pouched and peppered with liver spots, as were her bare arms. She wore an old yellow vest top over saggy checked shorts. Stooped, she had a walking stick. I was surprised I hadn't heard her enter.

She tapped across the quarry-tiled floor slowly. The chair scraped back and she planted herself opposite. Sniffing the foetid air, she viewed me as if I'd crawled out of a sewer.

'Yootha was Don's sister,' Cheryl explained with another black smile. 'Clay is her son.' And nephew to the late Don Birch, hence the odd familial similarity, I realised.

Cornered, I drew a breath, found myself shrinking into the seat. I gaped from one woman to the other. Heavyweight disapproval bore down on me as if I were personally to blame for Don's disappearance.

Disappearance.

Gathering my thoughts before they slunk away, I maintained stoutly, 'No body, no crime.'

'That's not what the police thought. Case remains open, unsolved.'

'For which I'm sorry, but how the hell could my mother have done such a thing? She was imprisoned in the Stone House.'

Yootha's laugh was a rasp, a distillation of dried twigs and sand.

'Girls were snuck out at night, isn't that right, Cherry?'

Cheryl gave a grim nod.

I remembered Tammy's words, about the men that "visited". Did they take the girls away to do God's knows what? Was Don Birch one of them? If it were true it seemed like an own goal for the women to talk so fondly of him. They were practically deifying Don Birch, building a shrine to him. What was I missing? Quite a bit, as it happened.

Yootha tapped the table with a grubby nail. 'My brother met your mother on the night of 3 July 1976 so he could finish with her.' She darted a sympathetic glance at Cheryl. 'I know because he told me.'

'Hang on, she was fifteen,' I said sharply. 'He had no business being in a relationship with her.'

'Don't you go getting all hoity-toity.'

'Sneering at us,' Cheryl said, with a poisonous gaze.

'So what happened?' I said, refusing to back down.

'He went missing that same night.'

'People do.'

'Not when he had a baby on the way,' Cheryl spat. 'Not when he had me in his life.'

My mind reeled. The way Cheryl painted it: she and my mother were willingly seeing the same man while both of them were underage. I could never imagine my straight-laced mother doing such a thing. It was inconceivable. She'd obviously been groomed.

But did that make her feelings for him any less real? I tried not to get sidetracked. *If* it were true, the likelihood of Birch going missing to extricate himself from what he regarded as a sordid ménage à trois was a distinct possibility.

'Maybe that's why he left.'

The slap was hard and fast.

'Shut your whore mouth.' Cheryl cursed.

Sharp nails had raked my skin. When I touched my face with the tips of my fingers, they were slick with blood.

'I-I'm sorry. I only meant that some men can't bear the responsibility of a child. It's not unusual for them to walk out of their lives and start new ones.'

'I know what *you* meant.' She glowered. 'You're protecting your mother. She did for him, I tell you.' Her voice rose into a roar. '*I* know it. *Yootha* knows it. The whole bloody county knows it.'

'But not the police, apparently,' I said with dry emphasis that was entirely missed by the women.

'They found blood in the smithy,' Yootha intoned. 'There were signs of a fight.'

I was disappearing through quicksand. Every time I posed a plausible explanation it was dismantled, plunging me deeper. I nursed my face, which smarted like hell. Yootha droned on.

'Your mother was clever, see. Cunning as a fox.'

'Ran in the family,' Cheryl said nastily. 'She had good old Eddy to help cover up her crime.'

Throttled by their accusations, I stared aghast. Was this the deadly secret my mother had spent her life protecting? Please God don't let it be true.

'Fact is,' Cheryl said, her cruel face in mine. 'Same night Don went missing, so did your mother. Nobody ever saw her again.'

'Vanished into thin air.' Yootha fluttered her gnarled fingers. 'Some folk thought she was dead.'

'Except,' Cheryl said, with flat contempt, 'she's very much alive and now we know why.'

CHAPTER TWENTY-NINE

'Take her away,' Cheryl commanded.

I turned and saw Clint and Chuck advance towards me.

'You can't do this,' I yelled, as they grabbed an arm each. 'This is kidnap and the police will come down on you so hard you'll be spending the rest of what's left of your old age in prison.'

Dragged backwards, my Vans skidding on the quarry-tiled floor, I bucked and lashed out. The grip on my arms tightened and a smack to the side of my head made my teeth rattle. Blind rage rampaged through me.

'Let go of me, you bastards. You don't know a damn thing. You just want someone to blame for your sad, pathetic fucking lives.'

I have never lost my temper in my life, but I lost it now. I was one spitting ball of fury made worse by Cheryl's stony and immutable expression. Yootha stared through me with rank disgust.

Out of control, I felt a rough hand clamp itself around my neck, forcing me down, as if I were a sheep being loaded up and taken to slaughter.

Bent double and thrust back out into the light, the pressure released. Jerking my head up, my stomach sank to my toes. There, in the yard, my car and only solid lead to my existence. All bright hope of rescue faded to shadow. The fire that had burned up inside me, extinguished. I was lost. In ten minutes, I'd vanished from civilisation. There had been no CCTV to record my movements. I had no phone, no means of communication. Nicola was out of reach. I'd upset my brother and his wife. Thinking of Alex and Dido nearly undid me. They seemed so far away. My mother was no longer speaking to me after I'd effectively trashed her relationship with a man determined to rinse her. And demented throwbacks, that had nursed grudges for decades, breathing new life into them and fanning the embers with each passing year, were holding me hostage.

Marched away from the main buildings, I was shoved into a steel-framed barn that looked like a recent addition. The weird thought that it had been erected especially for me scampered across my mind.

Sturdy, with a sliding lock on the outside, it contained straw bales, a camp bed with a dirty sheet thrown over it, a bottle of water and a garage-bought cheese sandwich, already sweating, with the crusts curling. A bucket and lavatory roll served as toilet facilities. I was too dumbstruck to protest when they snatched the watch Dad had given me from my wrist.

I listened as the doors were resolutely closed and then I sprang. I hollered at the top of my voice. I beat the steel walls with my fist. I kicked and punched and screamed until, wretched tears pouring down my face, I gave up. Entombed in silence, I collapsed onto the makeshift bed before my knees gave way.

My mother in a sexual entanglement with a man she'd murdered? It was inconceivable.

If she had nothing to hide, why lie?

The more I thought about it, the more irrational I felt. Was it possible that, in my mother's desperation, she'd viewed Don Birch as her ticket out of an institution that had so destroyed her? Who could blame her if she did? It would be a simple case of survival.

Shocked to my core, I didn't know for how long I stayed like that. Realising I was thirsty, I drank the water. It was warm and I didn't care. I'd last eaten the night before and, though I wasn't hungry, I opened the sandwich and took a bite, chewing mechanically. Physically, I wasn't in the best shape. My toes were sore from kicking sheet steel. My ankle was swollen. My hip was bruised. My ribs barked. My face and head hurt like hell where I'd been struck. My voice was raw from shouting and my hands remained a shredded mess. This was only a taster. If things didn't roll the women's way, frustration would boil over and it would get worse.

There were five of them and one of me and they were tied by an unbreakable bond of history, blood and shared experience. I didn't rate my chances. Out of Cheryl's boys, cocky Clint seemed smarter than Chuck who was, as even his mother agreed, positively gormless. He could still hurt. Clay, Yootha's son, was the one to watch. A piece of work, a man of few words and with a voice that rasped, like his vocal cords had been sanded down there was nothing slow-witted about him. I suspected volatility underneath that thin veneer of contained civility.

So what did they want?

Mum.

Where do I figure?

I'm bait.

But would she come?

Can't answer. If she's really a murderer she'll hang me out to dry.

Scared, I struggled up, walked three sides of the perimeter of the building and noted a wall of bales blocking the rear. There were no loose boards, or places that I could pry open, supposing I had the strength to do so. If I could pull out some of the bales to form a makeshift ladder it would take me to the top. Perhaps I could find an aperture to squeeze out of and shimmy down. I'd still have the long drive with which to contend and would only succeed if I weren't seen first. It would mean a flight in darkness.

Weightier than imagined, the straw was coarse and abraded my already damaged hands. Every time I heard a noise from outside, I jolted with fear. Eventually, I clambered up on bleeding palms and grazed knees. Desperation was a powerful driver.

The roof was solid steel and, had I the tools to punch or drill a hole in it, estimated the drop the other side around twenty feet.

Forlorn, I eased my way down and restacked the bales to conceal my doomed escape plan. I paced. I swore. Stuff like this didn't happen to people like me. But it had. Hysteria grabbed me by the hand, held me close, and whirled me around until, worn out, I slumped onto the earth, drew my legs up, wrapped my arms tight around them, and rested the good side of my face on my knees. I struggled not to give in to self-pity, and lost. Hot salty tears coursed down my cheeks.

My rescue relied on the one person who'd spent a life-time covering a crime, or at the very least running away from something in which she was surely involved. My throat felt as if I'd swallowed crushed glass. I was her daughter. Blood was thicker than water, wasn't it? Love bound us together.

What if it didn't?

PART TWO

CHAPTER THIRTY

Eleanor waited. She waited for Dido and Alex to stop fussing. She waited for Verity to return and tell her that it was all a big mistake. She waited for the phone to ring.

It's not true, she told herself. The man she knew as Roger would never deceive her. He loved her. He swore that to her only days ago.

And yet it would not be the first time a man had betrayed her.

'I've brought you tea,' Dido said.

She views me as if I had some awful illness, Eleanor thought. In a way it was not so far off the truth. How did you explain an affliction that had lasted a lifetime?

'Can I get you something to eat?'

'No, thank you, darling. Tea is fine.' She wanted Dido and Alex to leave, as kind and well intentioned as they were. She could not separate the muddle with them around. And, by God, she needed to think after the emotional chaos of the past forty-eight hours.

At first, she'd thought it was some kind of joke until Alex had told her how Roger had pulled the plug on Alex's business venture. Confirmation that the funds to her account were never transferred had sent alarm bells ringing. Still then she believed it was a misunderstanding, a result of human or technical error. Frantic phone calls to Roger, followed by even more frantic messages to his voicemail, resulting in deafening silence, and then she knew deep in her heart that all Verity's accusations were true. Shame gilded Eleanor's features at the memory. Guilt consumed her for not doing right by her child.

Why did she fall for a man like Roger? Only she knew. Of course, she did.

'I'll be all right,' she told her daughter-in-law, a brittle woman who colluded with Alex's weakness. Eleanor loved her son with the same fierce passion she had for her daughter, but she was not blind to his cutting- corners laziness and greed. 'Go home,' she said kindly. 'You've done all you can and your children need you.'

Dido's eyes brightened at the prospect of escape. 'If you're sure?'

'I'll be fine.' *Those words should be engraved on my tombstone*, Eleanor thought.

Skulking in the kitchen, like a teenager found drinking his father's best brandy, Alex readily agreed to leave the second Dido gave the word.

'Will you be all right, Ma?' His dark eyebrows drew together in embarrassed concern. 'I could call Hazel. Ask her to pop round.'

Please don't. 'That won't be necessary.'

'Well, if you're sure.'

'Certain.' Eleanor resisted the strong desire to clench her fists. *Go*, she thought. *Just leave.*

She hugged them goodbye and watched them flee. Closing the front door, she briefly rested against it. Her eyes closed tightly to prevent a cascade of tears from spilling down her cheeks.

Mustn't cry. Mustn't cry.

She went to the sitting room, cleared away the debris of two days of mercy meals and drinks, took them to the kitchen and washed up. She didn't use the dishwasher. She needed to *do*, to distract, and to calm her pounding thoughts.

This was the habit of a lifetime. Staying busy and deliberately active left no room for unwelcome conjecture.

She went upstairs and stripped beds, loaded the laundry into the washing machine. She eyed her chaise longue and the cushion containing the postcard, which Verity had so carefully sewed back into the lining, the purity of the needlework giving the game away. She hadn't reacted strongly then. She wouldn't react now, she thought. *Not until I am more composed.*

One last time she called the man she knew as Roger. She was told that the number was no longer in service, a step up from "leave a message". He'd already left the country, according to Alex. A bleak sense of rejection cut into her.

Stupid, stupid woman that she is.

Shame burned deep and long; for thinking that, in her twilight years, she was still attractive; for believing the pillow talk of a man who'd slept with her purely to rob her; for disbelieving and betraying her daughter; for squandering Giles's money when he'd worked so hard to leave her well provided for.

'I am so lucky to have found you,' he'd once whispered.

How could she explain that good fortune was all hers after a life of bad decisions, mostly made by others, but that Giles was *her* decision, her very best? She'd never had the courage to tell him that he'd given her a lifeline and an escape from the unspeakable things done a long time ago.

Perhaps this was karma, she conceded wearily, and nothing more than she deserved.

Eleanor stiffened, drew her shoulders back. Slipping out the postcard, she laid it on the desk in her bedroom. One image, two words and the name her mother gave her before her hippie father changed her name from Eleonora Kaminska to Eleanor Hannaford, fondly nicknamed Bliss.

Most memories faded. Some remained intense. She recalled glorious walks along riverbanks, playing outside, running naked and dirty, staying up late, gazing at sunrises and sunsets and watching her parents sleep away their lives. Home was a converted ambulance on a commune with lots of other people who lived in wigwams. She'd never tasted such freedom as she did then. Mum, with her green eyes, tangled hair and tattoos, always laughing and tickling her. Her dad was quieter, smoked a lot of strange smelling tobaccos, which she now recognised as weed. Spaced out, he loped everywhere on bare feet. He enlightened her and the other children about nature and he taught her to read. She couldn't ever recall learning arithmetic. From an early age she had the sense that numbers meant money and money was intrinsically bad. The day she was taken away to live with her grandparents because her parents were drug addicts and incapable of looking after a child was the day that idyllic life changed forever.

She willed away the past. Shock wore off, despair crept in and with it fear because, of the three important men in Eleanor Finch's life, all were dead. Two died from natural causes, the other . . .

Eleanor tried to mentally steady herself. The facade she had so carefully erected was already crumbling. She now wondered if the man called Roger was part of a bigger plan to trap her. *It would not be the first time*, she thought, with sick suspicion. And what of her daughter? Verity had taken off for a few days, according to Alex. To do what, exactly? She understood her child. She recognised her insatiable curiosity and desire for truth. In this regard, she was aptly named.

Fresh shame assailed Eleanor at the memory of arguments and blatant lies. Verity had no more believed her explanations than she believed the earth was flat. Why else had she gone through her belongings? A tremor of fear rippled through Eleanor at the thought of what else Verity might uncover. Please, please not that.

Where are you? She chafed inside. Call it a mother's instinct, but she knew in her soul that something was deeply wrong. She sensed that Verity had put herself in danger.

The old survival instincts kicking in, she reached for her bag and grabbed her keys. As an afterthought, she collected a fine voile scarf then headed for her car. First stop: Cheltenham.

CHAPTER THIRTY-ONE

Eleanor let herself into her daughter's home. She called out, hoping that Verity would stumble out of the bathroom, towel wrapped around her head, a facemask giving her the appearance of a ghost, or that she'd call back with a 'Hiya, I'm about to put the kettle on.' Silence greeted Eleanor, and it was crushing.

Absently, she swept up a magazine from the floor and placed it on the coffee table. She picked up a vase of wilting flowers and chucked them in the bin. A satsuma had gone mouldy in the fruit bowl. This, too, she picked out and discarded. She noticed Verity's phone, lying dead upon the work surface. She hunted for Verity's laptop but, of course, it was gone, as had her bag. If Eleanor had hoped to find clues, she was disappointed.

Biting her lip, she phoned Nicola. It went to voicemail and she left a message. Next, she called Rinelle.

'Mrs Finch, hey, um . . . what a surprise. How are you?' Rinelle asked brightly.

Eleanor gave a bland reply. She heard Rinelle exhale with what she assumed was relief.

'What can I do you for?'

'I'm trying to get hold of Verity.'

'She's not at home?'

'No.'

'Tried calling?'

'Her phone's broken. When was she last in touch?'

'Ooh, a few days ago.'

'Any idea of her plans?'

'Not really.'

Educated guess? Eleanor writhed in frustration. 'Did she mention going away?'

'You mean a holiday?'

'Not exactly. Was there somewhere she especially wanted to visit?'

'I don't think so.'

The line went quiet.

'Rinelle,' Eleanor said against her best intentions. 'It's really important you help me out here. If there's something you know that I don't, I'd be grateful if you tell me.' She didn't like asking Verity's friend to betray a confidence and yet, unless she did, she feared she would not be able to establish a lead to her daughter.

'Well,' Rinelle began, clearing her throat.

'Yes?' Eleanor jumped in.

'I know she felt a tad awks about Mr Scott-Jefferies. Maybe she's taken off for a bit to get her head straight. Not that I've got an opinion. I mean you're entitled to a life,' Rinelle said clumsily.

'It's all right, Rinelle. It's all over.'

'Oh.

'It's perfectly okay,' Eleanor said slowly, thinking this wasn't really helping. 'Was anything else bothering her?'

'Nothing she told me.'

Eleanor detected caution in Rinelle's reply. 'Would Nicola be able to help, do you think?'

Rinelle lowered her voice. 'She's not around. You know . . .' She let her voice tail off.

'Oh, I see,' Eleanor said uncertainly. 'If Verity contacts you or shows up, could you please get her to call me? It's extremely urgent.'

'Will do, Mrs Finch. And Mrs Finch?'

'Yes?'

'I'm sorry, you know, about what's happened.'

'Thank you,' Eleanor said stiffly, ending the call.

She stood motionless. Anything to stave off the circularity of her thoughts. She toyed with the idea that Verity was touring Cornwall, a favourite place when she was little, and one that reminded her of her father. Or she had taken a trip to London, to visit old friends. The idea of her poking around in places that Eleanor had long left behind was risible and remote, she told herself firmly.

Then why do my knees tremble and my hands shake?

Because every instinct proclaimed that Verity's natural curiosity and quest for truth had led her to stray into things she could never understand.

Unbidden, a kaleidoscope of flashbacks clattered through her mind. Darkness and lies; blood and death. Eleanor brutally banished them. Ever since her world had turned dark, she had pushed away the past. In the early days it was difficult to quash her most intrusive negative thoughts. She'd struggled with anger and irritability. She could not sleep. She'd felt as if she were living a half-life. A dull smile creased her lips. Everyone was awash with mental health issues. But were they really? Few were victims of genuine abuse. They knew nothing of isolation and violence and the random terror that struck out of the clear blue so that your lungs virtually burst through your ribcage with fear.

Eleanor jolted when her phone rang. Her stomach plummeted when she saw the identity of the caller. *Be cool,* she told herself. *Be confident. If you fake it with enough sincerity, you'll convey it.* She should know. She'd been doing it ever since she'd shed her fifteen-year-old skin.

'Hello, Hazel.'

'My darling, I've just heard the news.'

Alex. Eleanor bridled, wishing for once that her son would do as asked.

'That beastly man deserves to be horse-whipped.'

'I don't know about that,' Eleanor said mildly. 'I'm all right, honestly.' She did her level best to tame the shake in her voice.

'Of course you're not. Roger, or whatever name he masquerades as, is nothing short of a criminal. I've spoken to Justin and he's going to see if he can pull strings with the bank.'

'That's so kind. I fear he'd have to be a magician. It was my fault, Hazel.'

'Nonsense. I hope you're going to the police.'

Eleanor's throat threatened to close over. 'To report what? I was a willing participant; it's my fault.'

'If anyone is to blame it's me. It was my silly idea for you to date online. Please say you'll come to dinner tonight. We'd so love to see you and it's the least we can do in the circumstances.'

Eleanor had already tuned out.

'Eleanor, are you still there?'

'Sorry, yes. It's a lovely thought and thank you, but I'm taking myself off for a little while.'

'Damned fine idea,' Hazel opined. 'Somewhere nice, I hope.'

Somewhere you'll never believe, Eleanor thought.

'You'll call when you get back?'

'I will,' she assured her.

Eleanor ended the call and stared at the walls of her daughter's small home. For two whole years she'd lived in less space than the room in which she was standing. Four in the morning was worst. At any second she'd expected a knock at the door, arrest, re-incarceration, punishment. That day never came and when finally she'd escaped, with her grandfather's blessing, she'd never returned.

But now she must and it appalled her.

CHAPTER THIRTY-TWO

Eleanor pulled into Castle Street car park in Ludlow with a grave sense of foreboding. She remembered nothing of the journey, only that it took less time than she'd hoped.

Wrapping the voile scarf around her head, she stepped out and put an hour on the meter. A glance at the sky revealed that the weather was on the turn. There was a spit of rain in the air and thickening cloud was heavy, the suffocating atmosphere oppressive.

She walked along Castle Street, close to St Laurence's Church, to Upper Linney and the modest two-bedroom home that had belonged to her grandfather and Nan, Eddy and Nina Kaminski.

Someone had taken care of it, she observed. The glazed transom windows looked new and the red front door freshly painted. She suspected the cellar, her home for too long, had been converted into a home office. They were all the rage at the moment. She was not there to admire the renovation. She was there to honour the dead and remind herself that life in that little house had not been all bad.

Her grandparents had been kind people. They'd loved her. They'd fed her. Their home cooking had ensured she put a stone onto her thin frame within months. Her nan had a sweet tooth and taught her how to make macaroons and delicious cornflake treats coated in chocolate. She was shown how to cut open tomatoes, chisel out the seeds and pulp and mix it with grated cheese and pile it back in and bake it. She'd stuffed peppers too, and trickled cheddar into celery sticks. For the first time in her six-year-old life she'd tasted 'Wagon Wheels' and pies. Gone the strict diet imposed by her parents, which they'd insisted was good for her and, in reality, was only good for them because it meant they could spend the money saved on drugs. But Eleonora, which was what her grandparents had insisted on calling her, missed them just the same. Her clothes were too tight, her prayers too long. Much to her daddy's consternation, his in-laws were devout Catholics. Her father's beliefs had stemmed from the trees and the earth.

She'd found routine hard, school harder, and she'd been lonely. Due to her lack of education she was put back a year. Her only friends, and they weren't really friends at all, were little kids. One of them was a pudgy girl called Tammy Gray.

They said bad things came in threes and it's true. Her dad ran off to Devon, to Totnes, with a woman called Shia, and her wild and wacky mum died of a drug overdose a year later. Nan got sick and she passed away. Many, including Eleanor's grandfather, believed Nan died of a broken heart. The St Benedict signet ring Grandpa wore on his little finger did not ward off Satan and evil influences after all. Eleanor was ten years of age and she felt she was to blame for all the troubles inflicted on her family.

For two years she'd bunked off school. She'd slip out of the house at dusk while her grandfather was out playing dominoes with his friends and drinking Polish brandy. Sometimes he did an evening shift at the hotel where he worked and she could be gone all night. She drank and she smoked. She broke into building sites and abandoned homes because she could. On numerous occasions she was marched back home by police officers or neighbours. Some were kind. Some were not. Her granddad despaired. He railed and he raged. Occasionally, he would slap her. Delinquent, she was out of control and knew it and was powerless to do anything about it. In her head, she had a target on her back. All that was needed was someone to shoot the arrow and take her down.

And they did.

Three years were spent at the Stone House because her grandfather lost his patience and could no longer give her a home. Truth was he didn't want to, not because he was a bad person but because he ran out of road. She didn't blame him, despite the devastating consequences for her.

In the beginning it wasn't so bad. She found a friend in Cheryl Castrey, or so she'd believed. Eating sweets, they'd chat long into the night, plotting about making pots of money. They shared their dreams, which were one and the same, and talked about all the exotic places they would visit. Eleanor had assumed it would be the two of them. It had never occurred to her that she wasn't included.

'We'll head to Crete,' Cheryl declared, her mouth full of flying saucers, round pieces of rice paper, filled with sherbet. 'Greek boys are so good-looking.'

'But how will we get there, Cherry?'

'I'll think of something. Maybe we could hitch a ride on a cruise ship, or we could join the crew,' Cheryl said, eyes wide with excitement. 'Boat companies are always looking for waitresses. You could sing, be part of the entertainment.'

'Don't be soft.' Eleanor blushed, hopelessly flattered.

Guilt corrodes, but rejection bites and it's deep and it's hard.

Downcast, Eleanor abandoned her old home and walked in the direction of Market Square where she bought a ham sandwich and a bottle of water. She squirrelled them back to the car where she ate, without pleasure. She'd last viewed the Stone House online. She was surprised to see it up for sale, and aghast that the previous owner, Owen Jones, had bought and lived in it for decades. She'd shuddered at the image of the man, memorable for his rough hands and depraved desires. Nothing would be achieved by going back, she told herself. Why rake up bad memories? But she'd come this far. If she confronted those demons, would they leave her alone? Would they allow Verity to come back?

Tired of thinking, undone with anxiety, she let her eyes close. The Stone House loomed into view and with it the memory of cold washes, shallow weekly baths, metal beds, thin mattresses, whispered conversations and learning and learning and learning and discipline. She recalled standing half naked in a room in front of other girls while a male doctor examined her. Why he'd needed to peer inside her knickers she had no idea. She remembered blood and she remembered shame and the desire to do anything to escape, if only for a few hours. She pictured herself young and full of life and longing to be loved.

By anyone.

Eleanor's eyes popped open. She felt a little sick. It would be a lie to suggest that she'd slept around, although she'd had sex with too many men — not boys, she reminded herself. She hadn't been like Cherry who, according to her own lips, popped her cherry, ha-ha, when she was thirteen.

The hour was up. Eleanor started the engine and drove out of the car park. She picked up the A49 but did not head back home. She moved in the opposite direction, past a new Sainsburys and on past a Food Centre and a pub called the Clive. She put her foot down, exceeding the speed limit, before she changed her damn mind. She sailed past the turning to Onibury and Stokesay, with its fine manor house, and on to Craven Arms, a market town, until, several miles later she turned and headed down narrow lanes with high hedges, under a threatening, baleful sky, towards the Shropshire Hills and the Stone House.

CHAPTER THIRTY-THREE

It was no less imposing, Eleanor thought. As an adult, she'd hoped to dwarf it in her mind to manageable, unthreatening proportions. It proved an impossible undertaking and took her an enormous amount of courage to step out of the car. Was this what Cheryl wanted when she'd sent that postcard? Did she intend to punish her for what she did? Eleanor had no doubt that it was Cheryl who sent the cryptic message.

Skirting piles of junk and old outbuildings, Eleanor walked through knee-high grass and an orchard heavy with apples and heat. The sky had darkened to the colour of granite and a warm breeze was playing kiss chase among trees, a prelude to stormy weather.

The entrance to the secret passage was not overgrown at all. Owen Jones had kept it pristine as a sick reminder of what he'd orchestrated. She was bloody glad he was dead and hoped he rotted. Due to his twisted desires men of all ages gathered to collect the girls to do with them what they wished. Sometimes they were taken away for days.

Eleanor creased inside. Mistakenly, she'd thought the passage had provided a route to freedom, away from those hatchet-faced men and women who'd presided over her. She hadn't realised that it represented a man's hand over her mouth, the signing away of her virginity and innocence, and pain.

Amnesia from traumatic events had been her friend these past decades. Too grave to blot it out completely, she heard the crawl of old and sick men's voices, the bawdy, mocking laughter of the middle-aged, too. She remembered clothes ripping, skin tearing, blood running. Gasping, she screwed her eyes up tight, put her hands over her ears to dispel the sound of tears, screams, pleas and calls for help.

I shouldn't be here, she thought, shaking. It was too disturbing. Yet if she ran, what then?

With trembling fingers, she slipped out her phone and switched on the light function. *Not far to walk*, she reminded herself. *You did it before when you were young and vulnerable. You can do it again now.*

The narrow, winding passage took her to a room in the main house. Once, sneaking back in, the principal had caught her.

'Don't let me see you again.'

Not, 'Where were you? What were you doing? Who were you with?'

Because it had been common knowledge where she was, whom she was with and what she was doing.

Each time she'd made that journey she'd had one thought in mind, one single hope in her heart: escape. And, without exception, she'd been thwarted by one of Owen Jones's sentries posted at the throat of the tunnel.

The door at the end was bizarrely ajar. She waited and listened. Satisfied that she was completely alone, she pushed it open and walked into what was laughingly called a common room. In reality, a herding station. She recalled huddling around the single metal radiator when Cheryl first told her about Don Birch, a man who was going to change their lives. How horribly right she'd been.

'He's different to the rest,' Cheryl claimed.

'He's old,' Eleanor pointed out. 'Almost the same age as my dad.'

'So what? He's strong and handsome.'

'I wouldn't trust any man. They're all pigs.'

'Don isn't. And he's dead generous.'

'You'll do anything for a packet of fags and a bottle of cheap cider.'

Cheryl punched her arm playfully. 'You make me sound like a right slapper. All he wants is a kiss and cuddle.'

Eleanor rolled her eyes. *Won't be long before he's ripping off your clothes*, she thought, *like the rest of them*.

'Don't look like that. If you don't believe me, come and see for yourself tonight.'

'And what? Get grabbed by Jonesie and his crew?'

'Don will keep us safe, promise.'

And Don had — for a while.

Shaking away the memory, she crossed the floor to the staircase. Step by faltering step, she reached the first floor and teetered on the edge. What if someone came? What if someone made a connection? She wandered from room to room like a ghost, the chains of old conversations rattling through the corridors. She did not see the furnishings, the paintings on the walls, the furniture. She viewed it as it was before: bare, soulless, cold-hearted and beyond hope.

It was the sight of the sinks that did for her. Standing in line, they were first stripped of their clothes and then of their dignity. They weren't young women. They were lumps of flesh. It made them easy prey for the men who came.

And Don Birch was no different.

Eleanor recalled the first time he set eyes on her, his expression dark with desire and longing. His eyes were blue, almost navy, and he had a dimple in the centre of his chin. More often than not, he needed a shave. His stubbly cheeks and jaw looked as if they'd been sanded down with a nutmeg grater. He had short, jet-black hair with a resistant lock that always strayed across one eyebrow. To her surprise, he found her desirable and she realised that, young as she was, she had sexual power and it thrilled. It mattered not that Cheryl was standing beside her. 'You go anywhere near him and

190

I'll fucking kill you,' she'd said with a laugh, in a way that Eleanor was quite sure Cheryl meant. She'd seen Cheryl in action, scrapping with another girl, pinning her down and encouraging a weedy girl, called Penny, to take a pair of scissors to the girl on the floor's face. Eleanor baulked at the memory. Against her will, her mind flitted to another.

Acting the gentleman, Don had escorted them — that was the word he used — to his car, a green Cortina. On spring evenings, when the days were lengthening, he took them to pubs where they didn't ask questions and fed them crisps and Cherry B, and Dubonnet and lemonade. He told them about the big horses he worked with, how he gentled the skittish and difficult, how he loved working with iron and fire. He regaled them with tales of being bitten and kicked, which made him dangerous and yet dependable. You'd be all right with Don in your corner. His care and concern ennobled him and welded them together. They were a gang. They were "tight", as Verity would say. He protected his girls from other men and never laid a finger on Eleanor because Cheryl was his special girl.

Until she wasn't.

And Eleanor had become his secret, guilty pleasure. She'd wanted to feel bad, but she hadn't. She couldn't help it if he was sweet on her, if Cheryl no longer did it for him. Eleanor was enchanted, in love, and Don was in love with her. That's what she'd told herself then.

She recalled the deep joy and elation when Don told her that she was his, marred only by the knowledge that she was cheating on her best friend. Though she knew it was wrong, breaking off with him, something she briefly entertained, was unthinkable. The other girls were addicted to drink and cigarettes. She was addicted to Don.

Tall and broad-shouldered, his arms were strong due to his work, and never more so than when they encircled her. When he was an apprentice he'd once had the bone broken near his shoulder by a stallion. 'The humerus,' he'd told her. 'Nothing funny about it,' he added jokingly, his laughing eyes shining brightly from a permanently tanned face. And she would run her fingers over the scars.

She'd liked the fact that he was older and experienced, that there were lines on his face. This was a proper man, not like those creeps who used the Stone House like a brothel. His calloused hands were tender. Don Birch made her feel alive when she was frozen inside, when her life was in ruins.

Guilt assailed her: for loving him too much, and for never feeling that way again.

Incarcerated in that dreadful, barren institution, bereft of love, it was no surprise that her fifteen-year-old-self had sought affection and, yes, intimacy. Her only crime was that it was with the wrong man in the wrong place at the wrong time. But she'd never lied to Cherry. She didn't want to hurt her and, deep down, was scared of how Cherry would react if she found out. It used to amuse Don, Eleanor recalled. When she ticked him off, he would tease her, wrap his scarred arm around her waist, draw her close and tell her that, Cherry was a kid, but Eleanor was the woman for him. How she had burned with animal passion. How she had made plans for the future. How foolish and misguided she had been.

Eleanor didn't believe in ghosts. She *did* believe in the power of memory. Sometimes Don came to her when she least expected it. He appeared when she was asleep and when awake. Embarrassingly, he'd come to her on her honeymoon with Giles. He'd put in an appearance when Alex was born. Dinners with friends and Don would suddenly re-emerge, his presence so real and powerful she felt she could touch him. Was it a form of madness? Was being dead not enough for him? Why else would he remind her that he was still very much around? She knew, of course, why he haunted her.

Because, oh my Christ, for what I did.

In turmoil, Eleanor fled and headed back the way she came. She ran to her car and drove like a tormented soul until she turned left, shy of Craven Arms, and pulled over into the nearest gateway. She was holding her breath and let it seep out slowly between her lips. *Calm. Breathe soft. Breathe light.*

She called Alex who answered as if she was the bearer of bad news. She may well be if things turned sour.

'Ma, where are you?'

'Never mind me, has Verity called?'

'No.'

'Is Dido with you?'

'She's at the gym.'

Before he could continue the conversation, she cut him off and speed-dialled her daughter-in-law who answered. Eleanor heard the pounding sound of machinery, an exercise bike, or some such, against a ghastly background of rap music.

'Eleanor.' Dido puffed. 'Have you spoken to Hazel?'

'Yes,' she answered and posed the same question to Dido regarding Verity.

'Haven't heard a squeak from her,' Dido gasped. 'You sound worried.'

I am. 'It's odd for her to take off like this.'

'I'm sure she's absolutely fine.'

'You really think so?' Eleanor cursed the desperation in her voice. She didn't do needy and she didn't do helpless.

'Sure. She's feeling bruised, that's all. That man was quite horrid to her, you know.'

She knew and it was all her fault. How she regretted confiding in him about Verity's failed love affair. She only did so to impress upon him the importance of their special mother-daughter relationship. She thought it would lessen the impact of her suggestion for time apart. She foolishly believed it would be easier for him to accept. Instead, he'd wielded that knowledge like a weapon.

'Where are you?' Dido said.

Eleanor gritted her teeth and invented an imaginary friend she was visiting in Bath. Lies kept you safe. And she had lied for all her adult life and could see no end to it. She found it easy to deceive. It was like wearing a second skin.

'Good for you. Honestly, if she gets in touch, you'll be the first to know.'

She thanked Dido sincerely and gazed blindly at fields already harvested. In the distance she heard the burr of a combine harvester. Her vehicle should be safe enough, she reasoned, climbing out onto a single-track lane.

A warm summer breeze picked up and lifted the scarf from her hair. She secured it more tightly and forced herself to walk on unsteady legs. If she went back to where it all began, would Don leave her alone? Would he be satisfied? Could she pay her dues and depart, not with a clear conscience — that would be too much to ask — but with a sense of absolution?

I was very young, Eleanor reminded herself.

I never wanted it this way.

I didn't mean to.

I . . .

CHAPTER THIRTY-FOUR

An insect landed on my lower lip and I woke in a sweat to the noise of big machinery and what sounded like lots of tiny hooves clattering. Where the hell was I? With a thud, I remembered and let out a low groan of despair.

I'd spent another terrible night on the camp bed. Unaccustomed to the countryside I'd braced at every sound. Owls hooting. Sheep bleating. Dogs howling. Somewhere, outside in the rural zoo, cats scrapped. Without streetlights, night fell late and it was instant.

Stiff and dirty and needing a pee, I recoiled at the cloud of flies hovering over the stinking bucket, swatted them away, crouched, did what needed to be done and paced. They couldn't get away with this, could they? Something would break. Except it already had. My mother had killed a man, or so they believed, which in my saner moments I realised were two different things, but no less dangerous. Why else go to such lengths and abduct me?

Unbidden, hot tears sprang to the corner of my eyes. I wiped them away angrily. If I gave in to them now, I'd never stop.

Raging with hunger and out of water, I banged my fist against the nearest wall, creating a satisfying din. Maybe I could attract the attention of a postman, or an unwitting DPD courier, or an Amazon delivery driver — everyone had these, didn't they, even in these far-flung parts? It didn't take long for sour-faced Yootha to arrive with a tray of bread and jam and a mug of milky tea in a chipped enamel mug.

'You can stop that bloody noise,' she growled. 'There'll be consequences if you don't.'

I contemplated upending her makeshift breakfast, throwing the lot in her face, knocking away her stick and taking her. Had her son, Clay, not been lurking at the entrance, I would have done. He looked my way. Black stubble on his cheeks matched the darkness in his eyes. Gone the kindly stranger, alive and kicking the psycho.

'How long are you keeping me?'

'Depends.'

On their generosity, I guessed, not good odds.

'Can I phone my mother?'

'Eat.'

'Please?' Nice and pleasant and accommodating, not needy, not desperate.

'No.'

'Why not?'

'You're being moved.'

'I'm going home?' I suppressed a giddy laugh.

She treated me to the most resistant facial gesture I'd ever witnessed: an elevation of a grey hairy eyebrow. It made me flip.

'This is bloody ridiculous. Who, in God's name, do you think you are? Do you realise . . .'

'Eat and shut the fuck up,' Clay snapped. 'Mum,' he bawled to Yootha. 'Cheryl wants a word about vaccinating the lambs.'

She hobbled away, *tap, tap tap*. Clay threw me a warning look that turned my blood to ice. The doors were bolted. They might as well have been the gates to a high-security nuclear facility. I felt utterly trapped, with no chance of escape.

Alone and dispirited, I ate and drank to a soundtrack of banging, hammering and drilling. Incarceration sharpened my senses. Every noise was heightened. My vision felt sharper, my hearing keener. Stress, I realised, the proper stuff, not the small irritants that piss you off and which no longer seemed such a big deal. Meanwhile, the temperature in the metal building rose to stifling proportions. Perspiration dripped from my brow to my nose. I felt as if I were being slow-cooked in the suffocating heat. My head banged with dehydration. It took everything I had not to unravel. I'd been here a couple of days by my estimation and nobody seemed interested in letting me go anytime soon. I'd pretty much twigged this the second I was locked up.

I waited for a pause in activity and then hammered my fist against the sides of my metal prison, giving it ten whacks, listening to see if it got anyone's attention, and then repeated. A clicking sound I identified as the tip of Yootha's walking stick connecting with the concrete surface of the yard, followed by, 'Pipe down and stop acting up.'

'I want to speak to Cheryl.'

'She's busy.'

'Please, Yootha.' I'd read somewhere that forming a personal connection with kidnappers was more likely to guarantee fair treatment and, ultimately, survival.

She didn't answer and walked away.

I sat down. I stood up. I alternately fretted and fumed. A hostage to my emotions, I veered between courage and cowardice, false bravado and resignation. Underneath it all I was very frightened. I toyed with making myself a nuisance so that they would be glad to let me go then worrying that, if I pushed them too far, they'd do something really stupid and 'neutralise' the problem i.e. me. With that sober realisation, part of my spirit crumbled.

I began to fantasize about coffee, lattes and espresso and double macchiato. I'd kill for a caffeine hit right now.

Without warning, the bars wrenched open. Light sliced through the dark interior. The "boys" — not much older than me — strode in, took hold and marched me towards the cottage. The only visual addition to the general mess outside was a line of washing drooping inert in the heat. Buzzards freewheeled above my head.

But I had won a small victory and had Cheryl's attention. Buoyed, I entered the kitchen and, this time, was on what Nicola would have termed a reconnaissance mission. I noted dirty dishes piled up on a wooden work surface, blackened by water damage, benign-looking kitchen scales, old-fashioned, the metal pitted with use. I ignored the strong smell of fried onions in old oil, cobwebs in the corner, the grub and grime. I couldn't have cared less. My eyes flicked to the clock on the electric cooker: 11.40 a.m. I noted knives in a block, within striking range. Next to a tea urn and a jug with a chipped lip was a collection of mixed cutlery loose on a wooden table —spoons and forks, suitable for gouging and scratching. The large metal kettle, silently steaming on the range, offered the opportunity for me to throw it, scalding water and all, and, in the mayhem, escape. What would it feel like to have the contents of the open box of detergent, parked on the floor near to a washing machine, flung in your eye? Abruptly, conscious I too was being watched, Cheryl held my gaze. Her eyes shone and her top lip curled. She'd read me and her expression seemed to say: *Don't even think about it.*

Peripherally, I spotted a big chunky key in the lock on the back door, the sort I'd only seen in pictures of castle dungeons.

'You wanted to speak,' she said, her tone clipped.

'I need a toothbrush and toothpaste, somewhere to wash and have the use of a proper lavatory.'

'What do you think this is, the Hilton?'

'I want my basic human rights,' I said, which even sounded lame to my ears.

'Do you now?' Gone the smile.

'Please,' I said, feeling something hard lodge in the back of my throat.

'You've got some nerve.'

'Cheryl, I'm only asking for . . .'

'You dare to lecture me on what you think *you're* entitled to.' She didn't yell. She spoke quietly, slowly, full of threat. 'We could make things uncomfortable for you if you don't behave yourself.' It felt as if the temperature in the cool kitchen dropped by twenty degrees.

'Cheryl, I have no quarrel with you.'

'Then we're done.'

'But . . .'

'You do as you're damn well told. You will be quiet. You will behave. Do I make myself clear?'

'I—'

'For fuck's sake, get her out of here.' She bawled at Chuck and Clint.

Dismissed, I was lugged back to the barn. To make a point, Clint gave me a shove and sent me headlong into the dirt. Earth in my mouth, dust in my eye, I curled up and cried. I hated to think of what form "uncomfortable" would take. All kinds of indignities crashed into my mind.

Yootha came and went; the slab of bread and cheese she delivered left uneaten. Once a day, she'd remove the bucket and I was pretty sure she emptied the contents into the pond. I couldn't see a thing but I could hear and they seemed to do a lot of talking and reporting in the yard outside. Cheryl gave the orders for crops to be monitored for weed control and for potatoes to be sprayed. She took personal responsibility for checking animals, although it was Yootha who milked goats and decided which lambs were fat enough to go to market. I realised now the reason for the "hoof-march" earlier. There was a lot of noise of dry brooms sweeping and clearing and what I presumed was "mucking out". I intuited that the women carried out lighter duties, Clint and Chuck providing the muscle. They were the guys on the tractors and combiner. They were responsible for loading sheep for slaughter. Clay was the odd man out. He left early and came back late. Essentially, the family set-up, as dysfunctional as it seemed, was based on a matriarchy. Yootha was the weak link due to her infirmity. The "boys" represented the biggest physical threat. Cheryl, the great unknown, posed the greatest psychological risk. This was her revenge plan and when the Grade-A bitch gave the orders, everyone jumped and obeyed.

I considered faking serious illness so that they would have to call a doctor who could get me out of there. Maybe they wouldn't buy it. Maybe it didn't matter how poorly I seemed. I discarded the idea. Initially, I thought escape by night, providing I could find a way out, was my best option. Since then, I'd revised my ideas. During daylight hours, when everyone was busy and Clay was off the reservation, was my greatest chance of success.

Minutes crawled into an hour and maybe more when Clint and Chuck opened the doors and frogmarched me into a day heavy with heat and thick cloud. A relief to be outside in the fresh air, I gulped deep breaths and glanced up to the rooftops to search for alarms. None visible.

'Move.' Clint bellowed loudly in my ear, making me jump.

They hauled me across the freshly swept yard to a timber-framed barn. Dilapidated on my arrival, it looked sturdier today, a result of the earlier blitz of activity. Bleakly, the sleeping arrangements and bathroom facilities remained the same. I was really worried I might start my period and then what? Stress could really mess with your hormones so maybe it wouldn't be a problem. I could only hope. The garage sandwich was egg and tomato — not a winning combination. Water was upgraded to a jug and a mug. Nevertheless, my spirits lifted.

The result of a fast "make do and mend", the barn was not nearly as secure as the last. Built of wood, I'd no idea what, a bit rickety in places, resting on a concrete base that had degraded, there was a slim chance some of the lower wooden battens were rotten. If I could pull and prise away a couple of them, I could escape. The only problem: the structure was close to the cottages. Any sound I made would be heard.

I set about examining the best potential places for weakness. The entrance to the barn a no-go, the upper part of the structure looked solid. That left four walls, three of which were secure enough. The rear of the building was piled high with junk: heavy furniture, broken lamps, bedsteads and a discarded fridge freezer as well as other general crap.

As quietly as possible I picked up some of the lighter stuff and pushed it aside. Straining every sinew, I hefted an old tumble dryer, moving it minutely out of the way. I kept going at it until I created an aperture wide enough for me to wriggle through on my hands and knees and crawl along to the bottom of the back elevation. Glimpsing a shard of daylight was the best feeling ever. Near where one side joined the other, right in the corner, the concrete was particularly pitted, revealing a dirt floor. Wood had absorbed the moisture and rotted a couple of battens at the edges where nails, pinning it all together, stood proud. I reached out to give them a wiggle. They didn't budge. If I could only free one, it would serve as a weapon, should the need arise, I thought darkly.

Voices stopped me from what I was doing. I shunted backwards, bashing the back of my head and scraping my shoulders in haste to get out. Upright again, I piled chairs and a table in front of my makeshift tunnel and prayed to God nobody would notice.

As I crept towards the doors of the barn, conversation grew louder and more animated. I was starting to distinguish who was talking to whom by hearing alone.

'You sorted that Japanese pile of crap?' In his low raspy voice, Clay was obviously asking about my car. I had visions of it sold for scrap and crushed in a breaker's yard.

'Done,' Clint replied. He had a loud voice — he was probably deaf after listening to all that country and western at high volume.

'When you gonna let me have a drive of the Jag?' Slightly high-pitched drawl, it had to belong to chubby Chuck.

'Not until you get me my product. No rubbish, this time. Only the good stuff.'

'I'm seeing Spike tonight.'

Drugs. I pinched inside. Was it the same Spike who'd leered at me in Ludlow?

'See that you do.'

'What's happening with the girl?' Clint asked.

'Let her sweat,' Clay replied. 'Any funny business, you know what to do.'

Deep inside, I froze.

'And the mother?'

'Now we've got the carrot,' Clay said, sounding sly, 'stands to reason she'll come.'

'Yeah, but when?' Chuck whined. 'I didn't sign up to be no babysitter.'

'When Cheryl decides. The girls have waited forty-seven years for this,' Clay said, warning in his voice. 'Won't kill you to do what has to be done.'

Fuck, my gut twisted with fear, what did *that* mean?

'Right, gotta roll,' Clay said. 'Site meeting.'

'How's that working out?' Clint asked.

'Smooth. Perimeter's secured. Groundworks start today for the drainage systems.'

'What time will you be back?'

'Usual.'

I listened to the sound of boots on concrete followed by a vehicle starting up. The engine note was different to the Jaguar. It probably belonged to the mud-spattered pick-up truck.

From my new prison I had a better handle on what was going on and a greater sense of the dynamics, except that it didn't relieve the pressure. Clay was heading to his proper job away from the smallholding or farm, or whatever the hell it was. Relief that he had gone was swiftly replaced with the dread of his return. How long had I got in between? If I were going to escape, it needed to be now. I still had the problem of the long drive to negotiate and by no stretch was I in good shape, but I was young. I was fit (ish) and I was bloody desperate. I had two advantages: surprise and opportunity.

I had no tools with which to loosen the nails and pry open the battens. I stared at my hands, still wrecked and sore. Out of options, I slipped off a shoe and wished I were wearing a pair of solid boots with heels instead of my Vans. Next, I moved away the chairs and table, dropped to my hands and knees again and, placing my hand inside my makeshift glove, tunnelled my way through, my focus on the nearest nail. Wincing with each blow, I bashed away and tore a hole in the canvas of my shoe. The nail still refused to budge. In normal times, I'd have put it down to experience and decide to give it a try another day. These were not normal times. Panic grabbed me by the throat. Misery flooded my chest and, spun out, I broke down. I cried for being so stupid. I cried for my mum. I cried for my wrecked life. I bellowed at the world and shouted the injustice of my horrible situation to the skies.

The sound of noise outside brought me to my senses. Snivelling and backing out sharply, I dragged back the furniture and slipped my bare foot into my wrecked trainer just in time. Thank God, it was Chuck with his flat features and thick lids. He made a grab at my elbow with more speed than I thought possible for a slow man.

'You're wanted inside,' he said.

Tamping down my fears, I wiped my eyes, plastered on a smile and determined to play nice. Maybe I could try a charm offensive.

They wouldn't harm me then — *would they?*

CHAPTER THIRTY-FIVE

The sight of the old smithy winded her. Unnerved, Eleanor glanced fitfully around to see if anyone noticed the unhinged woman loitering at an ancient scene of a terrible crime. *Wasn't this what serial killers did?* she thought madly. But she had not come to gloat or revel or relive the horrors of the past.

It was boarded up, derelict and abandoned. She didn't need to force her way inside to remember. Standing there, in the mizzling rain, she pictured red-brick walls, a forge and hearth made of steel. She recalled rakes and hammers, pokes and slices to control the flames. She smelt coke and hoof oil and the leather from Don's apron as clearly now as she did then.

She remembered passion and lust in the dirt and straw. Most of all, she remembered that very last time she saw him alive. It was blisteringly hot, a relentless sun throwing death stares.

Her phone rang, startling her out of her reverie. *Please God*, she prayed, *let it be Verity*. She fumbled her mobile from her pocket and noticed the call was from a withheld number.

'Yes,' she answered anxiously.

With the mention of her old name, Eleanor froze and thought her legs might give way. She knew this day would come. She had imagined it many times. It was no less devastating.

'Cheryl,' she croaked in response.

'Been a long time.' Her voice was smoke and dirt.

Eleanor felt a pebble of guilt and grief lodge so hard in her throat it could never be swallowed.

'You know why I'm in touch.'

'Yes,' Eleanor whispered meekly.

'Say it. Because of . . .'

'Don.' It pains her to speak his name aloud.

'And why we have your daughter.'

Eleanor staggered and stared wildly into the distance. She saw nothing. She heard nothing. Her heart thundered as if it were being wrenched from her body. *Not my child*, she screamed inside. *Not my daughter. Verity never hurt anyone. Don't make her pay for my crime.*

'I want to speak to her.' Eleanor jammed the phone against her ear in a pathetic attempt to close the distance.

'Fair enough. She's on speaker.'

Oh my God, Eleanor thought. Verity was listening to every word. Eleanor heard a muffled noise: hushed conversation, the scraping back of a chair, a tapping sound on a tiled floor, then Verity's sweet voice, 'Mum, Mum, what the fuck?'

'Darling, are you all right, are they—'

'Enough,' Cheryl growled.

'Cheryl, listen to me, Verity has nothing to do with the past. This is between you and me. I'm so very sorry and can only beg forgiveness.'

'Save that for a fucking priest.'

'I'll do whatever you say. I can give you money, anything. I'll go to the police, tell them everything.'

'Like where you hid his body?'

Eleanor's eyes rolled in agitation. She could not tell, because she genuinely didn't know. 'Yes,' she lied.

'Then you can tell us now. Yootha's here with me. She'd very much like to give her brother a proper burial.'

'I will tell you. I will but, for the love of God, don't hurt Verity. Let my daughter go.'

'*Your* daughter.' Cheryl snickered. 'And what of *mine*?'

'I don't understand.' How could she? She had no knowledge of Cheryl's life since she last saw her. Unless . . .

'You are to wait for my next call,' Cheryl said threateningly. 'You will *not* go to the police. You will *not* speak to anyone. Get it?'

Eleanor was numb. In no position to argue, negotiate or bargain, she nodded her head.

'I said do you get it?' Cheryl repeated, her voice a roar.

'Yes, yes, I do.'

'Good, because if you don't you'll never see her again. On that, you have my word.'

The line went dead.

Eleanor pressed a fist to her mouth. She bit down hard and drew blood. Her head pounded and, suddenly nauseous, she vomited onto the country lane.

Body shaking uncontrollably, she wiped her mouth and retreated to the car. There, she ran through the conversation, frame by frame. Verity had heard an admission no daughter should ever hear, and in the most abominable way. And now she was in grave danger. Cheryl didn't want the police involved for one reason only: because she intended to enforce her own brand of justice.

You go anywhere near him and I'll fucking kill you.

But now there was an added complication. Her daughter for Cheryl's daughter was what Cheryl meant. And Cheryl's daughter, Eleanor realised with terrible clarity, was also Don's.

CHAPTER THIRTY-SIX

I was in hell.

Cheryl hung up and they pulled me by both arms from the kitchen and dumped me back in the barn. Too shocked to cry, too confused to think straight, my overriding emotion was one of fury.

At no stage did my mother deny, defend herself or apologise. She didn't say that she'd killed in self-defence, or that it was an accident, or an act due to the abuse she'd suffered. Disgustingly, she was prepared to buy off her victim's relatives, as if blood money would make a difference. Her offer to go to the police, something she should have done before entangling my dad in a bogus relationship and, ultimately, sham marriage, occurred four decades too late. I didn't give a flying fuck that me and my brother would never have been born.

My dad had integrity running through his veins. He'd never have married a woman like that if he'd known the truth. Guilty of the crime and so much more, caught up in some sick love triangle, she was a monster and I bloody hated her guts for what she'd done and for what she'd got me stuck with: druggie crazies with vengeance on their sick minds.

The choice before me was stark: stay and let those throw-backs do God knows what, or leave with my murderous mother who, no doubt in her delusion, thought we could go back to happy families. Screw all of them. I was getting out of here.

I returned to my task with venom. I tore at nails and wood where the nearest batten was crumbling until my fingers bled and I was breathless. It probably moved a couple of millimetres. Going at it again, a nail wiggled, moved and finally popped out like a resistant molar extracted by a determined dentist. It was around six inches in length and, although not particularly sharp, it would inflict serious pain if used appropriately. I grinned. "Appropriate" in common with "proportionate" had a proper ring about it, a mile away from what I intended. Suitably armed, the sense of euphoria bolstered my mood. I still had a problem: an escape plan. People broke out of prisons all the time, didn't they? How the hell did they do that? And then it came to me, courtesy of good old Eddy Kaminski. I'd invented the story about investigating World War II Polish pilots, although I hadn't lied about my interest. It was Dad who first told me about the great escapes of POWs from German prisoner-of-war camps.

I wriggled back out and, collecting the chipped enamel mug handed me that morning, tunnelled back in, selected the weakest batten and dug the rim into the cracked ground beneath. The clay earth was red and dense, scooping it up impossibly slow and hard, though the repetitive rhythm of positive action calmed me. I scattered the deposits into the gaps between the piled-up furniture. My stomach growled and rumbled and I only stopped when the insistent noise of an approaching vehicle bumped up the drive.

Fearing Clay, I shot back out again, rinsed the mug with what was left of the water and crept over to a crack near the door. Clay climbed out of the truck and strode towards the cottage as if someone had set light to his jeans. I couldn't see his face. The way he moved told me that something was up. This wasn't a bad day at the office. This was catastrophe.

Uneasy silence descended and I was getting hungrier and edgier by the second. Whatever was taking place inside, I hoped, was not going to impact upon me.

Sudden noise and the doors to the barn flew open. Bare-chested, muscled, tattooed and ripped, Clay strode in and, believing he was going to hit me or, by Christ, do something worse, I cowered.

He grabbed hold of my shoulders, shoved his hard stubbly face into mine. Close enough to smell his sweat, feel his animal heat, I stood rooted.

His top lip kinked in the semblance of a smile, the expression in his eyes hateful. They told me that he would like nothing better than to grind me into the dust. I surprised myself by speaking first.

'Revenge won't fill the void.'

'What do you know of emptiness, poor little rich girl?'

'I know about losing people you love.'

'Yeah, right. My mother and aunt had their lives ripped apart by your murdering mother.'

'And so have I.'

'Think I give a shit?' Staring into his face was like looking into the eyes of a wolf. 'Police are coming,' he said.

I stared, bewildered. Why was he telling me this? Had I misread the room? Was he really a good guy? Was the end in sight? Breath spurted hot and fast through my nostrils. *Please let me go.* And then he slayed me.

'Bones were found this afternoon.'

'What?' I mumbled.

'You heard.'

'Where?'

'At a building site.'

'It's not that unusual,' I said, remembering my dad telling me it was common. 'Most likely, belongs to an animal, a sheep maybe.'

'They're human.' Clay's voice was metallic. 'Word is that it's my uncle Don.'

Stupefied, tottering at the implication, I opened and closed my mouth. A normal family would tell the police about my mother and release me. End of. They weren't normal. They were warped and I was doomed. Unless . . .

'Police can't possibly have established his identity yet. Have they asked for DNA from Yootha?'

'What the fuck do you know about it?'

'I don't. I'm using my brain.' *Screw you if you don't like the slur on your intelligence*, I thought defiantly.

Clay's eyes narrowed to slits and his hands clamped around my neck, the pads of his thumbs pressed hard into the base of my throat. When he spoke he was an angel's breath away from my ear.

'We're gonna get plenty of visits from the law. So this is what you're gonna do, little girl. You will shut the fuck up, you hear me?'

The pressure suddenly intensified. My airways thinned. Black and white dots danced in front of me until my terrified gaze was filled with him and his hateful, malevolent expression.

'Not a sound. Not a squeak. You do anything to draw attention and I will burn this fucking barn to the ground. With you in it.'

My fingers shot up to claw at his hands. The soles of my shoes skittered on the ground. Strange grunts came from what was left of my vocal cords and then, as suddenly as he'd choked me, he let me go and turned on his heel.

Released, my knees buckled and I collapsed into the dirt. I didn't remember what happened next.

CHAPTER THIRTY-SEVEN

Eleanor's mind seized up and shattered into a million pieces. The last time she'd left this godforsaken place, she'd fled, half naked, and caught a ride on a cattle lorry heading to Ludlow.

She drove half blind with fear and struggled with a catalogue of images that crashed through her mind, uninvited. Don gasping. Don bleeding. Don falling. Don still.

She put her foot down, turning into the opposite lane of traffic. She screwed her eyes up tight, heard the blast of a car horn, and, opening them, veered back into the right lane.

Her arms juddered and her hands shuddered. *Verity*, Eleanor thought. *For her sake I must live.*

She parked in town and sat, gazing straight ahead, unseeing. Lying was like bathing in a warm bath, she thought, soothing and comforting and preventing the cold truth from rushing in. Since Cheryl had pulled the plug, Eleanor was left frozen, naked and exposed.

And so was her daughter.

Striving to be rational, Eleanor breathed slowly in and out and allowed her heart rate to settle. It took energy and guile to hide a person. There were practical implications, like food and basic hygiene. There was always the risk of discovery and the even stronger chance that the "concealed" will become "escapee". Her grandfather had gone to enormous lengths to ensure her protection, Eleanor recalled. He'd no fear of her making a break for it. Where would she go? He'd shopped for one person in Ludlow and for two people in outlying villages. He'd used out-of-town libraries to borrow books for Eleanor's incarceration. She had not been idle. She'd read voraciously, studied harder than she ever had at school. Books had been her friends and with reluctance she'd waved them farewell every two weeks. Grandpa told police, social services and those callous people at the Stone House that his granddaughter had gone walkabout, like she'd done so many times before. 'Sorry, not my fault,' he'd said. 'I cannot control such an unruly child.' She was simply another runaway to them, a troubled and troublesome creature that they'd be glad to cross off their lists.

But, held against her will, Verity's situation was very different. Eleanor had no idea how her daughter would react under such pressure. Would she crumble, or fight? Had she struggled when they'd taken her? It curdled Eleanor's insides to think of the terror Verity must have felt, the fear she still endured. Had she been taken clean off the street, her car rammed, or what? And what had happened to her vehicle? Would police discover it abandoned near woods, or burned out in a lay-by? And if they did what then?

Clearing her throat, she phoned the Charlton Arms Hotel. It was situated on Ludford Bridge, a short walk away from town, and with its own private car park.

She was in luck. There had been a cancellation for the Othello Suite, a room with a private terrace and hot tub. Eleanor knew she wouldn't be making use of the facilities; she took it straightaway.

'For how many nights, Mrs Finch?'

Eleanor hesitated. So much depended on Cheryl's mercurial disposition.

'Two,' she said. 'Maybe three.'

She made a payment over the phone and assured the receptionist that she would check in shortly.

Stepping out into the street, she found a chemist a few doors down from the Feathers Hotel. There, she bought a toothbrush and toothpaste, soap, shower gel, painkillers and a bottle of water. She paid for a bag along with her shopping and, scooping it up, drifted through town, barely noticing the changes, only that much of the historic buildings remained exactly the same as she remembered. No architectural vandalism here.

She discovered an old-fashioned-looking shop sporting "Ladies Fashions", where she bought two pairs of plain knickers and a shapeless pale green sleeveless shirt to replace the one she was wearing. With an idea scratching the back of her mind, she made a beeline for a voluminous polyester dress in an unflattering shade of purple with deep pockets and a curious side zipper.

Heading back to the car, she had a sudden craving for chocolate. There was a One-Stop convenience store on the corner of Tower Street and she walked that way until she halted abruptly in the middle of the paved street. Her jaw sagged. Her stomach felt as if it had plummeted to her feet. Her heart flew upwards and caught in her throat. An A-frame, outside a newsagent announced: HUMAN REMAINS FOUND COULD BE THOSE OF MISSING MAN.

Eleanor had retreated from the truth all her life. Each time it crept in it was so hard to bear it was hazy, and now it was in her face and there for the world to see, pin-sharp and focused. Without a shadow of a doubt, she knew it was Don. And if she knew, Cheryl would know it too and Cheryl had Verity's life in her hands.

Eleanor abruptly turned, barrelling into a youth with pixie features and a tongue like a blade.

'Mind where you're fucking going, bitch.'

Flustered, Eleanor apologised profusely and took to her heels. She didn't care about chocolate, still less about maintaining an exterior of calm and composure. The news ripped her in two. The universe had it in for her.

Somehow, she made the short journey over the bridge, with its weir and swans, and drove through the narrow entrance to the hotel, over the roughly surfaced car park. The terrace was busy with late-afternoon drinkers. There was laughter and animated conversation. What a world away.

Feeling conspicuous by her obvious lack of luggage, slightly dazed, she checked in. The room was, indeed, as glorious as she expected and lost on her.

She didn't believe Cheryl would phone that evening, but she took no chances and left her mobile within reach of the open bathroom door while she took a cold shower. With her body still damp and wrapped in a towel, she put on the TV and retreated to the bed where she perched on the edge.

The body on the building site was the first item of local news. A camera panned in on an area outside the market town of Tenbury Wells. Eleanor squinted at the screen and listened as a reporter, called Dai, and oddly wearing Wellingtons, revealed that site preparation had recently begun following years of negotiation with planners on what was originally pastureland. Dai shoved a microphone in front of a nervous-looking man with a weathered face the colour of old tobacco. Stress deepened the lines under the man's eyes and, camera-shy, he blinked like crazy.

'We understand that the land has been in your family for generations, Mr Farrington,' Dai began.

'S'right, but I knows nothing about no body,' he protested. 'My father, Percy, farmed this land, man and boy, and it passed down to me when he died, nigh on thirty year ago.'

'It must have been a difficult decision to sell.'

'Forced to, warn't I? Kids don't want to go into farming these days, too hard a life, not when they've got all them computers and gizmos. I did it to secure a future for my lads and safeguard my old age.'

Dai nodded and waved an arm vaguely behind him in the direction of a police car and officers. White-suited scenes-of-crime officers milled about like astronauts exploring a new planet.

Adopting a serious expression, Dai spoke directly to viewers, 'There's a lot of activity, as you can see, and forensics will continue for some time in what is deemed to be a complex investigation. While police are currently keeping an open mind, locals will no doubt be looking into the unexplained disappearance of Donald Birch, a local blacksmith some four decades ago. Back to you, Meera, at the studio.'

Eleanor chewed her bottom lip. Granddad knew old Percy Farrington. They'd played euchre together. Was this where he'd buried Don's body after removing it from the forge?

'Best you don't know, Eleonora,' Grandpa said, in answer to her anguished question. 'Now go to sleep and no going out.'

It had been two years before she saw the light of day.

Bile rose to the back of her throat. Grandpa hadn't told her that her young life was over. He didn't say that she would be emotionally disfigured forever. He didn't explain how she was to pick up the pieces when it was safe enough to leave.

A child takes an act of faith when it is born, she thought.

You trust your parents until they neglect you.

You trust your teachers until they abuse you.

You trust the police until they fail you.

Jesus Christ, during the years in hiding, she'd lived and breathed her past and felt the slow hand of death upon her shoulder daily. She thought only of Don and how she and he were inextricably linked, that they were both victims. Not that Cheryl, who she deeply feared, would see it that way. Or that Verity would see it that way either.

Eleanor glanced at her watch. How long before Cheryl contacted her again? With so much police attention, would she delay? Eleanor wondered what would happen if she were to walk into the little community police station and confess. She considered calling the emergency services to report the abduction of her daughter. She could do it anonymously, couldn't she? Would the police be able to rescue Verity before Cheryl took her revenge? Confusion filmed her eyes. Fear smudged her mind. In an agony of indecision, Eleanor didn't know what to do for the best.

But she knew someone who might.

CHAPTER THIRTY-EIGHT

I believed him. I'd read the threat in his eyes. Any attempt to raise the alarm and he would either kill me, or I'd be left to waste away and die here.

With a tight throat, I hunkered down and stayed absolutely still. Outside erupted in a frenzy of activity. It wasn't only the police that came. Journalists and a TV van turned up too. It was a circus out there. I heard Yootha bellow to some hapless hack, 'Have some respect for the family.' Chuck and Clint, more forthright, told someone to 'fuck right off, or I'll set the fucking dogs on you.'

Bones in a field did not mean they belonged to Donald Birch, I told myself. Bodies sometimes emerged that turned out to be the human remains of some ancient bod from centuries ago. I mean look at Richard III found underneath a car park, or the remains of gladiators found in parts of Gloucestershire. The skeleton found locally could as easily be some poor soul dispatched by a random killer. Didn't Fred West hunt his prey around here? And would the police be able to discern if it were male, or female after all this time? How come the family was so sure it was Don and not a more recent victim? Was it based on knowledge or blind hope? I was desperate to believe that it was too soon to jump to conclusions, never mind what Clay, with his murderous expression, maintained. All they had were rumour and hearsay, something of which they seemed to go in for in a big way.

Yes, that was it.

Except why was this dead place alive with excitement and energy and suspicion?

Running on fumes, I fell into a kind of slump borne of overwhelming desperation. Wrecked, I was tired to my bones with thinking and stress. Time had no meaning in here and I hadn't moved outside these four miserable walls in I didn't know how long, yet I'd never known such exhaustion. The frenetic part of my brain considered whether I was in my very own episode of *Lost*. Could a crew turn off the cameras sometime soon, pack up and go home?

Abandoned and desolate, with a mind in overdrive, I mourned the life I'd left behind: boring routines, without which I was confounded, spontaneous walks and shopping, soppy Alex and bossy Dido, my friends, my little home and, perversely, despite what I'd been told, what I'd witnessed, Mum — the old one, the one I knew. I wanted to smell her perfume. I needed her hug and to soothe me that it would be OK, like she did after Dad died and when Colm left. I remembered her coaxing me to rejoin the world and, faced with my continued stubborn refusal, she'd finally been "cruel to be kind", as she put it, and had insisted I go back to university to finish my final year.

'Go for broke, Verity,' she'd said. 'It's the only way out when you're in a hole.' And I guessed I had and I did.

Hot tears streamed down my snotty, dirty face. Despite what she'd done I still loved her and would continue to love her until I heard the truth. All of it. If she'd really killed that man, it had to be for a good reason.

But is there ever a good reason and who would believe her?

Sapped of energy and shaken by Clay's vile threat, I tried to take advantage of the craziness going on around me. If the family were so consumed by developments, they'd forget about me.

And I was right. Nobody came to feed me. The water had gone hours ago. I stank of body odour and despair.

Noise outside. The low burble of conversation cut through the warm night air. I heard Clay speak first.

'No work until this little lot gets sorted. Got some man from Forensics leading a team to recover stuff from the site. They're going through the soil like they're panning for gold.'

'Bloody hell,' Clint said.

'Cops said it would take time to formally identify the bones. They wanted DNA from Mum and asked a lot of questions.'

'What sort of questions?'

'If Don had access to a dentist.'

'Did he?'

'Not a chance.'

'And?'

'When he was last seen, what he was wearing, who he was with.'

'What did she say?' A thread of anxiety pulled at Clint's voice.

'Told them enough, but not the full story. Don't want our plan derailed.'

It went quiet until Clint spoke again. Gave me a chance to cotton on to a split agenda. While it was important for the women to know as soon as possible whether it was Don and if he could finally be buried with dignity, the timing could potentially screw up their plans to exact revenge. Did it put me in a better position, or not?

'Think it's really Don?' Clint asked.

'Ay, I do,' Clay said.

'It's a good few miles from the smithy.'

'Not if you've got a motor.'

'But she was only a kid.'

'That granddad of hers moved the body, didn't he? In it together. Plain as day.'

'Nah, according to Yootha, he was already on his way out by then. Big C, and all.'

'After what he put the family through, serves him right.'

They broke off at the sound of a vehicle coming up the drive. I assumed it was Chuck. I listened as it drove into the yard and stopped. Two doors opened and closed. Puzzled, I pulled a face, oblivious to the fact that there was nobody there to see my expression.

'All right?' I heard Chuck say.

Another voice offered commiseration, the accent broad and weirdly familiar. It was followed by grunts of gratitude, followed by the awful sound of a match being struck.

Fear barrelled through me like an express train. My eyes darted from the walls to the pile of junk. This lot would go up and incinerate me in minutes. My ears attuned to a definite inhalation of breath in and breath out and I almost wet myself with relief. Tobacco and cigarette smoke never smelt so good.

'Gotcha what you wanted,' Chuck announced.

'Shitting hell, keep your voice down,' Clay warned. 'Can't be too careful now the cops are all over the place.'

'What — are they still here?'

'No, you moron. I'm just telling you to watch it.'

'Oh yeah, sorry, Clay, but Spike here has a little proposition for you.'

My ears pricked with interest. Was sleazy Spike a local drug dealer? Sickeningly, I wondered if Clay were on something when he'd delivered his testosterone-fuelled warning.

'All right, but keep it schtum till we get inside.'

I waited until it was quiet and I'd properly adjusted to night vision then, feeling my way, I again set to the task of getting out of there. I would not be beaten, I told myself, as I persuaded, cajoled and forced one bit of wood away from another. I would not crack.

I dug at the dirt from underneath the wall of wood until an aperture the size of a hand's span appeared. I'd lost weight. My shorts were baggy and my thighs noticeably slimmer but

I'd not dropped enough kilos to force my way out through the opening. Not yet.

I dug and prised away some more until, lying on my tummy, I was able to squint through the gap, and observe lights on in an upstairs room in Cheryl's cottage. Someone was moving around downstairs at Yootha's.

Suddenly, the white glow of a security light lit up the night, shining rays through the gap and dazzling me between my sore eyes. It reinforced my view that no way could I escape in the dark. Lit up, like a Christmas tree, I'd be spotted straightaway.

Several pairs of boots emerged from Yootha's cottage. Loud talk and backslapping, hoots of bawdy laughter shattered the peace of the night. Looked like some deal had been cut, in which Clay emerged the victor.

The throaty roar of vehicles revving up and speeding out cut through the darkness. In the ensuing silence my hopes and dreams crumbled; my fear of what might happen next swelled. A man like Clay was extremely dangerous. A man like Clay, hopped up on God knew what, was also unpredictable.

The good news was that another plank of wood was definitely loose. I dug around some more, rested the broken plank back in place, felt my way back and finally, exhausted, lay down on the camp bed and pulled the sheet up over my face. Scared, I fell into an uneasy and troubled sleep.

CHAPTER THIRTY-NINE

Eleanor had no reason to believe that Enid had moved from the Sandpits estate, one of the most deprived areas in the country. Through an avenue of terraced houses, the sharp heels of her sandals click-clacked as she made her way along dogshit-strewn pavements.

Some properties were rendered, most with incongruous red-brick additions plonked slab-sided, end-on. Satellite dishes were notable for their multiplicity. Paved driveways, accommodating one car, were in various states of disrepair as if a bulldozer had bitten off large chunks. Enid's house was no different to the rest, though there was no car on the cracked concrete outside the front window.

An electric box, its door hanging off, was attached to the side of a brick extension that served as the entrance to the property. Eleanor understood the majority of these houses had downstairs bathrooms and gardens the width of tramlines, unless the owner was very lucky. Other houses crowded around, like a huddle of jawing women at a whist drive.

Her manicured hand trembled as she rapped at a painted green front door. A curtain twitched in the front upstairs window. Eleanor imagined the route from a bedroom, down the steep stairs, skirting a bathroom, the lounge, through the kitchen to the entrance. In her mind, she measured how long it would take a woman in her eighties to travel the distance. It was like one of those mathematical puzzles children learn at school. From inside, Eleanor heard the staccato of TV voices. She thought it might be a game show.

A security chain was unlocked. The door swung open.

'Thought it was you,' Enid said.

She had changed a lot in the intervening years, Eleanor thought, though, with her sly eyes and gruff disposition, she was still recognisable as the woman she knew.

'You coming in or going to stand there?'

Eleanor no more trusted Enid now than she did back then, but when your choices were limited, who else could she speak to in order to extract information? She bowed her head and followed Enid inside. The kitchen was clean and tidy, the lounge dominated by a fifty-inch television. It stayed on, mumbling low. A sofa and two easy chairs, in a floral design, collided with the wallpaper and red swirling carpet. If Eleanor hadn't already felt sick, she did now.

'Take the weight off your feet then,' Enid said in a voice honed by a serious cigarette habit. 'See you've done well for yourself.' She reached for a packet of Rothmans Blue Superkings. Her eyes never left Eleanor's while she lit up, inhaled and ejected two silver wisps of smoke from her nostrils. 'Money suits you,' she said, angling her head as if to fully appreciate Eleanor's transformation from street kid to woman of substance.

Eleanor believed this a strong hint that Enid would be open to payment for information rather than indicating her appreciation of the civilising influence of wealth.

'If you've come to confess, you're decades too late,' Enid said, altering her tone. 'Lucille, God rest her soul, passed on not long after that scoundrel, Eddy.'

'My grandfather was a good man.'

'Says who? Filthy foreigner covered for your crime. Assisting an offender.' Enid articulated each word as if she'd just learnt the legal lingo. 'Lucille was never the same again after you killed her boy and Eddy decided his blood was more important than Don's. What? Got nothing to say for yourself?'

'Nothing that would make a difference,' Eleanor said impassively.

'Try me. Bugger all else to do this evening.'

But Eleanor had plenty to do. She had to find her daughter. She had to rescue her. 'Enid, I haven't come to fight.'

'That's a relief, you a murderess and all.' Her gaze dissected Eleanor's pained expression.

'Would you believe me if I told you I didn't mean to? That it wasn't my fault?' There was so much that was too horrific to revisit, but this much was true.

'Don't you dare go blaming the dead,' Enid said with a snarl. 'Don wouldn't hurt a soul. He was a kind and caring son and brother, loved everyone, or have you forgotten?'

No, Eleanor had not. She also recalled the other side of Don Birch, the hidden, and the unspeakable. Would anyone believe her? Not now, not after all this time.

Enid squinted through a cloud of cigarette smoke. 'You know he's been found?'

'Do they know it's him for certain?' Eleanor asked quietly.

Enid rolled her eyes. 'Even now, after all you did, still looking to save your own skin.'

'That's not—'

'Hoping to God it isn't so you can dodge the law, 'cept you'll *never* be free.'

Eleanor could give Enid chapter and verse on the relative value of freedom and what it was like to live your entire life in a straitjacket of lies: it would be wasted.

'I only meant that it takes time for a body to be exhumed and formally identified,' Eleanor remarked as calmly as she could.

'You can but hope. Be a laugh if it isn't; all that fuss and commotion for nothing. But it will be him all right, stands to reason.' Enid's expression stiffened. 'Found on old man Farrington's land. Percy and Eddy were that close.' Enid raised a wrinkled hand and crossed two fingers to make the point. 'That's where Eddy took Don's body after you did him in.'

And she was probably right, Eleanor thought, shifting uncomfortably in her seat. She swore the floor beneath her feet rearranged itself too.

'But you already knew that, didn't you?' Enid spoke through tight lips, her expression one of disdain.

'No, I didn't.'

''Course not.' Enid puffed out and allowed the silence to crawl in.

'Where can I find Yootha?' *For where Yootha is, Cheryl will not be far behind.*

'And what makes you think I know?'

Eleanor read deceit in Enid's eyes. She had seen it too many times in her own not to be able to recognise it in others.

Because you stayed in touch. Because she is one of yours. 'Because you were good friends with Lucille.'

Enid stubbed out her cigarette and lit another.

'Did Yootha ever marry?' Eleanor asked.

Enid shook her head. 'Got a son though. Handsome man, Clay is the spit of his uncle.' Enid declared it with malice.

Eleanor swallowed. The idea of a man like Don was deeply disturbing. 'And Cheryl?'

'Married a farmer. A good man, he died a few years back. Her boys, big lads, work the farm.'

For someone who knew nothing, she was well informed, Eleanor noted. Enid always was a gossip.

She produced the postcard from her bag and raised it to Enid's rheumy eyes. 'Cheryl sent me this.'

The old woman reached for her glasses, perched them on the end of her veiny nose and squinted.

'Hereford cathedral,' she said, stating the obvious.

'They have my only daughter.' And as Eleanor said it, her heart swelled and she felt all that Verity was to her. She was her hope and her prayer. She was all that was good and light. She was the future. In a rough and ugly world where bad things happened to good people, there needed to be more young women like her.

'Can't help you.'

From the dull expression on Enid's face, Eleanor judged that Verity's existence came as no surprise. Enid was, in effect, colluding with the enemy. Community in action was generally considered a good thing, Eleanor believed, until it acted blindly to shut down the truth, alienate, repel and exclude.

'She is innocent, Enid.'

Would her plea, mother to mother, work where it had failed with Cheryl? And then she remembered Cheryl's daughter. As if reading her mind, Enid said, 'They buried Cheryl's babe at that terrible place.'

'The Stone House?' Eleanor felt a crush of fear within. She'd heard the rumours about girls giving birth and never seeing their infants again. Fearfully, she recalled Cheryl's words: *Your* daughter. And what of *mine?*

'Didn't even have the chance to have her christened,' Enid continued. 'At least the girl would have had someone and something to remember Don by and love.'

As if by telepathy, a picture of Don appeared on the television. Enid immediately sparked into activity and turned up the sound.

'Police won't confirm the identity of the body but locals believe it to be that of Shropshire blacksmith, Don Birch, who inexplicably disappeared in 1976, aged thirty-eight. Mr Birch was . . .'

Eleanor didn't hear another word. In thrall to the grainy picture of the man she'd loved, his power to reach out from beyond the grave robbed her of the air she breathed. Mesmerised, she experienced the stir of old passions. She felt the familiar tug on her heart and the terrible desolation of an irrevocable act committed in desperation.

The news moved on and Enid turned down the volume. Her tart expression gave no quarter.

Eleanor tamped down her emotions, a trick she'd perfected over a lifetime. Becoming upset would not help Verity. 'Enid, I'm begging you.'

'Bit late to ask for help now. You should have reached out to me a long time ago.'

Enid was as slippery as she'd ever been, Eleanor believed. She was the last person a young girl would approach and that was the point: there was nobody to whom she could have turned.

'What will they do to her?'

Enid coughed and shrugged. The gesture maddened Eleanor to the point she'd like to throttle the old woman until she revealed what she needed to know.

'Don't you care?' Eleanor pleaded.

'It's not about caring. It's about what's right. Rough justice, to be sure, but it is what it is, an eye for an eye.'

A sick memory of the Stone House, and the image of the girl injured for an unwitting slight, took shape before Eleanor's eyes. The girl had been terrified of Cheryl. She'd never identified the kid who had sliced up her face with scissors on Cheryl's orders, or revealed who'd orchestrated it.

Blinking the bloody picture away, Eleanor tried a different tack.

'How is Tammy?'

Enid slow-blinked. 'Right enough.'

'Still in the area?'

'She is.'

'Would she be able to help?'

'Doubt it.'

The urge to stand up and run in the face of a wall of silence was almost too much. Eleanor pressed her knees together and stayed right where she was. Enid had said she had all night and nothing better to do. Time to put it to the test.

'I'm struggling to make connections. How did Cheryl's path cross with my daughter's?'

'I wouldn't know.'

'But if Verity came here, perhaps someone tipped off Cheryl and Yootha. It's not inconceivable, is it?' Eleanor leant forward a fraction so that she could better watch the moves on Enid's wrinkled face. 'And if Cheryl has abducted my child,' she continued, steely, 'anyone involved would be guilty of *assisting an offender*.' The dry emphasis with which Eleanor delivered those last three words was not lost on Enid. The old woman's jaw slackened with unease. 'And if something should happen to Verity then . . .' Eleanor let the meaning drift and fixed Enid with a cold stare that confirmed she was, indeed, guilty of murder and had no qualms about committing another.

The hand holding the cigarette trembled. Colour glanced across Enid's raddled cheeks. 'I hear the family lives out in Herefordshire, somewhere near Preston-on-Wye, up an old farm track.'

Eleanor stood. 'I'll see myself out.'

CHAPTER FORTY

I woke to find Cheryl squatting at my side and staring at me, like a venomous spider. Behind her loomed Clay.

Unnerved, I shot up and, not ashamed to admit it, cowered. Had they uncovered my handiwork?

'It's okay, lovey.' Her soothing tones made my skin crawl. I hated the way she switched from bitch to saint in seconds. 'We just need you to be quiet for a little while.'

I nodded blindly. *Yes, I'll be good,* my face said. I hadn't forgotten those hands around my throat, the marks, I was sure, clearly visible.

'I know you will.' She leant over, traced a single finger lightly from my hairline to my cheek. I tried not to flinch. I tried to look docile and unconcerned. She wore her fake smile and glanced up at Clay who, to my utter horror, produced a length of black material. Bile flooded my mouth. Was he going to strangle me?

'No,' I said, flailing my arms. '*Please,*' I begged. 'You don't have to do this.'

'There, there, nothing to fear, Verity. Be a good girl and open your mouth.' Cheryl spoke like a dentist about to perform root canal surgery.

'No,' I shouted. The next was a blur of "Get off me" and "Fuck you". At one point, Clay was practically kneeling on my chest. It did me no good to struggle. I wound up flat on my back with a gag in my mouth that tasted of old socks, my hands and ankles tied together, and with a lot more bruises and scrapes than if I'd been compliant. Through a haze of hurt and humiliation, I could only surmise that my captors were to receive guests, by which I meant the police. If I was right, it signalled a development.

I watched them tramp back out. Alone, I struggled to contain my panic. Tears pricked my eyes and my nose started to swell. What if I couldn't breathe? Terror of choking or suffocating consumed my every thought. The rattle of a vehicle crossing the cattle grid briefly brought me to my senses. I heard a car drive in, park, doors open and close and unknown males speaking in low voices. In the dark, I'd discovered my hearing became more sensitive. Rolling over to eavesdrop, I shut my frightened eyes.

'According to Stuart,' a male voice began, 'while there's little to go on in terms of positive identification, the old fracture to the top of the arm is consistent with the nasty break Don Birch suffered during his apprenticeship. Once further tests have been carried out, it should hopefully provide the family with a degree of closure.'

'Good news is never a substitute for shit news, Matt,' said an older man, gruff-voiced, with a Midlands undertone.

'Ay, with more shit news to come,' the one called Matt said. 'A proper chicken and egg situation.'

'Best we leave it to the boffins to sort out.'

'And until they do?'

'Give them the standard spiel and say we're following all potential lines of enquiry. We only tell the family what we know for certain: Don Birch was murdered. How is open to interpretation, above our pay grade, and not something we discuss at this juncture.'

'Whichever way you look at it, someone badly wanted him dead.'

And then they disappeared I was left puzzled by what I'd heard and wondered what would happen next.

* * *

Eleanor had been up since dawn. The sky, gilded with weird cloud formations, was the colour of fresh crushed apricots. On the hour and every hour, she listened to the local news as she drove. Enid could be spinning her a line to deflect her from her mission. *She was devious enough*, Eleanor thought.

She travelled through unfamiliar lanes, some with passing places, some without, and steered the Range Rover down long narrow pot-holed drives to big farms and small farms. She visited the ordered, the manicured and the chaotic. It was too early in the morning to question people, even farming folk, without seeming peculiarly intrusive. Once the coffee hour was over, she was bold and asked direct questions about Cheryl Castrey and Yootha Birch, whenever and wherever. In return, she received blank looks and puzzled expressions. Some folk were helpful and misguided in equal measure.

'Oh, is that the Birches of Bartestree, or Stoke What's it?'

'Never heard of Castrey, is that a local name?'

'Ask the postman, if I were you.'

She did and he said he was in too much of a hurry to talk as he had a special delivery to make.

Some were guarded and suspicious.

A red-faced woman, who smelt of horses and leather, ordered Eleanor to clear off and warned her in flinty tones to 'Stop poking around in other people's business, or else.' It was not an encouraging start.

Eleanor tried a different approach, one more guaranteed to make an emotional connection. She whipped out her phone with a picture of Verity on it. 'Have you seen this girl?' she asked. Responses ranged from: *'You a copper, or what?'* and *'My, she's pretty . . .'* to *'I'd go to the police if I were you.'*

But Eleanor could not, and must not go to the police. She'd caught the threatening tone in Cheryl's voice. She believed Cheryl would make good on a promise if Eleanor didn't do as asked. An "eye for an eye", Enid had said. Eleanor could beg forgiveness for eternity and it would make no difference. Cheryl wanted blood, preferably hers. In its absence she would settle for Verity's.

Eleanor forced herself to picture where Verity was being held. She imagined a cellar existence, without daylight; a rusting shed with its windows blacked out. She hoped to God that they hadn't shoved her daughter in a hole in the ground. As a youngster, Eleanor had been haunted by the story of the sixteen-year-old heiress forced into a drainage shaft, cold, naked and hungry, by serial killer Donald Nielsen. *No, Eleanor thought, Cheryl needed Verity alive. Verity was part of her plan. Verity was leverage to make me do whatever it was Cheryl wanted as repayment for the life I took.*

Eleanor's mind churned at the memory. *Wasn't my fault. Didn't mean to. Didn't . . .*

For much of her life prevention of the past from colliding with the present had been a success. Her days were filled with Giles and children, house moving and house keeping, social functions and acquaintances, not friends exactly. Eleanor had never risked those. In more recent years, after Giles's death, she had found herself more unable to stop the truth from leaking in. Until there was Roger to make it all go away again. And now?

Eventually she broke off from travelling around the interior of her mind and stopped for a drink and an essential loo break in Hereford. Her shoulders buckled under weight of guilt. What right did she have to pause her search for one single moment when her daughter was in so much danger?

She paid by card in the car park, cut through to the centre of town, past a wine merchant, an estate agent, empty shops, and men from the Midlands selling fruit and veg. A military helicopter flew overhead. Two young police officers strolled by. Eleanor fought an irresistible urge to confess that she was a murderer and her daughter was being punished for her sin. As she drew near there was a crackle from a police radio and one officer, a woman, turned away and the other followed.

The moment tantalisingly gone, she headed towards Marks and Spencer where a busker was wailing outside. Up the escalator, she headed for the ladies' and used the facilities. A quick glance in the mirror, afterwards, revealed worry lines. She looked as if she'd aged a couple of decades in the space of a day.

Back out in the street, she ordered a coffee to go from a nearby café and found the tourist information centre. It was housed in the Town Hall, in St. Owen's Street, and handy for the car park. Old school, she bought an Ordinance Survey map and returned with it to the car.

She placed her drink in the cup-holder and spread out the map over the steering wheel. Quietly sipping, she homed in on areas she had already visited and those that remained. She planned a route to and through South Herefordshire and slipped out her phone, willing it to ring. Amazingly, it did. She almost dropped it.

'Yes?'

'Mum.'

Her heart plunged. Timing was everything in life, no more so than now, and she didn't have time to explain to her son what she was up to. Doubted she ever would.

'Where the hell are you?' Alex exploded.

Eleanor glanced out of the window and noticed the public conveniences. 'Somewhere nice,' she lied.

'We've been worried sick about you.'

'Well, don't. I'm perfectly okay.'

'Have you talked to the bank?'

A dull throb behind Eleanor's left eye let her know that a migraine was brewing.

'It's all in hand,' she replied. What "it" was she didn't say because "it" was irrelevant and meaningless. The money was gone. Her folly. Her fault. As Giles would say, 'Mea culpa.'

'So you're all right? You sound a little weird.'

'Must be the line.'

'Right,' Alex said, obviously unconvinced. 'Have you heard from Verity?'

She paused. Truth, or lie? 'I have.'

'And?'

'Alex, darling, I'm so sorry but I really do have to go. There's a traffic warden walking towards me.' She ended the call, started the car and prayed that Alex would not call back. She had never got the hang of speaking on hands free and didn't intend to start now.

Heading out of town and out into open country, the landscape felt more Welsh. Through the heat haze, she spied ghost hills in the distance. On the road, there were signs for Brecon and Kington. Unfamiliar with the area, she feared she had driven too far. And yet this would be as good a place as any to hold a young woman captive.

Glancing at her watch, Eleanor considered how much longer it would be before Cheryl called, how long before the police established a crime had been committed. For when they did, it wouldn't only be Cheryl Castrey knocking on her door.

* * *

By the time the police finally left, the gag in my mouth was sodden with saliva and my hands and feet had gone from tingly to numb. These were not my immediate concerns.

My mind churned with sick images of death and dying and I wondered how the hell fifteen-year-old Eleanor, not much more than a kid, had dispatched a strongly built middle-aged man. Now that the family had received the worst possible news and had all their suspicions confirmed I would become the personification of a punch bag. They'd want to take their ire out on me. More than ever I realised that I only had myself on which to rely. There would be no cavalry. No happy mother and daughter ending.

When Chuck lumbered in I feared the worst. His big moon face bore down on mine and, wordlessly, he removed the gag, untied my ankles and then my hands. So great was my relief, I even thanked him.

Freed, yet with the emotional temperature outside dialled to max, I didn't dare resume my tunnelling activities. Recognising the importance of maintaining a level of fitness, I sprinted the perimeter of my makeshift prison thirty times both ways. Appalled I was so out of puff, I flexed my legs, jumped on the spot and performed squats that made my knees creak. Press-ups were an unmitigated failure.

Much later, how much I couldn't gauge, Chuck returned with a tray of food. Perhaps he'd been appointed to deal with me because the others didn't trust themselves. For once, the food was hot: cottage pie with mushy peas. Looked a bit slimy. While my other meals could have been served at any time, this was more an approximation of an evening meal. Faintly worried and suspicious of what seemed an upgrade, I, nevertheless, wolfed it down.

As one hour slid into another, it struck me how much life in captivity is devoid of colour. Conversely, the fear it engenders vivid and bright. Was this a period of calm before something horrible happened? When would Cheryl call Mum? When would she agree to meet her and where? Would they chuck a sack over my mother's head and bring her here, like they did me? I desperately tried not to dwell on *it*, but focus on *me*.

A millennial, I had a life to live, stuff to do, places to visit, drinks to taste and conversations to have. I wanted to love again — no, I *needed* to. Odd to think that, busily mourning Colm, I'd failed to appreciate so spectacularly what I already had: a decent job, great friends, *life*. Judging by my current environment, I'd have made a crap farmer's wife. The thought raised a smile, a feat of hope triumphing over reality because I was as sure as I could be that, whatever Cheryl and her motley crew decided, I'd heard and witnessed too much. I knew their horrible secrets: a daughter born to Cheryl and mysteriously nowhere to be seen and a murdered man. Figuratively, I knew where the bodies were buried and was inextricably linked by virtue of my birth. Whatever I said to Clay in the car about not telling a soul was a blatant lie. If I got out of here, I was running straight to the nearest police station and, afterwards, I would climb to the top of that ugly office building in the Bath Road, and shout it defiantly across the city. I was going to nail those bastards and be seen to do it for what they'd put me through and as a warning to anyone else who tried to take the law into their own hands, like the vigilantes they were. It was easier to make plans about the fate that awaited my kidnappers than the one lined up for Mum. If she went to prison, as I knew she must if the police got to her first, a part of me would be lost forever. Would I visit her? Couldn't answer and with the fight abruptly deserting me, my mind tormented to near hysteria, I crashed out.

Later, I woke with a jolt, disorientated. I wished they had not taken my watch, my dad's last present to me. It was pitch black and the night weighed heavy. Lights were off in both cottages. No funfair style illumination outside. There was no "up with the lark" clatter and clang. Even the animals were asleep.

But there were definite sounds of scuffling. Fearing rats, I drew my knees up to my chin.

Then I heard a door open and close too quietly, like a drunk stumbling home in the early hours, desperately trying not to disturb those inside.

Wide awake now, I wondered why the security lights hadn't come on.

Straining my ears, I heard soft footsteps, getting louder as they drew closer. *Someone was going to the yard*, I thought. Perhaps an early morning start for Clay, or one of the others on a drug run — not that I knew much about the drug trade other than what I'd read on social media and in the news, which in my world often equated to the same thing.

When the bar across the barn door slid aside more loudly than seemed possible, I wondered if, by some miracle, I was to be rescued. Hope stirred. My spirits soared. I sat up, eager to make out my rescuer in the darkness and keen to get moving. Could it be Mum? 'Hello?' I cried into the tangle of darkness. Met by dead silence, fear churned inside me. Why were there no words of comfort, no reassurance that I was safe and that I could go home? Why no flashlight to identify it was really me, the missing teacher?

Too late to pretend to be asleep, I swung my legs round and planted my bare feet on the cool earth.

First, I heard a click then, nauseatingly, saw a flame. Was the smell of petrol by association, or was it for real? Whatever I believed, or felt, panic blitzed me as my eyes adjusted to night vision. Clay, bathed in blue and yellow, was not a figment of my imagination.

Bare-chested, he loped towards me with the stealth of a feline predator. Up close, I could smell whisky on his breath, sweat on his body. Despite the heat, I was icy-cold. Slipping my hand into the pocket of my shorts, I withdrew the nail. Not much of a weapon, more a comfort blanket, it was better than nothing.

'Got your attention.' He snickered.

'Keep away from me.' My voice shook.

'No way to talk to a man who protected you.'

'You call this protection?' I looked around and saw how tantalisingly close the open doorway seemed. Could I rush him? He wouldn't be expecting it. If I took him off-guard, I could run like hell.

'Reckon you owe me.' Clay's voice slurred. 'How would you like my tongue down your throat, little rich girl?'

'Fuck off,' I snarled. The nail itched between my fingers.

'You'll pay for that, slut.'

He drunkenly lunged. Balling one hand into a fist, I packed as much power as I could and struck him hard in the groin. As he doubled over, I jabbed the nail blindly into his face.

He screamed in shock and pain. 'Fucking bitch-cunt!'

And then I careered out into the night and I was fly-ing. I hurtled over the cattle grid. I didn't think of bare feet, sprained ankles, torn skin or stiff limbs. I paid no heed to the alarm going up and lights going on. I didn't consider the threat from dogs on the loose, cross men in vehicles giving chase. I didn't think of consequences, only that I was free. And all those things I wanted to say to those I loved and even those I didn't, all those experiences and adventures I needed to have, were within reach. My mind exploded with possibility. My heart soared with generosity. I would live and I would love, love, love. After everything that had happened, I was heading home and I was free.

And I was powerful. My legs worked like pistons. My arms swung in rhythm with every step. I was making fast progress. I'd reached the top of the drive and just beyond when an explosive noise sliced through the night, knocking the wind out of my lungs and cutting the power cables from my brain to my limbs. My hands flew to the top of my head as if to prevent it from falling off my neck. I twisted round.

Every light in the cottages was on. Outside was flooded with illumination. I narrowed my gaze, sensitive to a boot on the concrete yard, the snap of a branch on the drive, someone coming after me. This was not what had grabbed my attention and made my jaw drop in terror.

The figure that emerged was not Clay, as I'd imagined. It was Yootha. With the stock tucked tight into her shoulder, she held a double-barrel shotgun aloft and it pointed straight at me.

CHAPTER FORTY-ONE

After a futile search, not helped by road closures and diversions for essential highway maintenance, Eleanor found herself at the end of a steep drive. To her mind, it looked promising in that it was in roughly the right spot and there was no sign of a dwelling or farm from the road. She pulled onto the verge nearby and considered whether to drive or go on foot. She wondered how far the track extended. Some went on for miles.

The crackle of tyres from a big car captured her attention. She ducked down at the sight of a BMW with two suited men inside, who looked suspiciously like police officers. Eleanor harboured a healthy distrust of the police after Don identified two senior policemen, frequent visitors at the Stone House. When Leanne, a girl a year younger than her, had tried to report what was going on, she hadn't realised that her voice would never be heard, that her plea would be ignored and her complaint buried. Eleanor, later, discovered that Leanne had overdosed and died.

She waited for the car to pass before she straightened back up. She got out, walked up the drive a little way to a bend that took her to another. She attempted to visualise what lay at the top of the hill, beyond the tree line. If this really were the place, how would Cheryl react to an unscheduled visit? Would she set dogs on her? Would it make things worse for Verity? Would it trigger unforeseen and terrible consequences? She had taken risks all her life, but she could not risk the life of her child.

With a heavy heart, Eleanor returned to her car and headed back to the hotel, barren and empty-handed.

The next morning she visited her bank, the only one in town, and withdrew two thousand pounds, the maximum possible at short notice. The staff were friendly with only a slight suggestion of curiosity. She put the nice lady behind the counter at ease by mentioning that the money was for a spontaneous holiday in the UK. Devon, she maintained, to give the lie colour; it came so easily to her. It was less easy to explain that she wanted to collect nine thousand pounds the following morning. She talked quickly, conversationally, before she was deluged with a torrent of questions. She explained that her children and grandchildren required financial assistance. She made good use of the easily understood phrase: "Bank of Mum and Dad". Except there was no Dad and Alex had already exhausted her patience in this regard.

'Lucky them,' the cashier said. Her face fell when she noticed that a great deal of money had already left Eleanor's account. Eleanor kept talking, kept lying and reported that it was for a business venture, in which she was involved, a half-truth to conceal the lie. The cashier asked her to wait for one moment and left her post. A hurried conversation took place at a desk at the far end of the room. Eleanor plastered a smile upon her face and prayed. Giles was a wealthy man. She was a wealthy woman. She remained so, despite the con and loss of so much money.

The cashier returned and, with an edgy smile, assured Eleanor it would be ready for collection in the morning.

Eleanor thanked her and left. She shopped for a roll of clingfilm from the Co-op. This time, she bought chocolate. She returned to her room and, not only did she check the news on an hourly basis, she checked her phone. Cheryl's silence bothered her. In her bones Eleanor sensed that something bad had happened, though what she dared not think. Thankfully, there were no more calls from Alex, not so from Dido. Eleanor read her daughter-in-law's messages of concern etched with annoyance on WhatsApp. She sighed and deleted.

Not so easy to delete the fragmented pictures in her mind. Like wearing a fresh pair of spectacles with a stronger prescription, glimpses of what had been long buried assumed greater clarity.

Something had been up as soon as Don collected her that last night.

The blazing heat of the day had barely dropped more than a few degrees. Without a whisper of air, you could barely move without breaking out in a sweat. The night felt leaden on her shoulders.

He spoke little and when he did he was curt and distant. He looked rough and she detected whisky on his breath.

'Have I done something wrong?' she asked.

'No.'

'Why are you in a mood?'

'I'm not.'

'Where are we going?'

'Usual place.'

He drove fast and it scared her. When he slapped up the gears, she pictured him thwacking the rump of a big stallion.

'I was thinking,' she began.

'Don't.'

She turned and stared at him stupidly. His jaw was coated in stubble and a pulse near his left eye ticked. 'What's got into you?'

Scenery was flying by at alarming speed. Was this a side of Don hitherto unrevealed? Was this the real man beneath the charm?

They arrived at the forge, tyres spitting, her heart rate rising. The terrible sense of foreboding only served to undermine her further. This was silly, she thought. He loves me.

He said so. Didn't he? Actually, she can't quite remember when.

The driver's door opened and slammed shut. Don took a key from his pocket and opened the padlock securing the door to the forge.

'You going to sit there the rest of the night?' he called to her.

Slowly, she climbed out. She'd made an effort to look nice and wore the dress he'd specially chosen for her. An off-the-shoulder number, one he said made her look sexy.

He stalked inside and in trepidation she followed. From the floor, he picked up a bottle half full of whisky and necked it in great swallows.

'Take off your clothes,' he said, wiping the back of his hand across his mouth.

'What?'

'You heard.'

'Don, what's going on? What's got into you?'

'I'm giving you an order and I expect you to obey.'

She froze. He sounded like the others. She wanted to tell him not to be soft, that they were lovers, that she was his sweetheart, that he'd told her so. She couldn't think, let alone formulate words into a sentence. She stood mute.

His face darkened. His eyes so blue looked black in the reduced light. 'You're nothing to me.'

Her world imploded. Her bare legs and knees wouldn't keep still and her eyes darted towards the door.

'Damn you,' he shouted. 'Take them off.'

'Is it Cheryl you like better?' Her voice didn't sound like hers at all. It was high and quavery, like an old woman's. 'Have you met someone else?'

'Do me a favour.'

'Then what?'

He tipped his head back and laughed. 'You really don't get it, do you?'

She did not.

But now, Eleanor did, and she wondered, with an ache deep in her chest, if Yootha's boy was like his uncle.

* * *

There was a reckoning.

Rough arms snatched and grabbed and pinched me. Distraught, I protested loud and long and was dragged away, screaming. My bare feet grazed the ground. I was silenced with one backhanded slap that blacked my eye and another that made me bite my tongue, I snivelled. Pain made my eyes water. Blood dribbled down my chin. In shock, I was shoved past Yootha, who, alarmingly, still had the muzzle of the shotgun trained on me. Brought before Cheryl, like I was a criminal about to receive a life sentence, I saw that Clay was already there. He looked a lot less full of himself with Cheryl tearing verbal lumps out of him.

'What's wrong with you, you fucking pervert? You never *ever* damage the goods.'

'It wasn't fucking like that,' he bit back. 'She led me on.'

'I bloody didn't,' I belted out. Cheryl shot me a look that could melt ice. It said: *Shut up. I'll deal with you later.*

'Sure, she did,' Cheryl said, in a voice drenched in sarcasm. 'You're a liar, Clay. I won't have our plans fucked up, least of all by you. You keep your dick in your trousers or I'll saw it off myself.'

I didn't think it was a piece of theatre designed to appease me. With her dark eyes and darker expression, she looked terrifying and I was terrified. I had the sense that, when she was done with him, she would start on me. What would be the penalty for attempting to escape?

She continued tearing into Clay who stood, moody and belligerent, and finished with, 'Get out of my sight.' With a black look that said he was not done with me, Clay slunk past. When Cheryl turned her venomous eyes on me, I broke down. I couldn't help it.

'Cheryl, I'm sorry, please. I was frightened. I thought he was going to rape me and I ran. Please, Cheryl, I only want to go home.' Beside myself, I wrung my hands. 'Please, let me go. I've done nothing wrong. I . . .'

'Get her some water,' Cheryl said to Chuck. Sharply, she addressed me. 'Are you hurt?'

Was she blind?

'My eye,' I muttered. 'I need a doctor.'

'Nice try.'

'I can hardly see.' My right eye had swollen up alarmingly. Touching it with the tip of my finger was agony. I wondered if something was fractured. 'I think my cheekbone is broken.'

'Don't be such a baby. Going to have a bit of a shiner. It will heal,' Cheryl said, unsympathetic, as if it were no big deal.

A glass of water was pushed into my hand and I drank as best I could. When I'd finished, Cheryl asked, 'Did Clay touch you?'

I shook my head.

'No harm done then.'

She might as well have said *shit happens*. 'What's wrong with you people?' I burst out.

'I'll forget you said that because you're obviously very upset,' Cheryl said through gritted teeth. 'But you see, Verity, this is what happens when you break the rules.'

Before I could protest further, she continued, 'Get some sleep while you can. A few hours from now you'll see your mother.'

A few days ago, I'd have been elated. 'I don't believe you,' I said dully. Messing with my mind was all part of her cruel plan to make my life more intolerable, if that were possible.

'It's true.'

'I'm going home?' It wasn't so much a question, more a challenge.

She flicked a short tight smile. 'Not yet. Soon.'

This I really didn't believe. 'You can't keep me here forever.'

'That depends on your mother's co-operation.' Her expression was sly.

I threw her a defiant look. 'It depends on the *police investigation.*'

Cheryl's expression stiffened. I was tempted to reveal what I'd overheard about the question mark over cause of death, *'chicken and egg situation,'* one officer said. All this talk of murder, yet nobody knew how Don Birch had died. Unashamedly, I was grabbing at anything and everything that would change the narrative, exonerate my mother, and plant an unsettling seed of doubt in Cheryl's mind.

But Mum had *confessed*, a nagging voice in my head said. She hadn't denied her crime. Undeterred, I said, 'You're taking one hell of a gamble. Cops will be backwards and forwards, keeping you up to date with enquiries, asking more and more questions. At any time they could stumble across what you're up to. All my mother has to do is turn herself in and you're toast.'

Cheryl's face cracked into a grin, the accompanying laugh tinder-dry. 'Let's hope for your sake that she isn't that stupid.'

'Or what?' I yelled. 'What precisely are you going to do with me? *Fucking say it.*' My voice was a roar.

Inches from my face, she was breathing hard. Perspiration coated her top lip and she trembled. As dawn crept through the threadbare curtains, revealing the full extent of the rage on her face, I had the impression that she'd worked long and hard to contain her natural bent for violence. I hoped it pissed her off enormously to lose control, however brief.

First to drop her gaze, she stalked away. Undeniably shaken, I felt sharp satisfaction so that, when Clint dumped me back in the barn, I didn't feel as terrified as I should have done.

And then I set to work.

CHAPTER FORTY-TWO

I sensed a change outside and suspected there were fresh developments.

For the past few hours, by my reckoning, I'd stealthily shifted and distributed a lot of earth. The deeper I went, the more resistant the soil. My battle with nature spurred me on; I dug with the energy of the desperate. Two wide battens were loose and I'd made progress with an upright riddled with woodworm. With every creak and bump, I feared discovery. I stopped when I glimpsed the men emerge from the cottage. Clint was first, tucking the ends of his shirt into his jeans and disappearing into an outhouse; Chuck next, holding a pressure washer; Clay, a wide plaster on his cheek, last. Of the women, there was no sign. Didn't mean that they weren't up to something.

Chuck set about cleaning the Jaguar, Clay supervising the process, giving orders, although I couldn't hear a word he said. Under the cover of noise and activity, I returned to my task with grim determination. We were entering the endgame and I wanted to win.

* * *

Eleanor visited the bank as soon as it opened. The transaction was straightforward. Nine thousand pounds in cash in twenty-pound denominations was physically more manageable than she'd imagined. She stuffed the packages into a bag brought along for the purpose.

Before noon, Eleanor's phone rang. She answered and listened to the order to come without possessions, unarmed, so to speak. She was specifically warned not to bring a phone. Eleanor did not argue and did not enquire about Verity or ask to speak to her. Giving the impression this was straight business she buried her wildest imaginings into an unmarked grave.

Then she moved quickly.

She stripped off and, taking ten thousand pounds from her stash of eleven, secured the cash to her body with cling-film, wrapping it round and round. Stiffly, she put on the horrible dress and stuffed the remaining thousand pounds into its deep pockets. She grabbed a bottle of complimentary water from the room and nothing else.

From Ludlow, she took the A49, a busy road prone to accidents, and kept on going. Hot and uncomfortable, she had thirty miles to cover and must do it in fifty minutes. The cash burned against her skin. Her destination was Madley village hall, from where she was told she would be collected.

The base of her back was damp with sweat as she pulled in. In front of a hall that resembled a dormer bungalow, a dirty van, full of dents and with a long scrape down the passenger side, was waiting. Unnervingly, it had blacked-out windows. She made a mental note of the registration.

Two men stepped out: one lean and wearing a cowboy hat. It threw her. Don had often sported a Stetson. She'd admired his style because it cut him out as different to the rest. On this young man, with his dirty T-shirt and long shorts, it was a ridiculous affectation. A piece of straw popped out the side of his mouth. He gnawed away and his teeth were yellow. His accomplice was squat and overweight and his expression indecipherable. The familiar likeness was in their eyes. No doubt about it, these were Cheryl's boys. Eleanor was surprised. She thought Cheryl's offspring would be more attractive.

They approached. They didn't speak. They grunted.

Ordered out of her car, she complied. She expected them to frisk her, but they didn't. They took her car keys and guided her towards the van. Like the jaws of a predator, the doors snapped wide apart.

'I'm not getting in there,' she protested.

The tubby one looked at his brother in consternation. They hadn't bargained on resistance, it seemed.

'You are,' the one with the Stetson said, thumping the centre of her back.

Another push and she complied. They didn't help her to step up. She had to scrabble to climb inside, not easy with her increased bulk. She clouted both knees.

Used to transport builder's rubble and garden waste, the interior was filthy. She ferreted about and found an old sack to sit on. Prepared for discomfort, she was not prepared for the silent terror that washed over her. Mother love was the most potent of emotions. She would die for her children to protect them. And she very much feared that time was drawing near.

Unless she was clever.

The van moved off. Loud music assaulted her ears. With nothing to grab hold of she was thrown from side to side and the vehicle was not going that quickly. Focusing on the physical she had little time to dwell on strategy, although thanks to Enid's loose tongue, she had a plan. Whether or not, she would have the courage to see it through, she did not know. She hadn't yet factored in the variables. Much depended on Cheryl. The wild card was Verity.

At last, the engine note changed and the van took an abrupt turn as it travelled along a rutted road. Eleanor felt every lump and bump in the hard core. Finally, the van drew to a halt. She heard doors open and close. She braced, fully expecting to be let out. It was hot in the back, the air thick and humid, reminding her of that last fateful night with Don when she could hardly breathe because of the heat wave that consumed the country.

She waited and waited.

There was a nasty smell of petrol. Her hair was plastered to her skull and her cheeks were flushed. Parched, she badly needed a drink and wished she'd had the foresight to bring her bottle of water with her. *It will be all right*, she told herself, breathing rhythmically. *I've faced worse than this. It's no time to panic. Hold your nerve*, she thought, trotting out all the trite little sayings she had dispensed over the years. This was Cheryl playing mind games. Just like Don. It had taken her a long time to work out that they'd been in it together, and from the very beginning.

* * *

I was summoned. I glanced at my dirty fingernails, hoping they didn't give the game away, and plunged them into my pockets.

Once more, my minders, as I'd dubbed them, escorted me to the cottage. Travelling back and forth, I could probably walk between the barn and the cottage, blindfolded and unaided.

The van was in the yard, as was Clay's Jaguar. There was no sign of my mother, or my mother's Range Rover. Perhaps mercurial Cheryl had changed her mind.

Cheryl stood at the end of the refectory table, hands resting on the surface, her back to the window. She looked different. She'd made an effort and wore a magenta-coloured dress that flattered her figure and suited her colouring. Her make-up was carefully applied in soft shades. Gone the hard eyeliner and traveller vibe. Gold studs replaced hooped earrings. Even her nails were shorter and painted a muted pink. Significantly, the necklace remained, around her neck, her talisman.

She sat down. Yootha joined her and sat on her left, Clay, displaying a satisfying gouge to the side of his jaw, on her right.

A plain wooden chair was placed in the corner, nearest the sink. Told to sit, I sat. I'd have to get past Clay if I wanted to flee and that was never going to happen.

Cheryl twisted around to face me. 'Whatever is said in this room, you will stay quiet. You will not react. You will not address your mother.'

I said nothing.

'Do you understand?'

I nodded miserably. My face hurt, my damaged eye wept and my tongue was more painful than I thought possible. Cheryl didn't need to concern herself with my behaviour; Mum's was more problematic. I hadn't seen my mother for days. It felt like years. Would I recognise her when she came? The old mum would be horrified. She would demand action. She would be bold and brisk. And if that didn't work, she would grovel and plead. Would the murderous mum, the one who admitted to killing a man, who confessed to a crime and begged forgiveness, react in the same way? How far would she go to save me? I supposed the fact she hadn't scarpered and left the country was a good sign.

At a nod from Cheryl, Chuck and Clint trooped out.

All eyes turned towards the entrance. I was more anxious than before my driving test and first job interview, more nervous than before Dad's funeral at which I spoke. I was not alone. The air felt charged, electric. With steely expressions, both women tipped very slightly forward in their seats as we waited for the arrival of my mother.

* * *

With her mind on the brink, the doors flew open.

Eleanor blinked in the light and, stepping out with wary eyes, observed what looked like a junkyard. Cracked concrete, stained rendering. However tidy, whatever efforts made to closely sweep the yard, the brightest summer sunshine could never penetrate and warm this bleak, godforsaken place. Her heart broke for her daughter.

Eleanor was led to a small black-and-white cottage that seemed as if it had changed little in centuries. She had to duck to clear a low beam on entering.

Her gaze travelled through the room, past faces old and new, and fastened on Verity. Her girl was so drawn and thin, Eleanor was seized with cold fury. It took all that she had not to cry out in protest, run to her, sweep her up and carry her home. Instinctively, she knew to show concern would please Cheryl. Causing Eleanor maximum emotional pain was, after all, the object of the exercise, so she swallowed her rage and checked the thirst for reckless action.

Cheryl instructed her son, the one called Chuck, to frisk her. Gnawing with terror at the fear of him discovering the cash, she bit down hard and stood stoically while a stranger's hands felt over her body and, perfunctorily, between her legs. By some miracle he failed to differentiate between what he believed was flesh and the layer of money plastered closely to her skin.

'She's clean,' he declared.

In her old world such terminology was risible and the stuff of crime dramas. This was the real world and what she did in the next few minutes and hopefully, if all went according to plan, the next couple of hours, would either save Verity, or condemn her.

'I'd like to say it's good to see you,' Cheryl said, her eyes like darts. 'Waited a long time for this.'

'Aye,' Yootha agreed.

Eleanor glanced from one woman to the other. Cheryl had aged well. It came as a surprise. Eleanor believed that if rage were harboured in the heart, it would inevitably show on the face. She confessed she was disappointed it hadn't. Cheryl's deceptively warm mouth had changed little. There were more lines, of course, but she'd stayed handsome and the sultriness of her youth remained. Hard to believe it now, but they had been close once. Cheryl was her exciting, naughty friend and for a short and intense period of Eleanor's life, she'd loved her.

But that was before Don.

Yootha bore a striking resemblance to her mother, Lucille and had fared badly, Eleanor thought. The emotional scars on Yootha's face were all too visible, for which Eleanor was genuinely sorry. But it was the man, brooding next to Cheryl, who robbed her of air and certainty. With his dark looks, the dimple on his chin, his high forehead and dark hair, he was the spit of Don. A nasty abrasion on his face reminded her of the cuts, scrapes and burns that Don often picked up at work. It was like viewing a ghost. Unnerved, she struggled to keep it together. For Verity's sake, she knew she must. Could Eleanor play a role for which she was totally unrehearsed?

Cheryl raised her chin, sniffed the air, like a hyena scenting a wounded animal. Always was one for spotting weakness in an enemy, Eleanor remembered, and in Eleanor she had the perfect prey.

'Talk,' Cheryl commanded.

'About you?' Eleanor stood steady and strong. A calculated blow, she was pleased to see frown lines spreading across Cheryl's forehead and between her eyebrows, glad that Cheryl was fazed by her unusual opening gambit.

'About what happened,' Yootha cut in loudly, 'where it happened, how you did it?'

'Did what?' Eleanor asked.

'How you killed him, bitch.' Cheryl was white-lipped.

Eleanor glanced at Verity. Her daughter was perched on the edge of her seat. She, too, frowned in puzzlement. Her teeth rested on her top lip and her good eye was wide and wary.

'It was an accident.' Eleanor spoke in the same tone adopted by a child apologising for spilling orange squash on a cream-coloured carpet.

'That's a lie,' Yootha growled.

'I didn't intend to hurt him.'

'But you did,' Cheryl reminded her.

'He belittled me, made fun of me and then he attacked me.' And so much more.

'*Me, me, me* — you really expect us to believe that?' Cheryl's voice was one big jeer.

Yootha's face contorted. Her yellowing skin flushed with ire. Eleanor cared not for these women. Her only concern was Verity. She watched her daughter sitting with her chin tipped, a finger crooked beneath, something she did when engrossed. Deep inside, Eleanor realised her words had resonated. If nobody else believed her version of events, Verity would. At least, Eleanor *thought* so. She *hoped*.

'Do you want the truth, or not?'

'Truth?' Yootha could barely get the word past her lips.

There was so much to tell and so much nobody knew. Eleanor wondered if she should just come out with it and slay Cheryl in front of her oldest friend.

'Where did he die?' Cheryl asked the question.

'The forge.'

'How?'

'We fought. He hit his head.' *There was a great deal of blood*, Eleanor did not say. So much, she didn't know which was his and which was hers.

'You mean *you* hit his head?' Cheryl said, accusing.

'I did not.'

'Did you strike him with, a hammer, tongs, what?'

A chisel, Eleanor recalled. My God, if she only had a weapon now. 'I told you,' Eleanor replied implacably. 'I didn't hit him. He fell.' And she had been appalled by the damage. Staring at his lifeless body, she hadn't been sure which injury was the fatal one.

'You pushed him.'

'It was the only way to make him . . .'

'You intended to harm him.'

'NO.'

'You meant to kill him.'

'NO.'

'It was deliberate, wasn't it?'

'NO.' For Christ's sake, it was self-defence.

'You left him there to die.'

Eleanor stalled. Their ugly faces merged together as one. The only tears were in Verity's eyes.

'I wasn't much more than a child.' Eleanor thought how pathetic her excuse seemed now. For all her bluff and bravado, it didn't wash in her eyes and it wouldn't wash in the eyes of the law.

'Did you, or didn't you abandon him?' Cheryl railed.

In an empty voice, Eleanor whispered, 'Yes.'

CHAPTER FORTY-THREE

Mum resembled a very old lady. A horrible dress which I'd never seen her in before, was clearly designed to conceal the pounds she'd mysteriously piled on. It made me wonder for how long I'd been held captive. They say that time is misleading when you have no place to go. The pouched bags underneath Mum's eyes indicated she hadn't slept in weeks. I couldn't be sure whether or not she'd been crying.

To hell with Cheryl's orders, I itched to run to her until I saw Mum's shocked reaction to Clay. It was as if the quarry-tiled floor had shattered, opening up a sinkhole beneath, into which my mother plunged headlong. I'd never seen her look like that and, with a stab of sober realisation, I realised that Eleanor Finch, Eleonora Kaminska, Bliss Hannaford — whichever name she hid behind — was guilty as hell.

Blindsided, I watched helplessly as Mum seemed to give herself a shake and mentally get it together. Standing erect and poised, her voice was bold, her voice strong. Two words, uttered with a sarcastic twist, had Cheryl brilliantly if briefly floored.

Suddenly I wasn't so sure.

I watched the tick of a pulse in the side of Cheryl's jaw, the way her hands inexplicably tightened in her lap. I noted the confusion. Mum had seen it too. I could have screamed when Yootha ruined the moment and barged in with a list of morbid questions. But Mum was on a roll. Unfazed, she never wavered. She answered with sincerity and confidence, only buckling under the intensity of Cheryl's verbal onslaught, the cow. Spots of bright colour on her cheeks, Mum's voice sounded hollow when she admitted leaving Don to die. That really got to me.

A powerful individual, her own person, poised and certain and elegant: forget celebrities, Mum was the woman to whom I'd aspired. The person standing before them, shadowed by regret, was so much less. She'd barely spared me a glance, not until they wrung it out of her, and she looked utterly broken.

The ghouls around the table couldn't see beyond their own resentments and anger. For them, there were no mitigating factors. For me, this proved my mum was not the heartless soul they'd painted her to be.

* * *

There was no relief in telling the people who'd cared most for Don what they needed to hear, Eleanor thought. With one narrative in their minds, they would never accept what she said.

'What did you do with the body?'

'You know what happened.'

'Not what I asked,' Cheryl bit back. 'We know where Don finished up — in a bloody field. Tell us how he got there.'

Eleanor sighed, uneasy about betraying the dead. If there was a heaven, which she doubted, she hoped her grandfather would forgive her.

'Eddy promised he would take care of it.'

Yootha smacked the end of her walking stick against the quarry-tiled floor. 'I knew it. And to think that shitehawk lived among us with his bare-faced lies.'

Somewhere deep behind Eleanor, the lumbering youth with the moon face muttered, 'Filthy foreigners for you.'

She choked off a retort. Her gaze focused on her daughter; she urged her to be stronger than she'd ever been.

Goading, Cheryl returned to her pet topic. 'So Eddy protected you.'

Until he knew he was dying, Eleanor remembered sadly. She was seventeen years of age when he'd handed her his life savings in cash, and drove her in the boot of his car to New Street Station where he put her on a train to London. Goodbye was hard, and she never set eyes on him again. Years spent reading and studying in the cellar had served her well and she took a secretarial course. Staying under the radar, she educated herself socially and shared a basement flat with a couple of other girls off the Gloucester Road. Depending on whom she was dealing with, she variously called herself Hannaford and Kaminska, and never Bliss. It was so much easier to hide your identity back then. By the time she was ready to retrieve her official name, she'd already met Giles while temping at an architectural practice, fell in love, married him and became Eleanor Finch.

'And then you snared another man to hide your dirty secret,' Cheryl continued, droning on.

'That's not true,' Eleanor snapped back. 'You dare to question me, but what of *your* dirty secret: *yours* and Don's?'

Yootha shot forward, the walking stick rattling to the floor. 'What's that supposed to mean, Cheryl? What's she on about?'

All eyes upon her, Eleanor took a bold step forward. Cheryl leapt out of her seat. 'Don't you move, lady,' she shouted.

'The pair of you deliberately tricked me.'

'Shut up.'

Confused, Yootha looked from Eleanor to Cheryl and back again.

'She knows what I mean,' Eleanor said, tilting her chin. 'I was another in a long line of her sick little games.'

Yootha's yellowing skin deepened to the colour of burned ochre. She spoke with slow intonation. 'Che-ryl?'

'It's crap. Don't you see what she's trying to do? She wants to make us argue amongst ourselves. Split us up. Put nasty little seeds of doubt in your heads.' She plumped back down, seeking support first from Yootha and then Clay. Neither responded, or gave any visual clue that they agreed.

Eleanor stood steady, encouraged she had Cheryl rattled, if not yet on the run.

'What you're forgetting, Eleonora,' Cheryl thundered, 'you admitted to murder. Guilty as charged.'

'Then call the police.'

'What use would they be?' Yootha said, clicking her tongue. 'Presumed he was dead after seven years.'

Cheryl reached across and patted the older woman's hand in a show of solidarity, a deadly smile lighting up her face.

'You're nothing more than vigilantes.' Eleanor's tone was scathing.

Ignoring the barb, Cheryl said, 'We want proper compensation.'

Money, Eleanor thought. *It was always about the money and I don't have nearly enough.* 'How much?'

'I'm a reasonable woman,' Cheryl said with a sly expression. '£250k up front, £50k of it in cash, and then a stipend of £4k a month, a bargain for forty-seven years of misery.'

'I can't do that,' Eleanor said flatly.

'You can and you will.'

'You don't understand.' Eleanor spoke as if she was talking slowly to a foreigner with a limited grasp of English. 'Nobody transacts in cash these days. It's absurd to even consider it.'

Pleased by Cheryl's face flushing with the intended slight, Eleanor continued, 'Whatever would my accountant say, let alone the taxman? How would I explain a regular monthly outgoing?'

'Don't you people have cooks and cleaners and gardeners?' Yootha chipped in, her voice dripping with resentment.

'Possibly, but I'd need bank account details, sort codes.' She studiously disregarded the expression of horror on Verity's face.

Cheryl nodded. 'We can provide those.' Alarmed, Yootha opened her mouth to protest and, seeming to think better of it, stalled. Eleanor immediately pounced on the weak link.

'You're quite right to have concerns, Yootha. It would leave a hopelessly suspicious financial digital footprint. I'd look as if I were laundering money.'

'You leave us to worry about that,' Cheryl said, cold-eyed.

'Still can't oblige, I'm afraid.' Eleanor spread her hands in what she hoped appeared like a sincere gesture. 'I was conned out of a lot of money by Michael Yuill. You remember him, don't you?' she reminded them with a hint of a smile. 'My funds have taken a serious hit because of that man.'

Cheryl's expression darkened. 'Beg, borrow, or steal. We don't care.' She tipped her head at Verity, the implication clear. 'If you want to see your daughter again, that's the price.'

'Then we have nothing left to discuss.'

Eleanor refused to meet Verity's eye. Yootha's jaw dropped open. Don's lookalike, disinterested and bored by ancient history, old crimes and women bitching, slowly turned his glowering gaze on Eleanor, his expression one of menace. Intimidated, Eleanor was reminded of Don before she let him have it. Like a reflex response, it cooked up a storm in her mind, one she must tame. She dropped her gaze to the tattoo on his arm and realised he was ex-army. It made her feel worse.

'It's all right, Clay,' Cheryl murmured to the man on her right. 'She's bluffing.'

'Am I?' Eleanor stared at Cheryl.

'Why else would you come?'

'To see my daughter.' Eleanor paused for dramatic effect. 'For the last time.'

An audible gasp from the other end of the room almost knocked Eleanor off course. Before she bottled, Eleanor plunged a hand into her pockets and extracted one thousand pounds. She carefully laid the wad of notes on the table in two separate piles.

The man called Clay sparked with curiosity, his focus entirely on the hard cash on the table. Eleanor could almost see him processing how much was there and on what, given the chance, he would spend it.

'A thousand pounds,' Eleanor declared, 'for a last hug with my daughter. That's it.'

'You must think me stupid.' White-faced, Cheryl's lips looked almost blue.

Eleanor realised she needed to tread carefully. 'I think you miscalculated.'

'Sell your house.'

'I don't want to. It's a nice home and I'm very happy in it.'

Cheryl spluttered. 'Shares. You must have those.'

Eleanor pulled a face. 'Difficult to cash in without a lot of questions asked and forms to fill and, like I said, I fell for a man who cheated me out of a lot of money and continues to make my life difficult.'

'*I'll* make your life bloody difficult.'

Eleanor waited a beat. 'Then the only option is for us to help each other.'

Cheryl's eyes screwed up in confusion.

Resisting Verity's startled expression and adopting an eminently reasonable tone, Eleanor continued, 'Michael Yuill has returned to make life difficult for me. A big man and a bully, I need him taken care of first.'

* * *

Mum's biggest sin was to sell me out. She didn't give two hoots. I was tiresome collateral damage and, therefore, expendable. One last hug? She could fuck right off.

But Mum's hideous suggestion to have Yuill "taken care of" absolutely poleaxed me. The idea of Cheryl working with her in some murderous common cause spun me out. I was on overload with dysfunctional relationships a world away from anything I knew and that made any kind of sense. And thank God for that.

Cold grabbed the back of my neck. I didn't smell fear. I heard it, loud and clear and overwhelming. The sooner I got out of here, the faster I could leg it, from the lot of them.

Brain aching with anger and worry, I went through it all again in my head. What had happened while I'd been locked up in this godforsaken place? I'd believed Alex when he announced that Yuill had skipped the country. So why the hell would Yuill step back into her life? Even with murderous intentions, why take the risk of returning to terrorise a woman he'd just ripped off for thousands of pounds? It didn't compute.

Up until the money talk, I'd been with Mum all the way, thought she'd pulled a blinder. Eyes glowing with secret knowledge, goading Cheryl, claiming that Don's seduction was a sick set-up dreamt up by the two of them, it was a masterstroke. It pained me to think that while Don was whispering sweet nothings in a young Eleanor's ear, he was cackling behind her back. So ironic that the tawdry little plan would backfire so spectacularly. Cheryl was right about Mum stirring up a shitstorm of trouble in more ways than one. Yootha the malleable, the go-along to get-along, easily persuaded subordinate suddenly didn't seem quite so on board in the light of the fresh revelations. I wondered how long it would take for Mum's seed of doubt to take root and spread later. Sure as hell, I didn't want to be around for the fallout.

* * *

'I'm willing to pay,' Eleanor continued, directing her gaze at Clay.

'You want *him* to kill *Yuill*?' Cheryl's eyes shot wide at the prospect, as if it was the most outrageous suggestion she'd ever heard. Clay showed no such scruples. His cold eyes glittered and Eleanor felt his sickness inside her.

'Yuill is making my life a living hell and will continue to do so until he has drained me of every penny I have.'

A silent, hurried exchange took place between Clay, Yootha and Cheryl.

'Why Clay exactly?' Cheryl demanded, an unpleasant undertone in her voice that Eleanor stoutly ignored. 'And not my boys?'

'He looks like he can handle himself,' Eleanor replied and it was true. She didn't enquire how he would carry out the act, whether he would use a knife, a gun or his bare hands. It was irrelevant.

'If Clay agrees to come with me now, I know exactly where to find Yuill. Afterwards, I'll give you what you want.' It was odd to beg for protection from the woman who meant her nothing but harm. Cheryl couldn't care less about Eleanor's wellbeing: she was sure of that.

'And what do I get out of it?' Clay demanded to know.

'The going rate.' Eleanor spoke as though she knew what she was talking about.

Clay looked to Cheryl. '£10k?'

'Sounds about right.'

Eleanor agreed.

'How do we know we can trust you?' Cheryl asked. *That she hadn't dismissed the idea out of hand meant she was on the hook*, Eleanor thought. Keen to preserve what Cheryl believed was her investment, she was greedy. She always wanted a bigger slice of anything and anyone.

Eleanor reached for the side zipper of her dress and, pressing her fingers inside, tore the clingfilm with her nails, ripping the rest away with her fingers. Nine thick wads of notes dropped to the floor, to which there was a collective gasp.

'Fuck me,' the man called Clint said.

Cheryl gave Eleanor a dead-eyed stare and crossed her arms. 'Thought you said you were skint.'

'I said I'd suffered a loss.'

'Thought you said nobody dealt with cash anymore.'

Eleanor's sighed 'Do we have an agreement, or don't we?'

* * *

I could not believe my ears. Flashing with fury, I wanted to scream and shout at the lot of them. My mother was talking as casually about murder as a routine trip to the garage to sort the car out. She'd done it right there in front of me, no ifs, no buts and certainly no mitigating factors. Dead, killed, eliminated, neutralised, there were no other words for it. I'd tried to read her eyes to see if she was serious, but I honestly couldn't tell. She'd lied for so long, I doubted I'd ever be able to spot the difference. *Oh. My. God.*

The conniving way Mum had struck a deal over money, throwing good after bad, was off the spectrum insane. She'd settled it in the same way a mortgage adviser agrees a loan. How could she be that cold-blooded?

She'd obviously picked up on Clay's bad-boy status and selected the right man for the job. How was that all supposed to end? Didn't she realise the risk she was running and how dangerous Clay was? Did she have sinister intentions towards the man who so closely resembled her dead lover, the man she had, according to her, *accidentally* killed? After Clay had completed his mission, was she going to get rid of him too?

I was so busy tearing around inside my own head, ranting about the madness of taking Clay with her to do the deed that, too late, I realised she'd been given permission to approach.

And then, like the idiot I was, it suddenly dawned on me.

* * *

Cheryl nodded for Verity to stand. Eleanor started forward. Silently pleading for her daughter's trust, Eleanor prayed Verity saw that, despite all she had done, she was the same:

she cared as much as she did before, more so if possible, and that Verity was very much loved.

She reached out and cupped Verity's exhausted face in her hands. With dismay, she noticed the abrasions and swelling on her daughter's skin. Verity's eyes flooded with tears and Eleanor kissed her girl's hot, wet cheeks. More tears erupted and Verity let out a sob that broke over Eleanor like a cold wave. It reminded her of dark days, nursing Verity back to health from a broken heart. Don was not the only frightening episode in her life. But the fear that presented itself now was different. This was raw and beyond her control. This was about survival.

She firmly drew her daughter close. It was like cradling a tiny injured bird; Verity's ribs were plainly defined, her shoulders seemingly narrower, her collarbone more pronounced. Burying her face into Verity's neck, she did not smell the dirt and sweat of captivity. Verity smelled as sweet to her as a newborn. She whispered three words in her daughter's ear, felt her respond with a squeeze and knew the message had been received and understood.

'Very moving,' Cheryl said tartly.

Clay reached out and pinched Verity's arm at the elbow. Torn away, Verity let out a yell and a curse. Her small hands slapped and slapped and slapped again. It took everything Eleanor had not to growl and attack the man, who was to accompany her on her journey. *Like uncle, like nephew*, she thought darkly.

'Best get moving,' Cheryl declared. She turned to Clay. 'Report to me in twenty-four hours.' Clay grunted assent.

'And then you'll let my daughter go.' Eleanor did not ask. She stated it as fact.

'You have my word,' Cheryl said through half-closed eyes. *And your words are cheap*, Eleanor thought.

There was much scraping of chairs and Eleanor cast Verity one last look.

'Before you leave, *Eleonora*.' Cheryl spoke with deliberation. 'We know where your son and his family live. Fred and Kitty are so sweet.'

Inside, Eleanor's blood ran cold. Outside, she refused to rise to it. If she got things right, by the time Cheryl thought of pulling a stunt like that it would be too late for her to do a damn thing.

If . . .

'I'll take the van,' Clay told Clint. 'You and Chuck can pick it up from outside the hall later.'

'I get to drive the Jag?' Chuck's face split into a wide grin. *You'd think he'd had a big win at a casino,* Eleanor thought.

'Make sure you put her away first.' Clay jerked his chin in Verity's direction. 'And don't forget to stow the hay before you leave. Wind's blowing up.'

Waiting patiently, Eleanor watched Clay slip a leather jacket from off a hook, pull out his phone and punch in a number, the message cryptic and indecipherable to her ears: 'You in? Got a piece? See you.' The call ended and Eleanor felt his rough hands upon her. Memories swirled inside her mind. Unable to help herself, resisting the urge to lash out, she shook him off.

'You little . . .'

'Oi,' Cheryl warned. 'Mind you behave yourself.'

Pleased to see that the admonishment was not for her, but for him, Eleanor appreciated that Cheryl was guarding her investment. No point killing the golden goose before the egg was laid.

Clay grumbling behind her, Eleanor stepped outside. Before they reached the van, a hand clamped around the top of her bare arm. His eyes locked onto hers. 'Don't think you can play me. From now on it's my rules. You do as I say, you hear me?'

Eleanor glanced up at the sky. It was black and threatening and she heard the rumble of distant thunder.

'Of course,' she said, impassive. 'You're the man.'

CHAPTER FORTY-FOUR

Go for broke, Mum said.

I stopped snivelling and wiped my eyes with the hem of my T-shirt. There'd be time for tears later.

The whole "out to get Yuill" scenario was a clever ruse designed to get Clay out of the way. Mum had improved my odds of escape immeasurably. Once the boys left to collect the van, it would be me against Cheryl and Yootha — and a shotgun.

Carted back to the barn, I listened as the van started up and bumped down the drive. At the prospect of money in their pockets, Chuck and Clint were in high spirits. Hooting and larking about, they picked up the quad bikes and set off for the fields to lug in the hay like the jolly decent folk they were. *Not.* I was glad of the silence.

I had to hand it to Mum: she had me fooled about wanting Yuill dead. I was surprised Cheryl fell for it. Clinging to the idea that Mum was a stone-cold killer made it harder to think that she wasn't, I supposed. That was as far as I'd got with working it out. The big loose end: how could Mum sustain the lie with Clay breathing venom down her neck? She was in the gravest danger. I had to get out of here for me, but I had to get out of there for her, too, and Alex and Dido and the kids. I shut my eyes tight, tried not to think about what Cheryl intended.

Clint and Chuck would spend an hour, maybe more, sorting out the hay. I had zero knowledge of such things, but that's what I banked on. In that time I needed to establish an escape route and be ready to move. As soon as they left to collect the van, I estimated it would take Clint and Chuck around forty minutes to an hour to drive there, pick it up and return. It wasn't a given. I didn't know the exact distance. They might drive like maniacs — Chuck certainly fancied his chances with the Jag. They might stop off for crisps, or booze, or park up and smoke a spliff. Whichever way I looked at it I didn't have long to get out and reach the road.

And then what?

Out in the sticks, miles from civilisation, I could flag down a passing motorist and beg for help. *Look how that turned out last time*, I reminded myself grimly. Putting my faith in a complete stranger was a no-no. Truth was, I was so paranoid I no longer trusted the local population. Not any of them.

The interior path I'd carved to the back of the barn was a well-worn furrow. I quietly cleared the entrance of furniture, dropped down on to my hands and knees and tunnelled through. My nose pressed up tight between the cracks, I peered outside and saw a wheelbarrow with a spade inside, as if someone was about to garden but changed their plans, and then I almost passed out.

Front door open, Cheryl had come out of her cottage and was sitting on a chair in my direct line of sight. *Shit*, I thought. One false move from me, and it would all be over.

I didn't move. Tension in my arms spread to the muscles in my legs. Trapped, my limbs in danger of seizing up, I feared my calves would cramp. Breath seeped out between my cracked lips and even that felt risky. Statue-still, I didn't know for how much longer I could hold the position.

I swivelled my gaze to Yootha's cottage. It seemed very quiet. I hoped she was skinning a rabbit or plucking a chicken, or whatever country people did. Maybe she was having a lie down after an afternoon of revelations.

A huge clap of thunder startled the pair of us. Cheryl leapt up, took one look at the darkening sky, and scurried through the front door.

Grabbing the opportunity, I was seized by an acute attack of pins and needles. Madly flexing my legs, clenching and unclenching, precious seconds ticked by.

Desperate, I gritted my teeth and dug around some more. The earth was hopelessly dense and sticky. A season's worth of humid weather had done nothing to dry it out. I resorted to using my hands, scooping out stubborn slices of clay and scattering the deposits as fast as I could. I don't know how long I kept at it. The air felt heavier and heavier and I could smell rain. Another clap of thunder, this time right overhead. The rafters shuddered.

I pulled and pried at the battens, my fingers a mass of splinters and broken skin and nails. I was like a woman possessed. If I didn't get out of here now, I'd never escape.

Eventually, three of the main battens at the bottom were loose. Prising them apart would give me enough room to wiggle underneath. If it made the difference between liberation and incarceration, I'd scrape the skin off my back to escape, yet one big fat problem remained: should either of the two women step outside or glance through the windows, I'd be totally exposed.

Fat spots of rain began to fall, slowly at first and then at a more frantic pace, bouncing off the tired earth.

The noise of quad bikes signalled Clay and Clint's hurried return from the fields. A crazy idea to steal one to escape was quickly shot down. They were kick-start, like a motorbike. No way could I handle such a beast. Alex would have been okay — not me.

Yootha emerged from her cottage and joined the boys inside Cheryl's. I imagined them sitting around the refectory table, brew on, mugs apiece, shop-bought cakes and biscuits at the ready. They'd be in celebratory mood, toasting their good fortune. Cheryl would be banging on about Mum the murderer, Mum the provider of riches, the meal ticket for life. Yootha would nod, listen and agree and quietly wonder what Mum meant when she'd revealed her old friend's trickery. Hopefully, Yootha would wonder whether her brother, Don, would still be alive and kicking if Cheryl's nasty plan had never been born. I pictured her turning it over in her mind, mithering over it, chewing her up inside as it gnawed and chafed and suspicion drilled into her brain until, finally, when all was still and the immediate drama over, she would demand an explanation from the woman with whom she'd spent, and possibly wasted, her finest years.

I bloody hoped so. I fucking hoped Yootha ate Cheryl alive.

* * *

Eleanor was unceremoniously let out of the back of the van, handed the keys to the Range Rover and ordered to climb into the driver's seat. There was no question of her driving off and leaving Clay on the side of the road or, as stupidly, allowing him to give chase.

She buckled up. He buckled up. A big, brooding, slouching mass of humanity, he was an alarming individual. Not a man of sharp edges, Clay was a man encased in razor wire. Any attempt to reach him and she'd be shredded to bits.

Before she'd started the engine, he told her he needed to make a stop in Hereford.

'I'm not familiar with the city; where exactly?'

'Where I tell you.'

His truculence and hostility sucked the life out of her.

They moved off. There was no conversation. An attempt to play Classic FM, her usual radio station, was met with: 'Turn that fucking racket off.' She obeyed, without complaint.

They travelled in the direction of Moreton-on-Lugg, tracking the river, and then past Pipe and Lyde and the racecourse, before hitting a bank of traffic. Grinding to a halt, snarled up in queues on both sides, Eleanor sat quietly, Clay tense and belligerent beside her.

'Always fucking chaos,' he complained, knee jittering. 'Council's been jawing about it for years and years and still nothing done. How are people supposed to get on with their lives? It's a fucking disgrace. That's what it is.'

Eleanor didn't say a word, still less express opinion or sympathy. She was glad they couldn't move. It gave her more time — and it was of the essence right now.

Very slowly, they edged their way along two lanes that abruptly veered into one. The Range Rover had the advantage of size. Nobody tried to cut them up. If anyone was barging in, it was her.

A learner up ahead and an old Peugeot, all dent and rust, had broken down. It took them over thirty minutes to move a mile. With the patience of a five-year-old, Clay clicked his tongue, wriggled around in his seat, reminding Eleanor of little Fred and Kitty. *Cheryl's threat had better be an empty one*, Eleanor thought bitterly. Eventually, they got going.

'First exit off the roundabout,' Clay informed her. Sitting up straight, he was more alert now. 'Then second exit off the next.'

She followed his instructions meticulously. They were in a street of boxy terraced houses with Sky dishes attached to every surface and yellow and dying grass in the minimal front gardens. There were few trees and those that managed to grow looked sickly.

'Here,' Clay said suddenly. When Eleanor failed to respond because she had a van driver on her tail, Clay struck the dashboard with the flat of his hand and bellowed. 'HERE, you stupid slag.'

Eleanor tugged the wheel down hard. The Range Rover veered and bumped up onto the pavement, amid a flurry of car horns and hand gestures.

'Stay,' Clay said. 'Won't be more than a few minutes.' He rolled the collar of his jacket up against the pouring rain and stepped out.

Eleanor watched him race from the car to a house where a child's bike was propped underneath a dirty picture window. Its grey curtains were drawn tightly across, suggesting they were never opened.

The few minutes turned into fifteen. Eleanor counted every one of them. At last, Clay scurried out, wet hair plastered darkly against his head, one hand inside his jacket. He swung the door open, launched himself into the passenger seat, slammed it shut and withdrew a gun. Awed, Eleanor eyed it as if it was a statement piece in Hazel's new garden room. She was so ignorant she wasn't sure whether it was a revolver or a pistol. She was only thankful it was not pointed at her.

'What? Cat got your tongue?' Clay's smile was wide and taunting. He examined it, did something fancy that made a noise and made her sweat. Leaning forward, he opened the glove compartment and slipped it inside.

Not long now, she thought, her mood as dark as the sky above. When he ordered her to 'fucking get a move on,' she was happy to oblige.

* * *

My heart gave a little jump. Chuck and Clint had emerged from the cottage and were running against sheeting rain, towards the yard and the Jaguar. In they got, the engine started and then they were gone.

Rain on the tin roof rattled like machine gun fire. Noise was good. Noise meant I wouldn't be heard.

The bottom plank was easy. Rotted through, a section of it came away in my hands. I reached for the next one and did the same. A gap opened up through which a gust of wind blew dirt and rain into my face. One more to go, I raised myself up into a squat. Using the same technique, I grabbed the plank from beneath and, sawed it back and forth, leaning every atom of weight into it. It wasn't enough. Yowling with terror inside, I pulled and twisted, my skinned hands absolutely killing, until finally, with a crack, the wood split and I worked it free. The height of the gap was around twelve inches.

Flattened out and telescoping my body, face to the dirt, arms outstretched and fingers of both hands to propel, I used my toes to push forward, and wriggled and wriggled. Out the other side I stood up straight, dazed, and gulped in a lungful of fresh air, giddy with exhilaration.

Another blast of thunder above my head and the lights went on in Cheryl's cottage.

* * *

The only way to put him down and make him stay down was to hit him hard and fast so he never got back up, Eleanor believed. But this was the chic interior of her car, not a forge with blacksmith's instruments to hand and things that bludgeon, cut and burn. The only weapon she had was the one she was driving.

They skirted Ledbury and passed a petrol station and general store at Parkway. They were out on open road with undulating countryside on both sides, and not far from Bromsberrow Heath. Beyond, the M50, a two-lane motorway before it joined the M5 to Cirencester.

Clay insisted on having his window down though the air con was on.

Rain hammered against the windscreen. The surface of the road felt greasy. Visibility was poor and would be even worse on the motorway with lorries and vans kicking up dirt at speed. A fast car, a solid car, she was safer in this than others. Eleanor didn't want to be safe. She wanted danger. She wanted to reach a point of no return.

* * *

And then I froze.

Lights didn't spook me. There was no sign of the crazy bitches. The dogs didn't bark. They whimpered and hid from the coming storm. These weren't the problem.

It was ME.

What if I didn't make it? What if this time they found me and locked me up for good and threw away the key? What if they shot me and buried me in a ditch, disposing of me like Mum's grandfather got rid of Don? And what if everything, and I mean *everything*, I dreamt was true about my mum and all those good and redeeming bits, was a lie? What if I'd come up with a happy ending when there wasn't one to be had? Not ever.

I panted with terror. My soul felt in imminent danger of scarpering from my body, like I was dead already.

Temptation tricked me. So easy to scurry back inside; rearrange the planks, make them look good as new, destroy my tunnel and hide my deceit. I could pile the furniture back up, return to my little bed, my confined if not so cosy make-shift quarters with its stinking bucket and no toothbrush: *my* home. Nobody would ever know. I'd be good. I'd behave. I'd do anything they asked.

Rain belted down hard and fast, plastering my hair to my scalp, and dripped off the end of my nose. My heart did a bumpity-bump inside my chest. Paralysed with fear, I couldn't move forward and couldn't move back.

The sound of raised voices brought me roughly back to my senses. By then, it was way too late.

* * *

Through sheets of rain, Eleanor spied the River Avon, a sign for Evesham and, further on, 'Welcome To Gloucestershire.' Pylons loomed along the motorway. Bridges, ahead, topped with a mesh of steel girders that looked like pick-up-sticks.

The speed limit reduced to fifty miles an hour. Overhead displays warned that tiredness kills. A big yellow sign advised of road works several miles ahead and that essential work would be carried out at night. Motorists dodged and dived, cut each other up, and picked a lane. It was filthy out there. Appalling visibility, lost in a gauzy glow, headlamps made no difference.

Clay was not happy. 'Turn off. Gotta be another route.'

There was no other way, Eleanor thought. She explained this to Clay. 'And put your window up,' she said.

'It stays the fuck down,' he replied. 'That's the way I like it.'

Eleanor muted a sigh and, indicating, pulled into a gap in the outside lane. A man in a rental van drew right up behind her, bumper to bumper.

Clay twisted round. 'What the fuck is his game?'

Buckling under the weight of memory, Eleanor's hands tightened on the steering wheel.

* * *

'It's my game,' Don said.

'Game?' Stunned, Eleanor blinked in incredulity.

He viewed her with disgust, an ugly twist to his mouth. 'Don's Game, you can call it. Build 'em up and knock 'em down, like skittles in a bowling alley.'

Petrified, she started for the door. Burning pain across her back and she screamed out loud. She turned to see a horsewhip flash through the air. The lash caught the side of her face, narrowly missing an eye. Blood and tears trickled down her cheeks, urine down her thighs.

'That will learn you,' Don bellowed, grabbing hold of her by her hair, dragging her backwards.

Dropping the whip, he tore at her dress. Buttons flew. Seams burst. Wild-eyed and deranged, he reached for the lacy knickers he'd gifted her. She heard them rip. His nails gouged her skin. Contorted with lust, his face was in hers. Saliva crawled down the side of his mouth. And, my Christ, she could feel him hard and large against her.

* * *

Clay's voice jolted her back to the present.

'Fuckin' move, will you, dozy cow? We can go.'

Welded to the wheel, she didn't move, unlike her mind, which was nimble.

Clay pressed the button for the window to travel halfway up. She vaguely wondered if this was meant as a concession. Wrong. Clay reached across and slapped her once hard across the side of her face. It stung. It hurt. She didn't flinch.

'I said DRIVE.'

The engine was idling but Eleanor was going nowhere, not until she knew for certain. She turned to Clay. 'Did you touch her?'

'What you on about?'

Car horns blared. The van driver was bumper to bumper, flashing his lights. A glance in the rear-view mirror told Eleanor that the man was about to get out of his van at any moment and issue her with a torrent of verbal abuse. Clay undid his seat belt, twisted round, and threw his arms up in the air. 'Fuck you,' he screamed at the driver.

'I *said* did you touch my daughter?' Her voice was dark and chilling.

Clay smirked. 'What if I did?'

Eleanor pulled hard down on the steering wheel and drove. Bollards scattered. Temporary barriers shattered. Pressing her foot against the accelerator, Eleanor took aim.

* * *

I panted with terror.

Cheryl's cottage door burst open and Yootha, grim-faced, hurried out as best she could, Cheryl, with an ominous expression, flying after her.

'Yootha, come back. It's not what you . . .'

'Fuck off, Cheryl, you're a liar.'

'No, it's . . .'

They turned in tandem, astonishment in their eyes. Nobody moved at first, least of all me. I was weak. I was exhausted. My biggest enemy was my mind, which was intent on sabotage.

Cheryl needed no invitation to redirect her energy. I dropped to the ground, scurrying crab-like, fingers scrabbling for the nearest broken batten, howling with frustration. In a few fast steps Cheryl was upon me and I was flattened.

It should have been no contest. I was thirty years younger and necessarily fitter. But Cheryl was sturdy and well nourished. She was strong and I was not.

Her grip was like a vice around my neck.

'Get off me,' I shrieked. I struggled and wriggled.

'You silly little bitch.' Cheryl raked her horrible nails down my cheek, scratching and tearing skin. Stinging, it made my eyes water. Blood trickled down my face.

Rolling in the rain and dirt, earth went up my nose and into my eyes. My fists felt tiny against a spitting, mauling and rabid aggressor. Red-faced with rage, Cheryl bared her teeth like a feral cat, snarling obscenities, saliva flecking my mouth and chin.

Disturbed by the commotion, the dogs went wild, pulling against their chains, barking and snapping, eager to take a chunk out of human flesh. Out of the corner of my swollen eye, I saw Yootha hobble towards the pen, stick tapping. She was almost there, her hand on the gate.

'Leave the fucking dogs. Fetch the gun,' Cheryl yelled to Yootha who turned around to make the slow and ponderous journey back.

I lashed out and, with a lucky strike, rolled free and struggled dizzily to my feet. It bought me no more than a few seconds. A street fighter, Cheryl jumped up and came at me a second time. More determined, more resentful, she screamed and clawed and when she threw a punch, they landed — hard. A crippling blow to my belly doubled me up. Bile, hot and acid, rose up into the back of my throat and made me heave. All the rage and frustration, she'd nurtured over decades, was aimed at me. One mass of exhausted pain, it was all I could do stay upright. Rain punched the ground. The sky flashed with lightning, yet I could barely see.

Out of nowhere, a swinging blow put me on my back with a tremendous thump that knocked the wind out of me. Panting and victorious, Cheryl stood, slightly bent, hands resting on her thighs, out of breath, surveying her handiwork. I had a vision of her literally putting the boot in and stamping on my head. And I was too shattered to stop her.

Suddenly, Cheryl's phone rang and everything and everyone stopped.

I didn't know who it was, whether it was one of the boys, a crony, or a cold-caller. Out there, in the wet, an ordinary incident morphed into the surreal. Still it rang: incessant and insistent.

'Answer it,' Yootha bellowed. 'Could be Clay.'

Rolling over, I grabbed hold of a batten and held it tight to my body, got into a crouch and stayed crouched. Oblivious, all her focus on the important call, Cheryl fished the mobile out of a pocket, pecked at it, answered with a, 'Sod off,' and switched it off. Job done, she came at me again. This time I was ready.

Pushing up from my heels, putting as much weight and energy behind it, I swung the plank and whacked Cheryl square underneath her chin. A proper upper cut, the force so hard it split the wood and closed her eyes before she'd even hit the ground.

Empty-handed, cold with anger, I had the advantage.

But I still had Yootha to deal with.

* * *

Blood thundered through her ears. Her jaw clamped shut. Could teeth shatter?

Without his seat belt, Clay was like a meteor, or one of those pinballs in a slot machine, travelling at speed and random. He screamed and cursed, arms flailing.

The surface was uneven, greasy and puddled with water. Eleanor drove hard and fast, in a zigzag, throwing Clay against the windscreen, back against the seat, up against the head lining. His blind and desperate attempt to grab the steering wheel met with failure; she was driving too erratically and too fast. The sheer velocity of the moving vehicle defeated him. For a man used to control this was as uncontrolled as it got.

A sixth sense informed her that all traffic had stopped and open-mouthed motorists, rubberneckers, gawped. She thought she heard sirens in the distance. Please God; don't let any maintenance crew be on site. The sign said overnight work so Eleanor simply had to trust it was true. At top speed, she passed a road planer, a road roller and an asphalt-filling machine, big chunky beasts that could do serious damage. These were not her destination.

A tremendous thud, the suspension gave and the vehicle skidded and fishtailed. Clay let out a scream of pure terror. *Burst tyre*, Eleanor thought coldly, straining to keep control. She swore she could smell hot tar, although this was pure imagination. What was not fictitious: the smell of fresh urine, and this time it wasn't hers.

The bridge came upon them like an iceberg breaking free. Encased in scaffolding, it was undergoing repairs. A mesh of grey steel formed a barrier running along the approach on the passenger side. The way ahead narrowed and a network of iron poles loomed overhead.

Then everything slowed. The door to the glove compartment was open. Clay grinned. He yelled something that she could not make out. It was just him and her in a killing machine. The gun was in his shaking hand. He could not hold it steady. She realised he was aiming for her head, but any part of her would do.

She pulled down hard to the left. The bang was explosive, all consuming, and her hands came free of the steering wheel. Her body jolted against the seat belt. Shattering glass and grinding metal, the impact made a terrible sound. The space in which she sat closed in like a fist fast, and shrinking. *Airbags going off*, she realised.

She smelt hot steel and petrol and she smelt blood. She thought it was hers. The gun, she remembered. Clay had shot her. Everything hurt. She didn't know which part pained her most.

Turning her head was agony. Through fading visions, she saw Clay slumped, a pole impaled in his body. His lips were white and they moved but no words emerged.

It is done, Eleanor thought, closing her eyes. Back on that lonely road, the same one she'd travelled for a lifetime, Eleanor fled, lost in a world of pain.

CHAPTER FORTY-FIVE

Cheryl was down, unconscious for now, not out. Yootha was nowhere to be seen. I had the edge on the woman, in terms of mobility and age. Up against a weapon that blows holes in you, the odds were stacked in her favour. And double-barrelled shotguns didn't jam.

I tore towards the wheelbarrow, grabbed hold of the shovel and held it, like a shield maiden, in both hands. Plastering my back against the wall outside Yootha's cottage, I waited.

Every atom of my body throbbed with adrenalin. My palms were greasy and my arms and legs had the shakes. I felt out of my body, as if I were looking down on someone else with sweat running down her face, blood mingling with the falling rain.

Tap-tap, I heard. *Tap-tap.*

Like a forwarding party, the barrel emerged first at an angle; next, the walking stick, Yootha last. I held my breath and watched as she rested the walking stick against the balustrade.

Craning her head, ratcheting the shotgun from a broken position to operational, she muttered, 'Where's that blasted girl?'

With one hefty swipe, I showed her.

* * *

'Can you hear me, love?'

A mask was removed from her face. Eleanor's eyes fluttered open. She didn't know where she was. She thought she was in a big van. Oh God, that couldn't be right. There was a strong odour of what she believed was surgical spirit. Might be wrong. Nothing seemed the way it was supposed to.

On her back, surrounded by equipment, a man with a kind face hovered over her.

'What's your name?' he asked.

This was a good question. Am I Eleanor Finch, Eleonora Kaminska, Bliss Hannaford or who? They were all jumbled together in her head. *She's a mother*, she thought. *She's a widow*, she remembered.

'I'm a murderer,' she said.

'Must be the shock,' she heard a female voice say. 'You've been in an accident.'

'Is he dead?' Eleanor asked. It's really important he was.

'You're not to worry,' the kind man said. But Eleanor was worried. She was very worried.

'My daughter, Verity. You have to find her.'

Eleanor spotted a silent, anxious exchange. The woman spoke quickly.

'Was Verity in the car? Was there another passenger?'

'She's at the farm. She's in great danger. They have her, you see. They will kill her.' Agitated, Eleanor gripped the arm of the kind man. 'You have to reach her. You have to stop them. *Please, please.*'

* * *

The gun went off, scything the stormy air in two, and clattered to the deck. I pounced, swept it up and pointed it at Yootha. The stock bit into my shoulder and it was a lot heavier than expected.

Yootha squawked with rage. 'You won't get away with this. I've already phoned the boys.'

I should have run there and then. I couldn't take the risk. Not with those damn dogs whining and going wild. The second I was off she'd let them out.

'Move,' I said.

'You won't shoot me.'

'Want to bet?' I lowered it to her stomach. 'I've heard gut wounds are particularly nasty.' I gave her a hearty shove with the barrel. 'Inside,' I said. It felt good to give a taster of what she'd dished out. Better still to see the dread in her leathery face.

She backed away slowly and crossed the threshold.

'Walk to the dresser,' I said.

Following her inside, I toed the door closed and noticed, that, like Cheryl, Yootha left the key in the lock. A big chunky thing, I pulled it out, went outside, shut the door and locked her in. Stalking towards the pond, I hurled the shotgun into the thick pea-green slime, where it sank, and ran for it.

Crossing the yard, I sped over the cattle grid, feet pounding in my sodden canvas shoes. The drive was steep and a train wreck of puddles, some deep, some shallow, all of them capable of turning my ankle. It took energy and effort to dodge them.

Rain skinned my cheeks. My eyes strained to see. Coiled with fear, I tore down a bumpy track flanked by high hedges and rusting gates. In adjoining farmland, miserable-looking sheep huddled underneath trees for shelter. Abandoned machinery, old tractor tyres and piles of old bricks littered the verge. Castrey country, I thought. They left their grubby imprint everywhere.

I couldn't tell how long before Yootha struggled out of the back door, hobbled to the yard and let the dogs out, or Cheryl surfaced and found a way to hunt me down, or Clint and Chuck returned.

'I've already phoned the boys.'

My chest hurt and my stomach shrank at the thought of imminent capture.

But . . .

Fear could paralyse; fear could induce anger; fear could make you brave and drive a person to unimaginable lengths. I was bloody angry, seized with cold fury, murderous. Legs and arms pumping, my gaze locked onto the winding, undulating drive, searching for signs of a vehicle's headlights, yellow in the driving rain. I listened hard to the sound of an engine note up ahead, the noise of dogs snapping at my heels from behind.

Sheet lightning lit up the sky. It flashed again as I rounded a corner. The air was alive with electricity, sound and motion. I didn't know how far I'd run or how much further I had to go. The dirt track gave way to tarmac, indicating it was someone else's patch. The Castreys would never spend money when they didn't have to. This was good. This meant I was near the road.

Run, run, run, as if your life depended upon it — and I did.

At last, I heard traffic, faint at first, punctuated by the roar of a motorbike flying past; a little later, a whoosh of cars battling through the wind and rain; something heavier, next, a big lorry trundling along, transporting animals or fruit and veg.

The main road had to be close. One more corner, one more . . .

Beams of lights bounced off the hedges, heading my way. I ducked down, threw myself into a ditch and landed with a splash in inches of cold filthy water. Lifting my chin, water dripping down my neck, I could hear more clearly now. Not one, but two vehicles, travelling at speed.

And they were bearing down and closing in.

A blast of country and western and a flash of grimy white and the van streaked past. I pictured Clint, sharp chinned, a single piece of straw sticking out of his mouth, crouched over the wheels like a rally driver. I waited for the second vehicle, the Jag. As soon as it swept past, I was going to be up and out of my watery refuge.

Moving smoothly, the Jag approached and then it stopped beside me.

So close, I thought my heart would seize up. A single glance in the wrong direction and I'd be seen. One false move and I'd meet Chuck's gormless gaze. I willed him away.

Go away, you bastard, clear off.

Engine idling, the door opened.

He's seen me.

I ducked lower, sank my chin into the ditch, dirty water up to my nostrils. Shutting my eyes tight I pictured Chuck's thick-lidded eyes scouring the countryside.

Please don't see me. Please don't see me.

Lumbering footsteps came to a halt.

'Verity.' His voice was syrup smooth, as if he were calling a cat to come in for the night. 'It's all right. I won't hurt you.'

More footsteps, further away, and more creepy calling; more false promises.

Before I lost my bottle, I shot up out of the ditch, threw myself into the driver's seat and slammed the door shut.

Hair wet, turning his blonde to brown, Chuck turned around with the speed of an oil tanker, jaw slack, mind slow with confusion. Except he suddenly moved with more speed than I thought possible.

Fuck, fuck, fuck, my eyes fled over the dashboard. Where the hell was everything? It was as if I'd gone blind. Then I remembered Clay, how he'd imprisoned me. Underneath a screen, a panel set into wood. I thumped the first switch marked with the right symbol and the doors magically locked. I turned and stared into Chuck's angry face, his nose twisted, pressed up against the window, hot stinking breath on the glass.

'Open it, you fucking cow. Let me in. Open it NOW.' When I didn't he beat both fists against the driver window and tugged at the door.

Pedals, I thought, *two of them.* I'd never driven an automatic before. With the lack of clarity of a nervous learner driver, I glanced over my shoulder. I'd need to reverse. Shit, I'd always been terrible at it.

Chuck, meanwhile, had given up on trying to punch his way in and was engaged in animated conversation on his phone. Only a matter of time before Clint arrived with a sledgehammer.

Frantic, I belted up, searched the dashboard and central console. Might as well have been the cockpit for a Fighter Jet. A central dial, with letters, including "R" offered a clue. Seemed logical to me. It would even make sense to one of my primary school children.

Sticking my left foot down on what I guessed was the brake, I moved the dial to the 'R' position, gingerly took my foot off the pedal, touched the accelerator and I was in motion. 'Use all three mirrors,' my driving instructor had told me. 'Slow and controlled and don't push the gas.' Works brilliantly under normal circumstances, not when you're trying to escape maniacs.

I put my foot down a bit. The car shot backwards. *Fuck, the ditch*, I thought, *how far did it run?* Steering madly, and bouncing off a beech hedge, I discovered not very far at all.

Left and right, right and left. I was doing okay, making progress. Tyres spitting dust and gravel, I wasn't under steering or over steering. Muscles in my neck and shoulders juddered with strain and my eyes felt pickled with concentration. I needed to speed up. I need to . . .

A tremendous bump and I'd hit a fence post. I tried to knock it down and found I couldn't. Swallowing hard, I shifted the dial to "D" for Drive and glanced up to see Chuck striding towards me. I jerked forward. He kept on coming, smacked the driver's side window as he passed and disappeared.

Gripped by a wave of nausea, I put the Jag back into reverse; swerved a bend and belted around the next. The sight of the road nearly did me in. *Straight*, I thought, *keep it straight. Don't pull out and hit someone. Not now.*

Suddenly Chuck was behind me, standing like a sealed door at the entrance to a crypt.

'Check side to side and make sure you're free of obstacles, especially pedestrians,' my driving instructor always told me. Chuck wasn't a pedestrian. He was a kidnapper.

No hesitation, I closed my eyes tight, stuck my foot down, expecting to hear a massive bump. Reversing out of the entrance at speed, I caught sight of him sprawled, part of him in the hedge into which he'd dived, part of him eating dirt on the road.

I shifted the dial, found the hazard warning light, stuck it on and drove.

Cold and shock got to me. Teeth chattering, I didn't know how to put on the heating and wouldn't have stopped to find out if someone had paid me.

But I was free. I could go home. Whatever that meant.

CHAPTER FORTY-SIX

I could have covered the lovely policewoman in kisses.

The drive remained a blur of noise and grind and mayhem. I wasn't in my right mind and the weather conditions were atrocious.

The goal had been to get as far away as possible and I hadn't cared in which direction I travelled, how many corners I hurtled around on the wrong side of the road, how many cyclists I swerved or motorists I seriously pissed off. Against the frenetic pace of windscreen wipers going full tilt, the car had made warning noises like a submarine picking up on a torpedo strike. All sorts of switches lit up. Weirdly I'd stressed about running out of petrol. This seemed more important to me than was logical, considering the trail of motoring carnage I'd left in my wake. I was sure I'd run a red light, possibly several. It was a miracle I hadn't killed anyone.

Out on open road, I'd become aware of sirens and blue lights flashing, other motorists pulling up on verges and into passing paces. Me, I'd kept damn well going, foot down, red mist in my brain telling me to watch out for roadblocks, and stingers thrown across the road. I'd felt more like an escaping bank robber than a woman in jeopardy. Ignoring all attempts to slow me down, I'd finished up shooting across a junction, the car careering towards a roundabout. Hitting the kerb it sort of launched itself, all four wheels in the air, and had landed with a kerplunk. Dazed, I'd looked out to see smoke coming out of the bonnet and a sign promoting an antiques sale.

A policewoman in uniform had run towards me waving her arms and calling my name. That was when I knew, for certain I was safe. That's when I broke down. I clung to the poor police officer like a distressed three-year-old.

'Don't leave me, please don't leave me.' And she'd stroked my hair and hadn't seemed to mind my snotty nose leaving slime trails all over her uniform.

Eventually, I'd been wrapped in what looked and felt like tin foil, put in an ambulance and blue-lit all the way to the hospital. Examined by a doctor, wounds washed and dressed, given my first hot drink in days, I'd been put to bed in my own room where I pretty much conked out. Waking up was the horrible bit. I'd believed I was still there in that squalid barn, until I saw Alex's troubled expression and then his smile beaming down on me. Dido was sweetly holding my hand.

'Am I dead?' I asked.

'Verity, you're very much alive,' Alex replied warmly.

'Mum. How is she?'

Alex looked to Dido to answer. 'She's okay. Banged up, but she'll live.'

Relief seeped out between my lips. 'The man with her?'

'He didn't make it.' Dido's voice was sombre.

I'd like to say I felt something. Drained, I think I'd run out of emotions. 'Won't be needing his car then,' I muttered.

Dido's eyes popped with shock. Maybe she thought me heartless. 'Police said you were abducted. What happened exactly?'

I closed my eyes. How to encapsulate all that had been said and done? I loved Alex more than ever when he came to my rescue.

'Verity, you don't have to do this now.'

'She does,' Dido said. 'The police need to talk to her.'
'Are they outside?' I asked.
'In the waiting area,' Alex replied.
'Better get it over with,' I said.

CHAPTER FORTY-SEVEN

Eleanor sleepily watched the door. Her pelvis was fractured, now pinned; her right arm was broken, now set. Nurses came and went, took bloods, measured blood pressure and her fluid intake, administered pain relief and monitored her vital signs. She liked the soothing, steady beep of the heart monitor next to her. Doctors were solicitous, if a little wary.

But Verity was safe and that was all that mattered.

Eleanor remembered very little of what she'd said to the kind man, the paramedic. She'd spoken in sound bites: Castrey . . . farm . . . Herefordshire . . . Birch. It was enough because police urgently responded and found her daughter on open road, near Ross-on-Wye, in a stolen car. Taken to hospital, sadly, not Eleanor's, Verity was kept in overnight. Alex called to say that she was better than expected and had spoken to the police at length.

And now the police were going to speak to her. She wondered what that would be like. She was not a woman who would be humiliated by loss of standing in the community. Her fear was for how she would navigate her relationships with her children after what they discovered. The guilt and shame would no longer be hers alone and, if they abandoned her, and she could not fault them if they did, she would wither up and die.

A double tap at the door and it opened. A man and woman slipped inside. They were in plain clothes and looked official. Detectives, Eleanor intuited.

'Mrs Finch,' the man said.

Eleanor slipped a hand out of bed and pressed it down against the cool sheets, to ease her body more upright. In spite of pain-reducing drugs, every nerve ending reminded her flesh it bore wounds; a dull ache, deep in her bones, that they were broken and a long way from healing.

The man was tall, slim and had sharp hazel-coloured eyes. His sandy-coloured hair was thinning and receding, revealing a high forehead. Clean-shaven, he had a narrow nose and large jaw. He exuded dependency and trust. The woman, reaching for a chair, looked younger, same age as Verity, Eleanor estimated. Her hair was dark, shoulder-length and wavy, her face lightly tanned and there were laughter lines around her brown eyes. Eleanor concluded she was a happy individual, a good soul.

'I'm DCI Christian Rhodes and this is DI Andrea Warne. How are you feeling, Mrs Finch?'

The question took her by surprise. Obviously, she was not very well. This was not his reason for asking. *He wanted to gain her trust,* she thought — an uphill struggle.

'Not great,' she replied with a small smile.

'You've picked up some very nasty injuries,' Warne observed. She had a hint of a northern accent, short as when she spoke. 'Okay to call you Eleanor?'

Eleanor assured her that this was perfectly fine. It was a long time since she'd strung those two words together in the same sentence. Things had not been *perfectly fine* for most of her life.

'As you know, we picked up your daughter,' Warne said. 'She's doing remarkably well after what was a terrible ordeal.'

Eleanor liked to think Verity had inherited her survival gene. She hoped that this was all she'd bequeathed to her daughter.

'Verity was able to tell us a lot about what's been going on,' Rhodes said. 'And confirmed a number of details.'

'But now we want to hear your side of the story,' Warne said warmly.

The side of a story in which my daughter was abducted and held for ransom, or the side of the story in which I murdered a man, Eleanor wondered, *and possibly killed another.*

Warne appeared to spot her hesitation. 'Tell us about the lead-up to the accident.'

Accident was good, Eleanor thought. Accident suggested it wasn't her fault when she knew very well it was.

She stuck to the present and talked. She described the abduction of her daughter, the demand for money, and the threat if she didn't comply. She named all those involved, the players, as she thought of them, and took a complicated diversion into Michael Yuill aka Roger Scott-Jefferies. She admitted to her stupid infatuation and detailed the way he conned her out of a lot of money and, in doing so, opened the equivalent of Pandora's box and exposed her to Cheryl Castrey and Yootha Birch. She finished abruptly, out of breath, and was ashamed that her story had come out in an undignified mess. She wished she had done better by her daughter.

'You knew Cheryl Castrey well, is that right?' Rhodes enquired.

'A long time ago. We were friends, as children,' Eleanor added.

'What happened?'

'We fell out.'

'Must have been quite some row to last nearly fifty years,' Rhodes commented.

'Have you arrested her for the abduction of my daughter?' Eleanor asked.

'Castrey and her sons and Yootha Birch have been taken in for questioning.'

'What was Clay Birch doing in your car?' Warne asked.

'He wanted to ensure that I got the ransom money.'

'He threatened you specifically?'

Eleanor blinked. 'Yes.'

'Are you aware a firearm was found in your vehicle?'

'It belongs to Clay Birch.'

'You're sure it's not yours?'

Eleanor's eyes widened. 'Of course it isn't. I've never used a firearm in my life. Why don't you ask Birch?'

'We can't, Eleanor,' Warne explained. 'He died shortly after he arrived at hospital.'

Eleanor was pleased on one level and consumed by panic on another. *Arrest me for what I did, not for what I haven't done.* 'I can tell you exactly where he procured the gun,' she said urgently.

'That would be very helpful. Are you all right, Eleanor? Do you need a drink?'

'Thank you, yes.'

Warne handed her the plastic glass of water sitting on the bedside table. Eleanor drank deep and long.

'Better,' she said.

'The gun,' Rhodes reminded her.

Eleanor described the boxy terraced property in Hereford. She recalled the number on the door. She mentioned the state of the garden and the child's bike outside.

'You don't know who lives there?'

'I don't, I'm afraid.'

'And you've never handled a firearm?' Rhodes persisted.

Eleanor dry-swallowed. She felt the ground shifting beneath her. Never,' she confirmed.

'So what happened exactly in the car?'

'There were roadworks. We got held up. Lanes were gridlocked.'

'How did you wind up in the maintenance area?'

'Clay got angry and frustrated and wanted me to find another route.'

Rhodes frowned. 'You thought you could find a way out by driving through roadworks?' His tone was incredulous.

'No.'

'So?' He raised an eyebrow.

'When I didn't comply he got nasty and pulled the gun. I suppose I panicked,' she said, remembering how cold and calculating she felt. 'With nowhere to go, I crossed into the maintenance area and put my foot down. I wasn't thinking straight. I just wanted him to stop shouting at me and waving a gun in my face.'

'Do you remember what you said in the ambulance, Eleanor?' It's Rhodes speaking.

'A little.'

'What was the reason for Castrey's grudge?' Warne slid the question into the conversation. It's like a piece of bamboo driven beneath a fingernail.

'It's a long story.' And she was so weary.

'Can you start at the beginning, Eleanor?'

'For that, I'll need to take you back to 1976.'

'To when Don Birch went missing?' Rhodes said with a penetrating stare.

'To when I killed him.'

Rhodes stiffened and looked at Warne.

'We can't do this here, Eleanor.'

'Why not?' She wanted to talk. She *needed* to talk.

'For procedural reasons, Eleanor. As soon as you're fit enough, we'll need you to come to the police station for a formal interview.'

'But that might not be for several days.' She had to get it over with now.

Warne patted her hand. 'Best you fully recover first.'

'Am I under arrest?'

On suspicion of murder, they confirmed she was.

CHAPTER FORTY-EIGHT

I watched my mother sleeping.

Pale as the pillow on which her head rested, her face was a tapestry of cuts and bruises. Quite a bit of her body was broken. I wondered how much of her spirit was broken, too.

She stirred, eyelashes fluttering.

'Mum,' I said softly.

At the sound of my voice, and with the biggest smile, she opened her eyes. 'You came.'

I rested my hand on hers. 'Wouldn't have missed it for the world.'

We stayed like that for a little bit.

'How are you?'

'I'm good.'

'Are you sure?'

'Well, you know. Getting there.'

She held my gaze for a moment, the way she used to when I lied about not smoking.

'You're still at Alex's?' she asked.

'Yes, he drove me here today.'

'He's being a very dutiful son and brother.'

'Crisis obviously brings out the best in him,' I said with a grin.

'Yes,' she agreed. Suddenly, her smile lost its shine. 'Mum . . .'

'Verity, I'm under arrest.'

'I know.'

'I can't talk about the past. Not yet, but I will.'

'I know that too.'

'As soon as I'm well enough, I've agreed to go to the police and answer any questions.'

'That wasn't what I wanted to ask,' I said. 'All that stuff about Yuill putting the squeeze on you wasn't true, was it?'

She flashed a weary smile. 'Yuill is probably lining up his next victim on the other side of the world.'

'It was a ruse to get Clay away, wasn't it?'

She squeezed my hand. 'Verity, did he hurt you? I mean, did he, you know . . . He said . . .'

I saw tremendous pain in her eyes. 'He said what, the bastard, that he raped me? He didn't.'

'Thank God,' she whispered. And then I understood the present but I also understood the past.

CHAPTER FORTY-NINE

A week after the operation, Eleanor was released from hospital. Alex wheeled her from the entrance and helped her into the car. It was a Volkswagen Caddy, hired especially for the occasion to accommodate the wheelchair. Alex talked at ninety miles an hour. He asked how she was to which she responded that she was feeling better. Seemingly satisfied, he switched the conversation to Verity.

'We're concerned about her, Mum. Outwardly, she's brave and says she's doing all right but, boy, is she snappy. Bit my head off the other day for putting too much milk in her tea.'

'To be expected,' Eleanor said. 'She's been through a terrifying experience.'

'And you, Mum, how are you — really?'

Eleanor let out a deep sigh. Alex was convinced she'd had a brainstorm. Dido had suggested she went for tests for Alzheimer's. They could not and would not believe that she was guilty of the crime to which she'd confessed and for which she must now give an account of herself.

Alex didn't drive her home. His instruction was to take her to Hindlip, a central police station in Worcestershire. At their arrival, Rhodes and Warne stepped out to meet them.

It was a grand day, high cloud, warm sun, not too hot. Alex shook hands with both police officers, pecked Eleanor on the cheek and promised to see her later. She didn't have the heart to tell him that his services would not be required, that after what she said, she would be charged. To her anxious mind, this was a very real possibility.

Wheeled inside, the police ran through preliminaries. She was informed of her rights and asked to sign a custody record to signify whether or not she wanted legal advice. Eleanor declined.

'It's free,' a custody sergeant informed her.

Eleanor didn't want anyone to hear what she had to say, other than Rhodes and Warne. She signed a document to that effect. Asked if she were fit enough to interview, she assured them she was. They took her into a room where a recorder was switched on, the date and time logged and the identities of those present.

'You remember why you're here?' Warne asked gently. *She had a sympathetic face*, Eleanor thought. Perhaps they are not used to elderly murderesses.

'About Don Birch, yes. Where do you want me to start?'

'From the beginning would be good.'

* * *

'Say it again slowly,' Rinelle said.

'Which bit exactly?' It came out sharp. I'd mysteriously developed a short fuse — not me at all. Fortunately, it never set light around Fred and Kitty.

Alex and Dido had considerately taken the children out to Cotswold Water Park so that I could speak to my friends alone. For once, Nicola's shady activities took second place, not that we could talk about it anyway.

I was in my PJs, sipping iced coffee. Rinelle had brought biscuits and cake. Apparently, I needed fattening up. To be fair, I'd lost more weight since my release than during captivity. Effective it might be, but I wouldn't recommend kidnap as a diet plan to anyone. *At least*, I thought, *my sense of humour, if a little dark, remained intact.*

We lounged outside on deckchairs, the air fresher after the storm. Everything felt clean and lovely, mainly because I spent preposterous lengths of time in the bathroom. Nicola had sweetly brought me a Neal's Yard gift set to add to my ballooning collection of smellies. Can you become addicted to shower gel?

'How do things stand now?' Nicola said, heading off Rinelle's tussle to take it all in.

'The Castreys and Yootha Birch have been charged with kidnap, false imprisonment and extortion. Castrey's sons are feeling additional heat from an investigation into drugs offences.' I'd really enjoyed telling the police about their little druggy side hustle with Spike. No doubt he'd be getting a visit too.

'Right pair of Chuckle Brothers,' Rinelle said. 'How long will they all get?'

'Not long enough,' I said stonily.

Rinelle passed me a wedge of carrot cake. I eyed it as if it were doused in arsenic.

'Have you talked to your mum since her arrest?' Nicola asked.

'*Arrest?* Holy crap,' Rinelle burst out.

'She hasn't been charged,' Nicola said. 'The threshold for charging is the realistic possibility of conviction, just short of reasonable doubt.'

'How do you know all this stuff?' Rinelle asked, genuinely impressed.

'A healthy interest in crime comes with the job description.'

'So you're saying Mrs Finch might get off?'

'No, I'm saying, after all this time, it's difficult and it depends.' While Rinelle pondered that one, Nicola repeated her question to me.

I answered quietly that we'd talked in hospital. I didn't tell them about Mum's belief that Clay had raped me. It would horrify any mother, but with my mum it was on a whole different level. That's when I thought I knew about Don Birch, what he did to her, why she killed him.

'Did she *really* kill that man?' Rinelle's knuckles pressed against her lips.

'She says so,' I replied, non-committal. 'Seems resigned, strangely accepting of the police investigation.'

'Police will need evidence to prove it,' Nicola said. 'And that's going to be difficult after all this time. Brains decompose and memories fade.'

'Fuck's sake, Nicola.' Rinelle's mouth was full of cake.

'Nicola's right,' I said. 'Police are still corroborating information.'

'And if she did and they prove it, what then?'

I didn't answer.

'I mean,' Rinelle said, dropping her voice. 'If she hadn't done what she did, you wouldn't have been picked off that country lane and held prisoner. Aren't you furious with her?'

I couldn't argue the point. 'She's still my mum,' I said. 'And she had her reasons.'

* * *

Eleanor's voice was hoarse from speaking. She'd recounted her early life with her mum and dad. She spoke of living with her grandparents and of the terrible time when her father disappeared and her mother overdosed, the connections to her biological past severed. She expressed sorrow over her grandmother's death and how it threw her home life, already disrupted, into turmoil. She confessed to being unruly, a delinquent and a truant. She revealed the truth about the Stone House and what went on there. This elicited questions and she got the strong impression that her answers might contribute to a more general enquiry into historic abuses. Good.

She told Rhodes, with his serious face, and Warne, with her sad face, about Cheryl Castrey, about Don Birch and relationships formed and shattered. She told them, truthfully, that she had loved him.

'Did he know you were underage?' Warne asked.

'I assume so.'

'So he was like the rest of the men who visited?'

'Not to me. He wasn't like them at all.' Not in the beginning.

She reached for a plastic mug and drank water that tasted bitter.

'When you were at the forge with Don that night, you said he told you it was over and he tried to rape you. Is that right, Eleanor?'

Eleanor looked blindly at Christian Rhodes and then at Andrea Warne.

'Do you remember?' Rhodes asked.

Her stomach tightened. She felt a twist of fear inside. Oh my God, she remembered. It all came screeching back.

* * *

She was practically naked.

Screaming and struggling, she bared her teeth. The blows she landed made no impact. He was one seething mass of darkness and her pathetic attempts to protect herself seemed to add to his pleasure. She didn't doubt that when he'd raped her, he would kill her too.

'You stupid little mare.' He felled her with a single blow to her stomach that doubled her over and drew bile. A kick to her ribs sent her flying into the dirt. Wriggling away, belly down, arms flailing, straw in her nose, tiles grazing her knees. 'You really think you mattered to us?' he bellowed. Strong, too strong, he caught hold of her, swept her up, forced her back against the brick wall, his intention plain.

Hard and fast, she swung her arms up and, with straight fingers, dug her nails into his eyes. With a howl of pain, his hands shot to his face and he staggered backwards.

'I'll fucking kill you, you witch.'

Frantic, she swept a chisel from a workbench, swung it from side to side, eyes reaching for the exit. Lust and murder in his eyes, he positioned his body in front of the door, came at her again. One jab, and she'd sliced through his thin shirt, the edge of the chisel drawing blood. Raging, Don glanced down as if in amazement, then, fast as lightning, struck out and swiped the chisel out of her hand. It flew against something hard and heavy with a dull thud. Still, he kept on coming and she was bleeding.

Eleanor had one thought: if she didn't put him down and make him stay the fuck down, she was finished.

Bunching her hands into fists, she struck him again, harder this time. He rocked, lost his footing and toppled over.

There was a sickening crunch as the back of his head glanced off an anvil. Blood spooled from the wound onto the dirt. Blood dripped from the cuts to his chest. And he lay very, very still and she knew that he was dead.

* * *

'Eleanor, Eleanor, are you okay?'

She stared, open-mouthed. They stopped the interview.

'Let's take a break,' Rhodes said. 'Are you sure you don't want a solicitor?'

'No,' Eleanor whispered.

Half an hour later, they resumed.

Eleanor gave a faithful and honest account of Don's final moments. No detail was spared. After all these years it was the first time she had full recollection, the first time she had told anyone the whole truth. When she finished she was panting for breath. More water was administered.

'You were sure he was dead?' Rhodes had a habit of stroking his jaw when he concentrated, she noticed.

'There was a lot of blood. He was very still.'

'Did you check his pulse, look for signs of him breathing?'

'I was fifteen. I was terrified.'

'So you ran?' Warne said.

Like the wind, like a tornado, like a hurricane. 'I dressed as best I could and hitched a lift with a lorry driver on his way to Wales.'

'Do you have his name?'

'Rhys, that's all I know.'

'What kind of lorry?'

Eleanor shrugged. She really didn't remember.

'Did you have bloodstains on your clothes?'

'Yes, but it was dark.'

'Then what?' Rhodes nodded for her to continue.

'The driver dropped me off outside Ludlow. I was scared stiff because of what I'd done and what the people at the Stone House would do if they found me. There are dead babies in the grounds,' she said, her voice cracking. She reached for the water again and took a shaky sip. 'I walked a mile or so in the dark, no streetlights,' she explained. 'My grandfather was in bed and I didn't want to wake the street, so I threw a stone at his window. He was slow to wake and I had to do it several times. Eventually, he came down, let me in and I told him what I'd done.'

The horror on the old man's face was awful. Eleanor recoiled at the memory, which was etched on her psyche, along with so many other vile memories.

'You're doing very well, Eleanor.' Warne's brown eyes shone with encouragement. Of Rhodes, Eleanor was less sure. He spoke only when it was strictly necessary; she could not read him.

'Grandpa agreed to go to the forge. He said he would take care of it.'

'By *it*, you mean Don's body,' Rhodes said.

'Yes.'

'And as far as you know that's what he did.'

'Yes.'

'Did he say where he disposed of Don?'

'No. He never breathed a word.'

'But he knew Percy Farrington?'

'He did.'

'Are you surprised where Don was buried?'

'Not really; it makes sense.'

'How did he transport Don?'

'I presumed in the van.'

'Belonging to your grandfather?'

302

'Yes.'

'What sort of van?'

'Pale blue. I think it was a Citroen. It had one of those typical grills with arrow darts at the front.'

'Anything else you remember about it?'

'It had a beige interior.'

'Did he discuss what occurred at the forge?'

'How do you mean?'

'Well, when he got back did he speak about his reaction to seeing Don? Did he have difficulty loading the body? Your grandfather was an old man and Don, according to our enquiries, was a big, strapping fellow, and dead men weigh heavy.'

Eleanor felt a stab of anxiety. She knew how big and heavy Don was from when he hit her. Did they think she helped Grandpa bury the body? 'He never said.'

'He never discussed it?' From the expression on Rhodes's face he wasn't buying it.

'No.'

'Do you think Farrington helped him?'

'I don't know. I suppose it's a possibility.'

Rhodes didn't comment.

'There *was* one thing,' Eleanor said, feeling an overwhelming need to please. 'I didn't think so much of it at the time, but . . .' This was ridiculous, Eleanor thought, a stupid little irrelevant detail that will have no bearing on anything. 'No, it's nothing.'

Rhodes's stern expression declared *let me be the judge of that.*

'Anything you tell us is useful, Eleanor,' Warne assured her.

Eleanor curbed a sigh and said, 'Grandpa had a signet ring. Fourteen carat solid gold, with an image of St. Benedict engraved on it. He was very attached to it for sentimental reasons. A few days after Don's death, I noticed it was missing. Grandpa told me he'd lost it. When I sympathised, he was quite cold and said it didn't matter at all.'

The air filled with static. Warne exchanged a conspiratorial look with Rhodes who wasn't finished.

'Did your grandfather own a gun?'

She failed to understand his line of questioning and said so.

'Could you please answer, Eleanor?'

'A service revolver,' she stammered. 'He'd fought in the war, you see.'

'Did he show it to you?'

'Once.'

'Where did he keep it?

'In a box under the bed.'

'So you had access to it?'

She stared at both of them. Then she remembered how they'd questioned her about Clay's gun. 'I did not. I was incarcerated in the Stone House.'

'Except that night you weren't.'

'No,' Eleanor said, tamping down a strong desire to scream, '*because I was with Don at the forge.* He never knew my grandfather. We certainly never went to his house. Grandpa had abandoned me to the care system, remember?'

'It's okay, Eleanor. We realise this is upsetting,' Warne said.

'Well, it's ridiculous what you're suggesting.' She was aware a crack had appeared in her manufactured veneer. It could not occur at a worse time. Coursing with irritation, she licked the corner of her dry mouth.

'We have to cover all the bases. I'm sorry.'

'I understand.' Eleanor had a question of her own. 'Did you talk to the man who supplied Clay?'

'We did.' Rhodes was clipped. 'He's assisting us with our enquiries.'

'It was an incredibly helpful lead, Eleanor,' Warne gushed.

Eleanor smiled thanks, stupidly grateful for the compliment.

'Going back to that night,' Rhodes said, relentless. 'What did you do with your clothes?'

'I stripped them off, gave them to my grandfather who burned them.'

'What did you wear then? All your clothes were at the Stone House.'

'Grandpa gave me an old skirt and sweater that belonged to my nan and, afterwards, bought me new clothes. He was careful,' she added. 'He never bought anything locally.'

'And you lived with him?'

She explained how she had spent two years in the cellar until she was seventeen and he'd sent her on her way.

'He protected me,' she said simply.

Looking into their troubled faces, she wondered what happened now. Would they charge her, or what? Rhodes was stroking his chin again. His brain was like a computer, she thought. She could almost see him processing the myriad pieces of information, categorising and sorting into neat files.

'We'll obviously need to correlate what you've told us with experts and other evidence gathered,' he said. 'Given this is complicated due to the passage of time, you will be released on bail, possibly for several months . . .'

'Several months?' She was astounded. This wasn't what she expected at all.

'We have to conduct long and complex interviews with all the evidence to hand. A lot depends on reports from the forensic anthropologist and pathologist assigned to the case. Once we have the whole picture, you will return and we'll take it from there.'

'Do you have any questions, Eleanor?' Warne asked.

She shook her head.

'Thank you for your time,' Rhodes said, standing up. Warne wheeled her out.

CHAPTER FIFTY

A surprisingly cold October morning, during half-term week, we were sitting inside, drinking coffee. Mum had lost the money given to Yuill, despite Justin Tranter's best efforts. The bank took the view that she'd willingly parted with it and it hadn't helped that she'd lied to a cashier in a bank in Ludlow that it was for a business venture. Happily, the cash she'd handed over to the Castreys, and regarded by the police as a down payment for the ransom, *was* returned to her.

Mum's injuries had healed although she wasn't up to doing Pilates any time soon. She was sometimes a little unsteady on her legs. I privately put it down to anxiety. She had that *what will be will be* and *keep calm and carry on* vibe going on, the equivalent of horseshit, as far as I was concerned. I went along with it to please her, but I'd seen that lonely expression in her eyes. She was sixty-two years old and yet she had the appallingly lost and abandoned bearing of a little girl. Thank God for Hazel, I thought. She'd proved a solid friend and made sure that Mum wasn't on her own for too long.

Since Mum's interview, I'd spent most of my free days at hers, some nights too. We settled into a rhythm in which we spoke little. It wasn't Mum's way to dwell. We talked about the Castreys when police kept us up to speed with information, timelines and court dates. Thank God, Mum wasn't going to be charged with death by dangerous driving, which had seemed a distinct possibility. Extreme circumstances dictated otherwise.

One night, after far too many glasses of wine, she told me her story, the real one, and what happened on that hot night in July, 1976.

I could have cried. In fact, I did cry and it wasn't the booze talking.

'It was a clear case of self-defence,' I argued.

'I killed him,' she said, in that maddening black-and-white way of hers. 'I meant to do it.'

'*I'd* have meant to do it given the circumstances.' That's when I blurted it all out about Clay, about his threats, sexual and otherwise, and how I'd driven a nail into his face and how I'd preferred it if it *had* gone through his eye and into his brain. Me: the pacifist — *not*.

'Fear makes you do strange things,' I said, waggling a finger, seeing two of her, a dribble of red wine on my chin.

'Agreed, but it's not a mitigating factor.'

I couldn't fathom her thinking and I wondered if I were missing something. When I'd asked about her grandfather I received a character profile of the man, not exactly a full-blooded description of a human being. I guessed it was complex, what with him sending her away to that godawful institution.

'I'm so very sorry for what I did to you,' she said.

'It wasn't you. It was them.'

But she kept on apologising.

'More coffee?' she said, bringing me back to the here and now and looming threat of the future.

'Yes, please.'

When the phone rang I told her I'd get it. It was DCI Rhodes who asked to speak to Mum. They'd made a decision, I thought, blood freezing in my veins. *This is it.*

* * *

Eleanor listened to Verity who phoned Alex to tell him it was time, after which Verity drove her to the police station. Her daughter's motoring skills were considerably improved, Eleanor thought. She had flair and confidence and Eleanor felt in a safe pair of hands.

They did not speak. The silence was not companionable. It was edgy and laced with dread. Since the age of fifteen, Eleanor had known this day would come. She gazed out of the window and wondered if this was the last time for a long time that she would see streets and people and places she loved.

Rhodes was solicitous when they arrived. Warne was there too. She had caramel highlights in her hair. It really suited her. Eleanor noticed she had an engagement ring on her finger, a lovely solitaire set in a white-gold band. She wanted to congratulate her but it would be inappropriate. By focusing on the mundane and the inconsequential, Eleanor hoped to stall the inevitable.

Verity said she'd wait in the car. Eleanor gave her a hug that said *I never want to let you go.*

'Don't worry,' Verity whispered in Eleanor's ear. 'Whatever happens it will be okay.'

Eleanor tried so hard to believe her.

'You look in better shape than last time,' Rhodes said, pushing the door open for her.

'Still a little tender,' Eleanor said, 'Old bones.' Heat rose to her cheeks. 'What I meant . . .'

'Don't worry about it, Eleanor,' Warne said.

'Slip of the tongue,' she murmured.

Eleanor followed them into an interview room. They took seats. Eleanor was very still. She held her breath, looked hard and listened harder.

Rhodes was direct and cut to the chase. 'As you know, we've been looking into the circumstances of Don's death. Enquiries have been extensive and we've reached a number of conclusions. Don Birch received a relatively superficial head wound, Eleanor.'

Stunned, she felt her breath tangle in the back of her throat. 'But the blood.'

'Head wounds bleed a lot,' Warne said.

And there were cuts to his body, Eleanor recalled. 'Then how did he die?'

'Cause of death was from a gunshot wound to his chest that shattered his rib cage.'

Eleanor stared, open-mouthed. She couldn't get her head around it. 'Are you saying Don was alive when I left him?'

'That's the working hypothesis. Your grandfather obviously had means, opportunity and motive to — in his eyes — finish the job. Does that resonate with you?'

She closed her eyes. *Grandpa*, she thought. *No, he wouldn't have, would he? He'd seen enough killing during the war.* She told them this.

'But you were his flesh and blood,' Warne said, clearing her throat. 'There's something else.'

'Yes?'

'We found your grandfather's signet ring.'

'Right.'

'It was lodged in Don Birch's jawbone,' Rhodes said.

She was astounded. Grandpa would have been no match for Don. 'There was a struggle?'

'We can't tell. It's possible it was inserted post-mortem.'

He did it to shield me from prosecution, Eleanor believed. *It's what we do to protect our own.* 'So it wasn't all my fault?'

'No, Eleanor, we're satisfied that your actions were not intentional and premeditated.'

She didn't know what to say. How could she express enough gratitude for a life given back?

'Nevertheless,' Rhodes said, sternly, 'Given the gravity of the offence, we have no alternative other than to charge you for Actual Bodily Harm.'

Eleanor nodded dumbly. It had to be this way. Of course, it did.

'However due to the passage of time and your age,' Warne continued, 'you're potentially looking at a non-custodial sentence, a conditional discharge or short suspended sentence.'

'I won't have to go to prison?' Eleanor was awe-struck.

'No, you won't have to go to prison.'

CHAPTER FIFTY-ONE

I'd wanted to celebrate, party, throw some shapes, and hit the town. Mum wasn't keen so I threw a get-together at my place, drank cocktails, ate tapas, danced until I was sick and passed out. I invited all my mates. Alex and Dido came, too, and Mum was given the perfect out because Fred and Kitty needed a babysitter. And there was cause for extra celebration due to Alex's new business venture. Yes, really, and it didn't involve buskers. Using some of Dad's architectural contacts, he'd started an interior design company. Dido had handed her notice in with the "recud" company and was in charge of the purse strings. No more sponging off Mum.

But we didn't let Mum's newfound freedom go unnoticed. Hazel and Justin hosted a surprise lunch to which the family were invited. A genuine celebration of life, I wished I could bottle the expression on Mum's face and carry it with me forever.

'Why are you crying, Granny?' Kitty asked, her little face looking up in concern.

'Because I'm happy, Kitty, really happy.'

And I was happy, too, achingly so.

Afterwards, we sat by the log fire in the drawing room, the two of us. Alex and Dido had gone. Hazel was clearing up in the kitchen. Under strict orders, Justin had made himself scarce.

'That was lovely,' Mum said. 'Whose idea was it?'

'All of us,' I told her.

'It was such a surprise.'

'Wasn't easy. You wouldn't have agreed if I'd let on.'

'You know me too well.'

'I think I do now. I didn't before.'

She drew me close and kissed the top of my head. 'No,' she said softly. 'And I'm truly sorry for that.'

And she was and I got it. I was sorry for doubting her and painting her as some demented villain.

'When you do something unspeakable,' she continued gravely, 'you become someone you don't recognise.'

'Sort of if the cap fits, wear it,' I said hesitantly.

'Something like that,' she said with a frown.

'Does knowing after all these years that you didn't kill Don help?'

'It does, although it will take a little getting used to.'

'So what's next?'

'It's easy. No more men,' she joked, unusually irreverent.

'Seriously?'

She paused. I guess that's what you do after you experience the biggest wake-up call of your life. When she finally spoke her gaze was unwavering, her voice strong.

'I'm going to live, Verity, really live.'

I was glad for both of us. I hoped my mum went for broke.

THE END

ACKNOWLEDGEMENTS

As always, this was a genuine team effort. Firstly, many thanks to my agent, Broo Doherty, at DHH Literary Agency, for her enthusiasm and wise counsel. Thanks (again) to Graham Bartlett for expert police advice on bones, cold cases and the problems associated with proving events, and understanding the anatomy of investigating a murder when it's in the dim and distant past. Any mistakes, either technical or for dramatic purposes, are mine alone.

Finally, where would I be without my fabulous publisher, Joffe? (And they won Independent Publisher of the Year at the British Book Awards this time around). As ever, I'm indebted to Kate Lyall Grant for loving the story from the moment it was conceived, to Jasper Joffe for being Jasper Joffe(!) and, of course, the rest of the crew for beavering away on my behalf. Seriously, folks, couldn't do this without you.

THE JOFFE BOOKS STORY

We began in 2014 when Jasper agreed to publish his mum's much-rejected romance novel and it became a bestseller.

Since then we've grown into the largest independent publisher in the UK. We're extremely proud to publish some of the very best writers in the world, including Joy Ellis, Faith Martin, Caro Ramsay, Helen Forrester, Simon Brett and Robert Goddard. Everyone at Joffe Books loves reading and we never forget that it all begins with the magic of an author telling a story.

We are proud to publish talented first-time authors, as well as established writers whose books we love introducing to a new generation of readers.

We have been shortlisted for Independent Publisher of the Year at the British Book Awards three times, in 2020, 2021 and 2022, and for the Diversity and Inclusivity Award at the Independent Publishing Awards in 2022.

We built this company with your help, and we love to hear from you, so please email us about absolutely anything bookish at: feedback@joffebooks.com.

If you want to receive free books every Friday and hear about all our new releases, join our mailing list: www.joffebooks.com/contact

And when you tell your friends about us, just remember: it's pronounced Joffe as in coffee or toffee!

ALSO BY E.V. SEYMOUR

STANDALONES
MY DAUGHTER'S SECRETS
THE WIDOW'S BOYFRIEND

KIM SLADE THRILLERS
THE PATIENT
THE HOUSEKEEPER'S DAUGHTER